Dr. Brandt

BILLIONAIRES' CLUB SERIES

RAYLIN MARKS

RAYLIN MARKS

Copyright © 2022 by Raylin Marks

All rights reserved.

No part of this book may be reproduced in any form or by any electronic or mechanical means, including information storage and retrieval systems, without written permission from the author, except for the use of brief quotations in a book review.

Chapter One

Cameron (Cam)

This week in Jamaica was supposed to be a reprieve from the demand of my job as a pediatric neurosurgeon. What wasn't there to love about the white sandy beaches of the all-inclusive resort where we were staying? I was here for the sun and fun, but the latter had backfired on my ass.

I suppose I should've stopped the groom and questioned his *bright idea* of coming here after his fiancé dumped him a day before their wedding. Typically, however, guys didn't sit around and talk out their feelings. It was more common for us men to jump at the opportunity to turn a bad situation into a good one. You know, we've got each other's backs without questioning who was right or wrong in a relationship breakup—failed wedding or not. So, that's what I did.

I agreed to join the broken-hearted groom on vacation. Maybe Dennis would get laid and get over it; maybe he wouldn't. Either way, he requested that his groomsmen join him for a week, and I was happy to get away from work and Los Angeles for that time.

I felt pretty bad for Dennis after he said that his ex-fiancé was taking her bridesmaids to Dubai on what should've been their honeymoon, so how could any of us say no to him? Little did I know this fuck-knuckle had played all of us, and *we* were the ones going on his honeymoon trip. I didn't know much about what happened before the wedding day fiasco, and since I was just a last-minute stand-in and not a close friend, I didn't plan on going too deep with him about it.

Dennis was a resident at Saint John's Hospital, and if it weren't for him bumping into me when I'd had a little too much to drink one night after two days on-call, I would've never agreed to be in his wedding. I don't even know why I agreed when I was drunk. I barely knew the guy, and I was quickly finding out how different we were.

He did things that, even in my younger playboy, reckless years, I would've never considered doing. A prime example of that being that he'd also invited his fiancé's married bridesmaids to join us in Jamaica—in our shared villa—for what was turning out to be some weird-ass sex fest. That was *not* my style. No fucking way. None of this was what I'd signed up for, yet here I was, fending off drunk married women all night every time they tried to sneak into my room.

This was a nightmare. I called down to the front desk of the resort and requested a private room outside of this villa, and all I could do now was wait for them to call with the good news that I had a spot away from this insanity. I still had four days left on the island, and I sure as hell didn't want to spend them like this.

I was pissed, and God help anyone who tried to downplay Dennis's role in roping us into his honeymoon, turning this room into some weird fuck parade between the dumped groom, his groomsmen, and the bridesmaids. Perhaps if I got caught up on my sleep, I'd laugh at myself for being stupid enough to jump on a plane with these strangers. Maybe I'd even laugh about it one day with my *actual* friends. However, at the moment, I wasn't laughing.

I took a sip of my rum and coke, trying to wake up since this cursed vacation had consisted of me getting cat naps in between women sneaking into my room all night.

"Look who's finally awake and joining the party," Dennis said as he gripped my shoulder and took the barstool to my left. "We thought you were sick or something."

His squeaky voice didn't match his graying hair, but that wasn't even the most annoying thing about him at the moment. I'd left the villa an hour ago and gone to the tiki bar, hoping to get away from the fools I'd come with, but here he was.

This would be my first conversation with the fucker since I learned the truth about what'd happened to ruin his wedding—*he* was the one who'd cheated on his fiancé, and not the other way around like he'd led me to believe.

"You said that your fiancé was the one..." I paused and eyed his smirk, and then I twisted and leaned into the bar to face him. "Why did you make it seem like your girl had cheated on you when it was your stupid ass who cheated on her? At the hospital, you said that *those days* were over for you. I don't get it. Why bother getting married at all if you still want to fuck around?"

"Oh, please," he rolled his eyes. "I'm not here to get lectured by a surgeon who was screwing a nurse in—"

I narrowed my eyes and held up my hand after I gulped down the last of my cocktail. "First of all, Gabby was my girlfriend. Second of all, just because she was an ER nurse doesn't mean that I was supposed to take a vow not to have sex with her."

"That's not what flew around the hospital."

"Thirdly," I continued, "I never cheated on her. When we ended things, she decided to make it appear as though I used her as my personal fuck-nurse. It nearly cost me my job, but fortunately, social media saved my ass when I had to deal with the board about her complaints."

"How so?" He frowned.

"Because she posted everything but nudes of us on Instagram. She'd blasted that shit all over her accounts, and it saved me in the end. So, lesson learned. I don't date co-workers at that hospital anymore, much less fuck them for the hell of it." The story sounded so stupid when I said it out loud.

"Why did you break it off? Were you bored with her? You see, I think that's what my problem is. I got bored with Kelly," he took a sip of a martini that was as dirty as he was, "and I cheated on her. I don't know, I guess I got cold feet, but after my bachelor party, I realized that I wasn't made to be a one-woman man."

"That shit went down at your fucking bachelor party?"

Who the hell was this guy? He'd always seemed to be a decent guy, but I'd gotten that character assessment completely wrong. I guess you learn more and more about people when you're stuck living with them in a fucked-up situation for a week.

"She caught me for the fourth and final time after she sent a friend that I'd never met to the party to spy on me. Her friend followed me after I left with a few of girls who'd shown up at the bar." He shrugged. "I couldn't lie my way out of having my picture taken while checking into a hotel with my hand on some chicks' asses."

"No shit?" I humored him in disgust. He wasn't an ugly guy, but never in a million years would I expect him to attract multiple women at once—unless he was paying them. "I don't know who to blame in this scenario, you or your girl, who'd known that you'd already banged at least four other broads before her friend caught you on your bachelor night."

"Kelly thought she could change me." He arched his eyebrow. "Marriage isn't the answer to that, you know. Maybe I'm a sex addict. Maybe I'm the one who needs therapy."

You think?

I tapped on my glass and ordered another cocktail from the bartender. "Does therapy really help a man who brings his fiancé's married friends to Jamaica for a massive orgy? And yes, you are a sick fuck." There went our working relationship. "Excuses and self-diagnoses or not, you realize that this whole thing is another level of fucked-up, right? All of us are here on *your* honeymoon? I thought this was part of your *broken-hearted* groom's getaway since your fiancé supposedly took her bridesmaids to Dubai."

He sighed. "You clearly got it wrong."

"Clearly," I said, taking a gulp of my new drink.

"I'm not going to sit here while you say that I'm the dick in this situation. It was everyone's idea to join me on the honeymoon that *I paid for*—no refunds—because she made me look like an asshole. Even her bridesmaids agreed that she handled it dirty. I mean, who stalks their fiancé like she did when she used her friend to catch me? Huh?

Who does that to their future husband and then calls off the wedding?"

Jesus Christ. This motherfucker is delusional.

"A woman who doesn't trust her man. Obviously, it was for a good reason. Listen," I stirred the ice cubes in my glass with my cocktail straw, "I'll keep my mouth shut about all of it if you make it clear to the married bridesmaids that they're not allowed in my room. I would at least appreciate it if you can get the word out to the rest of your wedding party that I'm not fucking any of them."

"So, now you're suddenly a prude?"

I rolled my eyes. "They're married and are here without their spouses. There were three of them in the span of one night who walked into my fucking room naked—drunk off their asses—and woke me up for some fun in paradise. I don't roll that way."

Instead of trying to negotiate my way out of being sexually assaulted all fucking night, I should've been at the front desk, begging for a private room. I'd pay for a broom closet if it meant I didn't have to worry about someone grabbing my cock in the middle of the night.

"You're being a stick-in-the-mud, Cam."

"Well, I think the honeymoon is over for me," I said dryly. "I'm out, man. I swear I'll sleep in a fucking cabana if one of those bridesmaids comes into my room for the third goddamn night in a row."

"Just chill." He shook his head like *I* was the one who was being unreasonable. I was no choir boy, but I also didn't like people in my space unless they were invited—and none of the people in that goddamn villa were invited. "I'll take care of the hotties who came with me and my guys. It seems like you're the only dick that's shriveled up for the week, eh?"

"How about changing shit up for the final four days that we're here? Instead of fucking every last *married* bridesmaid," my eyes widened as I took my drink and stood from the barstool, "you can just go fuck yourself?"

I briskly nodded and bowed out. Maybe when I was a dumbass in my college days, I would've been down for this type of shit, but obviously, I'd grown up a little, and this wasn't my game.

As I walked through the bar, fuck-me eyes were coming at me

from all sides. A few of the bridesmaids were there from the villa—finally coming up for air, I guess—and it was almost like they were tracking me down. This *vacation* was fucking stressful. There was no way I was going to sleep with one eye open for the third night in a row.

"Cammy," I heard Tania call out, one of the more aggressive, naked bridesmaids. "Cam!"

I kept walking, hoping she'd be distracted by someone else on her hot pursuit to me. When I glanced back at her, she flashed her tits at me, making me run head-on into someone.

"Fuck!" I growled, trying to steady the woman I'd nearly trampled into the sand. "Holy shit! Jessa?"

"Cameron Brandt?" she chuckled.

"Oh, my God." I was in complete and utter shock.

I locked eyes with my stunning ex-girlfriend, and I couldn't help but smile when her bright blue eyes glittered as she laughed. I shivered internally at the welcomed sight of this lovely woman. She was the one who got away—and she was right in front of me.

"You look terrified like someone is chasing you." She smiled so sweetly as I stared in disbelief that I was looking into the eyes of the one woman I never stopped loving. "Are you okay?"

"I'm fine," I said in some foreign voice that I knew gave me away entirely. "This is quite a shock, running into you like this, and in Jamaica of all places…after all these years?"

An arm slipped around the back of my neck, bringing me back to my harsh reality. Fucking hell, how could I begin to explain *this* crazy-ass situation to the woman I'd crushed ten or more years ago? Why in God's name did I ever leave this beautiful woman? What the fuck was I thinking?

"Baby, you left me," Tania whined as she locked eyes on Jessa. "Who's this? Don't even think about it, girly. He's mine."

I wanted to throw the woman off me and catch up with Jessa, but I wasn't sure I had the right. How would Jessa trust anything coming out of my mouth when I vowed to love her and never leave her—yet that's precisely what I did.

Now, I was here with a drunk *and married* bridesmaid clinging onto me as if she and I were on our honeymoon, and I couldn't think so long as my Jessa's blue eyes were staring into mine.

"Is this your wife?" Jessa questioned with a smile, obviously eyeing the large rock on the woman's left hand.

"No," I quickly answered. "She's married."

"But she's here with you?" Jessa looked at me like the dirty son of a bitch it appeared I was.

Tania stuck her tongue in my ear, and I nearly threw her to the ground. "Are you fucking serious?" I said to the married woman. "What the hell is wrong with all of you bridesmaids?"

"What?" Jessa looked at me with wide eyes, and I could only imagine what she was thinking from the smile on her face.

"You and I are taking the master bedroom tonight," Tania said as she grabbed my crotch. "We can share it with the others. You want it, Cammy. Stop playing around."

"Cammy?" Jessa seemed to bite back her smile.

If Jessa had ever prayed for my ass to be punished for hurting her, she was watching the answer to those prayers come true at this moment. I was miserable, trying my damndest to focus, and Jessa seemed to find it all extremely amusing. That's what this was all about, right? Karma biting me in my ass like I deserved.

If that wasn't enough, I was now fighting off this bridesmaid like a rabid spider monkey. "I'm getting another room, and you're going back to that wedding party. I'm done with this shit."

"Why don't I leave you two alone?" Jessa said with a curious smile. "It was nice to see you again, Cam." She looked at the woman who was hanging like a drunken idiot on my side. "Enjoy your wedding festivities, or whatever it is you're doing here."

"This isn't what it seems." I tried to smile while refraining from throwing a bridesmaid off my ass. "Trust me."

"Have a good one." She laughed and grinned at me.

"Jessa, can we talk?" I looked like an idiot with a drunk woman trying to lick me as she stumbled over her own feet. "I mean, do you have a minute or two?"

"I think you might be the busy one," Jessa chuckled, watching the bridesmaid that I was unsuccessfully trying to keep at arm's length.

"You think this is funny?" I grinned back at her, hoping I could get her to agree to meet with me.

"I've never seen anything like this before." She looked at the girl, who was now sitting on the ground, holding onto my shorts like a toddler would cling to their parent.

"Neither have I," I said as I looked at Tania in disbelief.

"I really have to go." Jessa seemed weirded out about what was happening to me, and I couldn't blame her. I'd never been in a more ridiculous situation.

"I'll try to catch up as soon as I secure another room. The one I have now isn't working out."

"You do that." She winked before she turned and walked away, and I was instantly brought back to better days with my first and only love.

Thirteen years of college and med school taught me that resilience and good focus would get you what you want if you worked hard enough at it, and what I wanted now was Jessa. I hadn't seen her since I left early for med school, and I couldn't help but wonder what she thought of me after witnessing this scene.

I stood there—with an intoxicated, groveling bridesmaid holding onto my leg—and watched Jessa walk away. I'd had a lot of girlfriends and flings since Jessa, but no one had ever measured up to her. Now, I felt desperate to explain things to her and right all the wrongs I'd ever done. All I could do was hope to find her again and pray that she'd want to hear me out.

Cam

After a night spent searching the resort for Jessa, she seemed to be nothing more than a phantom after our shit-scramble of a run-in. There was no other way of looking at it. That fucking bridesmaid, clinging to me like a child with her tits falling out of her shirt—Jessa had seen it all.

Maybe Jessa *was* just a ghost. That was it. She had to be a hallucination brought on by my lack of sleep, some liquor, and profound frustration at my current situation. Why else would I dream up the woman I never stopped loving, the woman I hurt most selfishly?

I sat in one of the empty cabanas, staring at the stars glittering in the night sky. It was hours before the sun would make its appearance, and I was trying desperately to convince myself that our interaction was a figment of my imagination. It wasn't working, though, and this weak-ass coffee wasn't working either.

For the hundredth time, I pinched the bridge of my nose, knowing that I wasn't a man who created scenarios that didn't exist. I didn't live my life in frustration either—a trait handed down to me by my father. I was patient yet thorough in everything I did. Could I be pushed to my limits? Absolutely. Did this trip suck worse than I could've ever imagined and make me want to throw myself into the sea? Hell yes. However, despite my dismal circumstances, they weren't bad enough for me to hallucinate my long-lost love.

I'd seen Jessa, and she'd seen me, so however unfavorable the situation might've been, it happened. No such luck deluding myself tonight.

I leaned forward and rubbed my forehead. "Jesus, has it really been sixteen years?" I whispered to myself.

"Since when does the confident Cameron Brandt talk to himself?" Jessa's voice rang with humor.

My head snapped up to see her eyes glistening in the light of the full moon that rested peacefully above the ocean before me. I grinned, unable to withstand her beautiful smile and the reminder of the way I always loved hearing laughter in her voice when she talked.

"I've certainly turned into the worst version of myself, and here you are to amuse yourself with that," I said, turning and placing both feet in the sand to face the lounge chair she took next to me.

She arched her eyebrow while she pulled her long, blonde hair casually into a ponytail. "Of all the people in this world who know," she grinned playfully at me, "or should I say *knew* me so well, I could never amuse myself with anyone having so rough a time."

"Not even the man who promised never to leave you, yet that's exactly what I did?" I answered without hesitation.

She grew more serious. "We were both so young back then, Cam," she stated. "We had a lot of crazy dreams and ideas about how our future together might look. It turns out that fate decided we should live those dreams separately."

"You and your fate and always looking at the brighter side of things."

She grinned again. I missed how Jessa smiled at everything. Even through tears, the woman found happiness. "I'm fairly confident that in your line of work, *Dr. Brandt*, you're the same way now. Well, I hope so for your patients anyway."

I softly chuckled. "If I weren't, I'd have a lot of angry patients."

"So, which medical specialty did you choose? I know you took the internship for pediatrics, and I heard through friends that you graduated med school, but that's pretty much all I know."

"The path I should've chosen was to stay with you." I went for broke with that declaration.

"Answer the question, Casanova. Your charms aren't going to work with me." She smiled and then looked toward the ocean, more serious now. "Not now, anyway." And in the way only my Jessa could do, she recovered her curious expression and smiled back at me. "So? Doctor of..." She left her question hanging in the air.

"Well, after busting my ass, I graduated and worked through fellowships, internships, and everything else that comes along with becoming a pediatric neurosurgeon."

"Wow." She stared at me in disbelief.

"You say that as though it's a shocking reveal. I might've been a jerk, but I was always ridiculously smart, you know."

I tried my best attempt at humor, but the truth was that I wanted Jessa in my arms right this instant. I wanted to move past this awkward reunion and beg for her to take me back. It wasn't all about me, though. Sixteen years had passed, and what had happened to her in all that time?

"I'm not surprised that you managed to accomplish so much. You were definitely *ridiculously smart,* and sometimes you were just ridiculous." She flashed that half-smile of hers that always made my heart skip. "So, tell me what it is you do. Brain surgery?"

"Close," I answered. "I specialize in epilepsy and work with a pediatric brain and spinal surgery team. Do you remember how my sister passed away?"

"Of course, I do. She was born with a rare genetic epilepsy disorder. I remember you telling me that she passed in the night when she was five because she had a horrible seizure." She shuddered at the thought briefly before recovering herself. "Wow. Your parents must be so proud of you for going into this line of work."

"Yeah, of course." My parents had been killed in a plane crash a few years ago. They were flying with some friends to a ski resort in the Italian Alps when their jet went down, and it was the most devastating time of my life. However, I decided to keep that info to myself because I hated talking about it and didn't feel like bringing a storm cloud to rain on an otherwise lighthearted conversation. "Anyway, I wanted to pursue this career path since it is personal to me. And because neuroscience has exploded with breakthrough treatments, things are more promising than ever. I just want to help people so they don't experience the same grief as my family."

"Always thinking of others." She leaned her chin against her palm. "I'm glad to see you haven't changed much."

"Speaking of change since you and I last saw each other," I said, finding some bearings in this conversation, "what happened after I took off and left you to graduate college without me?"

"You might want to brace yourself for my exciting answer," she chuckled.

"From the look on your adorable face," I said when I saw her wide blue eyes dazzle, "I'm bracing for anything."

"I dropped out of college soon after you left." She held a finger up to stop me from blurting out my response.

Was it my fault? Did I fuck this up that bad?

"Jessa," I reached for her hands, and strangely, she let me hold them, "I'm sorry."

"Let me finish, dummy." She chuckled and stared down at my hands as they held hers. "It wasn't you; it was me." I watched her intently as her eyes returned to mine. "I had a lot of things come up that…" She stopped herself and shrugged. "It was for the best that we broke things off. You stayed on an incredible career path, and let's leave it at that."

"Bullshit." I became sterner, as if holding her soft hands brought me back to the days when I could call her out on anything as if she were still mine. "You had superior grades, and you wanted to be a dentist. What happened to make you drop out, aside from me leaving you in tears?"

"Life." She shrugged again.

"No. I'm not buying that."

"I have a son, Cam." She looked at me, and my stomach dropped.

"Is it mine?"

She smiled at the way I croaked those words out.

"No. Rest easy, champ," she advised me.

My stomach sank at the realization that my Jessa—who was definitely no longer mine—had not only been with other men, but one of those fuckers knocked her up? *It's been sixteen years, Cameron. She's not a nun,* I told myself. So much for the chill mentality that I so proudly proclaimed to have inherited from my father. I had no right to ask about Jessa's personal life, and I had no right to stake any claims on her. I had no right to do anything but sit here and listen to the last thing on earth that a man who was still in love with a woman wanted to hear. I did this to her—to us—to me.

"May I ask what happened? I left a year before you were set to graduate. Was I that easy to get over?" That last part came out all wrong. I knew that because I could taste the venom of jealousy in my mouth when I asked it.

"No," she said sternly. "You weren't *that easy to get over,* Cam, but I did move on. I might've made a few careless decisions, but I was young. I had a casual boyfriend, and I accidentally got pregnant. Jackson is the result of that. I regret none of it, and I would never consider it a mistake because Jackson is far from that. He's my everything, and even though I'm engaged to be married, Jackson will always and forever be my number-one guy."

"Engaged?" Fuck me. She wasn't lying when she told me to brace myself.

"To a man who will be a father to Jackson after all these years of him not having one."

"Who's the asshole who got you pregnant and just walked out on you?"

Her smile grew radiant as she glanced behind me, the sun now painting the sky as it rose. "I wish I had time to catch you up on everything," she patted my cheek, "but there's a wedding today, and I don't feel like talking about the failures of my past at the moment."

I stood when she did. "Jessa," I ran my clammy hand through my hair, "I have to see you again. Please don't just take off after dropping this in my lap."

"I've missed you, Cam. I've missed our fun days together," she said sincerely, "but we've both grown up, you in your profession and me with my son and being a single mom for a time. So maybe one day I'll be in Southern California again, and we can catch up properly."

"Fuck." That foreign taste of venom flooded my mouth again. "Jessa, don't leave. God, I beg you."

Her eyes widened. "Cam," she said softly, "it's fine. I'm so happy to see you again, but this was more of a friendly catch-up between two people who can hopefully be friends again and not two exes who can't get over their past."

"What if I can't get over it?"

"Nice try." She smiled, always seeing straight through me. "I'm sure I'm not the only one who's gotten around in the years we haven't seen each other. Like I said, maybe if I fly to Southern California, I'll hit you up."

"Here," I said, pulling out my phone. "Let me give you my number. If you're out my way, you're meeting up with me again."

"And I'm sure you'll be happy to meet my fiancé as well?"

I grinned. "The fact that you said fiancé gives me hope that perhaps something might happen, and you'll call off that wedding of yours."

"Oh? How? Because I ran into you, right?"

I eyed her, somehow feeling a bit more steadfast in this conversation. "If you only knew about the wedding party I came here with, then you'd believe anything was possible."

"Ah," she lifted her chin, grabbing her bag. "Like that lovely young woman last night?"

"Listen," I said, "are you leaving today, or can you at least have dinner with me?"

"If I had dinner with you," she said, "would you promise to respect that I'm getting married and not try to pull anything funny?"

"I'm not the Cameron you recall from our younger days. I grew up and matured a little, you know?"

"Well, if you respect my and my fiancé's wishes and don't play any games, then sure. As *friends,* I'd love to hear more about your job, and we'll keep it light. That's it."

"You don't trust me."

She ran a hand through her hair. "I trusted you once, and we both saw how that turned out."

"Touché," I said with a smile, and it was only because this woman was perfectly chilled out with a smile of her own. "Well, here's my number. I'm going to airdrop it to your phone. Hopefully, you can—"

"Got it," she said, whipping out her phone. "I'll text you if things don't go over tonight. Nice seeing you again, Cameron."

The way she said my name reminded me how quickly she could put my ass in its place. We'd both grown up. We both had gone down separate roads in life, but I had to believe fate led us to this resort simultaneously for a reason. I wasn't going to wreck a relationship—even though I didn't fail to notice that she wasn't wearing an engagement ring.

Buzz! Buzz! Buzz!

I glanced down at my phone and answered it when the chief surgeon on my ward called in. "If there's one person who never calls anyone, it's you. What's up, Chief?"

"They told me you were international, Dr. Brandt; is that still true?"

His tone was severe, leading me to frown. "It is. What's going on?"

"We have a pretty rare case on our hands. It's been referred to us by a doctor out of state. The patient will be here in three days if she survives. I know I'm stretching this, but this is your specialty, and the entire staff could desperately use your advice. Even me."

"That's saying a lot," I said. "Okay. I'll be out on the next flight I can get. This vacation was a bust anyway."

"Mr. Mitchell insists that you're taken care of. His VP, Mr. Monroe, has been vacationing close to where you are now, and Mr. Mitchell has seen to it that Monroe will stop to pick you up in Mitchell and Associates' private jet on his way home. I'll text you the information, and they'll dispatch your departure time and inform the pilots and Mr. Monroe. Also, I'll email all the information I have on the patient for you to inform yourself. That way, you will be prepared for our surgical team meeting in two days."

Without another thought, I was packed, ready to bounce out of my nightmare so I could help a little girl—a girl who, if Saint John's Chief of Pediatrics was requesting my opinion, was in a pretty fucking grim situation. I had Jessa's number, and once I was settled on the jet, I'd text her and make this up to her. I knew she, of all people, would understand why I had to leave. I wouldn't stand her up without notice or leave her like I did the first time. No. This time, I'd show her the mature man I'd become, even if only to keep her in my life as a friend.

Once I was settled on the private jet, waiting for my friend to board the aircraft, I pulled out my phone to call Jessa. And after Spencer Monroe had boarded and the staff on the plane shut the doors, the pilots had this bitch in motion faster than I could realize I gave Jessa my number, but I never asked for hers.

Fucking hell.

Chapter Three

Jessa

A week had passed since I'd seen Cameron, and I still couldn't get his handsome face out of my tortured mind...not to mention the spunky yet cheerful pitch of his voice and those deep blue eyes that his pitch-black hair had always highlighted.

Of all the people I could run into on a trip for my friend's wedding, it had to be him. This wasn't fair; I was over him. It seemed like a dozen lifetimes had come and gone since he left me, but for some reason, it also felt like no time had passed. My high school sweetheart had smacked me across the face, and I couldn't stop thinking about him.

Of course, this wasn't the first time I'd thought about Cameron Brandt since we'd gone our separate ways. Every now and then, he would pop into my mind when I looked at my son—our son—Jackson.

Jackson was unexpected and one hundred percent Cameron's son, but there was no way in this world I'd tell him that. Cam came from a proper and incredibly wealthy family. I knew what conclusion his parents would've come to about me and the situation if I had hunted down Cameron and told him everything.

Maybe it wasn't fair of me not to tell him, but after he left me so coldly—cutting me as deeply as a person can be cut—I didn't want anything to do with him again. Cam made it clear that he was done with me when he left, so why on earth would I choose to put myself and my unborn child through any more trauma? That's what I've always told myself, anyway. To hell with it. I'd seen therapists and been advised that I should tell him at the very least, but I knew Cam well enough to know it would just be a burden on him, make him miserable, and I wasn't going down that road.

I'd had plenty of moments where I regretted not telling him, but those came and went a long time ago, and I'd moved on. Cam loved me at one time—I knew that, and I felt that—but I wasn't going to see that look of defeat in his eyes when I told him about Jackson. So many people judged me, but I didn't care. They weren't in my shoes, and they weren't the ones who had to listen to Cameron's excuses to leave. *'I love you, and I know we made a promise, but this is my dream—my life—Jessa. Sorry. I hope you understand I have to do this.'* They also never had to spend what seemed like forever, mending my shattered heart. All those who said I was overly nice or not strong enough to deal with the situation head-on could suck it. They didn't know what I was made of.

Jackson was my life, and through my son, I gained a motherly instinct that made me stronger regardless of what anyone thought of me. Seeing Cameron again wasn't going to spark up the conversation that made me drop this bombshell in his life, either. Cam was Jackson's biological father, and that was it. The man who had stepped in as Jackson's father was Warren Branson, my fiancé.

Although Warren had some flaws with being the perfect man in a relationship, he proved his love through numerous methods. The man cared about Jackson and me and worked his ass off as a vice president for a global technology company, making life very comfortable for us. When he wasn't working late, he would cook dinner if I was too tired, and sometimes, he would pick up Jackson from school or join me on doctor visits, and most of all, he would snuggle up with me on the couch and force himself to watch a chick flick.

These weren't his only qualities. He was an all-around great guy from the first moment we were set up three years ago. Trust me, when it came to Jackson, I vetted the fuck out of any guy I dared to date and trust with mine and my son's future.

Like Cameron's sister, Jackson was born with a genetic disorder and suffered from severe epileptic seizures. After many grueling years, our neurologist finally put Jackson on a special diet to help prevent the seizures from happening as often as they used to. Thank God, too, because I'd spent so many years watching the seizures take over Jackson's life. This diet and medication were the breakthroughs we needed to get my boy healthy and happy again.

I didn't have to fight many guys off before I was set up with Warren. Men usually ran in the other direction after asking about my routine and how I managed as a single mom. Once they learned there was much more to raising my son than dropping him off at daycare and everyday things like that? Poof, gone. And good thing, too. They saved me the trouble of kicking them to the curb.

Warren was nothing like the other men. He seemed eager to meet Jackson and to learn more about my son and me. After six months, I finally let Warren meet Jackson, and I was so relieved that he instantly adored my son as much as he adored me.

So, that's why I didn't inform Cam about Jackson while I was at that resort. It was good that I lied and told him my son was another man's child, too. I didn't even need to drop that bomb for him to stand me up, leaving the resort without a word.

I wasn't too surprised when I realized he'd left. I learned a long time ago never to trust Cameron. Instead, it was better to wish him well and send my positive vibes into the universe after him. Forgiving the one who hurt you the most was the best therapy in the world, and that's why I wasn't sad when he vanished again. It's also why I had no desire to call him, even though I had his number. Cameron was a memory from the past—in the flesh—and that was that.

So, why was I sitting at my vanity in my Manhattan penthouse thinking about how Cam's jawline was perfectly formed by his neatly groomed beard? Beats the hell out of me.

"He was just an old damn flame," I softly reminded myself as I placed my drop earring in my ear. "That's it."

"What's it? What are you whispering to yourself in here, precious?" Warren's voice announced his entry into my dressing room.

"Precious," I said dryly, then turned and smiled at him. "I hate when you call me that, and you know it."

He raised his hands and brushed along the bare skin of my upper arms. "You look stunning tonight. I love this silk gown on you. You will surely astonish them all."

As Warren kissed my neck after fastening a new necklace he'd purchased for this affair, I closed my eyes, begging myself to *feel something* with this tender show of affection. Nothing.

Maybe he's right. Maybe my hormones are fucked up, and that's why I'm not that into sex or intimacy with him anymore.

He had to be correct. I loved Warren, and I knew how lucky I was to have him. Any one of the rich ladies at the gala tonight would've given their last fur coat to be with him. His dark blonde hair, muscular body, and soft jade eyes should've been enough to revive how I felt about this man during our first year together. Now, it was as if my body didn't have any fucking hormones at all.

I felt his hand slide under my dress, his fingers going to the spot that should've made me melt like butter while his teeth nipped at my lips, aggressively and seductively working to bring me under his sexual control. But he wasn't turning me on. In fact, I was fighting the urge to pull his hand away so I could get the fuck out of this room and to the party already.

Fake it to make it, I told myself, wanting to get this over with. It was either now or later when I was exhausted from the party. Might as well wrap it up now, so I could fall into bed after we got home tonight. Warren would be satiated since he hadn't gotten a piece of ass in the week Jackson had been in Seattle at my parents' house.

I hated that I felt this way, but I guess I should've been grateful that it was the only issue in this relationship—a relationship that I seemed to be forcing myself to be a part of since I saw Cameron again.

* * *

"Jessica, you look ravishing, glowing actually," Francis said, tipping a flute of champagne to her lips. "How's that handsome son of yours doing? He's in a private school now, correct?"

I looked at Warren's coworker's wife and grinned. "Actually, no. He's not in a private school. He—"

"Good lord, Jessica," Stevie said, another one of the wealthy ladies, as she snatched my arm, damn-near shouting for the entire room to hear. "We don't use the word *public school* in this circle."

I plastered on my best smile. I only had to tolerate these women at these particular gatherings. I always felt like I was suffocating by the end of them, unable to open up like I would around my friends. I was fake when these people surrounded me because their judgment knew no bounds, and I hated it.

"We don't?" I spoke.

The other ladies stared at me like I'd grown a second nose. "No," said another woman I hardly knew. "I'm shocked that Warren would allow that. While your son might have some *issues,* you two can afford to—"

I leveled the woman with an expression to match my rising anger. "Why don't we get off the topic of where Warren and I choose to send our son to school? I'm not going to listen to anyone tell me where I should send my son—with all of his *issues*—to school. Jackson is playing football again. The team loves him, and he's a huge asset to them."

"Jessica, darling," Francis said, her silver hair shimmering under the room's lights. "No one is attacking you. It's just that everyone here knows that private school is better for advancements in college and careers and such."

"While I can appreciate all your *humble* opinions on what's good for my son and what's not, Jackson is happy where he's at. That's all that matters. He's thriving in education as well as in sports."

"Well, then, we're wrong," another woman said. Her black hair was pulled back tightly, showcasing what must've been a hundred-thousand dollars' worth of Harry Winston diamonds. "Ladies," she eyed the group while her blush lips pulled up coyly on one side, "I'm sure there are better conversations to have over champagne than talking about public schools, private schools, and Jessica's son."

"Indeed," Stevie spat out in defeat.

These women and I were different breeds. We came from entirely different worlds, and it seemed like they could sniff me out instantly, no matter how expensive my gown or elaborate my jewelry was. They weren't the type to embrace people from different backgrounds, and the pretentiousness made me uncomfortable.

What the hell time was it anyway? It felt like it had been hours since we arrived. Awards had been handed out, leaders of divisions were recognized, dinner had concluded, and now, this conversation had gone on for too long.

I rubbed my forehead, feeling my palms grow clammy. Thoughts of Cameron and my feelings for Warren rushed around in my head. I needed air. I wanted out of this fancy hotel and would gladly welcome the noise of New York City's streets.

In a rush to get outside, uncertain if I was falling apart for no reason, I moved briskly out of the room, down the grand staircase, and out the main entrance of the hotel.

"Madam, is there a—"

"No, no," I raised my hand at the valet, cutting him off. "Just coming out for some fresh air. No need to call for the car."

This was the most foreign invasion of emotions I'd ever experienced. *Damn you, Cameron Brandt. You had to be at that resort, didn't you? I was just fine before I was reunited with you, of all the people in this world.*

I felt a tear slip out of the corner of my eye. On top of everything, the women inside reminded me of how lonely I was. I'd spent a fantastic week with old friends from Seattle at the resort; now, I was back in Manhattan. Moving to New York for Warren's promotion had taken me away from my friends, and on a night like tonight, I wished I could be with any one of them instead of being here.

I needed to knock it off. For God's sake, Warren and I were getting married—well, once I finally settled on a wedding date. So why was I feeling like some emotionally broken woman suddenly? Fuck this noise in my head. I had a son to think about and a decent man in my life. And yet, here I was, leaning against a brick building, hidden in an alley, watching the steam cover the dark road. I watched as it rolled and crept like a ghost blanketing the ground.

"No, I'm not going down this road," I said aloud. "Jackson loves his school. I was all about supporting Warren's career move to come here, and now I'm having an emotional crisis because I saw Cam? No way."

I stood up straight.

I was fine. More than anything, I was ready to see Jackson again. Only two more days before my parents would fly him home from Seattle, then everything would feel normal again.

Chapter Four

Cameron

I walked out of the meeting with our team, which specialized in consulting with families whose children were facing surgery. This case was different, and I'd spent the last two days and almost the entire morning going over all the scans on this highly aggressive brain tumor.

There were as many difficult aspects of being a pediatric neurosurgeon as there were rewarding ones. This meeting was a challenge to say the very least. I completely understood why the parents of five-year-old Crystal were wary of sending their daughter into surgery, and I hoped we'd reassured them adequately that we would take care of their precious little girl. However, time was of the essence to extract her tumor. It was growing rapidly, moving from the lower part of the back of her brain, and it had the potential of growing into the spinal cord.

"Do you think they'll go through with it?" Dr. Nadeer questioned, the neurologist who was first to meet with this family. "You did a fine job explaining the benefits that outweigh any risks of surgery in there."

As we walked out of the room, the surgical and consult teams following us, we left the family with our pediatric consultant to discuss this procedure without medical staff present. We answered all their questions, and now it was up to Mr. and Mrs. Johnson to decide whether they would proceed.

"I can talk about the benefits of saving their daughter's life and giving her a better chance at life until I'm blue in the face, but does it make a difference?" I turned to his worrisome expression as we walked toward the elevators, and I pressed the button to get us up to the floor where I'd do my evening rounds before leaving the hospital for the day. "Look, it's difficult to understand what this family has been dealing with. Their little girl has a grade-four tumor, and it doesn't matter what we say after a certain point. Our words don't make it any easier to trust us with their daughter's well-being. That's their baby, and in the end, we're just humans tasked to do something not many people can. They've been challenged enough by this tumor, and now they're forced to make what is probably the biggest decision of their lives. It'll take some more convincing on that therapist's part, but I'm fairly confident Crystal will be admitted tonight, and I'll perform her surgery first thing in the morning."

"I understand, Dr. Brandt," he said. "When I ordered the scans, I didn't expect it to come back as a glioblastoma multiforme. This must be such a devastating blow to them, and I know I can't attach myself like—"

I placed my hand on his shoulder and smiled sympathetically. "You've attached yourself to this patient as you would have any other. Getting close is both a blessing and a curse, I think. However, if we can't get attached, at least a little bit, then what's the point of working in pediatrics?"

The elevator admitted us onto the floor where most patients lived with us for months or stayed in recovery for days or weeks.

"How do you do it?" he half-smiled at me. "It seems as though every time we go through this with our surgical teams, you find a way to cope with every possible outcome."

"I'm not doing anything special. I'm just a man who does everything he can to save lives when permitted to do so. In the end, it's never my decision. I put everything on the table in that room, and I only hope it was well laid out. I also know that we work in a profession that tries to kick our butts at every turn. I won't let that mess with my mind. In fact, I'm on my way to see my little superhero fan, Kaleb. If I were still preoccupied with Crystal's parents, I wouldn't be useful to Kaleb or my other patients. Seriously, man, I have to let the powers that be take it from here, or I will lose my mind."

He grinned and glanced around the holographic rehabilitation room where we stood. "Well, I guess I've lost my own mind because I followed you into the recovery center as if this were where my next appointment is."

I chuckled. "Well," I pointed to where one of our nurses was playing catch with Kaleb, "if you'd like, you can throw the Nerf football with Kaleb. His coordination has vastly improved, and he's a fierce competitor. You're more than welcome to take him on."

Dr. Nadeer grinned, his white hair practically glowing from the lights in this brilliantly designed area. I couldn't help but chuckle at how he looked transformed from one of our most serious doctors into a half-human and half-cartoon version of himself.

"You're laughing because you know your patient will likely beat me at this game of catch, eh?" he asked, oblivious to my train of thought.

I pinched my lips together and dared not to laugh again. "I would never laugh at one of my patients kicking a highly-skilled neurologist's butt at a game of Nerf football."

"Look, Nurse Darcy," Kaleb said with an infectious laugh, turning his attention to where Dr. Nadeer and I stood, "it's an Oompa Loompa from the Chocolate Factory." He chuckled while I watched Darcy cover her smile.

"That's not very kind, Kaleb," she finally tried to scold the boy. Kaleb still wore the head dressing I'd wrapped this morning after checking the stitches and incision marks I'd made to rid him of a benign tumor.

Kaleb began singing the Oompa Loompa song, and I could tell Dr. Nadeer hadn't understood my patient's observation. His tanned skin looked orange, and his hair and eyebrows were so white they glowed. Now, all I needed was to see his bright white teeth, and then I'd be screwed by uncontrollable laughter.

"What's an Oompa Loompa?" Dr. Nadeer questioned.

"It seems he's got you pinned for a character from a family movie." I paused as Darcy brought Kaleb's attention back to playing catch with her. "I should thank you." I clapped him on his shoulder. "Now, I know his memory hasn't been marred after surgery. We just need to keep working on his fine motor skills."

"Well, Dr. Brandt," the neurologist said, "I will leave you to your patient. I am glad to be of assistance."

I grew serious, matching his demeanor. "As I said, you are no good to your next patient if you allow Crystal's current state to affect you. Give Mr. and Mrs. Johnson some time. Most likely, we'll be back in that room later, Crystal will be admitted, and my surgical teams will have that tumor out faster than it took her parents to make this decision."

"You're correct. I think I'll have a fresh cup of coffee, clear my head, and then prep for my next appointment in thirty minutes," he said.

As Dr. Nadeer exited, I saw a Nerf ball being thrown in a beautiful spiral directly toward my head from my peripheral. I reflexively caught the ball, then picked up my clipboard and vocally commanded the computer inside to pull up Kaleb's charts for the day.

"Not only can you throw the ball better than your favorite doctor," I teased while I used my thumb to scroll through Kaleb's charts swiftly, "but it appears you're a superhero yourself, kiddo."

"I'm doing great, aren't I?" the ten-year-old questioned.

"You've made more progress since I checked on you this morning than you have all week." I knelt and twisted the pointed part of the ball into his chest, prompting him to laugh.

"He's done very well, transitioning from the holographic ball to the Nerf ball." Darcy smiled at me. "Good call on that. His motor skills seemed to improve further with a more physical challenge."

"Is that so?" I eyed Kaleb. "Well, you've proven something that I never knew until now."

"I thought doctors knew *everything*," he said with a roll of his eyes.

"I thought *I* knew everything," I said playfully as I stood. "It appears I must humbly admit that even the most brilliant and gifted doctors, such as myself, don't know it all."

"That's a little scary," Kaleb shot back.

I grinned, loving how much his confidence and humor were on display. His parents would be delighted when they arrived to visit their son tonight.

"Trust me, kid," I arched an eyebrow at him, "there's nothing to fear when a doctor has more to learn. It's only a problem when a doctor thinks they know everything there is to know." I chucked the ball out to the holographic field, sending Kaleb after it so I could watch his movements and speak to my nurse. His improvements were impressive, and if all went increasingly well over the next few days, I'd sign off on his release from the hospital, requiring only weekly visits and scans while I monitored his brain for possible issues.

For now, my patient was on his way to a full recovery, and it flooded me with excitement that outweighed my concerns from Crystal's consultation. This was why I loved being a pediatric neurosurgeon. Kaleb was an easy example of that. When given a chance to help change and save children's lives, I thrived. Losing my sister compelled me to move into the specialty of epilepsy because, despite how wealthy my parents were, their money couldn't save my sister's life. Now, I got to help those who felt helpless. Giving children life-saving options—ones my sister never got—gave me the utmost satisfaction.

When I first met Kaleb and his family, Kaleb could barely go a few minutes without having a seizure due to the pressure the tumor was putting on his brain. Now it was removed, and I was standing here with a smile that stretched from ear to ear. I contributed to Kaleb's ability to live a full life, and that was the most rewarding part of this job. Well, that and playing with my patients in this fantastic technology room as they recovered.

"Dr. Brandt," the front desk assistant, Preston, called my name, "you have an urgent phone call from Dr. Nadeer."

"I'll take it in my office down the hall," I said, turning toward Darcy. "Tell Kaleb that I'm going to be able to help another patient because of what I learned from his amazing skills."

She smiled. "He'll love to hear that. Surgery?" she questioned.

"Let's hope. Of course, Dr. Nadeer wouldn't be calling me this soon after leaving as an Oompa Loompa otherwise," I chuckled.

"I'll upload the vitals, stats, and test results and send them to you."

"Let Kaleb know I'll be back to check on him in a bit."

With that, I rushed down the hall that led to the doctors' offices in this ward. I picked up the call, and from the triumphant tone in Dr. Nadeer's voice, I knew why he was calling. Crystal would be admitted into the hospital, and I would be up hours before the sun, scrubbing in. We'd be performing emergency surgery, and Crystal would be joining the likes of young Kaleb as a child whose life was drastically improved.

Today was a damn fine day, even if it was yet another day that I'd been distracted by thoughts of Jessa. A month had passed since our unexpected run-in, and there hadn't been one day that went by that I wished, above all things, that I'd grabbed her phone number instead of giving her mine.

I hated being cursed to wish I had her in my life again. I'd never felt heartache like this over a woman. Unfortunately, karma hated my ass when it came to relationships, and after what I had done to Jessa, I guess it was my turn to feel the pain.

I believe I finally knew what it must've felt like for her when I just up and callously walked away. God help me. She was engaged now, and she had a child. I had no business thinking about her like this. But hell, if I could knock this shit off, I would.

Jessa may have said we were just young and foolish back then, but I was no fool. I loved her—I never stopped loving her. I was just stupid enough to leave her in the worst way possible, and there's nothing I wouldn't do to take it all back.

Jessa

I walked out of my job, cheerful and ready to head straight to Jackson's game tonight. Being a receptionist at a dentist's office was a far cry from what I'd set out to be in life, but hey, we all have plans for our lives, and fate always seems to step in and change the game. It's all how you look at it, I guess.

I choose to look at the positive side of life. Everything happens for a purpose—a good reason—and what defines us is how we choose to deal with adversity.

I wouldn't trade being a receptionist for Dr. Meckler, even though the irony was that I was initially going to college to become a dentist myself. Funny how it all worked out. When I graduated high school as valedictorian, I envisioned myself sitting in the doctor's chair.

I'd have loved to have finished my schooling—I'd even done some evening online classes over the years—but with Jackson's seizures and treatments, I never had much time for myself. I didn't mind. He was my number one priority. I wanted him to live like an average kid who didn't suffer from this genetic disorder, and I was about to watch him live it up tonight at his football game. Nothing made me happier than watching him thrive.

Ring! Ring! Ring!

"Hey," I answered Jackson's call as I weaved my way through the brisk streets of the city. "What's going on?"

"Just making sure my number one fan will be at my game tonight," he said.

I smirked, nodding at the man I was almost shoved into while turning to hail a cab. "Ah. What's *really* up, Jacks?" I asked with a laugh.

"I love you?"

"Jackson Thomas Stein." The kid was no good at pulling one over on me, but he wouldn't be Jackson if he didn't try.

While Jackson was beating around the bush, I was about to be thrown into a damn tree by a grouchy old woman determined to grab the taxi I'd flagged down. I could hear Jackson's friends laughing and goofing off in the background as the hag tried to shove her way around me.

"Mom? Hey, Mom?"

"I'm here. Hold on." I held the phone against my chest and turned to the woman whose freshly shaped pink nails threatened to puncture my skin if I didn't back off this cab. "Hey," I eyed her with more shock than not. "Seriously, why don't we—"

"Listen here, you little tart," she snapped, and suddenly I was face-to-face with the nasty woman. "I waved the cab down first. You can wait. I might—"

"Take the fucking cab. Dear God."

"Fucking? How dare you speak to me—"

"All right, knock it off." A man from out of nowhere stepped between the old lady and me. "I think that's enough."

Honking, traffic, and a bitter old woman—combined with this dude getting in the middle of whatever was happening between her and me—were leading to mass hysteria. I'd rather walk eight blocks or eight goddamn miles just to get out of this situation.

"I said to take the cab." The quicker she got out of my face, the better.

"I was planning on it!" she snapped before she shoved her way into the taxi and smugly flipped me the middle finger before the cab drove away.

What a sweetheart, I thought, resisting the urge to be childish and flip her the bird right back.

"Mom?" I heard Jackson's muffled voice question again from where I held the phone to my chest.

"Right here," I sighed, putting the phone to my ear and smiling at the man who'd broken up the senior citizen fight I'd become an unwilling part of. "Thank you, sir," I said, hoping he knew I appreciated him hailing another cab for me to get the hell out of here.

"Just another day in the city. Have a good one," he said, waving as my cab driver pulled into the stopped traffic on the street.

"Hang on, Jacks," I said as I climbed into the taxi and gave the driver my address. "Okay, sorry. What were we talking about? Oh, yes. I'm going to your game if I can get home and get friggin changed."

"Friggin?" Jackson laughed. "Coming from my sweet mom who drops F-bombs on a poor *old woman*? I heard you."

I rubbed my forehead. "I'm sorry about that. I think that was the strangest encounter I've ever had in my life."

"When will you listen to Warren and me when we say that grabbing a cab is old news? Just call a stupid Uber and be on your way."

"In *this* city? What's the fun in that?"

"Well, maybe you won't go to hell for cursing out old women? That's elderly abuse, ya know."

"Yeah, yeah. Okay," I said with a smile. "What do you really want, Jackson?"

"I want to know if Paige and I can hit the movies tonight and maybe..." He held onto the word maybe for a bit too long.

"Maybe? Maybe what?" I asked with a little more firmness in my tone.

"Well, you and Warren have met her parents, and we just, well—"

"The fact that you're nervous to ask if you can stay at your girlfriend's house tonight should tell you my answer is *no*," I finished with a smile.

"Mom," he tried to settle me down with a sigh.

"Shouldn't you be in the locker room or something, getting ready for the big game tonight? It's the final game of the season, and here I am, about to go over how the word no means no."

"It's just that—well, what if we win tonight? That means I led the team to our finals and toward another championship."

I rolled my eyes. "There is no *I* in *team*," I said with sarcasm, knowing it would annoy him. "So, if the team wins tonight, Paige can join you with all of your teammates after the game like the cheerleaders always do."

"Mom," he pushed.

"Jacks, I don't care if Warren and I have met her parents or not. I don't care if the NFL drafts you tonight because of how well you play. You're not going to Paige's house."

"Damn it, Mom," he snapped.

"Oh no, you don't. Don't you dare curse at me. Get with your team, and we'll see you later at the game."

"Fine. Bye."

The cab stopped, I paid the fare, and the new skirt I wore snagged on the door as I jumped out. How did this lovely day go on such a rapid downward spiral?

Ring! Ring! Ring!

"Warren," I answered my fiancé's call. "Please tell me you'll be at the game tonight."

"Well, that's why I was calling," he said. "It looks like I have a hang-up."

"A hang-up?" I nodded and smiled as I walked through the lobby of our lavish building. "Please don't tell me you're working late again."

"I'm working late," I heard his smile through the phone, "but I'll be sure to meet my beautiful fiancée—who can't decide on a wedding date —at Jackson's game."

I blew out a breath of relief. "Good. In the last hour, I've dealt with nothing but crazy."

"Another patient giving you trouble because they forgot to floss, and the doctor is sending you to take care of the bill?"

"Huh? What does that even mean?" I said with confusion. Warren could be semi-funny at times, but most of the time, his attempt at humor was massively lame. "Nevermind. I'm walking into the house. Jacks is trying to sleep at Paige's house, and I almost got into a brawl with an old hag."

"Wait, what in the world are you talking about? Start with the old-lady brawl," he chuckled as I heard him greet his driver.

I breezed into our apartment, which had a combination of Warren's baroque tastes and my cozy farmhouse taste, and I plopped onto the sofa in the atrium. Somehow both of our styles worked, but it took a damn good interior designer to marry the two opposites.

"It was nothing, just an old woman being nasty by claiming my cab. She flew in on her broomstick and stole the damn thing."

"Shit, you did have a bad day," he said with a laugh.

"No." I smiled, feeling more relaxed smelling the fragrance of the lilies he'd bought me after we'd gotten into a stupid fight over something I couldn't remember anymore. "I was having a great day until that woman came around. Now, Jackson's trying to work some skill with staying over at Paige's because we *met* her parents." I rolled my eyes and half-smiled when I heard Warren laugh.

"And so, it all begins," he chuckled again. "Let him stay. Her parents seem just as responsible as we are."

"No, that's not the point, Warren." I sighed for what seemed like the hundredth time since answering Jackson's phone call. "If we allow this, he will take more and more liberties. He's only sixteen. Just forget it," I said, sitting up and slapping my palms on my knees. "I need to get ready to go. Let's all revisit this conversation later, shall we?"

"We *could* have the night alone?"

"Um, no," I said, marching toward the steps leading to our master suite. "You're not getting anything tonight." I smiled, hearing Warren's laugh. "I'll see you at the game."

"Love ya, babe," he said, and we ended the call.

I was at my usual spot in the stands, watching and cheering on my son's team as they led the game in the third quarter by fourteen points. I loved everything about football nights, especially watching my son play so well and throw the football with such ease and finesse.

The cool, crisp air had me chilled to the bone. I was counting on Warren to be here and keep me warm, but no dice. As usual, he got held up and had to go back to the office to handle a last-minute deal instead of putting it all to bed for the night and dealing with work in the morning.

I wasn't surprised, though. Warren's job held him prisoner, and that's why I was wrapped in my fuzzy, warm blanket, watching intently as the ball was being thrown in a beautiful spiral by Jackson. That was until everything stopped, and my ears rang while things went into slow motion as if I were watching a horror movie with my son as the star.

After the ball was thrown, Jackson was rushed by the biggest player on the opposing team. The guy got past Jackson's offensive line, and Jacks was slammed into the ground so hard that I felt it in my bones.

As any mom would, I stared in disbelief at first, and that's when I saw it. Jackson's body was rolling into a seizure as the coaches and team medical staff ran out to him. I bounded down the bleachers, skipping multiple steps at once, knowing that I needed to get to my boy as fast as possible. He hadn't had a seizure in so long that he was cleared to play ball, and now this?

I was on the field, running to him, when the ambulance drove onto the grass. Jackson was in the final jerks of this seizure, and tears streamed down my face as I had to stand back and let the medical team aide him.

"Mrs. Stein," I hardly heard Coach Wartham's voice. "This is Jackson's mother."

My head snapped over to the medic. Jackson's body was limp as the medic checked his pupils and called out the vitals to someone I couldn't focus on.

"Yes, I'm his mom," I said, my eyes never leaving my son. "Is he waking up?"

"His vitals are stable. We've got to take him to the hospital, though. He took a very hard hit, losing his helmet and getting hit in the head by another helmet in the process."

"I'm riding in that ambulance," I demanded as if they wouldn't let me.

"Yes, ma'am. We need to leave immediately. You can make any necessary phone calls on the way. Your son needs a scan, which is being arranged with the ER trauma team waiting for us."

"Thank you," I said through chattering teeth.

I climbed into the back of the ambulance while oxygen was strapped over Jackson's mouth, his eyes still closed. The medic reassured me that Jackson was stable, but this injury could be critical.

I numbly gave Jackson's medical history to the attending medic while the ambulance sped away from the stadium. I held his limp hand, feeling as helpless as always when he had seizures. This felt different, though, and I was scared.

It was Jackson's first seizure in a very long time, but he wasn't waking up. So many variables ran through my head, from brain trauma to concussions—they were things that affected Jackson differently than the average person because of his condition. It felt like my world was frozen, and all I knew to do was talk to my son to let him know I was with him.

God, please let him wake up and be just fine.

I must've chanted that over and over in my mind until the ambulance pulled up to the hospital, and I watched the ER and trauma staff receive my son. I had no idea what would happen, but my motherly instinct told me it wasn't good.

Chapter Six

Jessa

It'd been a week since Jacks's injury, and his diagnosis was better than I'd imagined. He'd suffered a concussion—which he'd managed to pull out of without further harm—but waiting alone in that cold, tense room for the doctors to come in still weighed heavily on my mind. Warren didn't even show up until after I'd been called back to see my son.

He'll be fine, Jess. It happens all the time, and we're already used to his seizures. Fuck Warren for being so dismissive on the phone about the situation that night. I was still pissed about it.

I hated to feel this way about the man, but I couldn't help it. Forgive me for being an *overprotective mom*, but I didn't care what anyone thought. We beat these seizures before, and now they were returning thanks to that fucking concussion.

"You doing okay tonight?" Warren asked after coming home early from work.

I tensed when his hand reached for me where I sat on my favorite lounging sofa. I was curled up with a knitted throw blanket, and my body was molded against the large throw pillow.

"Babe?" Warren called out again, and I finally looked at him with the same disgust I'd developed through anger and frustration since that night.

"What?" I tried to keep from snapping, hopefully preventing another argument wherein I received a delivery of flowers to *make it all okay* again. I sighed and pulled my hair out of the ponytail that was the source of my current headache. "I'm sorry. My head is killing me. I just need to go to bed."

I stood, but Warren was faster than I expected. He sat on the couch and pulled me onto his lap. I cringed when he began to rub my shoulders, wishing I could shake this mood.

"Damn, you're all knotted up," he said, rubbing my shoulders in a soothing motion. "Would you like me to call my therapist? Is this why you've been so cranky this week?"

Oh, right. You forgot I'm still pissed at you, and flowers didn't fix the problem this time, my thoughts rumbled through my mind.

I shrugged him off and rose. "I don't need your damn therapist."

Warren's eyes widened, and his features darkened some. "Then what the hell is your problem? It can't be Jackson because the doctors cleared him, and he hasn't had a seizure since the night of his concussion. So, what is it now?"

I heard the rising frustration in his voice, and the last thing I wanted was another fight.

I couldn't help but run my hands through my hair and grip the sides of my head. "What if they do come back?" I looked toward the steps that led upstairs, where I knew Jackson was doing his homework.

"Are we going to play the *what-if* game tonight and ruin the fact that I came home early with Chinese takeout?" He smiled playfully at me. "I saved you from cooking, and this is the thanks I get?"

I eyed him and his horrible attempt to make me lighten up. "While I appreciate that gesture, I need *you* to appreciate where I stand with my son at the moment."

"Your son?" He seemed offended by that. "I may not have the adoption papers filed, but it doesn't mean he's just your son, Jess."

"I'm sorry. I didn't mean to come off that way."

He stood and brought me into his arms. "I know this is upsetting, but even though Jacks isn't cleared to play ball, that doesn't mean we're going backward with his seizures."

"Maybe it's the way you responded that night." I pulled back and stared him in the eyes. "Maybe that's why I feel suddenly like it's just Jackson and me again."

Warren ran a hand through his hair. "We're back to this again, eh? I'm the problem?"

"You're not the *problem*. I don't know what the problem is," I tried to diffuse the argument I knew I'd lose—or just gain more fucking flowers from. "I don't feel right about any of this. I don't like it."

"I don't like that you're feeling so doom and gloom about everything, babe," he softened his voice and features. "Please tell me you're not like this around Jackson."

"Of course, I'm not. Jesus, why would you think that I would bring this around my son? The last thing he needs is his mom to fall apart."

"Then, pull your shit together," Warren teased, but, like everything he seemed to do lately, it wasn't funny.

"I need to go to bed. I'm going to check on Jacks, and then it's lights out for me. I'm done with this week."

"It's seven in the evening," Warren said.

"Good, I'll get a full night's rest before I go back to work tomorrow."

"Talk to me, Jessica. Is it me, pressuring you for the wedding date?"

Fucking hell. I forgot about that until now.

"I don't care about wedding dates. I wanted you to be there for Jackson and me that night, but work was in the way as usual. Hell, I think if I *did* decide on a wedding date, you'd have a snag with a deal and leave me standing at the altar, wondering where my groom is."

"What has gotten into you?" Warren slumped back down on the couch and propped his feet on the marble table in front of it. He grabbed the remote and pointedly ignored me. "Go to bed. I think your hormones have gone a little wild. You're just being cruel now."

He was right about one thing; I was turning cold toward him. I was taking shots at Warren just to be mean because I was angry about what was happening to my son, and I felt alone in my concerns for his well-being. This wasn't who I was, and I didn't like what the stress was doing to me.

"I'm sorry. Please just understand that it's tough not knowing if Jackson will have issues after the hit he took."

"Understandable." Warren was dismissive. "Get some rest. Maybe being at work will help you loosen up, and you'll realize everything that the doctors and I already know."

I dug out a smile I knew was hiding somewhere deep inside of me. "You know what they say about a mother's instinct, right?"

"Yes," Warren finally smiled. "I know that instinct is prompting you to want to kick my ass these days if I say the wrong things at the wrong times."

"I'm sorry for that." I really was, but I couldn't help feeling the way I did. I leaned over and kissed his forehead. "I love you. I'm sorry, but I'm going to go to bed."

He ran his fingers across my cheek. "I love you too. Look at me," he said when my eyes diverted from his. "We're all going to be fine."

That's when his phone buzzed.

"Text or email?" I smiled smugly, knowing someone out there was about to pull Warren away for the rest of the evening whether I stayed down here a moment longer or not.

"Give me a goddamn break. I have to go to London in two days," he snarled as he scrolled through the phone, staring at it as if it were the adversary I'd always believed it to be. "Those bastards couldn't close the acquisition of that business, and now they're bringing me in to do the work. I should fire all of them."

"You act like you own the entire company," I tried to tease and lighten his mood.

He looked up at me. "I'd love to take you with me. I have to be there for a week, but—"

"*But* nothing." I chuckled. "You know I'm not leaving Jackson right now."

"No doubt," he said. "Will you be okay if I take off for a week?"

"I'll be fine," I said with ease. "Handle your stuff. Maybe I'll run a bath and then head to bed."

"Okay, babe. I'll come up in a bit," he said as he got up to grab his laptop and start working.

As I turned and hopped up the steps, I heard a thud followed by grunting noises coming from Jackson's room.

"Warren!" I shouted, leaping up the steps.

Warren flew up the stairs as I threw open Jackson's door to find him in a seizure. He was on the ground and kicking against his gaming chair.

Shit! Why was he playing a game with a seizure warning on the box?

Warren and I got him on his side and made sure he did nothing to harm himself while the seizure ran its course. This was what I was dreading, and now I knew I wasn't losing my mind. I'd demanded further tests, but everyone was confident Jacks would be fine after his concussion. I guess I was the only one who saw that differently, so what was I thinking by not running with my instincts?

Nothing would stop me from getting a second opinion and having more scans to see why Jackson's seizures were back. Then, I would get him the help he needed. Medical science had advanced tremendously, and I knew there had to be a better neurologist out there who would be willing to help Jacks get past this.

Fuck me. Cameron! The memory of Cam telling me this was his area of expertise made me nearly shout out his name. All I needed to do now was figure out how to get us referred to my ex—who happened to be a pediatric neurosurgeon.

Suddenly, I hated myself for deleting the phone number he gave me. There was nothing I wouldn't do to be able to call him right now and get his help.

Chapter Seven

Cameron

I pulled up to Collin's place close to an hour after finishing my shift at the hospital. You'd think I wasn't born and raised in Southern California because I was dumb enough to leave during commuting hours, knowing damn well I would end up stuck in traffic for an hour just to go ten miles across town. There was no way around this bullshit, though. Taking side streets wasn't an option because they were under construction, and the only other route would've sent my ass into the desert.

"Hey, girlfriend," Collin smarted off, as he always did when he saw my Porsche. "Glad you finally fucking made it. I pushed out the dinner reservations, knowing your ass would be late since you insist on driving this Barbie car."

"This little Barbie car can take that fucken Bugatti you drive any day of the week," I said as I approached him in his driveway, nodding toward the closed garage where he kept his boy toy. "You know that," I rose my eyebrows to meet his usual bright grin, "I know that, and even the cop who pulled both our asses over on PCH knows that." I chuckled at the memory of the police unexpectedly showing up to a spontaneous drag race. Luckily, Collin's smooth-talking narrowly got us out of costly tickets.

Collin rolled his eyes and sighed. "Well, that race was cut short, or else I would have easily smoked this car—"

"Good God," I heard Elena call from behind us, a laugh in her voice. "I swear, if Collin isn't trying to taunt you into illegally racing, he's giving you hell for sleeping in or something."

I turned and grinned at Collin's lovely and full-of-life wife. She tucked herself into Collin's side after he welcomed her with an open arm. These two were the perfect match. Both had gone through hell and back—amnesia and everything—but fate pulled through. They persevered through obstacles that most people can't fathom, reinforcing that nothing can keep you apart when you've met your soulmate.

I'd like to think that could be true for Jessa and me. I really would. I had hoped for that night after night since seeing her again. I knew it was fate that'd brought Jessa back to me, and now fate needed to do some dirty work to get that fiancé of hers to move on and find *his* soulmate.

Jesus, Cam, I thought to myself. *Give this bullshit a rest.*

Since I'd seen Jessa again, my mind drifted to her constantly, no matter how I tried not to think about her. I couldn't get through an entire conversation lately without daydreaming.

Collin snapped his fingers at me, his eyes glistening in humor as he stared at me with a curious expression. "Toss me the keys to this 911, my man," he said, holding out his hand for the keys to my Porsche.

"I didn't realize you wanted to win a street race that bad," I chuckled.

"Yeah, in that case, forget it. Get your ass in your car, and I'll follow you to your place," he said, turning toward his garage.

Elena stood there and watched me carefully.

Shit, she must've caught my ass too. This wasn't good. Giving Elena reason to wonder why I was so distracted was one thing, but giving Collin a reason was entirely another. I knew he would make this the number one topic of discussion when we met up with the guys tonight.

"Whoever she is," Elena started with a smile, "she's one lucky girl, Cam. Now, go have fun with the guys."

My mouth dropped open. Yep, I was fucked. "It's not what you think," I stammered, trying to muster up some excuse. "Just going over a surgery in my head."

She nodded. "Ah, sort of like Collin does?"

"You're good," I chuckled.

"I'm Cuban, and I'd like to think we Latin people know a thing or two about passion. Also, I'm married to a neurosurgeon, and *you* are practically his twin," she said with a grin. "You're both easily readable, especially when you lie."

"Got it," I sighed. "Well, wish me luck with her, then, will you?" Yes, I was desperate. I was this close to heading down to the closest church and asking the congregation to pray for me.

"Always, Cam."

"See ya, Laney," I said with a laugh, seeing that damn devious look of hers. There was no doubt in my mind Elena was bound to spill her guts to the guys' wives when they got together.

Whatever, I was clearly obsessed. I felt like I'd been catapulted back in time, my feelings for Jessa as fresh and real as ever.

There was a reason fate brought us back together after all these years. That had to be it. Fate was at work here, and perhaps some karma, which was the part I wasn't exactly excited about.

My phone rang as I started my car and buckled up. The display on my dash showed the call was coming from my secretary, which confused me because I was sure she would've been scrambling around at this time, gathering her things and heading out the door for the night.

"Sup, Janice," I said, backing out and following Collin to the stoplight down the street from his driveway.

"Dr. Brandt?" she said with some hesitation in her voice.

"Janice? You don't sound well. Everything okay?"

"I understand it's after-hours with you being on call and all…" she trailed off.

"You also understand that I will never be upset when you ring my phone at any hour," I reassured my seemingly upset secretary. "What's going on?"

"Dr. Brandt," she repeated my name, "there is a woman here in tears, begging me to contact you, and—"

What the fuck? "Do you need to call security? Or have *me* call security to have her removed?"

"No," she said.

"I'm confused," I said, pulling the car over so I could figure this out.

Just as I wondered if Janice was being robbed at gunpoint or something, I heard a soft, familiar voice in the background that made my heart skip a beat.

Jessa. As much as I gladly embraced the idea that she was in my office, I instantly wondered why. How the fuck was this happening? Fate was at play, and with a smile on my face, I wondered if my Jessa had been fighting a mental battle over me since she saw me last, just like I had been doing on my end about her. What a beautiful ending to this lonely chapter in my life. Jessa was back and in my office, looking for me.

"What's the name of the woman?" I asked with a smile in my voice, giddy as fuck.

"Jessica Stein," she said softly. "She is here with her fiancé and her son. She says she knows you and that you are her last hope for her son, and she doesn't know what else to do."

My giddiness came to an abrupt halt. This wasn't exactly the reunion I'd imagined, but at least it was something.

I thought back to Jessa's daring and bold personality, remembering how she was fearless in getting what she wanted. But her son? What could've happened to bring her to my office for her son?

I went into emergency mode. "Janice, if it's an emergency, she needs to have her son seen in the ER."

I watched Collin's car do a U-turn and saw him pull behind me in my rearview mirror.

"She understands," Janice said. "She was hoping to meet with you, though. She said if you turn her son away, she's just going to fly back to New York tonight."

"Okay, I'm totally confused," I said, pinching the bridge of my nose. "Jessica Stein is a good friend of mine. Can you give her my cell number and have her call me? I'll handle this from here."

"Everything okay?" Collin questioned as he approached my

window. I raised a finger to politely ask him to hold on while I worked to end the call with my secretary, who seemed just as confused as I was.

I hung up, rolled down my window, and looked at Collin. "A friend of mine randomly showed up at my office needing help, and I might have to head over there. She's going to call, and I'll have more information in a second."

Collin's forehead creased with curiosity. "Do you think that is a good idea? I mean, you know her well?"

He went into chief neurosurgeon mode, and I knew why. This was entirely out of the norm, and it probably seemed like I was about to offer a favor because I wanted to get laid or something.

Jessa wasn't the type to do rude shit, though. If she was trying to contact me out of desperation, that was something on another level. I was *not* a man who questioned a mother's instinct to protect their children.

I answered the phone as soon as the New York area code showed up on the incoming call screen.

Chapter Eight

Jessa

It felt strange to let my mother-hen instincts take over and barge into Cameron's office like I did, demanding to speak to him like some deranged woman at a department store who wanted to speak to the manager, but I shoved that to the side. Being told it would be another six months before my son could see Dr. Tsang was the straw that broke this mama camel's back. That truth, however, didn't make me feel like any less of an ass at the moment.

After hanging up with Cameron, I was escorted to his office, where my insecurities pulsated through me with every tick of the clock as I waited for him. I had two options: I could run out of here and act like nothing ever happened, or I could face the consequences of my Entitled Woman of the Year stunt.

"I'm such a dumb ass," I softly mumbled as I rested my face in my hands.

"I beg to differ," I heard Cameron say with a hint of sympathy.

I snapped my head up, and my eyes met his deep blue ones. "Cam,"

I said with relief, and that's when the tears started streaming down my face.

After endless worry about Jackson's seizures returning with no help in sight, I finally broke down. Perfect timing, too.

I felt my skin burning with the touch of his familiar hand tenderly smoothing over my back. "Jess?" he questioned, making me raise my head to see him kneeling in front of me with a look of concern.

"I'm sorry," I managed with a sniff and a smile. "I don't know what possessed me to think I could insist upon you seeing my son like this. I'm embarrassed and feel like a fool."

Cameron tilted his head to the side and licked his enticing lips. "I like to refer to that as motherly instincts." He winked, and my heart rate sped up. He always had a way of dazzling me.

You're engaged to Warren! I internally scolded myself.

"I like to refer to it as that too." I rose, and Cameron stood, towering over me, as I managed to succeed in the desperate act of pulling my shit together. "I know there is a process for all of this—trust me, I get that—but I'm desperate, Cam," I said, my eyes fixed on his and my voice set with steady determination.

"I understand that. I also know you well enough to know that it would take a monumental situation to bring you into my office like this," he softly chuckled, most likely remembering the young college girl he dated who was once filled with drive and fearless grit. "Where's your boy?" he asked, glancing around his empty waiting area.

"He's with my fiancé. They're packing at the hotel and," I glanced at the silver watch on my wrist, "most likely headed back to New York on a flight that leaves in three hours."

Cameron frowned. "Without you?"

I nodded, thinking about how irritated Warren would get when I did impulsive things like this. In fact, I knew Warren *would* be on that flight, probably insisting to my son that I was a fool to believe Cameron would make any effort to help me. Warren had always liked to brag about how he was better at making decisions because of his logical way of thinking—his *business sense.*

Warren and I typically had a very low-key, easy relationship. But it seemed like ever since the going got tough because of the seizures, he disapproved of my reactions. I guess it was easy to be in a relationship where nothing was ever really happening—it was not so hard to be compatible while coexisting peacefully. I couldn't say I was a fan of Warren's behavior since the seizures started again, though. We were totally out of step, constantly butting heads, and I was in no mood for someone to be tripping me up while I was trying so desperately to get ahead and be proactive for my kid. I didn't appreciate the implication that I was behaving hysterically, and Warren seemed plugged into that idea for some reason.

"If we leave now, we can catch them at the hotel," Cameron said, bringing me out of my thoughts and back to the issue at hand.

"Let me text Warren and figure out where he's at."

"Great idea, tell them to meet us here. That way, I can chat with your son and give him an unofficial evaluation to get him on the books." He smiled at me as I waited for Warren's text or call back. "Since I'm not accepting new patients, you're lucky you're still the only beautiful woman who can bend me to her will with just a look." He grinned, the soft black beard on his face trimmed to perfection, bringing out the sparkle in his eyes.

"Thank God I still have that effect on you," I shot a smile right back at his handsome face and felt the old Jess return, insecurities gone in that second.

"You'll always have that effect on me, Jessa," he said, his voice lower and smoother than before.

That did something to me. I mean, it really did something to me. It had awoken an instant sensation within me that I'd not felt in years. Or had I ever felt this way before? No. No, I'd never had my breath taken away by a man for any reason, not like this.

Focus, Jessica! I demanded myself as my phone dinged when Warren's text came through.

"Son of a bitch," I said, reading the text. "What a dick!"

"He took an earlier flight and left you?" Cameron questioned.

"He's leaving either way. He said that if I want to embarrass myself, go ahead, but he's heading back to reality with Jackson."

"Why did he even come? What are you going to do?" Cameron

asked me, almost challenging me to see if I'd let my dick of a fiancé get away with this bullshit.

This was humiliating, and the fact that Cameron asked me what I would do made me question everything. Maybe Warren was right, and I was stupid to show up here. Cam already said he's not accepting new patients. Why did I fly across the country without reassurances? What kind of mother does that to her child?

"You know, I'm an idiot." I smiled at him, hoping that would get me off the hook. "If you'd like, I can buy you dinner for your trouble, but Warren is right. I need to head back to—"

"Fuck that shit," Cameron responded. "Pardon my directness, but Warren is a *prick*. If he weren't, he'd be thrilled that the doctor you searched out is willing to help you." He frowned, "You have a car?"

"I have an Uber app," I smiled, feeling a sense of peace wash over me, hearing Cameron confirm I wasn't entirely out of my mind for doing this—and that Warren *was* a prick.

"Well, no need for Uber," he said, dramatically raising his hand toward the entrance of his office. "I'm here, and I think you'll like the car I'm driving to get your ass to your fiancé and son before they jump the next flight out of here."

Usually, I would have given Cameron a hard time for whatever hundred-thousand-dollar sports car he was driving, but my mind was preoccupied with my fiancé's text.

"Why wouldn't he have called me?" I said after Cam and I were in his car, pulling out onto the street as though we'd just driven onto a racetrack.

"That I can't answer for you," Cam responded, eyes flicking up to the rearview mirror, most likely checking to see if a cop was on his ass for nearly running a red light.

"I'm sorry," I answered with a sigh.

"Never apologize," Cam said smoothly, making the anxiety that'd been building inside me, quiet down.

I smiled over at the familiar way he was driving. One hand on the stick shift of the Porsche, the other gripping the steering wheel, and eyes set with a hunger to chew up the miles on this freeway and close the distance between the hospital and us in record speed.

"Still trying to set records in sports cars?" I asked, soaking up this moment of familiarity.

"Always," he said, glancing over his shoulder and sliding into the carpool lane. "You still telling people how to drive while they set important driving records?"

I softly chuckled. It felt nice to have someone talk to me without being patronizing for the first time in a while.

"Important driving records?"

"You heard me," he said with a flashy grin I remembered well. "The last time you and I were on this freeway together, I hit one hundred and eighty. This time I plan to—"

"Get us killed?" I questioned with a laugh.

"Ha," he scoffed. "You've been away from me too long, Jessa." He arched an eyebrow at me, and I would've started to come undone at *that* familiar look, but the exit was coming up for the airport, bringing me out of some college hormonal awakening and back to the reason I was in the car with Cameron in the first place.

"I have no idea where we'll find them," I said, seeing cars go on for miles, offloading departing passengers to their terminals.

"Use that feature on your phone known as the call button, ring that ultra-considerate man you call a fiancé, and find out where they are," Cam said with sarcasm.

"Right," I responded as I called Warren's phone.

"Try again," Cam said with some irritation after watching me stare blankly at my phone when Warren sent me to voicemail.

"Yeah?" Warren answered on my second try. "We're walking into the airport now. Are you on your way, or are you—"

"I'm here," I said, looking through the crowds of people for my fiancé as soon as Cameron slowed the car where I pointed. "This airline right here, Cam," I said, trying to navigate. I suddenly spotted Warren, who made eye contact with me, then turned to walk inside.

"You did *not* bring that man all the way down here," Warren snarled into the phone after I stepped out of the car and walked into the terminal, trying to find my son and him.

"No, I didn't," I snapped. "He brought *me* down here after you left me. Now, can you please walk back outside so we can talk about Dr. Brandt's willingness to see Jackson?"

"Tell *Dr. Brandt* we are thankful for his willingness to see Jackson, but we're leaving. Seriously, Jess. If he were a decent surgeon, he wouldn't be participating in this bizarre fantasy you have, acting like the hero doctor who is coming to your rescue."

"No one is trying to live out a *fantasy*, Warren," I said. "Now, get my son outside so Cam can meet him. Hopefully, he'll have some open days soon to give him a full evaluation after calling for records."

"That's the thing, Jessica," Warren replied indignantly. "If the guy were a *professional*, he'd pencil you in *after* looking up Jackson's records. He wouldn't drive you to the airport in some douchey sports car, using Jackson as a ploy to prove his maturity to me."

"This isn't about *you*! Now, I'm standing in the airport right fucking now," I growled in some voice I'd never used on Warren before. "Where the hell is my son?"

"We're checking the bags," he snapped. "Get up here if you want on this flight with us."

"Stop fucking around, Warren, and get back here, I nearly shouted. "This is embarrassing." I ran my sweaty palm over my forehead and glanced around at the people bustling around the airport. "Warren."

Silence.

"Warren." I raised my voice even louder. "Warren!"

I glanced down to see the home screen on my phone. My fiancé had hung up on my ass. I should've expected this. It's what Warren did when things didn't go his way on a phone call.

Instead of allowing tears of frustration to surface, I remained steady in my cause to find my son. I didn't care if Warren was doing what he thought was best for Jackson; that wasn't his call to make, and I was furious.

"Call Jacks," I ordered my phone, my eyes staring at the security checkpoint.

"Mom?" Jackson answered. "Please tell me you're checking in. Warren is pissed and being an asshole."

"Yeah, he just hung up on me," I returned. "I need you to tell

Warren that you're staying here with me. Dr. Brandt is going to check you out, most likely treat you, and find some answers."

"Mom," Jackson said, trying to bring in some reasonable authority, "I know you're trying to do what is best, but if Dr. Tsang can't even get me in, what makes you think the more *famous* doctor will?"

"Because he's an old friend from college, son," I said, bringing in my parental authority. "Get out here and meet him. We'll take the next flight out if you don't like what you see or how you feel about him. Warren can kiss my ass for acting like this and making you believe this is all fucking bullshit."

"Good God, Mom," Jackson said.

"Sorry for the language, but I'm at my limit. Dr. Brandt is going out of his way to help us, and Warren is acting like the doctor is beneath him. I'm over it. Get out here. I want *you* to meet him and make the call on whether you want him to treat you."

"Hey, Warren, I'm heading back to Mom. She said we'll be on the next flight if I'm not into this Brandt guy," Jackson said.

I heard Warren mumble something to Jackson. Warren was still boarding the plane—even after I'd accomplished what we came here to do—and he couldn't be bothered to tell me himself. It was apparent that his goal for this trip was to prove me wrong and make me look foolish, and he was furious that I managed to do what I'd set out to do.

Why am I marrying this asshole again? I thought, feeling the heat rushing to my cheeks.

"Hey, Mom!" Jackson hollered. Bless that boy and his Spidey senses for picking me out of the crowd.

"Right here," I waved and hugged him tightly when he came close.

"Well, take me to this doctor you're willing to risk your fiancé for." He raised an eyebrow, looking at me like Cam had earlier.

I pushed away the instant fear that, for the first time, I was about to introduce my son to his biological father and Cameron to his son. I could only imagine what would happen if the truth of Jackson's paternity came out. Were the unknown consequences of that a risk I was willing to take? Absolutely. I'd do anything to ensure my son had his life back. Why else did I come all this way?

Chapter Nine

Jessa

Searching for Cameron, I rushed out of the airport, probably looking like I was fleeing the Feds.

"Where the hell is he?" I asked, staring at what seemed like hundreds of cars flooding into the loading zone at the airport.

"Hopefully, you got the good doctor's number, so you can just call him," Jackson said with a sympathetic grin. "Mom," his stark blue eyes leveled me, "take a breath and relax. I'm here, and you're here; that's all that matters."

I briskly ran my hand over his arm and exhaled. "Got it, Champ," I said. "Me and you."

He nodded assuredly, making me focus on the simplest of all solutions to my predicament: using my phone to call Cameron instead of looking around like a frantic idiot.

"Yes, darling," Cam teased.

"We're out front. Where are you?" I was too frazzled to bring myself to fully appreciate his light-heartedness.

"Parking garage," Cameron answered. "On my way to the terminal now."

"Okay. We're right where I got out," I answered.

"Be there in a sec," he answered.

"Shit, Cam!"

"Right here."

"I have Jackson with me, and you don't have enough room in your car," I informed him.

"No worries. I called an Uber, and they'll be here in twenty minutes. That gives Jackson and me enough time to meet so he can make sure he'll want me to be his doctor."

"Oh, my God. Thank you," I said in disbelief, looking around for the man who always seemed to be a step ahead.

"Well, if it isn't Jackson," I heard Cameron say over the sounds of car engines and squeaky luggage wheels rattling all around us.

"And if it isn't the doctor my mom hijacked to come and save my ass," Jackson answered while shaking Cam's extended hand.

"Jacks!" I said with irritation. "Language, please."

Cameron's grin lit his eyes. "Yes, easy on the language. We don't want to offend Captain America over here," he winked at Jackson as he cocked his thumb to point in my direction.

Why do I even bother? I thought, watching my boys as they laughed. *Oh, shit. My boys? Maybe I should've boarded that flight with* my fiancé *after all.*

"Can we?" I said, interrupting my thoughts.

"We can," Cameron said. "All right, kid. Give me the rundown. You into sports?"

"I'm an all-star player and MVP for my football team," Jackson said with his usual confident grin.

"That's what I'm talking about," Cameron folded his arms and gave Jackson his undivided attention. "Any other sports?"

"Basketball, also MVP," Jackson proudly proclaimed.

As I watched Jackson give Cameron the details of the life these seizures were stealing from him, my heart started to sink, a brutal reminder needed in this precarious situation.

"Nice," Cameron's eyes shifted to mine, then to Jackson. "Anything else?"

"Baseball," Jackson said as if he were now challenging Cam.

"Position?" Cam asked.

"Shortstop. Sometimes, pitcher," Jackson answered.

"MVP?" Cameron leaned in and playfully asked.

"Yes," Jackson chuckled sheepishly. "I sound like a complete ass."

"It's not bragging if it's true. And, if you give me the honor of becoming your doctor, I'd gladly work my ass off to get you back into all those games." He looked at me, "Sorry about that language, Cap."

"Fix this boy," I playfully elbowed Jackson, "and you can curse all you want."

"Hell yeah," Jackson said, and then I was in a big bear hug with my six-foot-tall son. "Let's see if we can crack the code on this shit."

I rolled my eyes at Jackson and Cameron, laughing at my expense. "How about we get you both checked into a hotel? Let's also try to refrain from cursing before your mom kicks both of our asses."

"I'll call the hotel we were in before Warren checked us out without giving Dr. Brandt a chance. Maybe they can extend the room there," I said, pulling out my phone.

Part of me expected to see a text from Warren—because that's what a decent person would do in this situation, assuming a decent person would be in this situation at all—but no. So, what the hell ever, and too bad for his ass because I knew I did the right thing for Jackson, and I felt that now, more than ever, this kid would be just fine. My relationship, however, not so much.

"Oh, hell no. My patients aren't staying in that shithole," Cameron said after Jackson told him which hotel I was attempting to rebook.

"It might not be the Ritz, but it's not a shithole," I answered.

"Fair enough. But I'd like you closer to the hospital," Cameron said, pulling his phone to his ear.

I stood there stunned when Cameron said the hotel's name to the person he was talking to on the other end of the line. The hotel was known for putting up Hollywood stars for award shows and things whenever they were in town.

"Cam," I said, shaking my head.

"One sec," he said to the person on the phone, "Yeah?" He looked at me as if I were going to put in a special request for some extra pillows.

"We're not staying there, and no, you're not paying for it either."

"Oh, I'm *not* paying for it." He raised his eyebrows in the daring, playful look I adored, a fact which he seemed to have remembered since he was using it as a weapon against me. "Yeah, for a week to start. Right. Okay, sounds great. Have the hotel send me the confirmation, and I'll forward that to my patient. Thanks."

I stood there with my arms folded as I watched Cameron study his phone and handle whatever business was on the screen he was fixated on.

"Well," I said, prompting Cameron's head to snap up, his humored eyes meeting my stern ones. "I know *I* am not paying for that, and my insurance company is *certainly not* going to approve of it. So, if you're not paying for the penthouse that you just booked for a week, who is?"

"Easy. Warren." Cameron chuckled with his new fan, Jackson, laughing right along with him. "Done and done."

"Seriously. Who is paying for that room?" I insisted.

"I think it's fair that Warren does since I'm sure the hotel he had you staying in wasn't delightful enough for the MVP to—"

"Cameron," I interrupted the man who still had the playful personality I'd always loved. "*Who* is paying for the room?"

I tried not to smile, but I couldn't resist it. Damn, I missed this guy. Always spirited and fun but serious when you needed him to be. He had a temper, to be sure, but something significant had to happen for that to show its face.

Warren was nothing like this man. Warren was serious, reserved, and, as of today, on my last nerve. I don't know why he'd been behaving this way recently, and I didn't know what to do about it because he was usually steady and typically supportive. What I did know was that this stunt he'd pulled—willingly boarding a plane without us—was going to be a big problem moving forward.

Before I could stop myself, a wave of emotion flooded me, and the sting of tears bit my eyes.

"Hey, now, Jessa. I'm only teasing." Cameron stared at me with shock. "The hospital pays for the stay if we call them and request the room for certain patients."

"It's fine." I sniffed, trying to shove away these unexpected feelings.

"Mom," Jackson said in a voice of concern, "are you okay?"

"I'm fine. I'm sorry, both of you," I recovered a fake smile. "It's just been a long few days, and I think I'm more relieved than anything."

"Awesome," was all Cameron said, and the awkwardness was over just like that.

After we were checked into the lavish room, which was as luxurious as the places we went for Warren's work galas, I glanced around and then started laughing.

"Maybe the tears come first, then the laughing before she knees you in the balls for all this?" Jackson said to Cameron.

"Already a step ahead of you on that assumption, kid," Cameron cracked with a nervous laugh of his own. "Jessa?"

"Jessa?" Jackson chuckled. "I've never heard anyone call her that one before."

Cameron laughed, and then his eyes met mine. We both knew why he called me Jessa—his Jessa.

"Not a word," I said as if he'd tell Jackson how he came up with *that* name for me.

He looked at Jackson. "If you want the story behind that name," he craned his head back to me, "you're gonna have to get your mom to cough it up."

"Ah, ha," Jackson teased me. "Another time?"

"Another time," I said with a smile. "But as for now, we're pretty screwed."

"How so?" Jackson questioned.

"Our clothes are on their way back to New York with Warren's shitty mood," I answered, unable to resist rolling my eyes.

"Damn," Cameron answered with the same shock any person would in this situation. "Well, it's a good thing I've got an extra bag of clean sweats and stuff in my car. Sometimes I'm on call for seventy-two hours or a week, so it's necessary. You both can fight over who wears my underwear after I leave."

DR. BRANDT

"Very funny," I said. "I saw a store in the lobby. Maybe I'll check that out."

"Good idea, and while I'm on my way out, I'll walk you down," Cameron offered.

"Thank you." I smiled at him, my gratitude for Cameron growing by the second.

"I can run down and grab the extra clothes," Jackson said, his smile and generous personality matching his father's.

"Why don't I go get that so I can see what we can borrow of Cameron's?" I said to Jackson. "I'm also going to check out that clothing shop in the lobby and pray they have underwear, or you and I *will* be fighting over Cameron's." I wanted a moment alone with Cam to tell him how much I appreciated everything he had done since he took my call.

"Okay. I'm going to check out my bedroom while you're gone. You can have the room closest to the kitchen in this pimp pad. It's a pleasure to know you, Dr. Brandt," he said, extending his hand to shake Cam's.

"The pleasure is mine, Jackson. And call me Cam. Now, enjoy the pimp pad," he chuckled with a wink.

I'd forgotten how amazing Cam was with kids. He could get on their level and relate to them. Cameron had never behaved like the billionaire's son he was. That wasn't the kind of man he was, and I could easily sense that he hadn't changed. Cam was fun, charming, and genuine, and he had a dynamic personality that made women do anything to get his attention.

Okay, enough of that. All of this is a good reminder of the player who broke up with you, I reminded myself as Cameron and Jackson ended their conversation, and Jackson walked down the hallway to the room he'd chosen.

"So," Cameron said with a curious expression, his eyes now a deep shade of blue.

"So," I hung onto the word, unable to resist a bashful smile in response to his look that held me hostage.

"When were you planning on telling me I was a father?"

Chapter Ten

Cameron

There was no doubt in my mind that Jackson was mine. The kid even played the same positions in the same sports that I did once upon a time. Even without comparing our athletic-star qualities, you'd have to be blind not to see the genetic resemblance.

I'm a father.

Jessa hadn't been able to say a word, even as we walked to the elevator. It wasn't until the elevator bell dinged and the door opened that she was able to squeak out my name.

"Cam..."

I smiled at her to reassure her I wasn't pissed. "I have no right to be angry that you never told me, Jessa." I was cut off when another couple joined us in the elevator.

I glanced over at her as she stared straight ahead. Her cheeks were flushed, and she couldn't have been more irresistible than she was right now. Her beautiful sky-blue eyes glistened from the tears threatening to spill out. I couldn't resist reaching for her hand and holding it as we waited for the elevator to take an eternity to bring us to the lobby.

I knew I loved Jessa. All those feelings had been stirring since I saw her again, growing from a simmer to a rapid boil with every passing moment. Seeing Jackson and staring into his eyes—eyes we'd inherited from my father—seemed to have focused my feelings. He was *ours*.

The elevator reached the lobby, and we exited. We walked through, and I scanned the place, wondering if there was an ideal spot to question a long-lost love about why they decided to keep their son's birth and entire life a secret. I was guessing there wasn't.

"The way you're clenching my hand makes me think that you're pretty pissed off, and rightfully so," Jessa echoed through my thoughts, pulling me out of them.

I instantly released my grip around her tiny hand and pulled my shit together. How should I feel about this? Fuck if I knew. I just knew I missed this woman like crazy, had her halfway back in my life, couldn't stand her fiancé, and wanted to help her son—my son. *Our* son.

"Truth be told, I don't know how to feel," I answered her honestly as the earnestness in her eyes held me captive.

"Most men would be angry if their ex-girlfriend never told them they had a child. Maybe they'd be mad about child support or custody or something."

I ran a hand through my hair. "Well, I'm not feeling any of those things, so I'm not sure if I'm *most men* or not."

"You've never been like most men, Cam." She smoothed her hand across my cheek. "I'm sorry I never told you, but you left to pursue your dreams and—"

"You were always too good to me, Jessa. Why would I have *ever* been such a selfish dick to leave you to raise my son?"

"*Our* son," she smoothly cut me off to correct me.

"Our," I smiled. "Why didn't you just tell me? Jesus." I ran my hands through my hair, clenching the sides of my head and spinning around. "How did you do it all by yourself? Please, God, tell me you had support and finished school."

Before turning back to Jessa, she was already in front of me, showing me a severe side I'd never seen before.

"Cameron Mark Brandt." She cut me off in the same tone my mother would use to scold me. And, like when my mother used that voice on me as a little boy, I couldn't help but smile. Call me juvenile, but the sight of an adult scolding me had always made me want to laugh.

I interlaced my fingers, still holding onto the back of my head. "Gonna come at me with my middle name now, eh?"

"I think this situation calls for it." She folded her arms and continued to level my ass with this authoritative gaze she so cutely wore. "You have every right to be upset that I never told you about Jackson, but what happened in my life after you split is my business. You left and didn't look back, remember?"

"Jessa," I said softly.

"I wasn't going to hunt you down because I was pregnant. That wasn't where my head was at the time. I was hurt and missed you, but I was also young and immature. I was heartbroken and angry, and the last thing I wanted to do was hunt down the guy who'd dumped me on his way to a better life at a better school." My grin was long gone by this point. She couldn't have made me feel worse if she'd punched me in the gut. "We both made decisions, and they eventually led our separate paths here. From this point on, what we decide to do can either help or hurt our son. Jackson is number one on my priority list, now and always, and I would move heaven and earth to make him better. Of course, now that you know that you're his father, we can work through that together if you'd like. Or not. But I'm most concerned about Jackson and you treating him—saving him as only you can. Is that still something you're willing to do?"

"Well, shit." I folded my arms to mirror hers. "Looks like that conversation is over."

"I'm not trying to dismiss your feelings, Cameron. But it has been a long couple of months since Jacks's seizures came back, and there is nothing any of these other doctors can do. I'm a desperate mom in need of a gifted man's help, a man who just so happens to be my son's father. I will be here for any questions you have about him if you're interested in being a part of his life, but for now, I beg of you to keep this between you and me—"

"Who does Jackson believe his father is?" I asked, curious.

"A friend from high school," she answered as if she'd had to answer this question millions of times.

"And you don't think he sees *any* resemblance to me?"

"I'm not sure. I haven't been alone with him long enough to learn if he's connected the dots."

"And if he has, and he asks?"

"I won't lie to him," she answered.

"But isn't that what you've already done by not telling him I'm his father?"

"I only kept the identity of his father from him because he never asked. He'll come to me when he's ready."

"And if he's ready now?"

"Then I'll tell him now. Listen, Cam," she said, her eyes filling with tears again, "I've been doing this for sixteen years, and in that time, he hasn't expressed an interest in learning who his father is. Instead, he's been focused on sports and getting scholarships. Now that the seizures have returned, he's been trying his hardest to get his life back, praying for a miracle so he can fulfill his dreams."

I knew there was only one thing to do: put Jackson's health needs first. Nothing was more important. Fix the problem, and everything else will fall into place. This wasn't about me, and it wasn't about Jessa.

"Okay. What medication is he taking, for how long, and when did it stop working?" I stared at Jessa as I would any other patient's parent. But this wasn't any parent; this was my Jessa. This was my son.

That's when it hit me.

"The list of med—" she started.

"My sister was five when she died. Shit." I closed my eyes, refraining from anger. Jessa knew I had a sister born with epilepsy, and her death inspired me to go into this field of work. "You know my sister Charlotte was born with epilepsy."

"Yes," she answered.

"Shouldn't that have been reason enough to hunt me down and ask a few questions?"

"Truth?"

"I would appreciate that, yes," I said, a bit harsher.

"Sir?" I heard the valet call, finally driving my car up for me. "Your car is ready. Sorry about the wait."

"I'll need a moment," I said, seeing that my car wasn't parked to hold anyone up. "Thanks." I nodded after he kindly left me to wrap this up with Jessa.

"I was an idiot," she said, a tear slipping down her cheek.

I instantly wiped it away. "Don't insult yourself," I returned. "Let's just leave it where it is. I'm here, and I will help *our* son."

I needed to figure out how best to approach my care of Jackson with St. John's since they didn't look favorably upon surgeons treating their family members. I needed to get out of here, sit with the guys, and ask for their advice. Hopefully, they were all still at Darcy's. If nothing else, I could use a stiff drink. I walked to my car and grabbed my bag from the trunk.

"I'm going to take off," I said as I handed her the duffel. "He's a chip off the old block, Jessa. A handsome young man, great athlete, and a well-mannered personality."

"He is."

I got in the car and headed out of the parking lot, calling the guys as I pulled out onto the street.

I only had to try two different numbers before someone finally answered.

"What's up, douche?" Jake, the heart surgeon, said.

"You guys still at Darcy's?"

"Just finished dinner," Jake answered. "Is everything okay? Collin mentioned something was up, and you sound like hell."

"I'm on my way." My voice had an unmistakable edge.

"Sounds bad, man. Did the stalker ex-girlfriend hold you hostage in that office of yours?"

The humor in Jake's voice elevated my mood.

"Turns out I'm a dad."

"The fuck?"

"I'll explain when I get there."

"Yeah, I'll set us up with another round."

"Thanks, man."

If there was one night I was grateful to meet the guys at Darcy's, tonight was it. I needed time to organize my thoughts, but I also needed to talk.

I didn't want to be angry at Jessa about her secrecy, but I'd lost sixteen years nonetheless, and I knew that sooner or later, I was going to feel that deeply. All I could do in the interim was to try to sort out my feelings and keep my cool for Jackson's sake.

Chapter Eleven

Cameron

I planted my ass in my seat at the table permanently reserved for the guys and me. It was back in a corner, surrounded by windows, and mainly used for privacy from the rest of the patrons in this restaurant. Given the high profiles of my friends—and the staggering amount of money we spent—the establishment had no problem ensuring we were always cared for.

The guys didn't say much as I downed the scotch they'd ordered for me like a glass of water. I ran the back of my hand over my wet lips and motioned to the waitress for another, something entirely out of character for me. As I sat in silence, surrounded by curious stares, I stared at the empty glass I clenched in my hands as if it were a magic ball that could give me the answers I needed.

In the time it took me to drive here, I'd gone through an array of emotions, and now, I was utterly overwhelmed and more than a little confused. I had more questions than answers. Could I still operate on my boy, knowing he was mine? Should I try to become the father this boy deserved in his life? Would he want me to try? If I got Jessa pregnant sixteen years ago, knowing how careful we always were, could I have *other* unknown children running around out there?

"Cam," I heard Jim say. James Mitchell was CEO of Mitchell and Associates, which owned St. John's Hospital, and he also happened to be Jake's brother. I could tell by his voice that it wasn't the first time he'd called my name.

"Sir, your scotch," the waitress said.

I smiled to thank her before looking around the table. I was surrounded by Collin and Jake on one side, two world-class surgeons, and Jim, Alex, and Spencer, top executives and tycoons, on the other. To say I wouldn't be able to bullshit my way through this conversation was an understatement. I might as well have been sitting with the CIA. These guys could read me like a book.

"I don't know where to start," I stated honestly and with a defeated tone I didn't recognize.

"Well, if you said that in a consultation with our surgical teams at St. John's, I'd have to—"

"Shut the fuck up, Spence," I said to the VP of Mitchell and Associates. The look of enjoyment on his face at my expense was mildly infuriating. "Seriously, you fuck women like your dick depends on it, so you should know that you can easily be in my shoes."

"My dick does depend on it," Spence shot back a shit-eating grin. "Listen, man," he softened up, letting a glimmer of sympathy show on his face, "I'm just trying to lighten your ass up. So, what the hell is going on?"

If there was one thing Spencer Monroe was known for, it was switching gears almost instantly, especially if the environment called for it. Spencer was a talented son of a bitch like that, though, and I think every one of us cocky assholes envied that talent more than we cared to express.

"Start with the fact that a woman showed up at your office and forced your secretary to call your cell phone," Collin said. "Then, you change your plans, head to your office to meet this *old friend* of yours, and after a couple of hours or more, Jake gets a call from you demanding we keep the bar tab open because you're now the proud father of a bouncing baby boy." He finished with a grin that he must've known I needed to see, given this was most likely the longest the guys had ever seen me not smile.

I downed the second glass of scotch, feeling the warmth of the liquid working its way into my bloodstream. Finally, I felt I could talk reasonably.

"I know it sounds like some chick I fucked ended up finding my office and is claiming I'm the father of her child—"

"Um, last I checked, the documentary crew that Mitchell and Associates are using to promote the pediatric wing has blasted all kinds of fun facts about you, not the least of which is that you inherited Daddy Brandt's *billions*. You don't have to be an *actual* brain surgeon like you and Collin to know that might attract the masses. It just so happens that you're also almost as devastatingly handsome as the rest of us, and you're great at your job, so let's not pretend that the truckloads of women you've managed to bag aren't going to try to capitalize on that. Am I the only one who isn't surprised by the new baby revelation, or am I just bitter because my documentary scarred me for life?"

I stared at Jake, shocked I'd let him run his mouth for so long, especially when it came to the insinuation that Jessa would use my fame and the ridiculous amount of money I'd inherited from my father to coerce me to help her son and fund the rest of the child's future.

"That's not the case with this one," I said. I practically dug my fingertips into my forehead while closing my eyes. "I can see the boy is mine. There's no refuting that fact at all."

"Then start talking because I've had enough mysteriousness for one goddamn night," Alex finally spoke, right on cue for his nature. He was sharp as a fucking tack and twice as shrewd. He could only sit quietly and let any of us ramble in circles for so long before reining us in and making us get to the point. He was a problem solver to the core and a no-nonsense one at that. "Let's have it, Cam. I've got a wife and twin sons at home who will likely join us at this table if I stay out any longer on a Friday. Don't make me push my luck too far," he finished with a grin.

"So," I said the word with an exaggerated sigh, "the woman in my office tonight came in with her sixteen-year-old son, who is suffering from epilepsy. She is the woman I fell in love with in college. Things between us ended badly. Long story short, I transferred schools and kind of abandoned her."

"Okay," Jim spoke again, "you were an average college guy furthering himself in a career, being selfish, not ready to settle down, and going to college elsewhere. There is no guilt in that. If you think you should feel like shit over that, you get a pass, buddy. We've all made those mistakes in life, learned from them, and became better men for it."

"Fine." I felt myself getting edgy again. "This woman was the love of my life. Unfortunately, she found out she was pregnant soon after I left. She sacrificed her future—a very bright one—to leave mine alone by not telling me about the boy, and now here we are."

"Sounds like you're in a pretty damn good spot, Cam," Collin said, the muted light in the area somehow not dulling the blond in his *just fucked-looking* styled hair. "Looks like you both are in a great spot to start again. She seems to trust you anyway."

"Also sounds like she's an amazing woman for having to put her career on hold to raise a child and not going after your money. I assume she knew your father if you say you loved her. I've known you for a while now, and you've never mentioned love and women in the same sentence before," Jake added with his usual smile. "I say go for it."

"That's the thing. Not only have I taken an oath to not perform surgeries on family or friends—"

"You take that oath for a kid you don't know?" Jim asked.

"No," I answered truthfully. "But he is my son."

"Biologically," Collin added. "You know why we take that oath, to stay away from emotions while we operate. Trust me, it *is* personal, and I know that very well because of Elena. Girlfriend at the time or not, I nearly went gray from fear that I would kill my soul mate when I was forced to operate on her *twice*. That will fuck with you; I know it fucked with me."

"So, now that excuse is out of the way. What's the problem, other than you need to figure out how to be a dad to a sixteen-year-old? Does she hold this against you?" Alex asked.

"Exactly," Spencer added. "Where's the dilemma? Use the kid to win her heart back if that's what you're aiming for and what you want."

"Of course, that is what you'd say," I shot back to Spencer. "But I'm not using a child to win this woman's heart. In fact, I have no right to her heart since I already broke it once. She's engaged to a complete dick and has already chosen—"

"And there lies the root of our problem," Jake smirked and raised a glass to my perplexed face. "Looks like there's some competition in the mix, which will make fighting for your woman's heart much more rewarding for you."

"I have no right to step in and fuck with her life. I already did that once," I answered.

"But," Spencer smirked at Jake as if they were plotting some evil plan to let the billionaire playboy doctor get what he felt he had rights to.

"But, what? It's off the table," Jim spoke up, the familiar voice of reason. "The woman is engaged, and her son needs your medical expertise," Jim leveled me with his knowing stare, "not your playboy bullshit, trying to win back his mother."

The third scotch I finished liked where Spencer and Jake's heads were. Jessa was mine, Jackson was mine, and I *would* impress the shit out of them and win both of their hearts because they were both mine.

I raised my glass. "They're both mine. I will fix the boy, marry my girl, and be the happiest man on the mother fucking planet."

"Cheers to that," Alex said in a menacing yet humorous voice. "I think I'll enjoy *this* particular shit show more than all of the others."

Jake chuckled. "To the great Cameron Brandt," he eyed the men around the table. "May the odds *forever* be in your selfish favor."

Half-drunk or not, I knew this was a stupid idea. Why couldn't I have owned this like a man, gone home, and thought long and hard about the right way to handle this? Why the hell did I come here and cry like a bitch about my problems? The guys were going to get a kick out of every wrong move I made now.

Chapter Twelve

Jessa

The weekend seemed to last a year. I couldn't get answers for Jackson soon enough, and despite the luxurious accommodations, I'd hardly slept a wink since Cam booked Jackson and me this penthouse suite.

Now that it was officially five in the morning, I felt I could justify getting out of bed and making coffee while waiting for Cam's secretary to call me and schedule my son for his appointment.

Once I set the coffee in motion, I strummed my fingers on the counter, staring at my fingernails while a string of worries ran through my head like they were trying out for the Olympics. Making its way to the top of my anxieties was Warren and his *"k"* response to the text I'd sent him with the details of Cameron taking on Jackson as a patient.

I felt a weird spasm in my stomach, realizing that Warren was acting like he didn't care about what was going on and there was zero support from him. It wasn't the first time Warren had pulled a cold-hearted move, but we always found a way to make up and move forward. This was hitting me very differently, though.

I wiped a tear that'd streamed down my cheek, feeling hurt that Warren was treating Jackson and me this way. A lot of what attracted me to the man was how he provided security and cared for us. Even on his worst, busiest workday, he was always reliable. He was always there, whether by text or phone call or by surprising me and showing up in person. I'll be damned if I could understand why he was acting like this now.

I knew it wasn't because he was jealous of Cameron. I didn't think so anyway. If he knew Cam was competition for him, he'd find a way to work remotely so he could be here with us. How fucked up was it to think that if he was at least jealous, I could have the man's support?

Ring! Ring!

I nearly jumped out of my skin when the phone rang, and I saw Warren's caller ID show up. I didn't want to answer the call; under other circumstances, I would not have. But I was in such a precarious situation, needing support like never before, and part of me wanted to be able to explain his horrible behavior away. I wasn't sure I could deal with drama on top of everything else, so there was only one way to find out how to move forward from here.

I answered. "I thought I'd never talk to you again."

"Ha," he said dryly as if he needed to continue making a point that he was displeased. "So, what's the deal with Jacks?"

"I'm supposed to get a phone call around seven or so from Cam's secretary to set up an official consultation."

"Ah, so *Cam* is not calling you himself to set this up?" He mocked Cameron's name.

I was wrong to give him the benefit of the doubt. He's pissed and *jealous.*

"No," I returned flatly. "Why would he? I texted you that he confirmed he would take Jacks as a new patient. Doctors don't do in—"

"Does he know that he's Jackson's father yet?"

"Jesus, Warren, why did you call if all you're going to do is continue your dickish behavior? This isn't about me hooking up with a boyfriend who ditched my ass a million years ago. This is about getting Jacks the best treatment possible."

"Right," Warren said in a low voice. "Well, does he know that he didn't only skip out on you, but he also left his son behind in the process?"

"Why does it matter?"

"You're kidding me, right?" Warren shot back.

"I'm not. And yes, he knows. Jacks looks exactly like him. He'd be blind if he didn't see the obvious resemblance."

"And with this information, what does he plan on doing?"

"He plans on taking Jackson as a patient. So why the hell are you calling me and acting like this? If you were worried about Cameron, you shouldn't have pulled that stunt at the airport. This is my son's life hanging in the balance."

"You're acting as though it's owed to you to have Cameron Brandt take him on as a patient, and you've pulled a hell of a lot of shit since you've been trying to demand an audience for Jackson. Do you think he's doing this for anyone but himself?"

"What the fuck is that supposed to mean?"

"How can you be so naïve?"

"If you think I wouldn't walk over hot coals to get my son help, then I don't know what to tell you." I knew what he was insinuating, and I couldn't have felt more disgusted. He was insulting both Cameron and me, all because he was feeling insecure. I didn't know where this breakdown in our communication had started, but I was positive I'd never felt farther away from him. If he was trying to get me to see things his way or be sympathetic to him, he couldn't have gone in a worse direction.

"Anything else?" I questioned, tears pooling in my eyes again.

"You know where I stand. Don't say I didn't warn you if things don't work out for Jacks."

"Warn me? What the hell does that mean, Warren?"

"You know what? It doesn't matter. You'll do whatever you want, regardless of my opinion or feelings, so this is on you."

"What are you *warning* me about?" I questioned again.

"The guy probably wants to get laid, Jessica," Warren sighed. "I saw what he looked like, and he looks the type who would take that as payment from a gullible woman like yourself."

"You're such an unbelievable asshole," I stated bluntly.

"Well, someone needs to keep your head out of the clouds. Jess, professionals like him don't just take patients and do friends a favor. Can't you see that? For Christ's sake, the man's a world-renowned pediatric neurosurgeon, and you're treating him like he's a hook-up for discount movie tickets. He's doing this all for a piece of ass; trust me on that."

"You know what?" I finally spoke up, stopping Warren mid-lecture. "I know you're pissed, but this isn't fair to Jackson."

"Oh, so what's fair, then? His mom hooks up with his dad, whom he doesn't even know about yet, and then insists that this man will perform magic on him, fix him, and all will be well in his life again? It doesn't work that way, Jessica, and you know that."

"What I know is that not trying doesn't work for me. You, of all people, should know that when it comes to Jackson having a chance at the life he deserves, I'm willing to throw it all on the table."

"Even our relationship?"

"You're the one doing things to threaten that, not me."

"If you're the woman I want as my wife, you'll respect that I have a problem with this. I know you think I'm being an asshole but put yourself in my shoes. Imagine how it feels, knowing that my beautiful fiancée is with her ex-lover and *their* son, and I'm not there to protect you both from this man should he have other motives."

"We don't need your protection. I'm not a damsel in goddamn distress, and I have never been. What I *am* is a competent woman, listening to the insecure ramblings of a man who is being extremely selfish." I contained my emotions as best I could, so I didn't end up screaming at him the way I wanted to. "Furthermore, I think I'm smart enough to know if a guy is doing me favors for a piece of ass. This conversation is ridiculous, and I'm not having it anymore. If you want to support Jackson and me, as you *used* to be keen on doing, then get out here and do it."

"Yeah, well, I'm working. Someone has to pay the bills, right?"

With that last dig, Warren hung up on me. I was so sick of his shit, and I knew I didn't deserve it. I deserved better. Fuck him.

There was a lot at stake here emotionally, and now, my future marriage was in jeopardy. I couldn't get swallowed up in those thoughts, though. I needed to be focused and clear-minded and set up Jackson's appointment with Cameron and see all this through until the very end. My relationship drama would have to wait.

Chapter Thirteen

Cam

In the week since Jessa had come into my office, I'd been faced with the need to process more emotions than I could count. Unfortunately, I didn't have the mental capacity to deal with all of them, so I stuck with the one thing I *could* process. I had a patient whose scans I was going over for the fourth time, and he needed my skill.

Of course, this patient happened to be my biological son, and every time I'd seen him since our first meeting, I saw myself. It was bizarre to stare at a sixteen-year-old version of myself; it was also a curse.

"Dr. Brandt, Jackson Stein is here with his mother," my receptionist alerted.

"Yes, thank you," I said, rising to my feet. "Let's hope this goes smoothly."

"Good luck, Doc," she said with a curious smile.

She had no idea how much luck I would need. After learning the boy was mine and reading up on his condition, I walked a fine line by meeting with Jessica and Jackson without my surgical consultation team. I hoped this was a smart idea, taking more of an intimate approach than a professional one.

Jackson's only shot at halting these seizures was through surgery. It would also mean a lifestyle change and could be the most challenging mountain he'd ever climb in the fight to get his life back.

"Shit," I mumbled, my hand gently covering the door handle to the consultation room where Jessa and Jackson waited.

I took a quick moment to clear my thoughts. I had to be confident, or there was no point in meeting with the two on a more personal level to get them to agree to this life-changing surgery.

"Cam," Jessa's eyes lit up as I walked into the room.

Thank God this woman had some soothing, soul-energy charm that worked on my ass, or I'd let my twisted-up emotions run over the top of me. Since looking at Jackson's charts, I'd done my best to disconnect from my feelings for the woman. Those selfish thoughts of her and Jackson being mine had faded, and my medical instincts had been dominating since.

"Jessa," I returned her sparkling smile and eyed Jackson's, "and Jacks," I said, sitting down and using the name he'd requested.

"So, we got a phone call stating you wanted to meet us on a more personal level. I'm probably being a bit negative, but I'm not sure if that's a good thing," Jessa said skeptically.

I maintained my composure and internally thanked my years of practice in this field because I didn't waver under her or Jackson's look of concern. It was my job to fix him and banish any fear of what they may be thinking. I should've followed protocol and brought the team in here, but I went with some weird instinct and met with the two alone. My gut instincts never steered me wrong, so I wasn't going to backtrack now. I was going to pace myself and move forward.

"Yes and no." I clasped my hands on the table in front of me. "I can't stand when medical professionals beat around the bush and don't get to the point, so I will get right to it."

Jessica seemed to bring that warrior-like motherly instinct to the table as soon as I answered her. Good, she needed to be strong to handle the news I was about to deliver.

I looked at Jackson. "For this, I'm going to ask you to bring forward your competitive nature, which I know you possess since you are an all-star player in multiple sports."

"Yep," Jackson answered, eying me like I was about to deliver his death sentence.

I could've been. It was a matter of perspective at this point.

"As you well know, your medication has been unable to control your seizures, and your MRIs have not been helpful either. After going over your lab work and scans repeatedly, I had my neuro team do some additional research into why this is happening when there is *no reason* why you should be having seizures."

"That's the thing," Jessa interjected. "The doctors find nothing, and so they prescribe a new medication. The last one he was prescribed made poor Jacks walk around like he was half-stoned all the time." She smiled sympathetically at her somber son, whose eyes were still locked onto me.

I subtly grinned, hoping to soften up Jacks some. "Right, and that's because there is no medication that can ease what the neurological teams have found. Jackson, you have what we call a hemispheric cortical dysplasia, otherwise known as HCD." My eyes shifted back to Jessa's. "This is a very frustrating cause of epilepsy because while we are advanced in epileptic findings and research, this one slides under the radar. You need a trained eye or a doctor who refuses to give up on finding it."

"You won't give up," Jackson finally spoke.

"Hell, no. I won't give up," I answered. "But I need to be sure you won't either."

"*I'm* not giving up. I wouldn't be here with my mom, trying to fix myself, if I were the type to let this beat me. What exactly are we talking about?"

"I'll have the surgical teams show you diagrams and a video of how this affects you. You'll want to become educated on it." I knew he and Jessa weren't interested in anything but details, so it was time to dive in. "This is a very subtle condition, and one either needs to be exceptionally skilled to find it or know what they're after because it will not show up on scans. Luckily for all of us, I am exceptionally skilled, *and* I've dealt with this before. Basically, your brain is being altered in specific circuits, and it is not functioning correctly. The electrical storm will fire up at random, prompting a seizure. There is no way to block this electrical storm with medication as the neurons are abnormal, so my job will be to disconnect them."

I paused for their reactions. I was about to drop the hammer concerning the type of surgery needed, and I wondered if less was more in delivering this information. I didn't want to scare them into this surgery, and I certainly didn't want to overwhelm them. Hence the reason I didn't have fifteen members of my team in here staring at them as I delivered this news. Surgery was always the last resort, but the fact that I'd found this almost instantly might have made it seem like it was first on my list. That wasn't the case. Unfortunately, there were no other options for Jackson but to go under the knife.

"What type of surgery are we looking at, Cam?" Jessa's voice was direct.

I nodded at Jessa and pursed my lips. "I want you both to know that I do not take this lightly. It may be frightening to hear and process at first, but I've done numerous surgeries of this nature, and they have all been successful."

"Okay," Jackson said quietly.

"A hemispherectomy of Jackson's left hemisphere will need to be performed. I will go in and disconnect the *bad parts* of the brain in this surgery. The seizures will improve and end from that alone."

"At what fucking cost, Cameron?" Jessica appeared to have snapped, and now, I was facing a ferocious mother without my surgical team to step in and help me keep her and her son reassured throughout this consultation.

What part of me being some damn hero doctor and doing this on a more personal level was a good idea again? God help me. I'd never done this shit alone; even worse, I could be screwing this up for Jackson by trying to handle it on my own.

"Listen, I know this is frightening to hear because I—"

"You just told us you were basically *removing* a hemisphere of Jackson's brain, Cameron. The term *disconnecting* is just how you put it to make it sound like my son would have to live life with only one side of his brain functioning."

"Yes," I was direct and easing my way into responding to Jessa in the same tone she was using to keep her as focused as I could in this terrifying situation. "I want you both to meet with my patient, Lisa Jameson. She was in Jackson's situation four years ago. I want her to share her story of how the surgery helped her. Even though it took hard work, she got her life back. I know nothing sounds hopeful about losing the function of one side of your brain, but there is hope. Though we may not like the journey or path we're forced to take, there is a reason for that path and that journey. I'm the type of person who believes we all come to these decisions for a good reason."

"Cameron," Jessa stood, "I apologize if I started off on an unprofessional and unconventional foot. I am. It's probably why you felt you could casually come in here and talk about disconnecting half of Jackson's brain. I'm sorry, but this is not good enough for me. I will not gamble with my son's life or make him spend the rest of his life trying to retrain his brain to compensate for the parts that don't work anymore. He doesn't deserve that."

"What does he deserve then, Jessa?"

"A chance at the all-star games next year. To go back into sports without fearing something will happen and trigger a seizure again. Anything but having to probably learn to walk again."

"Mom," Jackson rose and took his mother into his arms as I stood across from them and watched silently. Their bond reminded me of what I shared with my mother before she died.

As I watched them, I felt helpless. I wanted to be there for them, a supportive helpmate for Jessa or a father to Jackson, but I was the one delivering the bad news. Instead of being able to comfort them, I was forcing them to feel like they only had each other.

This was a strange feeling that I didn't like at all. I could only stand there and observe and wish I had the luxury of holding them in this time of need.

Jackson needed this surgery, and I knew that. The clock was ticking, and it was only a matter of when, not if, the seizures would take over, and then he wouldn't have this fighting chance. It was my duty to ask the only questions that mattered right now.

"I know this isn't easy news to hear," I started, listening to Jessica sniff and pull herself together to take me head-on. "But as these electrical storms and these epileptic seizures continue, the *good and healthy* side of Jackson's brain will struggle to develop further. So, it is vital that we use what time he has left in the still-developing brain to allow his right hemisphere to train itself to develop and do the job of both hemispheres. You both need to know and understand that things will get progressively worse if we don't take the luxury of operating soon."

"Luxury?" Jessa spat.

"Luxury," I answered her. "Most doctors find these issues when it's too late. By then, the patient is disabled because things progressively worsen with age. I'd say we found this just in time. This will no longer be an option within a year or so, and then he'll be facing a lifetime of these seizures."

Something softened in Jessica, almost as if I were suddenly speaking her language. I don't know what triggered the change, but I was damn grateful she appeared more receptive, and there seemed to be a fighting chance.

"If Jackson wishes to investigate this further, we will want to see these *videos* and look at all the available information. Also, if Jackson wants to meet with your patient, I will gladly support him." She looked at her son. "My first instinct is to say no to this and pray we can find another way, but I know that reaction comes from my fear. You and I have looked for quite a long time and prayed for answers, and though it's not the answer *I* want, Jackson, this isn't my life. It's yours, and I want you to live it to the fullest no matter what. Cameron is right; this is your journey, not mine. I will support whatever decision you make and the direction you want to take."

"Well," Jackson briskly rubbed his mom's arms, "you will have to support the decision because I'm still a minor and on your insurance."

"Jacks," she playfully punched his arm, "I'm serious. Yes, you're a minor, but at times you have the decision-making skills of a wise adult. I want you to take some time to think about this, though."

"We'll watch the pieces that Dr. Brandt recommended, and we'll speak with his patient. Trust me, I'm taking my time before I decide to unplug any part of my brain." He chuckled and rolled his eyes, then he looked at me, the buffoon standing there watching this moment as if I were outside, looking through a window at the two most important people in my life. "Let's finish discussing the details of this surgery and the *odds* I'm up against. And then we'll move forward.

I would do anything for them, and as I let that warm and fuzzy feeling wash over me, a man was ushered into the conference room and introduced as Jessa's fiancé.

Chapter Fourteen

Jessa

When Warren walked into the conference room, I realized something: I didn't have time for his games. A few days ago, maybe part of me would've been relieved to see him—the man who was supposed to be an anchor during hard times—but today, I wanted to shoo him away like a fly. He was a distraction, and I was very much annoyed by him.

My son was facing a life-changing surgery, and I needed to be on top of my decision-making game. I needed to focus on how to counsel Jacks as we headed into unfamiliar territory, forced to make a decision that no one would ever want to. An impossible choice.

Warren had the nerve to make this all about our relationship when we spoke on the phone, and now he decided to show up like nothing had happened. I could hardly stand to look at him.

"So, what exactly are we looking at here, Doc?" Warren asked Cameron as the rest of us stared at Warren silently, wondering where the hell he'd manifested himself from as he took a seat.

"As I informed Jackson and his mother, the left hemisphere of Jackson's brain is what is complicating things for him." Cameron didn't skip a beat, and I was grateful. "Medication will not prevent this hemisphere from remaining in this state, and his seizures will worsen. Fortunately, this isn't the first time I have seen this issue; it's what is known as hemispheric cortical dysplasia. I was able to encourage a trusted neurologist to look for that while we studied the scans I ordered."

"So, that's why Jacks's other pediatric neurologists couldn't find this?" Warren said, nodding as if he understood perfectly. "This is a bit overwhelming, I must admit." Warren smiled across the table at Jacks and me. "How are you feeling about it, son?"

Son?

I wanted to roll my eyes into the back of my head.

I looked at Cameron—knowing Jackson was *his* son—and wondered how that comment made him feel. Maybe I shouldn't have cared. Jackson is his biological son, and that's it. Since I last spoke to Cam about Jacks being his, Cameron had been in some distant-doctor mode, which was perfectly fine. The only thing I needed from Cameron was his expertise in epilepsy and for him to help Jacks. That was it.

However hard I pushed that rationale into my mind, it didn't stop me from staring at the good doctor's facial expressions and noticing that he'd given no sign that he was bothered by Warren's statement.

"I'm nervous. I want to meet the patients who've had this surgery and hear how they dealt with it." Jacks reached under the table for my hands, which were clasped into fists on my lap. "And you're going to speak with the parents, Mom. You're trying to put on this strong, brave front, and I can see right through it."

I grinned at him, and all the drama in the room faded. It was just Jacks and me, and that's all that mattered.

"I will definitely need to do that." I smiled, released my hands from the death clutch, and held my son's. "I want you better, living the life you deserve, but the solutions to get you on that path are quite overwhelming."

"It is all very overwhelming," Cam said in a soft, non-doctor tone. He exhaled with a casual smile, and I could tell he wanted to say more but didn't. "All right, I think Warren is up to speed a bit," he nodded at Warren to confirm before glancing at his smartwatch. "Right now, the rest of my surgical team is arriving. I'd like to have my secretary send them in." He looked over at Jacks. "These guys are going to make you feel a bit better about your decision to trust your brain in my hands," He winked and grinned at Jacks, both men sharing the same expression.

"Why don't we do that," I smiled at Jacks, gaining back some of my confidence. "Let's see if it was a good or a bad idea that I hunted down Dr. Brandt."

"I think it was your amazing motherly instincts. I'm just sorry that I acted like such a jerk after you sought out this help for our son," Warren said, cutting off whatever Cameron was about to say in response to my comment. "I was wrong to question your instincts."

Nice try.

"If there's anything I know in my profession," Cam's eyes locked on mine, and something kept my eyes fixed on his, "it's never to question a mother's instincts." He looked over at Warren with a subtle arch of his eyebrow.

Warren nodded, and the two men were locked in a silent standoff for a moment.

"And I'm glad I learned that lesson now rather than when you're my wife, and I could screw it up worse." Warren smiled warmly at me.

"Right," was all I could say in response.

I truly could not believe he was pulling this act. The bullshit spilling out of him couldn't have been more repulsive. I'd admittedly let too much bad behavior on his part slide throughout our relationship, but Warren had picked the wrong time to put me to the test these last weeks. I'd never been more stressed about my son, nor had I ever been more determined to do whatever it took to help him. I didn't know what Warren was up to, but one thing I knew for certain was that I'd never been treated more disrespectfully by anyone.

As Warren, Cam, and Jackson spoke, my mind drifted. I'd been apathetic when it came to Warren for longer than I cared to admit, but seeing him walk through the doors as if he hadn't thrown a bitch-fit because he wasn't in control made me feel anything but apathetic. Instead, I was pissed that he could march in here as if I were the type of woman who could be manipulated into giving over my power so he could feel like more of a man. The longer I looked at him as he sat there, pretending to be the devoted fiancé and father, the more I didn't recognize him—the man I first fell for. And sadly for him, I didn't care.

I couldn't and wouldn't waste another moment of stress, concern, or worry on this man. I didn't have the emotional capacity for it. And with Cameron having the answers we needed, knowing this would be a steep mountain for my son and me to climb, there was no way in hell I would stay in a relationship that would pull me away.

"Jess?" Warren said with some humor in his voice, interrupting my thoughts. "I always wonder what goes on in that beautiful mind of yours when you space out like this." He crossed his arms as he leaned back in his chair.

I stood, irritated by his stupid comment. "Space out? Hardly," I leveled him with a stare that quieted the room. I didn't mean to be so bitchy, but it was involuntary. I couldn't have been more over the guy if I tried. "I'm focused on the information Cameron has given us to help my son get his life back." I looked at Cameron, "Thank you for this. Jackson and I will talk more about it," I shouldered my purse, "and we'll also talk about him speaking to your patient. That might be a good way to get the confidence he needs to make an informed decision." I looked at Jackson and smiled, "Let's head to the beach or something, eh? This is a lot to process."

"I don't mean to interfere with the decision-making process," Cam stopped me. His eyes held me in place, and I felt a sense of calm rush through me. "But I do know—well," he stammered, glancing back and forth between Jackson and me, "I am very confident about performing this operation, and I hope you consider that when you make your decision."

"I do understand, Doctor Brandt," I smiled. "I know you well enough to know that if you didn't feel confident, you would've already referred us to someone else."

"Okay. Well, I'll have my office call you with your next appointment with me in a couple of days," Cam said as I made my way to the door.

"Sounds good." I was being cold, but this was a lot to process. My son was about to lose an entire brain hemisphere to stop the seizures that no medication could help.

I had to get out of here, and looking back at Warren, I knew I would have to deal with him too.

I just needed my mind to unwind a little, and with Cameron setting up our next appointment in a few days, I had plenty of time to chill out and handle the hurdles in my way. Namely, Warren, because the more I thought about him being here to support Jackson and me, the angrier I became.

"Hey, Jacks," I said. I spun around to face my son, who was following me out of the doctor's office.

"Yeah?" Jackson said, his expression showing curiosity and concern.

"I know I said we should head to the beach, but—"

"Already done!" Warren exclaimed with victory.

"What's already done?" I asked, annoyed by his interruption almost as much as his presence.

"I just reserved a beach house for us for the week." He shrugged and grinned at me as I stared at him in shock. "I'll look at extending the stay for however long we need once decisions have been made with Jackson."

"That's a pretty bold move, especially for you." I stood there in disbelief, not wanting to cause a scene by launching into the tirade I'd wanted to unleash on him for weeks.

I just needed to keep my mouth shut until I knew how I wanted to deal with Warren.

The beach house Warren had reserved for us was lovely and welcoming to my frazzled nerves. Jacks loved the place, primarily because of the infinity pool built into the veranda that overlooked the shore.

I tried to see what the neighbors' terraces were like, and it seemed a popular idea to swim in a big, fat pool while watching the tide roll out and in. Not a bad life at all, if you ask me.

I grinned, feeling the fresh, salty air blow across my face and through my hair, feeling relaxed, even if only for this moment.

"Wine? It's Malbec," Warren said, holding two glasses of dark red wine and walking out where I sat on a lounge chair, my knees pulled up into my chest while I absorbed this sudden peace I felt.

"Oh, sure." I reached up and grabbed the glass from him.

"I understand you're under pressure, Jessa. I feel that too. Perhaps that's why I've been such a dick. I know that Jackson needs help, and," he paused and stared into his glass, "well, it just sucks that I can't be the one to help him."

"I think we're at the point where it doesn't matter who the hero is. What matters is Jacks getting help."

"I understand, but you see what I'm up against, right?"

I tucked a strand of hair behind my ear and returned my gaze to where the sun began to set on the horizon, creating a bright sparkly effect on the rippling water beyond the shoreline.

"It's not about you, though, is it?" I sipped my wine, irritated at Warren's words, but I could tell that the man, who had zero sense of humor, was trying to lighten the mood with silliness.

"You know I'm kidding, right?"

"Mm-hmm," I responded, feeling the Grand Canyon-sized distance between us. "Do you think he's as nervous as I am about this?" I questioned Warren about Jackson, who'd excused himself earlier to call his girlfriend in New York.

I thought of my son's bright smile, bringing a smile of my own to my face. This kid was undoubtedly a strong boy, and given everything he'd gone through already, I knew he must have felt stronger than I did.

"He's nervous," Warren answered. "He's going to need his mama's strength, though, more than I'm sure he'll ever care to admit."

"I feel numb."

He sipped his wine, crossed a leg over the other, and ran a hand through his meticulously combed hair. "I get that. It's hard to imagine the surgery he'll have to go through. Do you trust Dr. Brandt enough for this? I guess that's the pressing question."

"Cameron is a lighthearted jokester. That's how I knew him, anyway. But he always had this air about him when it came to school and his future career, and when that kicked in, the humor faded, and he got shit done. He's precise. Always has been."

"You didn't answer the question," Warren stated.

"I didn't answer the question how you wanted me to," I snapped, feeling my nerves on edge. I gulped my wine, hoping it would chill me out. I didn't have the energy for a fight.

He sat up, dropping his legs over the side of his chair, and turned to face me. "Do you or don't you trust this man to perform this surgery?"

"I don't know," I answered truthfully. "This is huge, you know? It's not something I ever expected to face, even after accepting that my son had epilepsy. It's just too much right now."

"I understand that, but if you have no faith in the surgeon, what is the point of any of it?"

"The point is to get my son his life back, Warren. Whether or not I trust Cameron, I just don't know."

"I'll help you out a little." He pulled out his phone. "I took the liberty of researching this man."

Oh? Because I wasn't responsible enough to? How condescending can this fucker be? Someone give Warren a medal. He Googled. He's so responsible.

"Go on," I said, knowing Warren was waiting for me to give him my undivided attention. God, he could be so full of himself sometimes.

"Well, I think you already know the history of the college and universities he attended."

I was so goddamn annoyed with this conversation.

"Of course, I know this. I also know that he's made global news with spinal and brain surgeries, Warren. The man's a genius in this profession. And he knows this too, or he wouldn't recommend we meet with his patient. I just need to accept this is Jackson's journey. I'm just not sure I'm there yet."

"Hold on," Warren rolled his eyes as his phone started buzzing. "Got a call."

I welcomed his business intrusion because I wanted to stop talking more than anything, which was contrary to how I'd previously felt when his work interrupted a serious moment. Ordinarily, I would've been upset by something like this, but as I told him earlier, I was numb, especially regarding him. I honestly couldn't muster any feeling about him or what he had to say.

I placed my wine glass on the end table and picked up my phone. I opened a search to find testimonials about Cameron, curious about what I might find.

I clicked on a link that brought me to Cameron's bio, ignoring the black hair, blue-eyed, gorgeous man's ridiculously hot picture, and found the testimonials section.

> *"Dr. Brandt has remarkable skill and talent. His bedside manner was impeccable, and his love for children was apparent in every interaction with our son. We couldn't be more thankful for Dr. Cameron and his help."*

I smiled, imagining how Cameron was with his patients and enjoying this little peek into what previous patients thought about him.

> *"We were faced with no other option but to have spinal surgery for our daughter. Dr. Brandt was a positive, guiding light throughout the process. He went out of his way to treat us like dear friends, taking time out of his day (or day off, in our case) to make sure we were okay to move forward with the surgery. He listens and is considerate of his patients and their family's needs. If it weren't for his constant reassurances (and trust me, we needed the reassurance), we would've had difficulty deciding whether to go through with the surgery."*

Another one...

> *"Dr. Cameron Brandt is an angel on this earth. We couldn't be more grateful for him, being there every step of the way since our lives changed with our daughter's unexpected diagnosis. He had a way of connecting to her that put all of us effortlessly at ease. He treats his patients as if they were family. We will forever appreciate you, Dr. Brandt. God Bless you!"*

All the testimonies read like this, and by the time I finished reading them, I had a larger-than-life smile. I was so proud of Cameron for pursuing his dreams. Reading success stories of the lives he'd changed filled my heart with happiness.

Now, all I needed to do was to allow him to help my son.

· · ·

That night, I lay flat on my back in bed, Warren sound asleep on the other side after his head hit the pillow. When he climbed into bed, the look on my face must've been a clear signal that I was *not* in the mood for him to try anything sexy. Of course, I couldn't have been colder all day if I were an iceberg, so I wasn't surprised when he lay on his side, snoring almost immediately.

I lay there, thinking about Jackson, knowing that with these significant changes came fresh starts. Jacks would inevitably have a lot of work to do if he decided to have surgery—a ton of recovery and different therapies—and, more than anything, I wanted to be in a good place mentally for him when he did. I wanted to be in a good mental place no matter what. Jacks deserved that with or without surgery.

I looked over at Warren, realizing that, as much as I loved him as a person, I was not *in love* with him anymore. I loved the safety and security that he provided, being the anchor to keep me grounded or the partner to reassure me that things would be okay, but were those things enough to overcome the other feelings—the jealousy, the condescension, overall sense of going through the motions, or being prioritized beneath work? Could I be my happiest self while feeling those things? Because Jacks deserved the best of me, and I hadn't been my best in a long time.

Maybe I'd wake up tomorrow and feel differently, but I didn't think so. It had been over for Warren and me for quite some time. I just don't think he and I could admit that. It was undoubtedly the logical explanation for how he ditched us in California. People who love each other don't do shit like that.

Strange as it may seem, I wasn't upset about it. It was time to put my attention where it was necessary. I didn't want to lose Warren's support at this crucial time, but I couldn't be my best with him. Jacks deserved the best of me, and I deserved it too.

Chapter Fifteen

Cam

"Great, and I'll expect to see you in surgery bright and early tomorrow morning," I teased the new resident on my floor, watching her flushed cheeks turn another shade of red.

"Are you just saying that so I don't go out with the girls tonight, Dr. Brandt?" Kelly bashfully played back.

I stopped and turned to face her. Her soft green eyes shied away from staring up into mine. As beautiful as this young woman was and as insane as my hormones were these days, I was thankful that I viewed her as a little sister type. Fortunately, I wasn't the type who was easily tempted to fuck around at work. I knew myself well enough to know that the ease at which I was able to move on from casual relationships would be a problem in the workplace, and I didn't need HR breathing down my neck.

Something about Kelly reminded me of what my little sister might've been like if she'd had the chance to grow up, and I appreciated our strictly platonic friendship.

"Well, *Dr. Palmer*, if that keeps you out of Mark's bed, then yes. Surgery starts at four in the morning." I folded my arms and watched her face turn beet red. "Ah, ha," I said with a laugh.

"What! How would you know anything about that?" she whispered as if he were standing on the other side of me.

"Oh, I don't know, maybe it's the fifteen different shades of red your cheeks turn while talking about him every single day." I turned to walk toward the office I used when I was on call. I desperately needed to brush my teeth after the coffee I'd been downing the entire night started to leave a disgusting aftertaste in my mouth.

"No," she said, feistier. "How did you know that I was planning on…you know. Bed."

She paused, and I smiled, punching the lever to open the automatic doors, admitting us into the lounge area.

"You give yourself away completely, you know? Your facial expressions, and then having these moments where you're so defensive that you easily forget how schedules work and so forth."

Her face scrunched up in this adorable expression. "That's ridiculous. You guessed. And then you just were being *you* by trying to get me back here at four in the morning."

I smirked, "Who else is going to buy me breakfast after a long four days on call?"

"Cameron," she said, rolling her eyes. "You know I'll be here if you need me. So, what is it?"

"You know I'm messing with you. Enjoy your night out with your friends. I'm going to catch a nap before the next call comes through."

Before Kelly could respond, my phone rang. I picked it up when I noticed it was my secretary calling.

"Janice," I answered. "How'd the past few days go? I'm impressed you haven't called me over the past few days since I've been on call."

"You know the drill, Dr. Cam. Emergencies only, right?" Janice responded with a half laugh.

"Yeah, right. We know how hard and fast *that* rule is," I teased. I'd always made it clear if she needed to reach me, she should do so no matter what.

"I was calling because Jessica Stein finally called to schedule that appointment for Jackson to meet with Lisa."

I'd been ready to get out of here in an hour so I could sleep for twenty-four hours, but now, I was wide awake.

It's about fucking time! I was beginning to wonder if Jessa had lost the number to the hospital or if I would have to hunt her ass down myself and figure out if I'd scared her and Jackson off so bad that they went into hiding.

"That's fantastic news. Okay, I'm off for two days, but why don't you see if Lisa can meet with them the day after tomorrow? I'll come in on my day off. I really want this young woman to breathe a little hope into Jackson's situation."

"Sounds great. Ms. Stein said she was available any day."

"Excellent. Then so long as Miss Lisa can make some time for us, we'll be golden. Is there anything else before I go?"

"Some prescriptions for Haylee Brown need refills. Other than that, everything is buttoned up nicely over here at the office."

"Send the scripts to me, and I'll have them refilled. I'll see you when I'm back in the office next week."

"Perfect."

"Also, text me the updates on when Lisa will meet with Ms. Stein and her son."

"You got it, Dr. B."

My long-ass on-call week had finally come to an end. I was too tired to think of anything besides sleep at this point, so I ordered an Uber because I was too sleep-deprived to get behind the wheel.

I was bone tired but relieved that Jessa and Jacks were moving forward. This was not an easy surgery for anyone to accept, and I was grateful that they were brave enough to hear Lisa's story.

Chapter Sixteen

Jessa

This week felt like it'd lasted a year, and I hadn't even faced the longest part yet—Jackson and me meeting with Cameron's success story patient.

After Warren and I called off the engagement and ended our relationship, I had my ups and downs. I was grieving the relationship but was confident that it needed to end, and Warren agreed. We had become stale and stagnant in our relationship, the romantic aspect of it anyway. Something was missing, and it had been for a long time. I guess caring for a son with a medical condition while one caretaker was a workaholic was a recipe for disaster.

At one time, the chemistry between Warren and me was fire, but that flame had burned out long ago, and neither of us was prepared to do anything about it until now. We preferred to split amicably than to let our resentments grow into full-blown anger. Remaining friendly was important to me because Jackson didn't need any undue stress.

Warren left for the airport in an Uber the day before I called to set the appointment to meet Cameron's patient. Warren wanted to stay for the consult, but in the end, we both determined it was best if he stepped away now rather than involve himself and make it harder to separate after the surgery.

We were both young. He was a very eligible bachelor, and I knew it would be selfish of me to hang onto him when I was no longer in love with him.

By the goodness of his heart, Warren didn't leave us destitute. So, here I was in the beach house he had rented for an additional week, giving me time to make arrangements for what came next. He was set on ensuring we found a place to live and making sure I had an income. He put me on his company's payroll, which gave me medical benefits to cover Jackson, and paid me a ridiculous amount of money to transcribe ledgers and prepare notes and things for his weekly meetings.

I was acutely aware that most breakups didn't happen this way—cushy, remote-work jobs with hefty salaries and benefits packages weren't typical for broken engagements—and I couldn't have been more grateful.

A clock was ticking on this beach house, so I perused rental listings in the area, rolling my eyes at the cost of living in Southern California.

I had to find Jackson and me a place to live for under two thousand a month, preferably in a part of town that didn't take a million miles to commute to the hospital.

Not an easy task, as I was finding out.

This wasn't going to be easy.

"Are we calling an Uber to get to the hospital?" Jackson asked.

"Already done," I answered with a confident smile, feeling the best I had since the breakup.

"How much longer are we going to get around in an Uber when we should buy a car, Mom?" Jackson asked. "It's not very cost-effective."

"You're sixteen years old," I said with a smile. "Stop acting like you're twenty-five."

"You've always said I act older than my age, and now you're insulting me for it?"

The one trait you didn't inherit from your father, the man who forever acts like a big kid, I thought, looking at Jackson and seeing how much he resembled his father.

"It's not an insult, kid," I said. "You've always kept up with the adult conversations, and sometimes I forget you're only sixteen."

"Well, take advantage of my wisdom, then, because I'm pretty sure these Uber fees will add up to more than what Dr. Brandt paid for his Porsche."

"Don't worry about buying a car right now, Jacks. First, we need to decide if you will be comfortable with this surgery. After that, depending on your decision, we'll worry about finding a place to live. Then, finally, we need to decide if you want to stay here and go through rehab or maybe go to Seattle near my parents. Believe it or not, I *have* given this some thought. I'm not just out here running around, throwing twenty-dollar bills into the wind."

Moving near my parents in Seattle was not on the top of my list, but I wanted Jackson to have options. This was not about me.

"Okay," he responded distractedly, grabbing his phone from where it buzzed in his pocket.

I checked the Uber app, seeing our driver was down the street, and I shouldered my purse.

"Jacks, let's head out." I shoved the last of my bagel in my mouth and marched up the steps toward the door. "Jackson," I called again, wondering where the hell my boy went.

"Right behind you," he said sadly, prompting me to look back and see what had happened.

"Everything okay?" I asked as I shuffled through my purse to find the keys to lock up the place.

"Paige just dumped me. Perfect timing, right? I'm on my way to find out what life will be like after losing half my brain, and she sends me this. So, yeah, everything's great."

"Oh, shit," I said, my heart broken, seeing this look of grief and fear crossing Jackson's face.

Without warning, I reached out and hugged my son.

"Mom, don't," he said, standing there rigidly as I clung to him. "I'm fine. I really don't care."

I stepped back and studied his bright blue eyes, "Saying you don't care just means that you—"

"Mom," he said, cutting me off. "Let's just go. I don't want to talk about it. I'll be fine. Can we please meet with this Lisa girl and hear more about this surgery? Please?"

His eyes pleaded with me, and I knew it was best to shut my mouth and go with the flow for now. I wasn't going to try and play mother protector of the year because I could feel my fears growing the closer we got to meeting this girl.

We sat in the car and drove in silence. I didn't know what to say anymore. I was scared as shit, realizing this surgery was a reality. It wasn't some abstract conversation anymore. It was real, and someone who'd gone through it wanted to tell us what we could expect.

Reality was a bitch, and she was breathing down my neck.

I wanted to text Warren like I would've before, just to get some reassurance, but that wasn't exactly an option anymore. I hated that I'd come to depend on that man's strength after all these years.

I knew the only way to gain confidence was to embrace my fears and these uncomfortable, scary moments. I didn't have a partner to bolster me anymore, which was okay. I didn't need anyone for that. I had to be strong again. The tests of faith were coming, and I had to be ready.

Once we reached our destination, I inhaled a breath of confidence and stepped out of the car.

"Well, where to go now?" I said, scrolling through my emails and trying to find the one that detailed this meeting.

"Fifth floor, consultation room B," Jackson said.

"How the hell do you remember every damn thing?" I questioned with a smile, feeling nervous with each step toward the hospital.

Something told me that I would hate this place soon enough, that I would associate it with Jacks's surgery and all the worries that went along with it.

I shook my head briskly, expelling these negative thoughts from my mind.

"Dr. Brandt, you're needed in OR-3. Dr. Brandt to OR-3, please," the intercom announced over the hospital speakers. It didn't take much to figure out that Cameron wouldn't be joining us for this consult.

That was fine. I didn't need the distraction of the man's looks right now. Something told me that I was a little weak in the emotional department and that all it would take was Cam's charming smile for me to melt.

That was definitely something that did not need to happen. Though, if I were honest with myself, I would've enjoyed seeing him.

"This way, Mom," Jacks directed while I worked to keep up with my kid's long strides.

"This hospital is lovely," I said, seeing the technology that was integrated into the large pillars but somehow not standing out so boldly.

The place was bright and airy, welcoming in every sense of the word. There were tall windows placed strategically throughout to show the weeping willow trees, fountains, ponds, and every neatly manicured part of the hospital grounds outside. It was peaceful and serene, and I felt my smile grow wide, feeling more confident.

Perhaps that's why this hospital was built this way, to breathe hope and confidence into anyone who walked through those doors. I knew I needed it, and it was certainly working on me.

We walked through double glass doors that automatically opened as we stepped toward them. A young man was sitting at the receptionist's desk amongst three young women, whose laughs were silenced as we walked in.

I grinned. "Hi, I'm Jessica Stein, and this is my son, Jackson. We're here to meet with Dr. Brandt and Lisa Jameson?"

"Dr. Brandt was called into surgery moments ago," the young man said, bringing his attention to his computer screen. "One moment while I look to see if we will be rescheduling your appointment."

I stepped back and looked at Jackson, who flashed his handsome smile at the younger blonde woman sitting next to the man helping us.

By the look on her face, specifically the flush in her cheeks, it was obvious that my son had the same effect on women that his father did.

"Ms. Stein?" the young man said after making a quick phone call as he clicked through screens on his computer monitor.

"Yes," I stepped back up to the white marble counter.

"Okay, we'll have you back in a moment. Dr. Palmer will be assisting in Dr. Brandt's place. If you'll follow me," he rose, took off his headset, and walked around his desk. "I'll take you to her."

I pursed my lips and shrugged at Jackson, realizing that having a different doctor was probably for the best—for me, hormone-wise.

"Right this way," the young man guided, motioning toward an open door to our left.

My eyes widened as we entered. The meticulously neat office space was every bit the Cameron that I knew and remembered loving so deeply. When we lived together for a short time in college, I got to experience the neat and tidy—to a fault—side of Cam. Some of his habits had permanently rubbed off on me, but I never got quite *there* with how painstakingly clean the man could be.

A pretty blonde woman sat behind a desk, taking a call. Her stethoscope hung around her neck and lay on her lab coat, leading me to assume this was Dr. Palmer. She looked over and made a motion for us to come in.

"If you'll have a seat," the young man advised while Dr. Palmer smiled and gave us a thumbs up. "Dr. Palmer will be right with you."

"Thanks, Manuel," I said, finally noticing the young man's nametag.

"My pleasure," he smiled, then dismissed himself, closing the door behind him.

"Great, and then we'll go ahead with those assessments. I'm confident that before you move forward, Dr. Brandt will want to review these images." Dr. Palmer said with a knowing laugh. "Yes, right. Okay, I'll see you this afternoon, and I'll let Dr. Brandt know that we'll meet in conference room ten with the family. Perfect. Sure. Okay, goodbye."

She hung up the phone and rose, walking briskly around the large walnut desk, prompting Jackson and me to stand.

"Hi, there. I'm Dr. Palmer, and it's very nice to meet you both," she said sweetly, extending her hand to shake mine and then Jackson's. "Dr. Brandt wanted me to extend his apologies for not being here. He was unexpectedly called to assist in emergency surgery."

"I hope everything is okay. We heard the hospital page him over the intercom when we got here," I said, a bit worried that since Cam was a pediatric specialist, something must've gone wrong with a child.

"Everything will be fine," Dr. Palmer reassured us. "Now, I'm quite excited to be the one to introduce both of you to our sweet little Lisa." She smiled, and I could tell she was raptly changing the subject. "I think you will marvel at her strength, tenacity, and positivity. She is an amazing young woman." She glanced down at her delicate, gold wristwatch. "But before we meet with her in a couple of minutes, do you have any questions for me? Again, Dr. Brandt is sorry he isn't here, but let's face it, he's a bit boring, anyway." She flashed a charming, mischievous smile, prompting a laugh from Jackson.

"We really don't have any questions," I said. "I'm sure I'll think of them at the worst possible time, like while Lisa is telling us about her successes in recovery."

"Always," Dr. Palmer grinned.

Out of nowhere, I felt a twinge of jealousy, wondering if this beautiful doctor and my ex-boyfriend—the player from hell—had ever engaged in a relationship.

God help me. This was not the time or place for this utter nonsense. Jealousy was the ugliest emotion and even uglier when it wasn't warranted. Yet, here I sat, sizing up this perfectly lovely, charming woman who was only doing her job. A job that she no doubt busted her ass to get.

I needed to get a grip. I shook the green-eyed monster off my shoulder and decided I would blame my momentary lapse in sanity on memories conjured by Cameron's pristine office.

Yeah. That was it.

Chapter Seventeen

Jessa

When we walked toward the room where Lisa waited for us, I was more anxious than ever. I had no idea where these feelings had come from because I was surrounded by all things zen in this hospital. There was no call for this. Nonetheless, my heart was racing, my palms were sweaty, along with all the other exciting symptoms accompanying nearly chucking up your guts in front of God and everyone.

As we followed Dr. Palmer into the private sitting room and I laid eyes on the young woman, my fears vanished.

Her black hair was cut into a pixie-like bob, accentuating the pointy features of her face. Her eyes were a vibrant green, and her complexion a soft pale color. The rosy-red blush of her cheeks made me grin. This young lady was a physical display of health and happiness, with no traces of a medical condition that led to life-changing surgery.

"Hi, I'm Lisa." She snapped to her feet and nearly danced over to where Jackson and I stood next to the doctor.

"I'm Jessica," I said smiling, "and this is my son Jackson."

"Call me Jacks," Jackson said, much more forward than I imagined he would be after meeting someone for the first time.

Lisa's energy was intoxicating, though. She was filled with excitement and radiated positivity. I don't think there was any way someone could be negative around this girl.

"Hey, Dr. Palmer," she said, hugging the woman I had developed a jealous streak for minutes earlier.

"How's our favorite gem?" Dr. Palmer questioned.

"Good," she said. "Where's Dr. Brandt? He promised he'd be here, and I haven't seen him in forever."

"He was called into surgery," Dr. Palmer said, "but I'm going to make sure he buys you that bag of Kettle Corn he promised the day you left us."

"Mm-hmm. He owes me," she said with a silly smile.

"Lisa, where did you want to begin the interview?"

"Interview?" She rolled her eyes and giggled, "Dr. Palmer, you are way too professional sometimes. It's just me, and Dr. Brandt said to keep it casual." She looked at Jackson and me. "You guys want to go outside? The breeze gardens were always my favorite when I was in rehab here."

"Sounds great," I said, trying to loosen up and go with the flow.

"Here, Jacks," she said with a darling smile, "walk with me."

It was an endearing moment, and I was grateful for this opportunity.

"They are cute," Dr. Palmer said with a hint of sass as we walked behind the two.

"They are," I answered. I saw the girl's slight limp on her right side and noticed that she didn't seem to have movement in her right arm.

My heart rate raced, and this time it was somewhat justified. Cameron hadn't mentioned these possibilities when he went straight to the idea that surgery was the only answer.

I didn't want to jump to conclusions until we heard Lisa's story, but I was happy we were headed outside where I could get some fresh air because I felt myself beginning to spiral.

I knew the surgery would have some life-changing effects, so why was I surprised that one of them was potentially staring me in the face?

Fuck. Why is this happening to Jacks? How are we supposed to do this?

I felt like punching one of the beautiful willow trees we passed by.

I tried to steady myself, knowing that if I spoke, I had no idea what manner of unfiltered things might come out of my mouth.

I wanted to march back into that hospital, find Cameron, drag his ass out of surgery, and demand he tell me why he didn't warn me about these side effects. Jackson's future in sports would be out of the question, at the least.

As I selfishly ruminated on these horrific thoughts, anger firing them off one-by-one in my head, I heard Jackson laugh.

I felt like I was in a daze, but my thoughts were pulled out of this hole of selfish hopelessness when I saw Lisa throwing her head back in laughter.

"Dr. Brandt said that it took about six months after her surgery for her to be able to speak again," Dr. Palmer said, bringing my attention to where she stood smiling at my son and Lisa laughing at the swans in the pond, swimming in circles.

"That was me after my surgery," Lisa said with another laugh. "I was walking in circles instead of swimming in circles, though."

"Was it frustrating?" Jackson asked. "I read that I might lose function of my right leg, possibly the entire right side of my body, with a hemispherectomy."

"Which side is Dr. Brandt going to operate on?"

"The left," Jackson answered.

"It's possible. Only Dr. Brandt can answer that question for you," she answered him.

"True. Was it hard, though? To go through with it or to go through rehabilitation?"

I folded my arms together as Dr. Palmer and I sat on a nearby bench, listening to the two talk.

The thought of Jackson having this surgery, going through painstaking recovery, and having potentially severe side effects terrified me to my core. I was a mother. Biology demanded that I do everything in my power to keep my child from harm. It would go against nature for me to feel anything other than fear in this situation, but I reminded myself that this wasn't about me. This was about Jackson, and he didn't seem scared. If anything, he seemed intrigued.

"Lisa's mother was a lot like you," Dr. Palmer said. "At least that's how the story goes. I've only been here for a year, and Lisa's surgery was performed four years ago."

"Four years ago?" I said. Knowing that Lisa still had some paralysis after that length of time made me wonder if Jackson would ever be able to play sports again. I'd been holding to hope that surgery was the solution to that problem. I didn't think that it might take away the possibility entirely.

"Yes, and she's come a very long way. But Dr. Brandt has always said that timing and age are critical in performing these surgeries. He operated on Lisa when she was fourteen years old, and still, even though she was young, it took a lot of work in rehab to get her where she is today."

"And that is?"

That may have come off bitchy. I didn't know, and I didn't mean to, but it was hard to put a lid on my concerns.

"She brags that Dr. Brandt challenged her in ways that most doctors wouldn't. She is quite a competitive child. Cameron thinks she must've talked her mother into allowing her to have the surgery just to prove to the doctors that anyone could recover at her age—older or not. I think Cameron's first challenge was telling Lisa the only wheels she'd have were her wheelchair wheels."

"That's a bit callous, don't you think?"

"You haven't seen Dr. Brandt with his patients, or you'd understand."

"No, I haven't."

"He's known for finding his patients' weakness or challenge points," she said, ignoring my blunt remarks. "So, with Lisa, he knew that if you told her she wouldn't have something, she'd prove you wrong. Cameron told me that it nearly crushed him when he challenged her because even as a fantastic surgeon, he wasn't sure if she would be able to walk again. It was a real possibility that she'd be in a wheelchair for the rest of her life. But when her parents told him that reverse psychology worked like a charm on their daughter, Cameron went to work.

"He didn't want to upset Lisa, but he needed to challenge her greatly to train her right hemisphere to work harder. She needed it to pick up where the left hemisphere once did the work. She remained diligent, focused, and most of all, driven with willpower that blew Dr. Brandt's mind. It didn't take long before she regained the function of parts of the right side of her body. She found her little laugh and smile again too."

I smiled, hearing Lisa and Jackson in a happy conversation. Jackson didn't shy away from the hard questions.

"It's okay to be fearful for your son, you know?"

"I understand, but it's not fair to him for me to be upset by this drastic change in *his* life. I don't want him to have the surgery, but because my son is sixteen, and this isn't my life, I don't know how to feel about making the decision. Am I willing to risk constant, crippling seizures over the potential side effects of this surgery?"

"It's wonderful that you consider his feelings; however, in the end, he's a minor, and you're the one signing the papers. So, if you're not one hundred percent convinced that your son should go through with this surgery and you back out at the last minute, whether he wants it done or not, that will be a heavy thing for you both to deal with."

"What are you saying?"

"I saw the look on your face when you noticed Lisa's limp," she said, practically reading my mind and having the answers lined up for my questions. "The sight of it rightfully shook you. I've been with parents who were very confident and comfortable with their children having surgeries—different ones than a hemispherectomy, of course—and even they have backed out at the last minute, some of them leaving mine or Dr. Brandt's care altogether. Unfortunately, fear has a way of taking over emotions, and sometimes poor decisions are made. This is why Dr. Brandt wanted you both to meet with Lisa. Lisa's mom called off the surgery the night before it was scheduled, but with the help of our neuropsychologists and Dr. Brandt's relaxed demeanor, they convinced her to go through with it."

"What would have happened if they didn't do the surgery? What form of epilepsy did she have that called for a hemispherectomy?"

"She had Rasmussen's encephalitis, a degenerative disease. It damages tissues, eating away at one side of the brain but never making it to the other. If it had been left untreated, she would have suffered paralysis on one full side of the body and had uncontrollable seizures. It took about a year before Dr. Brandt was able to fully gain Lisa and her family's trust to move ahead with the surgery. The younger they are, the better it is to operate on them since the brain is still developing and the left and right hemispheres are still growing."

"Dr. Brandt mentioned that if we wait too long, there's a chance he won't recover as expected?"

"Correct," she answered. "Jackson is sixteen, and that really is the maximum age that this surgery will be performed. After that, there are more risks, and the percentages of excellent recoveries start to go down."

"Funny, Cam didn't mention that when he insisted this surgery was the only answer."

I was irritated again, but I knew it was just a flood of emotions taking over me. Still, Cameron could've been a little more forthcoming with information like that.

"Dr. Brandt most likely knew that if he were, you would never have spoken to Lisa or given this a shot." A curious expression crossed her face, "Do you call him Cam?"

I nodded. "We went to college together."

"Oh, nice. That makes sense. That guy has a knack for getting into your head before you even know what's happening."

"I take it you've dated, then?"

Jesus Christ! Shut up! I thought, feeling like an idiot for blurting that out.

"Oh, no. No," she said with another laugh. "Though he is easy on the eyes, our relationship is very platonic." She arched a playful eyebrow at me, most likely feeling sorry for me and adjusting her bedside manner to accommodate my stupid and immature comment. "Besides, he's made it clear to nearly everyone at this hospital that he will not date anyone here."

"Oh, wow. Well, I guess that makes him a bit of a stand-up guy. I always imagined that the good-looking doctors get to have all the fun."

I stopped and shut the fuck up. What the hell was wrong with me?

"No, Dr. Brandt is most certainly not like those hot doctors you watch on those drama shows on television," she laughed.

"I appreciate what you've said today. I mean, before this weird sidebar about Dr. Brandt," I admitted.

"You're going to be okay," she said with a reassuring smile. "We're all here for you and Jackson. You need to understand that."

"I think I do," feeling my nerves unwind for the first time since walking out here. "It's going to take a bit, though, to process this."

"We expect it would. The best part is that you both came today, taking the first step in the journey to learn more about the surgery and knowing that Jackson is not alone."

"Yes," I said, returning my attention to the pond.

I was going to be okay. Jackson would be okay too. I had to accept that and overcome these fears, and that would take time.

Chapter Eighteen

Cam

Being called in for Jonah Williams' emergency surgery was not what I'd expected when I woke up this morning. Calling the time of death on a patient is something we are trained to separate ourselves from emotionally. I dealt with the loss of patients in numerous ways, mainly by moving on to the next. Focusing on death never helped the next patient in my line of work, and I had to focus on the next patient because the reality that a child was gone would be too painful otherwise.

Dr. Novant requested my assistance in an urgent situation once he realized his surgery was not going as expected. This didn't happen often, but we knew there was a seventy percent chance young Jonah wouldn't survive this surgery, which was a contributing factor to why I disagreed with Dr. Novant's decision to move forward. However, despite my opinion, Dr. Novant was confident about the procedure, as were the medical teams.

A good surgeon shouldn't have considered surgery as their first or second answer. This case was different from most, though, and I understood why Dr. Novant wanted to go in and remove the malignant tumor. The patient's life expectancy was not good, and surgery was the answer to hopefully giving the young boy a chance at life. It crushed me that there were no other options because I knew we would find them if we took the time to look.

Jonah's parents would've agreed with me, but their journey to get to this point had been burdensome, and I knew they were running swiftly out of options. So, considering the boy's family and, more importantly, reviewing the findings in Jonah's MRIs and scans, I understood why Novant cut. It's also why he pulled me to the side and requested I be on standby in case the surgery got away from him.

Through our protocols at St. John's, I was placed on standby, so if the worst-case scenario happened, I'd be called in to assist, hoping for a miracle. But now, here I was, seven hours after calling the time of death, thinking about how precious and fragile our lives were. I could say that Jonah was no longer suffering, and no one would know that was true more than his parents. But that wouldn't take away the pain of his loss. Nothing would ever take it away. And nothing I could say would bring any relief or comfort to his family. The loss of a child would never be anything but tragic.

When my sister died, I saw what it did to my parents. My parents stayed together, but they were completely disconnected. My father dove into his work, building an empire that threatened to put Mitchell and Associates out of business, and my mother self-medicated. They managed to keep up appearances in their social circles, but their grief hung heavy in our home until the day they died.

I got into this line of work to do what I could to keep families away from experiencing that level of anguish. I didn't want anyone to know what it was like to feel like they were drowning in despair, but, to my greatest disappointment, I couldn't save everyone.

I sat in this empty operating room, thinking about my son and how he was suffering from the same epileptic condition that took my sister.

I had to help Jacks, even if only because he'd inherited his genetic disorder from my family. There was so much more to it than that, though. Time was of the essence. I was taking risks by allowing the decision-making process to drag on and on, and Jackson didn't have that kind of time. His brain was nearing its maturity, and if I disconnected his left hemisphere, the right might not learn to adapt and take over the left's functions.

"The fuck are you doing in this OR, man?" I heard Jake Mitchell say. He was most likely hunting down my ass for a favor. "Hey, I need a favor."

A smile spread across my face, wondering if I should've changed careers and become a mind reader.

"Shocker," I said, looking up from the swivel chair where I sat alone in this room. "What do you need?"

Jake looked around the room and then back to me. "Everything okay? Seriously, what are you doing in here?"

"It's where I come to think sometimes. It's quiet," I said. "And yes, I'm fine. Just going over some things in my head about an emergency surgery today. I lost a young one, and I'm just determining what more could've been done and what could've been done differently. You know the drill."

"I know that drill all too well." He crossed the room and pulled himself onto the OR table, sitting across from me. "It's good to get that shit out of your head. You know, sometimes it can also be good for your sanity to bounce some of it off a brilliant doctor like me," he teased. "Tell me, how the fuck did you lose a patient in surgery? I thought you were going to meet with the success story kid and *your* kid. I didn't know you had surgery."

"Long story, but I was on standby for Novant's surgical case today. The patient's odds weren't great, to begin with, but they were even worse *not* going in."

"Hardest cases, man," he said, "How's Novant handling it?"

"Not sure. I bounced out of there after the surgery. I was hoping I could get ahold of Jessa and see how it went with her and her boy today."

"*Your boy*," Jake teased, obviously still attached to my big ideas about winning back my ex and being more than a biological father to my son. "Or has that changed?"

"Nothing's changed," I said. "I guess I'm just a bit more focused on the kid right now than my selfish desires."

"That's a good thing, but something tells me that will pass once you get past your loss from today," he said.

"It could," I smiled, "which is never a bad thing. I'd give anything to have another chance with this woman; not too sure I'm deserving of it, though."

"It's the humble mindset that will get you the girl, that's for fucking sure," he said. "Why don't you bring her and the kid to Monterey with all of us this weekend?"

"I'm not in the mood to load them up into a private jet with a bunch of strange billionaire besties to go whale watching and shit. Besides, I'm not in the mood to have her fiancé join the festivities."

"Then don't invite his ass," Jake said with a laugh. "And, for the record, I'm not strange. The others, well, you're not wrong about them."

"Jake," I tried to lower my voice, hoping to end this conversation politely, "I'm sure you remember that *Billionaires' Club* bullshit you idiots were labeled with before you settled down and got married?"

"How could I forget? The highlight of my youth," he said with a roll of his eyes.

"Let's just say that Jessa has always been the toughest on my spoiled ass, so proposing we join the rich kids previously known as the *Billionaires' Club* on their private jet will mean I will never hear the end of it." Jake laughed. "What the hell are you hunting me down for anyway? What do you need?"

"I have a patient who I recently performed open-heart surgery on," he said. "Anyway, the dude's a pilot, and he gives flying lessons and shit. So, I was rounding up the boys to see if you all wanted to join in and get some lessons."

"Huh? Dude, you know I have my pilot's license," I laughed. "And why the fuck are you trying to round up the gang for flying lessons? You suddenly run out of money and need to go in for a group discount?"

He grinned. "If I wanted the discount, I'd have *you* teach my ass how to fly," he said. "It's just to change things up a little, you know. Hey, it could help with that fatherly bond you've been yearning for?"

"Jake, I know we haven't talked much since I drunkenly proclaimed that I would win back the girl and become the father of the year, but there's too much going for him medically to fuck around with shit like that."

"Don't say I didn't try," he said.

I couldn't help but wonder why Jake came searching for me. He could've texted me if he wanted to ask me to take some adult Chuck E. Cheese adventure in flying, but he didn't. And none of us ever had time to go hunting each other down at this hospital, so what the fuck was going on?

"That's not why you're here. Why are you in pediatrics, man?"

"No reason, really. I had to sign off on some charts after being on call. I wondered where your stupid ass was, and when someone mentioned you were in a dark, empty operating room, I thought it best to check on you. And I was right. You look like shit. I'm glad that some color and life is returning to your handsome, boyish face, though," he said, sliding off the table. "Think about going up to Monterey. I think it might be a neat trip for your boy, at least. You know what it's like, being in a strange town with no friends, facing a life-changing surgery?"

"Yeah, I don't know what that's like," I answered.

"My point exactly. Bring the kid and your girl, even the fiancé, and let us judge if you're a good candidate to take on fatherhood as you suggest."

"I'll let you know." I just wanted out of this conversation. "Jess and her son met with Lisa this morning, and I need to see how that worked out."

"And just like that," he snapped his fingers, "the lights come on, the doctor is in, and my work here is done. Good luck in getting that surgery scheduled, my man."

Jake practically skipped out of the room, leaving me standing there and shaking my head. Now that my head was out of the clouds and I was grounded, I knew exactly why Jake was here. Word spreads quickly when you lose a patient and even faster when you go MIA. If it weren't Jake, who was free when he got word I'd lost a patient, Collin would've been in here with some pointless conversation, trying to get me to stop replaying the surgery over and over.

I had to give the man some credit, though. He managed to snap me out of it.

Now, I needed to focus on the next patient, and that was my boy. He needed this surgery, and I wanted to know what Jessa and Jackson thought of their visit with Lisa. Were they on track to make a decision, or were we going to load up in Jim Mitchell's private jet and set off to Monterey to watch whales and shit?

Chapter Nineteen

Jessa

I pulled on my sweater, loving the West Coast weather more than I cared to admit. Well, Southern California's coastal weather, anyway. There was virtually no humidity, just brisk temperatures and light, breezy air.

It was quite a stark contrast from what I was used to in Manhattan during the late August months, which consisted of humid temperatures, and me begging for the sultry summer to end quickly. Fall in New York was my favorite time of year; not too hot and not too cold. That was the perfect weather to wear the sweater I was pulling on, and lucky me, in this part of the country, I got to wear it mid-summer in the evening.

It was the little things. And that's what I was focusing on these days, the little things and finding joy in them. Like this silly brown cashmere sweater that absolutely did not go with the current season—and most certainly did not go with the fashion of Southern California—but it brought a smile to my face, and that's all that mattered.

Smiling these days felt like a bit of a struggle since getting slapped in the face with the reality my son was facing, but I hid my emotions from my very observant son. Then, last night, I heard him crying in his room. It was to be expected, though. We'd met with Lisa that morning and didn't talk much about it after we left the hospital.

I had heard him crying after I'd finished drying up tears of my own. The sad part was that we were both afraid to show emotion to the other, which I knew wasn't good. We needed to come together to work through our fears and reservations. We wouldn't be able to make a sound decision—or any decision at all—if we didn't.

Again, I wanted to text Warren for some advice but knew it was best to leave him alone. I'm the one who decided to go this route, making my own decisions on behalf of my son and me. Besides, I had Dr. Palmer's number, Lisa's number, Lisa's mom's number—though I'd never met her—and the obvious number, Cameron's, if I needed any help or advice.

"Mom?" I heard Jackson call. I saved my work and sent the final transcript that Warren needed for his afternoon meeting today. It was seven-thirty in the morning in California, and given that *my new boss* was three hours ahead of me, my workdays started early and ended early.

"Mother?" Jackson said. He seemed to be in good spirits this morning, a big change from when I held him last night and let him cry into my shoulder.

"Yep, yeah?" I said, sending off the last email to Warren's secretary and turning back to see Jackson wearing his favorite Knicks jersey. "Is there another game tonight?" I questioned.

"Nah." He playfully tugged on my ponytail. "This jersey just puts me in an unbeatable mood. That's why it's my good luck shirt," he said. "Is there breakfast?"

"Oh crap," I said, pushing back and standing up. "I'll fry some eggs."

"No biggie," he said. "I can do it."

"Jacks, let me make breakfast," I said, hurrying into the kitchen.

I snatched the spatula out of his hand and was shocked when he turned and looked at me with frustration.

"Why would you do that?"

"Do what?" I said, grabbing the eggs from the fridge and bending to grab a skillet from the cabinet.

"Take this from me."

"Jacks?" I questioned. He was pissed, and I couldn't understand why.

"Pretty soon, I won't have use of my right hand. Don't you think I should enjoy it while I still can use the fucking thing?"

"I—Jacks," I started, not knowing how to respond. I stood there, my heart racing and breaking simultaneously. The thought never even occurred to me.

"It's fine. Just make breakfast and call me down when it's ready." He turned and left before I could say anything.

Shit. Shit. Shit.

I felt selfish for not considering what my son was dealing with. *Maybe if I weren't so in my head all fucking day, I'd know my son was just putting on a brave face, knowing that his life is about to be changed forever. Oh, my God. I need help with this!*

And as if God answered me in that split second, my phone rang.

It was Cameron.

"I think God answered my prayers or something. That's why you're calling," I said without thinking.

"I could argue that I'm not the answer to anyone's prayers, but then we'd both know I would be lying." I could hear the smile in his voice, but I wasn't in the mood for Cameron's charms.

"Yeah, okay."

"Jessa, you don't sound too hot, and that's why I'm calling. Forgive me for not calling yesterday evening, but I had a bit of a rough morning after being called in for an emergency assist on a surgery."

"Yeah, well, maybe you should've called. If you had, I might know what to say or do when it comes to my son, who has to deal with the mental fuckery of losing movement in his arm." There it was. I officially snapped, and Cameron was the poor man who would be on the receiving end of the fear-based vitriol poised to spew out of my mouth. "Perhaps it was that you failed to mention that you would be performing other surgeries instead of following through with the ones you've set appointments for. Do you do this to all your patients? You know, bail on them when they need you most. I guess some things never change. You must have this scale of importance where you rank things in your arrogant brain. I mean, I felt the brunt of that when the importance of going to your fucking dream college versus staying with the used up, throwaway college girlfriend—"

"I never said—"

"Ah, ah-ah," I interrupted him. "I'm not done yet, Dr. Brandt." I exhaled, my rage giving birth to some demon that had apparently been growing in me since Cameron left me years ago. My voice changed into some diabolical tone like I was possessed, and now, Cameron was about to hear everything I never knew I needed to say. "If running off to the next best thing is more important than helping my son, then I don't give a *fuck* if you're God's gift to surgery, you have the most successful cases, or even if you have the mother fucking cure to cancer, I will *not* allow you to perform this life-altering surgery on my son." The demonic voice that'd taken over me seemed to fade, but my anger wasn't gone. "I'd like to offer you a suggestion: when you say you're going to be there for a patient, be fucking there. It'll serve you well to know that you can't play with your patients' minds like that and hurt them like you're the very type to do."

"Anything else?" he said as if he were taking notes.

"Yes, you're an asshole," I finished, feeling my heart pounding in my throbbing head.

"May I speak?" he questioned meekly.

"Yes. Yes, you may speak, Cameron."

"First," he spoke carefully so as not to wake the demon in me again, "it was rude of me to miss our appointment yesterday, and no, it is not something I do to all of my new patients."

"Just my kid, right?" I said, annoyed at the excuses I knew were about to be delivered.

"No," he said. "This was a rare case. I was not happy the surgery was moving forward, and given that there are laws that prevent me from disclosing too much to you, I can say that, despite my best efforts, we lost the patient. Otherwise, I would've most definitely followed up with you last evening. I'm sorry it took me until this morning to do so. I can tell that, due to my lack of effort, I've evoked your hatred of me leaving you once again. Unfortunately—"

"Did you just say you lost the patient yesterday?" I questioned, my rational brain seizing control again in this demonic tug-of-war.

"Yes, and even so, I am sorry I did not call you. I didn't expect it would affect me as it did, which is no excuse. I deeply apologize."

"Oh, Jesus, Cameron. Don't you dare apologize for that. I'm the one who should be apologizing. I was wrong to go off like that. I don't know what's gotten into me."

"Hey," I heard his smile through the phone, "if that's how you handle doctors who are negligent in their duties towards your son, I'll take it all day long. Trust me, I know I was wrong in this situation. I could've had my secretary text you or done something more than not saying anything at all. Nevertheless, I learned a little something from this phone call, and I feel I must repay the favor now."

"How so?" I still wasn't in the mood for games, but I would do anything to get Jackson feeling better, and I needed a better understanding of how to be a solid support system for my son.

"What are you two up to tonight?"

"Um, I don't know. Jackson was going to use a fake I.D. to sneak into a strip club, and I figured I'd go to a singles bar and find myself a new boyfriend," I said sarcastically.

"New boyfriend? I didn't know you and your fiancé were into that sort of thing," he said humorously.

"Warren and I ended things last week," I announced and regretted it the moment I did. "And I'm *not* looking to get into another relationship, so you can forget about being excited."

"Excited?" he said, rightfully confused by my assumption.

"Shit," I said, closing my eyes in embarrassment. "I'm sorry. You most likely have a girlfriend, or a wife, or who knows. You're gorgeous and probably exploring the idea of men these days. Why not? Everyone is beautiful in this town. Why limit yourself, right?"

Nice, Jessa. Keep it up. As if you haven't embarrassed yourself enough for one conversation.

The silence on the other end of the phone would've been deafening if I hadn't heard Cameron restraining himself from bursting into laughter.

"Nothing seems to have changed with the woman I never stopped loving, let me tell you. You're still able to talk out of control and make wild and very false assumptions when you're pissed off."

"So, you're not into dudes?"

For fuck's sake. Shut the hell up already!

"Fortunately for the ladies, I still dig chicks. And fortunately for *your* cute little ass, I still dig you too and I am not dating anyone—male or female."

"How did we get onto this subject?"

"Your wild assumptions, still pissed that I left you in college, no hope for second chances, and me standing you and your boy up yesterday morning."

"Right, good. But I went to those assumptions because—"

"I have a beach house, and it's around where you and Jackson are staying."

"How would you know where we're staying?"

"I peaked at the medical charts," he said. "Anyway, it's five or six houses from where you're at, just a fun walk down the beach. I'm off at seven tonight, and I'd love to cook you both dinner. We'll sit, and I can answer any questions that may have come up since you left the hospital yesterday."

"You know, Cameron Brandt, if my son weren't so upset, and if I had any clue how to handle this situation, I would turn you down."

"I know without a shadow of a doubt that you would turn all this down. But I am reaching out to offer some help that may ease any fears that have arisen since meeting with Lisa yesterday."

I ran my hand over the top of my head and chewed on my bottom lip. I looked out the ocean window, knowing that this place gave good vibes, and if we were going to talk about this shit, we would all be comfortable opening up here. I just needed to be careful not to get *too* comfortable with Cam.

"Fine. What time do you want us there?" I conceded.

"Fish Tacos at my place at eight-thirty."

"We ate that last night," I said with a smile.

"Fine, then, *chicken* tacos?"

"Bleh. You know I hate chicken."

He laughed. "Well, you're fucking with me, so I'm fucking with you." He laughed again. "Listen, I have to get back to meeting my patients in the office. It's going to be carne asada, then."

"There you go ignoring—"

"I had *you* scheduled to call first thing when I got to the office. I have my first patient at eight. I'm getting off this call at seven fifty-five to do a quick study on charts before I meet with them. So, no, I didn't fuck up priorities this time."

I shook my head. "I'm sorry about your patient from yesterday. Really."

"Thank you," he answered, more serious now. "You and Jackson have a nice day, and I'll see you both tonight."

We ended the call, and I wanted to think of someplace Jackson and I could go to get his mind off things until we met with Cameron tonight. He'd been adamant about searching for a car since he wasn't into Ubering everywhere anymore, so maybe that's what we'd do. We could make our way to a used car lot and see if we got lucky.

Chapter Twenty

Cam

It was no surprise that Jessa would take her anger and frustration out on me this morning. I understood why she decided to sit me on my ass for not being there for her and Jackson. I wasn't making excuses for her, but I knew the fear that was ruling her at the moment. I'd seen this with many of my patients' families. They were frightened, in shock, and usually went through grief stages while deciding upon surgery for their children.

Regardless, I couldn't go back in time and fix any of this, so what was the point in even thinking about it? I could only go forward, and that meant doing something a bit more intimate for her and Jackson, using this time to address their concerns and maybe even talk about the issues plaguing them with fear.

I glanced up, past my outdoor kitchen barbeque, and took another drink of my beer, enjoying the aroma of the carne asada on my grill.

I used the tongs to flip the skirt steak and watched the flames rise over the meat, the sounds of the ocean complementing the sizzle of this delicious-smelling steak that was making my mouth water.

I glanced down at my watch. Jessa wasn't here yet, and I was beginning to wonder if it would be rude to sneak a taco before they arrived. I was starving.

"You know, every time you fire up that barbeque and send those fancy aromas into my house, I contemplate whether or not it's your way of sending an invitation to have me over for dinner."

I smiled. My neighbor, Linda, was always looking for an opportunity to get inside my house and, more specifically, my pants. Unfortunately for the lonely housewife, I liked my dick *and* balls right where they were. I didn't need her workaholic husband ripping them off after finding out I'd been banging his neglected wife whenever I came to my beach house.

"I might just take that smile of yours as an invitation," she pressed. She sounded buzzed, which was not a surprise.

"Sorry, Linda. I'm going to have to turn you down once again." I took another sip of beer and laughed. She tossed her beautiful red hair over one of her porcelain shoulders, revealing that she'd stripped off her bikini top before we'd started this conversation. She'd probably been drunk before the sun had set tonight. "You might want to throw on a shirt. A patient of mine is coming over in a minute or two, and I'd like him to imagine that I have decent neighbors."

"*Him*, huh?" she purred.

I would probably have to call the neighbor to my right to deal with Linda. Ruby Grantham was a sharp, no-bullshit elderly woman. She'd all but adopted me in the last few years, and this wouldn't be the first time I'd used her to handle my horny-ass neighbor.

"Yeah, *him*," I answered, agitated that Linda was drunk, half-naked, and oblivious to pick up on social cues. "He's sixteen, and his mother will probably kick my ass, your ass, and some random stranger's ass if she finds you out here, bouncing your tits around."

"You're no fun, Cammy," she teased. "Why can't you be a *regular* neurosurgeon, not a pediatric one? You should be inviting older, male patients to your scrumptious barbeques."

"Tick-tock," I ignored her ridiculous drunken remarks, not wanting to encourage anything else to come out of this woman's mouth. "Seriously, please cover up."

"Oh, Cammy," she squealed, tap dancing on my last nerve. Her tits bounced all around while she giggled and put on a display for everyone walking on the beach on the other side of our terraces.

Glass surrounded her balcony, making any number of activities visible to anyone walking in front of her home.

With my bamboo privacy fence—which I was currently wishing was ten feet tall instead of four feet—I couldn't see if this lady had exposed everything for the peaceful beach walking community or if it was just the bikini top that she'd stripped off.

"Oh, dear God." I heard Jessa's familiar voice from below and cringed. I wondered if I should duck and not reveal this was my place. I could call her and cancel or face the fact that my neighbor was a lunatic.

"Fucking hell," I growled, then glared at Linda. "Clothes on, *now!*"

I turned off the barbecue burners and jogged down the back steps of my home. I met Jessa and the wide-eyed Jackson with a smile, hoping to distract from the eyeful they'd just received.

"Hey, Dr. Brandt," Jackson politely acknowledged me, trying to shake the flush out of his cheeks caused by Linda's tits.

"Hey, kid," I said, covering my smile.

"Lovely neighbors," Jessa said. But, unlike Jackson, she was *not* flushing, nor did she appear amused. "I hope we're not too late?"

I narrowed my eyes at her unamused ones, "Not at all. In fact, I wish you were later and had also chosen not to look for the place from the beach. It seems that might've avoided a spectacle."

"Well, it was a lovely night, perfect for a stroll on the beach. We figured we could find the place easily from here. Turns out, we did, thanks to your lovely neighbor alerting us to this place with her high beams."

"High beams, huh?" I smiled at her and watched her cheeks flush red in response. "Well, she does seem pretty fucking high tonight."

"And I'd tell you to watch your language, but your lovely neighbor has already stripped away the last shred of innocence my son once possessed."

"If it helps, those *high beams* are just the result of botched plastic surgery." That wasn't exactly true. If I had to be honest, Linda's rack must've cost her and the husband a fortune, not that he ever seemed to be around long enough to enjoy them. Linda was probably just trying to get her money's worth by flashing them to anyone within eyeshot.

"How is that supposed to help?" she questioned while Jackson seemed amused.

I shrugged. "I don't know. They're fake as hell, like looking at a naked barbie doll or something."

"Fake as hell?" Jessa eyed me. I'd forgotten this look, her feisty, charming, yet challenging expression. She was so damn beautiful.

"Fake as hell," I stated as if it were a well-known fact.

"They looked pretty real to me," Jackson said, dodging his mom's attempt to swat him playfully for his remark.

I burst into laughter. Damn, I loved this woman with all of her silly bullshit. The best part was that I could see in her ocean-blue eyes that she knew there was no point to this conversation.

"It's not funny," she said, arching her brow at me.

"It's not. I apologize, and I'm going to be pissed if she ruined your appetites because the carne asada is done, and I'm ready to eat."

"I'm good," Jackson said, rubbing his hands together.

"I'll bet you are," Jessa said with a knowing grin. "Let's eat before your neighbor decides to introduce herself to my son. I had no idea people who lived in homes like these would act like that."

I motioned toward the direction of the steps that led up to my balcony, "Don't ever assume how people might act after drinking vodka tonics from their ocean-view terrace all day."

"Nice surfboards. Are these all yours?" Jackson asked as he pointed under the deck where eight boards were neatly stacked.

"Three of them are," I answered, walking over to my favorite one. It was a Rip Curl shortboard that I hadn't gotten out in too long. "The rest of them are my buddies' boards."

"How long have you surfed?" Jackson asked.

"Since I was a bit younger than you. I practically grew up out here with a surfboard in my hands," I answered.

"So surfing is sort of like your sport, then?"

I grinned. "It's not really my sport, more like a favorite hobby. In fact, I was a lot like you when I was younger. I was blessed with pretty damn good genetics and played football, basketball, and baseball. Surfing was more of an outlet from feeling too much pressure from the other sports. I was always expected to perform at the highest level of competition, and surfing was always a nice break from all that."

"Which sport was your favorite?" he asked.

"Easy," I smiled and slipped my hands into my pockets, "football. There was just something about throwing a spiral down the line and nailing my receiver in the numbers."

I watched Jackson's eyes light up, and I realized everything had faded around me as we talked. I saw my father in him but even more of myself. I'd been referring to him mentally, possibly outwardly, as *the boy*. I'd been trying to compartmentalize things to keep him as a patient in my mind. I needed that so I could function with precision while performing his surgery. I couldn't attach emotionally to him, or the surgery could become extremely risky, knowing I held my son's brain in my hands.

Even so, I wouldn't allow anything, not even the surgeon's mindset in me, to take this moment away from me. I was intrigued, proud, and honored beyond words to stand here and, at this moment, begin forming a bond with my son.

"So, you were quarterback too?" he questioned with some giddiness, prompting me to laugh.

"All-star, just like you are."

"Were," Jessa said.

She'd killed this moment the instant she referred to Jackson's athletic accomplishments in the past tense.

I glanced at her, confused and half annoyed that she would interject such a negative point into the conversation. Then it hit me, and I was brought back to my surgeon's mindset, reminded of why I pressed the two to come to my place for dinner tonight. These were the questions they wanted answers to. Their fears stemmed from the uncertainty of Jackson's future and ability to accomplish his goals. They needed reassurance.

Before I could respond, I saw Jackson's eyes roll back in his head, and I lunged to catch him before he fell back against the surfboards he'd been looking at moments ago.

I squatted down, holding Jackson and guiding his convulsing body into a safe position while he fell under the control of the seizure.

Though scary to those unfamiliar with seizures, the most essential part was watching to ensure he didn't asphyxiate while convulsing. I turned Jackson's tightened body onto his side while he jerked and convulsed to allow him to breathe easier, and Jessa spoke calmly as she told him he was going to be okay.

It took just under a minute before Jackson's brain quieted, and the electrical storm had passed, which allowed him to pull through the last of the seizure.

"He's probably going to want to sleep for a while," Jessa said, informing me as if I were a stranger helping her boy. "Would you mind giving us a ride back to our place?"

I saw the remorse in Jackson's eyes. "No, I wouldn't mind at all, but it looks like Jackson's pissed about having to leave already," I said in a teasing tone, trying to feel him out and assess how he was functioning after the seizure.

"Jacks, we should probably get you home and to bed. Are you thirsty?"

Jessa was an amazing mother, and that went without saying. However, unless Jackson needed to be spoken to as if he were a two-year-old, I would have to help break her from this. She might've been uncomfortable having this happen in a strange place, especially after she made a point to refer to Jackson's sports accomplishments in the past tense.

"You cool with resting on my couch, kid?" I asked, trying to feel the boy out. I wanted him comfortable, and comfort for a patient with epilepsy was also being aware that their seizure didn't inconvenience anyone or serve to embarrass themselves in one way or another.

"I'm cool with that," Jackson said, his speech a bit slow but steady enough not to raise alarms with me.

"What about you, Mom?" I said, looking back at Jessa, her eyes glossy. I could tell she was holding back tears.

"We may need a ride home later," she said with a smile at Jackson, "he's usually pretty weak after one of these things."

"That's why we're going to put an end to them," I said. "You can't be some devastatingly handsome kid and be weak in the knees by these annoying seizures, can you? We need you strong and healthy so everyone can fight over having you be their Prince Charming one day."

"True," he said, rolling his eyes at his current situation and probably my goofy prince charming statement.

"Can I get him some water?" Jessa asked.

"Yeah," I said, helping Jackson to his feet after seeing him struggling to get up. "Let's get Prince Charming up to the couch." I looked at Jackson, seeing a bit of discomfort or embarrassment leave his expression, "You hungry, kid?"

"Nah," he said with a shy smile. "I am sorry that happened."

"You do realize that my entire livelihood revolves around *that* happening. It is quite literally my life's work. Now, stop apologizing for shit you have no control over, and let's get you settled."

I was always driven to help make lives better and give children their lives back, freeing them from medical conditions that intruded on their normalcy. I still felt that way, but the desire to help Jackson was stronger, him being my son or not. He was a good kid; I could sense that a mile away. I could also see that these seizures were beating him down, and knowing his condition, they would only get worse.

I knew Jessa was concerned with the boy's ability to play sports and do many other things that might be at risk after a hemispherectomy. Palmer and I had discussed what she'd talked about with Jessa, so I already had a heads-up prior to meeting Jessa and Jackson tonight.

It was also why I decided to go about it all this way, with dinner and all, because I needed to get Jessa to open up and let me understand her fears and concerns. Then, through the powers of my carne asada marinade, I would work to convince her that this surgery, and the *new* lifestyle that Jackson would have, would be worth so much more than his sports career.

I knew it wouldn't be easy—hell, I'd gotten a scholarship from playing ball, so I understood the mentality—but Jessa and Jackson needed to see that sometimes our lives have these unexpected turns for a reason. We never know what the reasons are, but I'd seen enough through recovering patients to know that the reasons would manifest later. You just had to let shit play out.

Jackson was a good kid, and I knew there was a reason he likely wouldn't play sports again after I disconnected the left hemisphere of his brain. I just needed him to see that life didn't stop after this surgery. Life would go on, most likely in a direction he would've never taken.

Chapter Twenty-One

Jessa

When we walked up the steps to Cam's beach house, my nerves were still tense from Jackson's episode.

"Where can I get him some water?' I questioned. Jackson was always thirsty and highly exhausted after a seizure.

"Already ahead of you," Cameron said, walking over to his outdoor kitchen, which was nicely situated on his patio.

He was back before I could blink, handing the water to Jacks. "How's the grip?" Cameron asked.

"Okay. Not as good as it should be, though," Jacks answered.

"You just need to rest a little bit, buddy," Cam said, walking to the sliding glass doors and leading us into his home.

"No kidding," I heard Jacks answer with a smile in his voice.

It was almost eight in the evening, and if we were at home, Jacks would've probably been out for the rest of the night after having a seizure this late. It was his second seizure of the day, forcing me to acknowledge how badly he needed the surgery even though I was struggling to accept that, by going forward with it, he would lose the ability to do what he loved, play sports.

I needed to talk to Cam.

"I have a game room and theater downstairs. This level has an indoor pool, spa, gym, and, best of all, lounge seating. You know, all the good stuff for enjoying the view of the shore. Upstairs is all bedrooms, so if you just want to crash, pick your room," Cameron announced while we walked through his immaculately decorated home.

"Wow, you sound like you're selling us this beachfront real estate, Dr. Brandt," I said with a smile, seeing Jack's lips turn up into a lazy grin.

Jacks smeared his hand over his forehead and took a sip from the bottle of water Cameron had handed him. "I'll just chill here," he said, walking across the large living area surrounded by opened floor-to-ceiling sliding glass walls.

The cool breeze flowed nicely from the shore over the patio lining each side of this square home. The house wasn't too cold, given the wall that didn't have the ocean views, and it had a long custom gas fireplace that had warmed the room just enough to knock any extra chill out of the air.

I walked over to where Jackson sat on the chaise part of Cam's soft cream-colored sofa. Everything was so relaxed in this home. But of course, it was Cam's, and I would expect nothing less than a Cape-Cod style beach home décor. It was airy, spacious, and spotless with zero clutter.

"Damn, looks like you're still Clean-Cam, eh?" I teased.

I was met with a dark stare from Jackson when my motherly instincts took over, and I grabbed a throw from the other side of the sofa and placed it over Jacks as if he were three.

"Seriously, Mom?" Jacks said as if I'd embarrassed him in front of a girlfriend.

I heard Cameron stifle a laugh, prompting me to turn back and look at him, watching me piss off my poor kid.

"Moms, right?" Cam said as he smiled at Jackson with a wink. "Don't worry, my mom would've done the same thing to me too, kid."

"Sorry, Jacks," I cringed at my behavior. "Instinct, I guess?"

Jacks yawned, his eyes looking heavy, and I knew it was time to let him quiet down and relax. "Mm-hm," he said, gazing out at the horizon and watching the sun's fiery sparkles on the water as it began to set.

"We're going to be just outside; you cool in here?"

"All good, Mom," Jacks mumbled in response, doing everything in his power to stay awake after the seizure.

This was normal. Routine. His life, and the reason I wanted these seizures eradicated. They stole so much from him, and it killed me to watch him go down like this, knowing that most kids his age were out enjoying their summer nights while mine was drifting off to sleep, unable to enjoy the night he was looking forward to.

"This way, Jessa," Cam said, standing in the open area across the room. "The porch wraps around the house, and all roads pretty much lead to the beach patio."

I glanced one more time at my exhausted and now passed-out son.

"I'm sorry we ruined dinner," I said. "It seems that carne asada you were barbequing out here was on track to be delicious until the damn seizure ruined things."

"You always apologize for things that are out of your control?" Cam questioned as he walked through his patio. Party lights were strung throughout, adding a lovely ambiance.

"No," I said defensively. "Well, I have no idea. I apologize if I feel bad for upsetting someone or disrupting plans." I shrugged.

Cam fired up his kitchen grill to heat the meat he'd had on the grill before he came to greet us, then walked to a nook area into which a large stainless-steel fridge was inset. "Beer? Water, tea, juice?"

"Beer is good," I answered with a smile.

He reached in, grabbed a beer, twisted off the cap, and handed it to me.

"Don't ever apologize for your son having a seizure." He brought his beer to his lips, eyed me, and then used the barbeque fork to flip over the meat.

"I just feel bad, Cam," I said. "You went out of your way—"

"Jessa, don't worry about it," he cut me off, turned off the flames, and pulled the meat onto a large platter that he'd prepared for us to make our steak tacos. "But you will have to apologize to me if you don't eat this delicious meal that I spent a whole twenty minutes preparing. Follow me. The table is set over here."

He led the way through banana leaf trees lit with outdoor pink and blue lighting.

We followed a narrow brick path through landscaping that must've cost thousands upon thousands of dollars, concealing a private eating area with views beyond the patio of the ocean. It was a trip to see how tropical and lush this spot was, knowing that just through the trees to our left, the crazy boob-lady lived. You would never guess there were homes so close by with the privacy of all this landscaping and the outdoor brick fireplace that sat off to the back of the table.

"This is really nice," I said, sitting and placing a napkin over my lap.

"Thanks," Cam said. He took a serving of rice, beans, and two steak strips and placed them on my stone plate. "Cilantro? I know you hate sour cream, but I can't remember if you like cilantro?"

"Love it. Where's the guacamole?" I asked with a smile.

"Shit," he said after popping a bite of steak into his mouth and licking the flavors off the tip of his fingers. "Give me a sec."

He jumped up and disappeared through the tropical forest of trees behind us.

I sat there, inhaling the salty air. I didn't know what I would do without this refreshing, therapeutic ocean air after we moved. I was becoming way too spoiled by it.

"Don't think about that shit now. One stressful issue at a time," I said under my breath.

"So, when did you start talking to yourself?" Cam asked.

I narrowed my eyes at him after he smiled, sat, and then set a large stone bowl in front of me filled with guacamole.

"Jesus, did you cut down an entire avocado tree to make this tonight?" I questioned while my stomach growled at the sight. I couldn't dip a tortilla chip in it fast enough.

"One would think. Trust me, it tastes a lot better than it looks," he said, nodding toward the steak on my plate that I hadn't touched.

"It looks delicious, sorry," I said.

"Sorry again, huh?" he questioned, arching an eyebrow of disapproval at me.

"That bothers you?"

"I just don't understand what the fuck you feel you need to apologize for?"

"Hurting your feelings by not eating your food," I stated while he shoved nearly half of his taco in his mouth and held up a finger for me to pause.

I grinned and proceeded to construct my steak taco while Cameron worked on chewing down his large bite of food.

"I don't know. Enjoy it because I know you don't ever remember a time when I apologized for shit with you," I said.

He smiled and dabbed his napkin into each corner of his mouth. "Exactly." He scooped some salsa with a chip and threw it back as if this were his last meal. "I guess what I find so bizarre is that you feel responsible for my feelings?"

"No," I answered, "I feel responsible for *hurting* your feelings."

"Right," he said as if his point was being made, "and who said you hurt my feelings? Who gives a fuck if you hurt them or not? I'm a grown-ass man, and I can take it if someone doesn't like something I do or don't do."

"Fine, then," I rose to meet his challenging banter. "If you can handle it, then maybe you'll be fine with me saying that I didn't appreciate having to learn the *hard way* that Jacks will most likely be paralyzed for God knows how long after this miracle cure of a surgery."

Cameron had eaten one and a half tacos in the time it took me to get all that out, all while putting a healthy dent into the guacamole.

"Now we're getting to a place where we can actually have a conversation." He placed a whole, guacamole-loaded chip in his mouth, and his dark blue eyes widened in humor as he chewed it up.

"Damn, when's the last time you ate, a year ago?" I laughed, sat back, and proceeded to nurse my beer.

"I ate this afternoon, but lunch sure as hell didn't taste as good as this does," he winked, then leaned back and took a sip of his beer. "So, I need to understand what Jackson feels about the surgery. I'd hoped to get a little more out of him tonight, but the reason I need to perform this surgery in the first place got in the way of that."

"If I'm honest—"

"And sorry?" he interrupted.

"Whatever," I rolled my eyes. "I'm scared and sad for him."

"Just scared and sad, huh?"

That response caught me off guard, "Yes, what were you expecting me to be?"

"You seemed pissed off earlier," he said. "You have every right to feel that way."

I grew more serious. "I *am* pissed off. None of this is fair to Jackson. The only way to stop him from having constant seizures isn't by medication. *Oh, no, no, no.* That would be too easy. He's got to have half of his fucking brain removed instead. That's the solution."

"And if that wasn't unfair enough," Cam said. His eyes locked onto mine, but his demeanor was cool as a cucumber. "He may not even walk again, much less play sports. It's fucking bullshit, I know."

"You know?"

"I fucking know. I've performed this surgery. You, yourself, met with one of my former surgical patients. So, you know what I've seen in Lisa alone."

"Right," I said. "It's not fucking fair."

"You'd rather have Jacks back on medication? After reading his charts, he was on, what, twenty pills a day to control them when they were steamrolling his ass?"

"That's why he was walking around like a zombie."

"But at least he was walking around, not having to deal with possible paralysis straight out of surgery and all the fucking work that goes along with rehabilitation?"

"Yep." My frustration was rising, and I was glad I hadn't eaten much because I was feeling sick. "What are the odds he may not survive the surgery?"

"Given that Jacks will be in my care and the care of my surgical team, the odds are very good, but there is always a chance of death in any surgery."

"Why the fuck are you acting like this? I thought you had us over for dinner tonight to help us decide on this surgery."

"That's precisely why I invited you over for dinner, Jessica," he said.

I was talking to Cameron the surgeon, the no-bullshit doctor, and he was an absolute dick.

"Is this how you pep talk all of your patients into having surgery?"

"Only the ones who will be on the fence for about a year or two while trying to make a decision."

"Huh? That makes no sense."

"It makes perfect sense. There are no gray areas here. Parents need to make a firm decision about whether they want to go ahead. Those who aren't sure tend to call it off the day before, and I try my best to avoid that."

"I'm not like most parents."

"You're a textbook fear-driven parent, Jessa," he smiled. "It's not a bad thing, but it can be if I don't take care of this shit up front." He took another sip of his beer, "You need to be faced with everything your mind will throw out at you to put a stop to this. This is a fucking serious surgery. It's not to be taken lightly by the family or the patient. Unfortunately, Jacks is at the top end of the age for which we will perform this surgery. Within a year, he will no longer have this option, and there will be no other choice to help him. It fucking sucks, I know, and I wish there were more time to decide, but fuck me, there's not. I would strongly advise that you not take long to decide."

"Cam, sports are his life just like they were yours," I said sadly. "It's the life I was trying to get back for him, and now that isn't going to happen either."

"I completely understand that but shaking your fist at the sky and screaming that it's unfair won't change a goddamn thing," he said softly. "Not every disease has a cure or even a treatment. But, lucky for Jacks, his condition is treatable. Will it leave him with a deficit? It very well might. Is that better than dropping into a seizure multiple times a day? You bet your ass it is." He shifted in his seat. "It's up to Jackson to find his drive to beat the odds. I, for one, am not programmed to let something defeat me, and I'm hoping Jacks may have gotten some of those wild genetics from me because if he has, he might beat all the fucking odds."

He laughed after he saw me smile in confirmation that Jacks was just as stubborn and determined as his father.

"He's got my blood in him, too," I said proudly.

"Well, fuck," Cameron said, taking another sip of beer and staring at the ocean.

"Well, fuck you too," I laughed at his dramatics. "It's probably why I know he'll be fine coming out of the surgery."

"You realize that his speech and smile will be impaired when he wakes up from this surgery? It could take nearly a month of solid determination just to get those two motor skills back."

"Oh?"

"Yeah, so while you're proudly proclaiming the boy has your genetics and will pull out of it fine, we won't know until after he apologizes for being unable to speak for a month."

"Oh God," I rolled my eyes. "There is not enough beer for your inability to be serious about anything."

"You needed a break," he grinned. "I could see the wheels turning in your head. Your eyes were nearly crossed, trying to stomach all of this shit, and I needed to knock you off balance a little bit."

"Be honest, Cameron. I need to know what we're up against."

"All right, then," he said, and then I wished I hadn't asked for his candor. "Given his age and how mature his brain is *at* this age, honestly, he may never speak again. He may never regain function on the right side of his body. This is all dependent on the right hemisphere of his brain being able to pick up the functions that the left hemisphere normally is responsible for." My hand instinctively covered the tiny gasp that escaped from my mouth as tears formed in my eyes.

"Jessa, I want to spend more time with him," he said.

I brushed away the rogue tears and nodded.

"I need to see how strong he is," he continued. "It's not like there are any other options with this medical condition, as this hemisphere of his brain is storming and actively dying. But if you want reassurance, I need more time with him."

"Yeah, okay," I said.

"In the next couple of days, my friends and I are taking a trip to Monterey Bay to see the aquarium or some shit like that. You and Jacks should come. It will be fun, and aside from my friends, who I'm confident will adore you and Jacks, it will give me more time to assess him and form a better opinion. I don't want to sugarcoat anything; I've got to shoot you straight because I do not want to give you false hope."

I sighed in defeat. I was numb and didn't care if we went to an aquarium, a park, or a fucking schoolyard for Cam to get more time with Jacks. Cameron offered to go above and beyond to assess the situation, which could only help things.

"It doesn't matter whether you know Jackson's personality or whatever the hell you're looking for. What matters is the fact that he must do the surgery either way. He's virtually fucked."

Cameron stared at me sympathetically, then his lips parted into the sexiest smile, "Virtually fucked?"

"You heard me."

"Loud and clear. Well, shit," he rubbed his hand over mine, and I felt a spark of tingling sensations underneath his perfectly manicured fingertips. "Let's hope to God he's got more of my optimistic personality than yours because if that kid's got a lot of you and not me, he is fucked."

"You're such an asshole sometimes."

"He's my kid too, Jessa. I mean, biologically. As I was talking with him tonight, I felt something insane, like some fatherly bonding."

"Good grief," I couldn't resist running my hand along the sharp line of his jaw, "you're adorable, Cameron Brandt. I love you."

Oh fuck, I did not just say that out loud!

Worst of all, I said it with sincerity and tears in my eyes.

Cameron's expression showed that all bets were off, and my ex just heard what I think he'd wanted to hear since we first saw each other at that resort.

Chapter Twenty-Two

Jessa

"No, I mean, I love that you're helping Jackson."

Cam studied me with the most adorable, humorous expression. "No, that's not what you meant," he pressed with a look of curiosity.

"Um, yeah." I stared at him. "Yeah, it's exactly what I meant."

"No," Cameron insisted. "We weren't even discussing me helping Jackson when you dropped that hot potato in my lap."

I rose, getting flustered, "I didn't mean to say—"

"Didn't mean to say what you meant?" he said, standing up with me.

"Cameron, I'm not doing this with you." I shook my head like I was trying to shake the crazy out of my system. "I won't let you hurt me again. I promised myself that I would never go down this road again with you, charming, hero doctor or not."

He reached for my arm, which I instantly pulled away from him, "Hear me out."

"Hear you out? Hear *you* out?" I stepped further back, the anger resurfacing from the day he messaged me to break it off. "No, Cam, I will *not* hear you out. In fact, I tried to question you after I thought your *break-up* message was a damn joke. And you know what I got in return?"

"Jessica," he pressed.

"Don't *Jessica* me, Cameron," I said, knowing my gaze was icy. "Do you know there is only one emoji in all of the fucking emojis that I despise more than anything?"

"No, but I should be happy to know you've taken your anger for me out on an emoji instead."

I folded my arms. "The thumbs up emoji," I said. "I *hate* that emoji because of you. So, yeah, you *and* that damned emoji. So I guess I hate you both equally."

Cameron covered his smile. I hated when he was on the verge of laughter and trying to conceal it without breaking eye contact. This stupid expression is why I had a handsome son sleeping on Cam's sofa.

"I don't mean to be a stickler here, but I think back then, they were called emoticons," he said as seriously as he could.

"Seriously?"

"Well, fuck," he said. "I don't know about the *emoji*, but *I* would at least like to try to win your heart back."

"It's like I put all this energy into a response, and all I get is a fucking thumbs up? How goddamn rude can someone be? I'd rather get the middle finger emoji."

"You told me to be safe and to follow my dreams, no matter where they lead."

"I know," I said, eyes wide with shock that this dick still wasn't getting it, "and that got me a stupid thumbs up? It's bullshit, and now I'm fucking pissed again."

"Jessa," he said, staring at me with some sad expression, "I read what you wrote, and I knew if I saw you, I wouldn't leave, and I wouldn't have been able to say goodbye. So, after reading what you wrote, I just tried to end it as easily as possible for both of us."

"And you *really thought* a thumbs up was the way to do that?" I sighed. "I need to go. And I didn't mean to drop an *I love you* bomb just now. I'm going through a lot, and I'm convinced I may be having a mild nervous breakdown."

"You may be because I had no idea that a thumbs-up emoji would be why I can never have another chance to prove myself to you."

"It would take a whole hell of a lot," I said, softening up a little, the panic of saying *I love you* fading. "I never expected our relationship ending would make me hate an emoji, but it has, and it's going to take a whole hell of a lot to—" I stopped and looked at the sudden sincere sadness on Cameron's face. "Why did you really respond that way, like what we had wasn't a big deal?"

His lips tightened. "Because I knew I was making the biggest mistake of my life by leaving you. What we had was a *very* big deal to me, Jessa. After reading what you wrote, I cried for the first time since my sister died. I didn't want to leave you, but I knew I couldn't pass up the opportunity." He cocked his head to the side, staring at me, then looking back to the house, "I can't say that I regret my decision because I don't believe in regrets. We all make decisions that lead us where we need to be. If I hadn't gone, I wouldn't have the career I have now, and I wouldn't have been able to help all the children I've been privileged to help."

I remained silent as Cam grew more somber.

"Jessa, I have to believe that there are bigger forces in the universe at work. Maybe I left while you were pregnant with our son so I'd be able to save him one day. It's a thought, and I've seen too many miracles in my day-to-day work to dismiss it."

Cameron's excuse was something that I'd ordinarily counter with a snide remark, but it resonated deep within me. Cam wouldn't have tried as hard as he did to succeed if he knew I was pregnant, which was why I never told him. He would've stayed with me and missed out on all the incredible opportunities that ultimately landed him as the top pediatric neurosurgeon in the country. And if that had happened, there would be no one to help our son now. Looking through that lens, it seemed like divine intervention.

"What are you thinking?" Cameron asked curiously.

"You're right," I nodded. "When I think about it that way, I get it.

But I think we should keep all this focused on reuniting for Jackson's health and not our relationship."

"What if Jackson's health depended on our relationship?"

"Now, you're just making shit up," I softly laughed. "Listen, I need to get Jackson home. I need some time to think."

"Come with me to Monterey. Allow me an opportunity to gain a bit more trust—"

"Cameron," I said softly, "you don't need us to go on a road trip with you and your friends to assess Jackson's strengths and weaknesses for this surgery. Please stop trying to do this."

"Do what, Jessa? I want to get to know the kid a bit better. I'm virtually bound by law with my friends' kids, and I'd like to take these next two days off to spend some time around Jackson. I want to help him trust me as his surgeon."

I narrowed my eyes at him, "Bound by *law*?"

"Mm-hmm," he nodded with fake-serious eyes, "these kids are no fucking joke. I don't think I've ever met a five-year-old as lethal as Jacob Mitchell's son. With his icy gaze, that kid could likely freeze you where you stand."

I rolled my eyes, "Icy gaze? What is he, the frost king?"

"It's what I've got him labeled as anyway," Cameron said.

"I'll see if Jackson's feeling up for it."

"Great," Cameron said with more excitement than I imagined he should have. But then again, this was Cameron; he was a big kid in a grown man's body ninety percent of the time. "I'll have a car pick you two up tomorrow and bring you to the airport."

"Airport?"

"You're not going to want to drive there if you don't have to. It'll be worth it, trust me."

"Last time you asked me to trust you, you dumped me with an emoji."

"Now you're just making that story eviler than it really was."

I shrugged.

"I think this will do Jackson good," Cameron said, nearly marching me up to the house as if we were leaving for the airport this instant. "With what I have planned, this could help Jacks explore other passions outside of sports."

"Huh?"

"You'll see."

* * *

When the car pulled through the security entrance of the private airport—and not a regular airport—I shook my head at Cameron's bright idea.

"Has he lost his damn mind?" I said, glancing around at all the parked, private airplanes.

"No way," Jackson said in a low voice of excitement.

"Exactly, there is *no way* we're going up with this adrenaline junkie of a man in one of those planes. Good God, Cameron."

After some Googling, I read that Cam's parents were killed in a plane crash years ago, and I was confused that the man would dare to take one of these glorified tuna cans into the air. Was he insane? Maybe he was, but I sure as hell wasn't. I was *not* trying to die today.

"How would you know he was an adrenaline junkie?" Jackson questioned me, reminding me that I should *probably* tell him his surgeon was also his dad, whom I'd dated in college.

"Don't worry about it," I said, holding my ringing cell phone up to my ear as I called Cameron.

"Hey, I see the car you're in. Tell Branson to pull around the side, and I'll meet you back there," Cam said.

"I'm telling Branson that we're turning around, actually. I'm not flying in some small-ass plane," I said.

"Jessa," he sounded annoyed.

"Nope," I was stern. I was *not* doing this. "Cam, I do not wish to bring up the death of your parents—my deepest and most sincere condolences, by the way. I shouldn't have had to read about that on the internet, but that's for another time—but please know that I cannot begin to imagine what you're thinking."

"That I'm not afraid," he answered dead seriously. "I won't let the shit that scares me stop me from living. I got my pilot's license to face it head-on so that I can move forward."

"Fine. I'm not afraid of flying." The car pulled to a stop.

"Bullshit," he said, scaring the crap out of me when he jerked open my door. "Yeah, you are, and that's why we're doing this."

"There are so many colorful cuss words I could spew at you, but I won't because I wouldn't want Branson to judge me harshly."

Cameron chuckled, "Branson? I thought you'd be more concerned about how your son would judge you."

"Jacks wouldn't judge me because Jacks has also pushed me to my limits with decisions such as this, and he has already heard the dark side of my foul mouth unleash hell and fury for his bad decisions."

"Thanks, Branson," Cameron said, giddier than a kid jumping on a trampoline. "Okay, I'd love to take you to Monterey on my plane, but it's in maintenance and won't be ready until next week."

"Maintenance?" I said as Jacks and I followed Cameron, who led the way through the hangars.

"Yeah, routine. They check everything out and ensure things are sound on the plane. Now," he said, moving on and not letting my irritated mood derail him. "I know you fear private planes, and I'll give you that; however, we're not traveling that way."

"Oh, even better," I said, not knowing what Cameron was up to.

"No freaking way," Jackson said excitedly.

"Hell, yeah," Cameron said, wiggling his eyebrows. "We're going in this chopper."

"Are you out of your damn mind?" I said, pulling the strap of my purse tighter against my neck on my shoulder. "Cameron, what the actual fuck?"

"Don't tell me you're afraid of helicopters too? Shit. This thing has a jet engine, a—"

"I just don't understand why we're not flying commercially. I swear, sometimes I can see that spoiled rich boy that I remember oozing out of you."

"Remember? What the hell, Mom?"

"Yeah, *Mom*. What the hell?"

"Mom?" Jackson pressed, but this wasn't the time to get into all the details of why I was seemingly so knowledgeable about his doctor. The only way to get the boy off my ass about me knowing more than I led on about his surgeon was to give the surgeon his way. And that meant we were all about to go flying in a mother fucking helicopter.

"Let's just go," I said, eying Cameron. "I'm trusting that you're as good a pilot as you are a surgeon. If you kill us, I will kill you."

"I'll hold you to it," Cameron said. "All right, Jacks, you're sitting up front with me." He looked at me as I stepped in and sat in the first leather executive seat I could find.

"This is quite impressive," I conceded.

I was the first to admit that I'd had a short fuse lately, but I didn't want to be a wet blanket all the time. There was a time when I wasn't so cautious, and maybe now was a good time to resurrect some of that. Jackson was more excited than I'd ever seen him, and watching him interact with Cam this way hit me in my soft spot.

I didn't want to get too attached to these feelings, but for a split second, seeing Jackson flying with his dad in a helicopter made me think of what could've been if Cam had never left and we'd been a family from the beginning. Of course, I pushed the thought away as soon as it intruded on me, but I couldn't deny that there was a part of me that'd always wondered what it would've been like.

Cameron had never shied away from Jackson being his. Instead, it seemed like he was embracing it. Something told me to relax and let Cameron assess Jackson, and while he did that, I could determine how Cameron was with Jackson.

It was probably a horrible idea trying to imagine Cameron bonding with his son like this, but it was something that felt so right I wouldn't push it away. They always say to go with your gut instinct, and my gut instinct was telling me to trust Cameron.

I only hoped it wasn't a mistake.

Chapter Twenty-Three

Cam

In my profession, I took to all my young patients as if they were my own. I even thought I had figured out what it was like to be a parent, but I was learning just how fucking wrong I was about that.

Jackson reminded me so much of myself that I sometimes couldn't believe it. Seeing yourself reflected in your child was nothing short of miraculous. It was for me; now, I was on a new-dad high that I never wanted to come down from.

"I could've flown that helicopter too, you know?" Jackson said as we all got into the car that awaited us at the small airport in Monterey.

"Oh, I'm sure you could have." I bent to lift Jessa's travel bag, placing the last piece of luggage in the back of the Tesla I'd arranged to be dropped off here for my personal use the next two days. "Okay, let's get this fun little vacay underway," I announced, holding the passenger door open for Jessa to sit. Jackson, in true gentleman fashion, took the seat behind her.

"Good grief," Jessa said, rubbing her arms that were folded tightly across her chest, "it's cold as hell here."

"If you're going to cuss, Mom, at least do it right," Jackson teased from the back seat. "Last I checked, hell was hot."

"Last you checked?" I said, pulling out of the airport. "Shit, I had no idea one could check that place out."

"You know what I'm saying," Jackson said with a laugh.

"Why don't we pull off the subject of hell and admire this beautiful stretch of California coastline, shall we?"

"Oh?" Jessa said in a high-pitched tone, filled with humor, "I'm sorry."

"Don't be sorry," I said, acting like some dipshit family man, enjoying having Jessa and Jackson in the car with me as we traveled to a home owned by one of Jim Mitchell's clients. "Now, are we hungry? Bathrooms? Anything before we head to this lovely home?"

"Home?" Jessa said with confusion. "I thought we were going to the aquarium or something?"

"Don't you dare worry your cute little heart, Jess," I said. "We'll have you at that aquarium and finding Nemo before you know it."

"So, how do you both know each other, anyway?" Jackson questioned, prompting me to look at Jessa immediately, hoping she'd throw me a lifeline.

She smiled as if the boy sitting in the back seat were another man's, and I was just the chauffeur. "College, I told you. Cam was a good friend of mine."

"Ah," Jackson said. "Best friends?"

The kid was prying, and I was okay with that. This part was not my fault. Jessa was going to have to face the music at some point. The wisest thing for me was to let her handle this the best way she knew.

We were on this mini vacation to help them gain some courage about the surgery, and the distraction of finding out who I was to him could spin things out of control. But here we were. This whole thing could go south quickly if we weren't careful. As much as I wanted Jackson to know everything, I was more concerned with his health and didn't want anything to sabotage his decision to have surgery.

"Best friends," I said, smiling over at Jessa's amused expression.

"Now, back to where we're staying." I changed the subject, grateful that Jackson didn't press the issue. He certainly didn't inherit his ability to drop things from his mother; that much was obvious.

"Yes, where are we staying? I packed clothes for warm and cooler weather, like you said," Jessa informed me.

"Well, this marine layer will burn off soon, and it'll warm up once the sun breaks through. That's pretty much why you have to pack for all four seasons on this peninsula. It will reach about seventy-eight degrees today after the sun breaks through, and it'll be a perfect day. Until then, gotta cover up."

"It's so beautiful here," Jessa said as I kept on Highway One toward Carmel-by-the-Sea. "The cypress trees are incredible."

"If you look down at the shit-stained rocks," I said, pointing to where the gray ocean surrounded numerous rocks covered in sea lion, seal, and seagull shit, "those black mounds are sea lions and seals."

Jackson laughed while Jessa rolled her eyes, "Shit-stained rocks? You should be a tour guide up here," Jackson said with another laugh. "Oh, shit. I see one, maybe two!"

"Shit-stained rocks or sea lions?" Jessa asked Jackson before looking at me. "Thanks for that, by the way."

"No problem," I smiled. "The seals are super cute." I pointed toward another shit-crusted rock, "Check it out. There's about fifteen over there."

"Not for spotting the marine life," she arched a reproachful eyebrow at me, "for—"

"I don't think I—wait. I see them! They're on the closer shit-stained rocks," Jackson added with a laugh.

"For *that*. Thanks for that," Jessa said.

"For what, calling the rocks what they are? Shitty rocks?"

"Cameron," she exhaled, lowering her voice, "I do my best to refrain from cursing around my sixteen-year-old son, so could you please respect that too?"

I eyed her and sighed. "You've done an amazing job raising him," I said. "However, he's going to curse either way. So, you need to pick and choose which ones you will allow."

"Exactly, Mom," Jackson said, joining my team.

"No, not *exactly*, Jacks," she said. "The second I let you, you'll be dropping f-bombs on every other person you see. Besides, it's extremely unprofessional for Dr. Brandt to cuss in front of children."

I smiled at Jackson through the rearview mirror as he rolled his eyes and put his earbuds in, pointedly ignoring the tirade his mother was about to launch into about our usage of foul language.

"Seriously, Captain America, you should relax a little bit," I teased Jessa, only to have the power of the mother hen stare my ass down and pin me to my seat.

"I think it's best if you focus on your job as a surgeon who wants to help me and my son, and I'll focus on being Jackson's mother."

"Why don't we meet in the middle?" I pressed, not knowing what hole I was digging myself into.

"Why don't we *not*?"

"You have done a fine job raising him; I will say that," I informed her, taking the safer ground.

I'd have to be a fool to sit here and act like I could win an argument with a single mother. God built these women to be mentally stronger than anyone on this planet, and I would lose this battle should I foolishly choose to fight it.

"Thank you. I'd like to keep raising him right if you don't mind?"

"I get it. Subject change," I conceded, smiling at her softened expression. The Jessa I knew wasn't quick to jump on anyone's case, so it was easy to deduce that the strain she was under made her testy. "I think we're going whale watching tomorrow morning. Someone mentioned something about whales in the bay or some shit?"

"Oh, for the love of God, Cam," she said, nailing me for saying the word *shit*, I'm sure.

"What?" I announced, "he's got his earbuds in. Jesus, Jess."

She rolled her eyes, and I couldn't help but smile at how adorable she was. It was highly attractive, but I felt bad for pushing her when she was already at her limit.

"Okay, allow me to censor your mouth like this," she said in a calm yet borderline lethal tone. "Would you talk like this around your patients?"

"Fuck no." I didn't want Jessa to think I was some dumbfuck who would be so unprofessional around his patients. I covered my mouth, feeling like an asshole, and glanced in the mirror to ensure Jackson had his earbuds in. "Sorry," I said with a guilty smile.

"My point exactly. Treat him like he's a regular patient, and we'll be fine. You must understand that, especially at his age, kids will constantly push the limits, and that last thing I need is some kid who cusses like a sailor."

"True," I pursed my lips. "I've seen some disrespectful kids come through my hospital, and it's quite shocking when they cuss their parents out. Not to mention disrespectful."

"Ah, look at you. The pediatric neurosurgeon, learning something new every day."

"Hey, I never claimed to be the smartest man," I answered with a grin. "If I were, I certainly wouldn't have left you."

"Let's not go down that road, shall we?"

I grinned in response, but there was no way I would put the brakes on something I wanted so badly, which was her. If fate was busting its ass to bring us together, who was I to stand in the way?

Chapter Twenty-Four

Jessa

After we pulled up to the phenomenal home, built on the cliffs of Carmel with nothing but coastline in front of it, we were greeted by all of Cameron's friends as if we'd come home for a family reunion.

The wives of Cam's friends were so kind that, at first, I wondered if it was an act. After suffering the bullshit of Manhattan's high society for so long, I didn't expect much from the behavior of billionaires' wives. Part of me had been dreading this, meeting women who would probably sit around and talk about their kids' private schools or interior decorators' designs for their third and fourth vacation homes.

To my pleasure, I was very much mistaken. These women couldn't have possibly been more delightful. I couldn't remember the last time I'd met a group of women who enjoyed each other's company so much. They were down-to-earth, charming, and funny, and they made me feel very welcome.

"Good God," Avery said, her brilliant blue eyes sparkling against her pitch-black hair. "I swear if we don't find something for these men to do, they will start making rope swings to fling themselves into the ocean from up here. Seriously," she laughed, taking a sip of freshly brewed coffee.

"What the hell are they talking about?" Ash asked, craning her neck to see where they were.

Avery and Ash were married to the Mitchell brothers, Jim and Jacob. Jim, Avery's husband, was the CEO of the global empire Mitchell and Associates. Jacob was the chief cardiothoracic surgeon at St. John's, where Cam worked. Both men were undeniably drop-dead handsome, and their wives were equally as beautiful.

"All I know is that they seem to have pulled some shit on Collin, and that's always a good time. We should get in there," Collin's wife, Elena, said with a mischievous laugh.

Collin was just as gorgeous as the Mitchell brothers, but with blond hair instead of black. Collin introduced his wife as his Cuban goddess, and from where I sat, she looked like one. I don't think I'd ever been so envious of someone's skin tone and natural beauty. They were all just as lovely on the inside as they were on the outside, which was the most important part, in my opinion.

"I have to know," Elena said, walking into the room and sitting on the arm of the couch next to her husband, "what has Dr. Brooks so blown away?"

"No joke, Jacks here says that some kid flew a Cessna after the pilot blacked out. He landed that son of a bitch and everything," Collin answered her.

I smiled, knowing what game my son was playing. That kid would do anything to prove video games were good for you. My eyes drifted to where he and Cam sat next to each other on the sofa, their backs to the windows that overlooked the ocean rolling into the cliffs below.

It was a beautiful sight; the heavy fog drifting along the shoreline that went on for miles, rocky bluffs lining the entire view this home was built to enjoy, and Cameron and Jackson. My heart suddenly skipped a beat, and my breath caught while I enjoyed the identical smiles of father and son.

Cam's arm was relaxed behind Jacks while he sat casually in a humored conversation, resting an ankle on his knee. He was so devastatingly handsome, and I had to stop myself from drooling here and now.

Goddamn hormones.

"So, the kid landed the Cessna safely because he knew how to fly a plane in a mother fu—" Jake stopped himself as soon as his brain caught up with his mouth, and the daggers from each of the mothers' eyes fell on him.

"Go on," Cameron said with a laugh, enjoying that Jake was in the cussing hot seat. "Mother fuh? Hmm?"

I smiled while Jim rolled his eyes, his two-year-old daughter Izzy, looking at her uncle Jake from where she sat on Jim's lap, apparently waiting for him to screw up and get busted too. Izzy's older sister, Addy, was very well-mannered compared to everyone else in the room, a bit reserved and shy for a ten-year-old, but I sensed that she was feeling things out. Izzy seemed a bit more mischievous of the two; that was apparent.

"Don't say the f-word, Dad," Jake's son, John, said as he walked into the room.

This boy was a little stud, and, like Jacks was Cameron's mini, John was most certainly Jake's little doppelgänger. They both sported short, stylish black hair and bright blue eyes that leveled you with a glance. However, the difference between Jake and his son John was in their personalities. John was only five years old, but the kid acted like *he* could be the chief heart surgeon at St. John's, not his fun-natured dad.

"I won't, son." Jake took it as a challenge, and suddenly it felt like the room was in a silent standoff over whether Jake would recover himself or not.

"No, you won't," John said, then his piercing blue eyes met with Ash's humored ones. "He's not in trouble, Mommy. He didn't say it this time."

"*This* time?" Ash said, her auburn hair dancing on her shoulders. It was obvious she was trying not to laugh. "Good grief, can we all just pack it up and head to the aquarium for Addy's birthday party before *I* drop the f-bomb? How in the world does this happen every single time?"

"What?" I questioned, confused.

"One of these guys lets a curse word slip, and the next thing you know, we're doing this. Kids are defending their father's mouths, and the moms are looking like the bad-word police," Avery said to me with an arched eyebrow. "Let me be the first to say that I don't give a fuck who hears me drop the f-bomb because I'm a grown-ass woman, and I am who I am. My kids don't need me pretending to be someone I'm not, and I'm sure as hell not going to sit back and act like any words are off limits when we all know I'd be the first one to bankrupt myself if there were a swear jar sitting around."

Jim laughed and blew Avery a kiss.

"The family fortune would've been long gone if Avery came within ten feet of a swear jar, and we all know it," Jim said.

"God knows it's hard enough for the rest of us to keep our *colorful* language to ourselves, but for Avery, it's impossible. She's the only one who gets away with it," Ash laughed. "Which is *baloney* if you ask me because Mom gets to be the heavy when the bombs start dropping."

I grinned at Ash. She wasn't wrong, and it did suck to be the bad guy all the time. But at least I wasn't the only one dealing with this. Sometimes I felt like such a prude, and that is precisely how I'd started this trip, by making demands of Cam about cussing.

The worse part was that I swore in front of Jackson semi-regularly, so it wasn't like my son's innocence was being violated. What a stupid point for me to try to make. It seemed evident that I'd been trying to flex my control in the situation because I felt so *out* of control in my life. Why else would I choose to die on such a dumb hill?

The aquarium was a stellar idea. We all blended in like the tourists we most certainly were. The kids held onto their parents' hands as we passed by massive tanks of endless, exotic fish. Rows of children on school field trips were being ushered around, stopping to gasp at the occasional shark that swam by. The soothing sounds in the background and the dark, cool rooms in this two-story aquarium were almost hypnotic.

Everyone split up into groups, and Cam, Jacks, and I stuck together. I eventually wandered upstairs and sat on a bench in front of a huge tank, leaned forward on my knees, and watched a sea turtle swim with slow strides, pulling each leg through the enormous tank's backlit water.

"Relaxing, isn't it?" Ash said, slipping in next to me on the bench.

I sat up and smiled at her. "I could take a nap here," I joked.

"No shit," she said with a smile. "So, Cam told us a little bit about your history together. I hope you'll forgive him for that."

"Oh, I don't mind," I said. "I suppose I'm surprised he would mention that his ex-girlfriend was in town."

She laughed. "Well, I think he was more or less preparing the guys. I mean, Jacks looks just like him, and all those ding dongs would have had something to say about it."

I grinned, "It's probably a good thing he told them because I haven't told Jacks that Cameron is his father yet, and I'd hate for him to find out that way."

"Oh, really?" Ash said. "Are you concerned he'll be upset by that?"

"You know, it's not like I've been keeping it a secret for his whole life. I would've gladly spilled those beans ages ago. It's just that he's never really asked, and I never felt the need to push it on him. It makes the situation now a little unintentionally sticky, I'll admit." I never anticipated we'd be in this position; having to reveal that Jackson's biological father was also the man trying to remove half his brain seemed a bit like a soap opera, but here we were. "I figured he'd get curious about it one day, but until then, he was perfectly happy to accept my ex-fiancé as his father."

"Fiancé?"

I shook my head, realizing how strange that bit of information must've sounded to a woman I'd just met. "Yeah, we broke up last week."

"God, I'm so sorry," Ash said, covering her heart.

"Don't be. Ending that was one of my better judgment calls. It wasn't the healthiest relationship, and it was better to part ways, especially before Jacks goes through this surgery."

She smiled, "Well, I'm here if you need anything. I know we just met, but I went through a similar situation when I moved to LA after my dad had a heart attack."

"Oh, wow," I said. "So, you came down here with no friends too?"

"No friends *and* my dad's doctor ended up being a previous one-night stand," she said with an eyebrow arch, then she shook her head and laughed and brought her attention back to the massive two-story aquarium we faced. "I was a fish out of water, and my only quote-unquote *friends* were a couple of evil bitches I worked for at an art gallery. And, as these stories go, those chicks happened to have a thing for my dad's surgeon," she ran her palms over her jeans, "Dr. Jacob Mitchell."

"Ah," I smiled. "Well, Cam and I are just friends. There'll be no relationships other than that for us. There's just no way I'll go down that road again."

"I understand that," she nodded in understanding, "and who knows where everything goes. But I want you to know that you have a friend here no matter what. I'm here if you just want some time for yourself or someone to get massages or pedicures with. Hell, I'll even pack peanut butter and jelly sandwiches if you want to go to the beach for a picnic," she chuckled. "I truly understand the stress and heartache of processing medical issues while living in a foreign place. I did all of that and then decided to date Jacob to *add* to the stress." She nudged my arm with her elbow. "I'm glad you're here. We're going to make sure you're okay."

"Thanks, Ash," I said sincerely. "You have no idea how much I appreciate it."

"No problem at all. And last I saw, Jake and John were with Cameron and Jacks in the exhibit where you pet the manta rays. I'm going to head back if you want to join me?"

"Sounds great."

I enjoyed being around Cameron's friends. They were warm and inviting, and we had a great time goofing around. Sadly, all the fun came to a screeching halt when Jackson had a seizure while we ate lunch at a beautiful restaurant overlooking the bay.

"Will he be okay?" Avery asked, trying not to show her shock and fear.

"Yeah. He's got two neurologists barking orders at the restaurant staff, so he's in good hands." Collin and Cam were working in tandem to take care of my son. "He'll be fine, but we'll have to head to the house because these episodes drain all his energy, and he's going to need to sleep."

"Cam, why don't we sit him up over here?" Collin said before he looked at me as I approached with a glass of water. "You good, Mom?"

"I'm fine. Thanks, Collin," I answered. I knelt by Jackson's side where Cam sat protectively near his son, watching him as he lay next to the table where we ate fish and chips moments ago.

"Hey, kiddo." I smiled at Jackson, seeing his eyes in a daze. "Whatever am I going to do with you?" I asked, running my fingers through his thick black, wavy hair, and smiling at his bashful grin.

Jackson shrugged and grabbed the water, sipping it slowly, then shook his head. He looked up at Cameron, who was on his knees directly across from where I knelt.

"I'm sorry," he said.

"You should be," Cam answered, smiling, and trying to act annoyed all at once. "I was in the middle of a good story when, apparently, you weren't getting enough attention and pulled this shit," he winked and finished with an adorable smile. "You know, if you wanted to get that hot girl's attention across the room, you could've just smiled at her. You know your dashing eyes would've done the trick, right?"

"Nah," Jacks smiled and took another sip of water, "I'm good."

He was still a bit out of it, which was expected after an episode.

"Ha," Jake said, joining our little party on the floor of the fancy restaurant, "damn fine move. I was wondering if Cam here would ever stop talking about that ridiculous chopper ride up here. How you doing, kid?"

"I have a pretty bad headache. Sorta ready to go now," Jacks answered.

"Good idea. I'll go get the car," I answered.

"Absolutely not," Cam said, looking over at Jake, "Can you, Col, or Jim get the Tesla? We'll wait for you in front of the restaurant."

"I've got it. Keys?" Collin said, stepping toward us and holding out his hand. "Where are you parked?"

"In the parking garage by the Cannery Row bridge," Cam said as the men moved around, clearing a pathway for us to take the side exit of the restaurant.

"Jim's outside with the kids. Addy got a little concerned about Jacks and started crying," Ash said as we moved through the restaurant.

People couldn't stop staring at us. It was like we were walking a corpse out of the place. I tried not to glance around because seeing all those eyes would only piss me off, even though, I suppose, it was a normal reaction after witnessing a medical emergency. Unfortunately, some people weren't exactly empathetic, and I had to avoid saying something to those people so as not to embarrass my poor son further.

This was normal, though; this was life since these seizures started again. The interesting part would be the next, though. Warren and I had lost a few friends over Jackson's public episodes—*good fucking riddance.* But worse than Warren's friends being embarrassed by them, Warren was too, and there was no hiding it, no matter how hard he tried. It wasn't easy to deal with, that's for sure, but this wasn't Jackson's fault. He didn't ask for this shit, and *he* was the one who was affected by it the most.

This was the part where I waited for the shock and horror to die down and watched how Cam's friends started casting side glances at the mention of having Jacks in public with them. Whale watching was tomorrow, and since little Addison was a bit traumatized about what'd happened to *her buddy*, whom she'd been joking with before the seizure, she might be afraid to have him along.

Jim also seemed extremely protective of his little girl, and I was waiting for the excuses to come: *Why don't we just pass on the whale-watching excursion tomorrow?* or *Are you sure he should come along after that seizure yesterday?* All that would start happening sooner than later. And not far behind that, Cameron would either be rightfully upset at his friends' reactions or that we'd made a spectacle of ourselves in front of his friends.

"Is Jacks going to be okay?" Addison asked, pulling me out of the string of PTSD thoughts plaguing me in the worst way.

"He'll be fine, sweetheart," I said.

Then she hugged me tightly, "I'm sorry that happened to him."

"I am too, honey," I said, hugging her back. "He'll be fine, though. He just needs to sleep for a while at the house."

"Okay, I was ready to leave anyway." She smiled and then rolled her eyes, "Don't tell my dad, but I didn't want to go to that one place for my birthday cake."

My mind softened up from my defensive thoughts, expecting all of Cam's friends to reject us after embarrassing them.

"Why not?" I chuckled. "That little bakery smells delicious."

She shrugged. "It's pretty good, I guess." Then her eyes widened, "Why don't we get the cake and bring it back home?"

"Honey, you don't have to stop everything for us. Why don't you get your cake and eat it at the park by the ocean? You sounded very excited about that earlier. And if you have leftovers, I'm sure your buddy Jacks will love some when you get back."

"Nope," she smacked her lips. "We're going back to the house, and we'll have cake when Jacks is feeling better. It's not fair if he misses out and we go play without him."

I stared at her, entirely shocked that the little girl would be so considerate. Most adults would run away after witnessing a seizure like Jacks just had, but this sweet little girl wasn't budging on the fact that she wouldn't allow it to ruin Jackson's day. She didn't care that it was cutting the second part of her birthday in half.

"Okay, then, Miss Addy. Run it by your parents, though. Jacks will be asleep for a while, so why don't you play around here for a bit, and then you can decide what you want to do," I said.

"We're going to take the kids back through the aquarium," Ash said. "Jim overheard Addy talking to you a moment ago, and I think he's right. So why don't we let you, Cam, and Jacks head back to the house and give you three some peace and quiet? We'll come back with cake and stuff in a few hours."

"The house is stocked up nicely," Jake said, standing next to his wife. "But if you'd like, the guys and I could go back with Jacks and Cam, and you can stay with the ladies if you want?"

I watched Ash smile and look up at her devastatingly handsome husband. "Nice try, wimp. You're stuck going through that aquarium one more time, just like the rest of us. And yes," she smiled back at me, "it was John's idea to do the aquarium again. Gotta love how these guys like to get out of the hard stuff." She winked, then looked over at Jackson. "Wow, he's not missing a step, is he?"

My attention was brought back to my son. This was the easiest time I'd ever had while dealing with Jacks having a seizure. Cameron was sitting next to Jacks, joking and engaging him. It's like the rest of us didn't exist. It was just Cam and his son.

This moment took my breath away. It was the most beautiful sight. Jacks was laughing with that extremely exhausted look, but he seemed so damn happy with whatever Cam told him. Likewise, Cameron had his own beautiful smile, chuckling at whatever he was telling his son. It was as if this were one of the best days of his life, but I had no idea why.

Having a son with this medical condition had always made me feel like I didn't quite fit in with the rest of the world, but I felt like I fit somewhere now.

I fit right here in this moment with the man I'd loved so profoundly so many years ago. As I watched him share my burden of caring for our son, I knew I still loved him. I don't know if I'd ever stopped or just packed all those feelings away and hid them deep inside because they were too painful to process.

I'd never thought of myself as a girl who needed a hero. Still, as I stood there, watching my son's worries floating away and feeling the relief that comes with being unburdened, I wondered if maybe everyone needed a hero sometimes.

As quickly as I let these feelings sweep me away, I put them back in their box and packed them away deep inside myself. I couldn't get caught up in this. There was no way I would get all mushy and let my guard down because the second I did, I would end up paying the price for it.

"All right, Mom," Cam said, breaking through the ice wall growing around my heart, "the car is here, and we're getting this kid home. I've got bets placed on the NBA game later, so Jacks needs to take a nap before he can watch my Lakers take down his Knicks."

I smiled again, and the battle to keep my guard up commenced. Would I or wouldn't I allow myself to love this man again? Our eyes locked, and the way I felt scared the shit out of me.

Chapter Twenty-Five

Cam

The car ride home was primarily quiet. I had tried to initiate conversation more than once during the drive, but Jessa wasn't engaging. I didn't know where it all went wrong. Perhaps she was reaching a breaking point with Jackson's seizures, given how disruptive they were to his daily life.

I'd seen many different reactions from parents in these situations, so it didn't surprise me that she was preoccupied after the latest episode. Instead of prattling on about nonsense, I remained quiet, thinking about what I'd picked up from Jacks in the short time we'd spent together thus far.

The kid was undoubtedly positive and seemed to have inherited my competitive streak, which was apparent in his athletic proficiency. However, I was most interested to see his willpower and ability to stand up in the face of adversity. I wanted to see a fighter's mentality because, after this surgery, it would take the heart of a fucking lion to get his life back.

In this short time, I couldn't say whether the kid would let this surgery mentally beat him, but his positive attitude was a good start. Most kids his age were preoccupied with getting laid and video games, throwing temper tantrums if they didn't get whatever they felt was owed to them.

Jacks couldn't have that entitled mentality if he wanted a strong recovery. Hell no. This surgery would bring me to my knees at this age, not to mention what it would've done to me at sixteen. Thankfully, Jacks seemed a lot more mature than I was at his age, and he wasn't an all-star because his mommy was screaming at the coaches that her son deserved it. He worked his ass off for that; I saw that in his eyes. Those attributes would serve him well in recovery.

"He's out like a light," I said to Jessa after we pulled up to the house. "I'll grab him."

"No," Jessa said, speaking for the first time since we rolled onto the scenic 17-mile Drive. "He can wake up and walk in. He's good."

His mom made him work past the crippling episodes. She didn't baby him or cater to it, and that was good for him.

"Jacks," she said, shifting in her seat to look back at him and rouse him. "Hey, it's much more comfortable on a bed than in the car." She chuckled.

"Ugh," Jacks protested. "I hate this."

"No shit," I answered. "I can carry your precious little butt into the house if you want?"

"God, no. I mean, unless you're offering a piggyback ride," Jacks managed to tease, prompting me to laugh and step out of the car.

I turned and opened Jackson's door. His eyes were slightly opened, and the exhaustion from the seizure was present, but he dropped his feet out of the side of the car and rose.

He stretched and then smiled at me, "Knicks are going to wipe the Lakers off the basketball court tonight. No tears when they do."

"You must be sleepwalking," I teased, "because that would only happen in your dreams, kiddo."

"Mm-hmm," he answered, then yawned while he rolled his eyes.

"I'll help you in the house. But, unfortunately, you must be under five-feet tall to take the piggyback ride, so you're going to have to hoof it," I said.

"I'm going to take the trail down and go for a walk on the beach," Jessa said. "I'll be back in a bit."

"Hold up," I called out. "I'll head down with you. You want a beer or something?"

"That sounds nice," she answered. "Maybe a blanket and a glass of wine would be better."

She gave me a look that made my dick suddenly throb. Fucking hell. Of all the times my dick decides to come out and play, it's when we're stacked on top of each other in this house. I hadn't responded sexually with Jessa since first seeing her at that resort, and now, when we're all in this home like a bunch of fucking vacationers, the damn thing decides to finally give me a fucking pulse.

"Everything okay?" Jessa waved her hand as if trying to bring my mind back to earth.

Oh, just having an internal argument with my dick. All fucking good here.

"Yeah, I was just thinking…" I paused. "Don't worry about it. I'll be back with a blanket and some wine."

"I was kidding," she said with a laugh. "I wondered why you sort of blanked out just now."

Because I suddenly want to fuck you under that blanket after we've had a glass of wine? Because I'm suddenly hornier than ever? And, most of all, because I think you're the most beautiful woman I've ever known, and I was such a goddamn fool to leave you?

"Okay, cool. Be back in a sec," I said, then turned to walk toward the house where Jacks was already fifty steps ahead of me.

"All right. The room's up here, Champ," I said, walking up two sets of floating pine steps to reach a loft where two separate rooms were situated.

"Champ?" Jacks said in a tired, humored voice. "Funny, that's what Mom calls me."

I smiled. "Yeah? She called me that in college too because I kicked ass, sort of like those Lakers are going to do this evening."

"Can I ask you a question?" Jacks said when we reached the third floor, and I turned left to the room where he'd be staying.

"You just did, but please, do ask another," I teased, raising my arm to admit him into the corner room. The view of the cliffs and the ocean was out of this world.

There goes that sex on the beach idea, I thought, realizing you could see for miles from this window. It was like a goddamn lighthouse or something.

"You and Mom?" he started, and his curious expression killed any sex drive that had possessed me from out of the clear blue sky minutes ago.

"Were good friends in college," I said slowly, begging him with my eyes not to *get it* right now.

He scrunched his face up with a look that made my stomach knot.

Jesus Christ, kid. Please do not put it all together here and now, I thought, knowing he was worn-out but scared as hell I was about to answer for being the deadbeat dad he never cared to meet.

"I don't know. I'm just tired," he said.

Then he shook his head as if trying to rid himself of a question he was too afraid to ask. A question that I was too chicken shit to answer.

"You look it," I smiled and ruffled his thick, black hair, another thing he'd inherited from his grandfather and me. "Get some rest, and hey, what's your favorite snack to eat while watching the game?"

He chuckled. "I don't know. I never got to chill out and watch a game like that before. I had to watch on my phone in my room because Warren was always watching the news. He hated watching games."

Why does that not surprise me?

"Well, that sucks for him," I said. "There's nothing like eating chicken wings and chips and dips while drinking beers and watching the game in the luxury of your own home."

Jackson's face lit up. "I love nachos. Maybe I'll be hungry for something like that later, but I need to take a nap first," he finished. "You and mom enjoy your walk or whatever on the beach."

"You're a good kid. You know that?" I said, and I thoroughly meant it.

"Thanks. I think you're a pretty good doctor, too. And thank you for helping me through the seizure today. Sorry I sort of ended everything early."

"I *am* pretty fucking pissed that I couldn't go back through that aquarium again," I smirked.

He laughed. "Better watch that mouth around my mom, Doc." He shook his head, "Sorry she's been jumping your case about that. I have no idea why she is, either, because I've heard her use every word in the book. It's weird."

"She's a great mom, and I can say that with authority because I've met many amazing moms in my profession. Yours is one of the best and most caring ones I know."

"Sounds like you might have a thing for her," he said with a yawn, and I started to think I was keeping the poor kid up when all he wanted to do was close his eyes.

Seizures were no damn joke. Not only did they pause space and time while you went through them but coming out of them took your ass out also. It was like having your brain suddenly be rebooted.

"Get some sleep, buddy. We can shoot the shit later," I said. "Oh, and don't tell your mom I'm a closet curser."

"Ha," was all he said, and that's when I left to let the poor kid get some rest.

I wasn't prepared for the feelings I'd been experiencing since I'd been here with Jackson and Jessa. I was reminded of the fond times I'd spent with my father before I went away to college and the mornings that I'd spent drinking coffee and talking with my mom—family things. I hadn't felt anything like this since my parents passed away, the warm and fuzzy feelings, and I didn't want to fight it. It was like I'd been hypothermic, and someone had wrapped a warm blanket around me.

I had these renewed yet different feelings for Jessa. How did any of this happen? I mean, I never would have described myself as lonely before. If I wanted a woman's company, it wasn't hard to attain. Go out, have some beers, and bring whichever gal I'd choose to the nicest hotel suite around until it was time for me to go again. Voila. Done and done. No strings and no one to disrupt my career and the kids who needed me to be the best doctor I could be.

No, I wasn't lonely; I didn't think so, anyway. On the contrary, I was the happiest asshole on the planet. I owned lots of real estate, two Cessna airplanes, and a luxury helicopter company that flew tourists all over the coast. I even hired a man to run my father's company after he passed away so I wouldn't be distracted by it.

Hell, outside of being a very successful pediatric neurosurgeon, I found a way to enjoy life and live it to its fullest. I was the poster child for living each day as if it were your last, and because of that, I wasn't going to deny these feelings.

I wanted to believe that Jessa was feeling this way too. She had a look in her eye when I locked eyes with her before we got into the car, a look that made me think she was staring into my soul, and she loved what she found.

There was a reason fate brought my girl and son into my life. And I wasn't going to ignore that.

Even though we were in a house with my friends, I didn't give a fuck. I would find a way to start new with my Jessa. The past was in the past for a reason, but the present was where I thrived. My decisions in the here and now would create the future, and that future was looking brighter than the sun moving toward the horizon.

It was time to bring this bottle of wine and blanket to my lady and prove that we were back in each other's lives for more reasons than one.

"Hey," I said, trying to act casual and not like some guy who'd been reading inspirational quotes on Instagram all day.

"I was kidding about the wine," she said, shaking her head and laughing.

"You are so beautiful. You know that?" I said precisely what I felt when my eyes searched her sparkling ones. "I was such a dipshit to walk away from you."

"Yes, you were," she arched a playful eyebrow at me. "Now, pour me a glass when we get down to the beach, so I can enjoy it without falling."

The house was on the cliff, but the trail to the beach was anything but treacherous, thanks to the wooden stairs leading safely down.

Once we reached the bottom, I poured the merlot and handed her the glass. "Hopefully, this will enhance your walk. Listen," I grew more serious, "I want—"

Fuck. My brain froze. What the hell was I going to say? More than that, why was I so goddamn nervous?

"You *want*?" Jessa answered with a laugh. She took a sip of her wine while I poured mine fuller than usual. "Maybe you want to tell me why you're acting so weird?" She took the chenille throw blanket from my hands and wrapped it around her shoulders. "How about this? I want to take a walk and enjoy this crisp ocean air while I watch the waves crash into the shit-stained rocks."

I smiled and set the wine bottle down next to where I'd kicked off my shoes in the sand. Jessa's shoes were tossed off to the side, and once I put everything together, I walked toward her on the wet sand.

I slowed some, taking in this view of the woman as she moved gracefully along the shoreline. The wind breezed through her hair, tossing her golden locks in circles, as she watched the waves spraying up after crashing against the rocks in the ocean.

The fog muted the sun, making it chillier than it should've been.

"As I was saying before," I announced as I came up to her side, "You're a good mom. I mean that."

"Thank you, Cameron," she said, her eyes slightly more relaxed after a few sips of wine. "And you're a great doctor. I'm not just saying that, either. For you to take on Jacks as a patient, then diagnose him so quickly, and take this personal time with him, it means a lot to me." Her features became more serious, "I wish I were confident about this surgery, but I'm hoping that will come. And soon."

"Jackson has six months to a year at the absolute most before I cannot operate on him," I said, my mind functioning much better in surgeon mode than lover-boy mode. "That doesn't mean I want you to take that amount of time to decide. However, I can see his spirit will pull him through recovery, and even though some areas may be problematic, there will also be areas where he will recover better than I anticipate."

"Yeah," she answered, pulling her fingers through her long hair. "I'm just going to need a bit of time. Thank you, though."

"For what?" I asked, wondering if her brain was misfiring like mine was currently.

She licked her lips, and I ran my bottom lip between my teeth, holding back my sudden craving and desire to kiss this woman.

"For helping Jacks with his seizure today. Your friends, too. All of you were great." She stopped walking and turned to face me. The blanket was wrapped tightly around her, and she held it just beneath her neck. She looked past me to the ocean, studying something beyond the white-capped waves as they rolled into shore.

"You know, Warren would've let that ruin our entire trip. And his friends would've never invited us out again. It's happened more times than I care to admit."

My face fell. I was pissed at what she'd proclaimed, but more than that, I was saddened by it. I suddenly felt like I'd abandoned the most beautiful soul in the entire world for my selfish interests. She and Jackson would've never had to endure that if I'd only stayed.

"I should've never left you," I blurted out again.

I'd said it for what seemed like the hundredth time. Did it even mean anything to her at this point? I wasn't sure she knew how serious I was; maybe that's why it was so easy for her to move on from the subject.

"Don't," she said with determination.

"No. I won't have you push me away for that. It's *how* I left you; that's why you never told me about our son, Jessa. I put you in a horrible position, and it wasn't just by getting you pregnant and leaving. It was my selfish bullshit that stopped you from interfering with my life. I'm sorry for that from the bottom of my heart. I truly am."

I reached out for her soft face and thanked God she didn't push me away. My eyes followed where the back of my fingers traced along her soft cheeks, and my heart picked up, feeling a jolt of energy course through my hand as I touched her.

"I forgave you long ago for texting me *after you left*." Her breath caught, and I could tell this tender moment was doing the same things to her as it was to me. "Let's leave it in the past," she said, her face leaning into my hand.

"I never finished loving you, baby," I said, meaning every word that came out of my mouth and somehow feeling like I had permission to call her that again.

"Please." Her eyes closed, and as I bent to kiss her, I noticed a frown on her lips. Then, her eyes reopened. "Please, don't do this," she pleaded with tear-filled eyes.

"I will not break your heart again; I promise you. Jessa, please give me another chance. I have no idea what hit me today, but I feel like my family has come home. I never felt like I wasn't whole before until being with you and my son today." I smiled at her expression as it began to soften. "Being on this silly birthday trip, I know that you and Jackson —" I shook my head, mentally begging myself to explain this feeling to her correctly. "God, I don't know how to say this, but this all feels *right*. I've had a void in my soul and didn't realize it until I spent this time with both of you. I've never needed anything in my life as much as I need you and my son, Jessa."

She studied me for a moment, then her hand traced along my jaw as she examined my eyes. "Cameron," she shook her head, "these emotions are probably coming from being around your friends and their families, knowing that Jacks is your son. And the guilt that you feel for leaving me piled on top of that is amplifying it. It's probably some weird, parent high you're on or something. It will go away."

I shook my head. "Don't tell me how I'm feeling. This isn't some fleeting thought. I feel it deeper than anything I've ever known. Please don't push me away."

She chewed on her bottom lip and shook her head while studying the ocean again. "It's not just my heart you'll break this time; it's Jackson's too."

"Do you think I don't know that? I wouldn't dare hurt that boy, and I swear to God, I'll never lose you again if you give me the chance to prove I'm a better man."

She walked past me, then turned back and smiled. My chest tightened with anticipation that I was doing this too hard and too fast. I could quickly lose her by speaking every thought I was suddenly feeling. This was very abrupt, but something told me that I had to speak up now or I never would.

This was my moment of truth, and I only hoped she would answer by allowing me to try and prove that my words matched what was in my heart and soul.

Chapter Twenty-Six

Jessa

Today, everything seemed to take a different turn. For the first time, I *saw* Cameron not only as Jacks's surgeon but also as a dad. I'd already been fixated on how lovely it was for all of us to be here together, how natural it felt, and those feelings intensified when Cam sprang into action to help Jacks during his seizure during lunch.

I couldn't get up from my seat fast enough to help Jacks when the episode started, but Cam—who was in mid-conversation about Jake's yacht coming into the bay tonight—stopped everything and bolted around the table, catching my son before he could hit the floor. In the flawless art of not missing a thing, Cam was rolling Jacks onto his side, concealing him from people watching him convulse and gently talking him through it.

I saw past the *doctor* in Cameron at that moment. He was trained to help in these situations, but I saw that he did so this time with the compassion and concern of a father. There was no mistaking the difference, and I noticed it immediately because I'd been waiting for someone to treat Jackson with that tender consideration for his entire life.

A gust of icy wind blew up, bringing my attention back to Cameron's soulful gaze.

"Don't do this, Jessa," he said, some frustration in his tone. "Don't push me away."

I shook my head. "I need to focus on Jacks and decide about this surgery," I said, feeling my motherly instincts kick in to protect me from the reckless decision of rekindling a romance with the handsome doctor who could have any woman he wanted. "You need to get your thoughts away from trying to be in our lives for more than just Jackson's surgery."

I was harsh, but I had to be. Nothing about this walk on the beach had warranted conjuring a love that had fallen apart the day he left me. I could not get caught up after a simple trip to that aquarium, nor could I continue thinking about Cameron fitting the bill as Jackson's father today.

It was a relief to have an epilepsy specialist be in our presence when Jackson went down, and it was wonderful to be in the presence of a man who didn't let the seizure ruin his entire day. But that's it. That's all this was. No more and no less, and I wasn't getting swept up in some fantasy land.

"Will you ever forgive me, or am I doomed forever for hurting you so badly?"

"That's not what any of this is about. You know that."

"No," he snapped back, frustration rising in his face. He stepped away from me and ran his hand through his hair, searching the gray ocean for answers. "I'm sorry," he said, his blue eyes filled with a sadness that I didn't expect to see. "I know those are just words, and you need to see action for me to prove that, but you won't let me in."

"Don't do this to yourself. We've been on different paths for years now. It's all too much, you know, trying to bring back what we once had. We're here so you can get a feel for Jackson's personality and see if he's mentally strong enough to overcome the aftereffects of this surgery, *not* to get caught up in feeling like you need us to be a family. It's too heavy, and I won't—I can't," I felt tears welling up in my eyes, accepting the truth of what I knew. "I just can't live my life through the things that feel good for the moment. And you and I have always felt good, Cameron, but it's a pipe dream. There are too many obstacles that I'm unwilling to jump to try and make it work. The idea of being in a relationship with you again—honestly, it exhausts me."

Cameron folded his arms in front of him and continued to stare at the ocean, so I went on. I needed to make sure he understood that this wasn't a situation where you could date your ex, rekindle the relationship, and if it worked, it worked. No. I had way too much on my plate as Jackson's mother, and bringing Cameron Brandt back into my life romantically only for me to wonder if he was going to commit this time was not something I could do.

I couldn't even begin to fathom how difficult life would be after Jackson's surgery, and adding relationship issues wasn't going to work. So I had to end this all before it got started.

"I know this sounds callous," I said, "but you must see it from my point of view. I have a son with a medical condition, and a responsibility to focus on getting him better. I can't get caught up in a fairytale, dating my ex in the hopes that my son will have the perfect father in his life—"

"Just stop, Jess." He turned to face me, his face unreadable. "I get it. I fucked it all up. So, from this moment forward, I will honor your wishes and return my focus to assessing Jackson's strengths and weaknesses. I'm sorry I caused you any unneeded stress." He stepped back. "Believe me, it was never my intention."

I felt Cameron's disappointment, and it made me feel horrible, but it was better this happened now than after I'd fully opened my heart only to have it broken again.

I didn't trust Cameron. How could I?

It was heartbreaking to watch him walk away and back to the house, especially after hearing the excitement in his voice of wanting to give it another try. And, as I watched him go, I was acutely aware of the ice wall I'd built around my heart to protect me from him. The warm side of me knew that I was just scared, but I didn't know how to bridge the gap. All I knew was that I was utterly wrecked after he left me the last time, and I never wanted to feel that way again. Goddamn right, I was scared. I couldn't function with that level of heartache ever again.

I turned away, unwilling to watch what could have been my future walking away from me, and I refocused my thoughts. My son was in bed at four in the afternoon, his day shot to hell after his seizure, and I had no business standing out here arguing about love declarations.

My responsibility was to Jackson first. It had been since the day the doctor placed that beautiful baby boy in my arms, and he locked eyes with mine.

Later that evening, the group had returned from their day in the bay, everyone in great spirits. After turning Cameron away and burying myself in the stress of everything I had to face in life, I just wanted to go to bed.

I had no desire to sit in the room where I could hear everyone enjoying the basketball game, especially Cameron and Jacks. I felt depressed and disdain for myself; I'd not only rejected a man's love and affections, but now I'd been wallowing in my gloomy mood, alienating myself from having a pleasant time.

What are we even doing here? I mentally questioned myself, detached from everyone while I washed the dishes in the kitchen.

Actually, in the brilliant act of being in the most pathetic pity party of my life, I was *re-washing* the dishes, to be exact.

Tears started to fill my eyes for the hundredth time this afternoon, and I tried to keep my composure when I heard someone behind me.

"Hey, Jessa, you're missing out on the Knicks being in the lead." Avery laughed, "Jacks is schooling everyone in there, too, by the way."

"He's good at that," I said with a laugh, keeping my eyes focused on the soap bubbles until I could dry up these sudden tears of frustration.

"What's going on?" she questioned, and I could hear the concern in her voice.

"Nothing," I sniffed. "Ugh." I shook my head, frustrated that I couldn't just knock this shit off.

"Here," she said, pouring me a glass of wine, "this usually gets the tears flowing faster. Then, once it's out of your system, you're freed up to handle shit again."

I grinned at her, grabbed the glass, and took a sip. "Don't they call that self-medicating?"

She laughed and raised a perfectly shaped eyebrow, her blue eyes so piercing and beautiful, "I run a women's home that deals with those types of things, and I can tell you that this isn't self-medicating. Turning to booze to make the troubles disappear is where we draw the line."

"Ladies?" Ash called, bouncing into the kitchen with the usual pep she always seemed to have in her step. "The kids are settled in, and it's time we relax."

"I didn't realize the children went to bed so early," I spoke. "It's only seven."

"I was referring to the gentlemen," she teased. "Seriously, though, half the time, the kids are babysitting them and not the other way around."

I softly laughed, feeling my gloomy mood lift a little, and I took another sip of wine. "I could see that."

"You don't want to," Avery chuckled. "Come on. There's a kick-ass balcony with full views of the ocean. We can talk shit while we're up there, too."

I followed the ladies, welcoming the chance to clear up my shitty mood.

"So," Avery said as we sat in the white Adirondack chairs that matched the look of this uniquely crafted home, "what's the deal with you and Cameron?"

She smiled at me, and her expression had such a caring and charming look that I could easily see she was rooting for us to make things work.

"No deal," I smiled in return. I tucked a strand of hair behind my ear and looked out to the horizon. "I'm just grateful that he was willing to take Jacks on as a patient and go above and beyond to get to know him better by bringing us on this outing." Avery casually rocked in her chair, watching me curiously. "And I appreciate all of you being cool with us intruding on Addison's birthday trip. Sorry that it went south after lunch."

Both women's expressions hardened a bit. Was I being a bitch? I thought I got out all the bitchy behavior when I leveled Cameron with my icy rejection.

"First of all," Avery said, the blunter and more uncensored of the two, "thank you for putting up with all of us." She took another sip of wine and crossed her leg, "It's wonderful to have you and Jacks here. I just hope it's going okay for you. Cam mentioned a bit about the surgery, and I can see why he'd want a little one-on-one time with...your son."

I smiled at her pause when she referred to Jacks as my son, not Cameron's. I liked these ladies, and as I pulled out of my funk, I felt more relaxed and curious as to what Cam's friends were told about our past.

"So, out of curiosity," I started, "what has Cameron told you about our relationship and that Jackson is his son? I know you all know, and it's certainly hard to miss with him looking so much like Cam."

Ash smiled at me. "Cam mentioned that he knew instantly that Jacks was his. He saw his dad in him, actually."

I had never thought about how much Jacks resembled Henry Brandt. I wonder if that was difficult for Cam, seeing his father, whom he loved so much in his son. It had been six years since Cam's parents lost their lives in that plane crash, and Cameron must've still felt that pain. I couldn't imagine all the grief he'd gone through alone by losing his parents so tragically, and I never knew.

Stop thinking negative thoughts for a change, I mentally ordered myself.

"He definitely has those striking blue Brandt eyes," I said, knowing that was the damn truth.

Eyes that could bring the strongest girl to her knees with just a wink.

"He said that he was a fool to leave you. He regretted it every day afterward," Avery finished.

"And that he's a firm believer that fate brought you back together," Ash added with a knowing grin. "So, don't be surprised if the handsome young doctor tries to fix your heart *and* your son's medical condition."

"He's a good man," Avery said, her scratchy voice filled with sincerity. "I recall the first time I met him," she laughed. "Please, don't let this bother you. This story involves a rich lady he brought to some gala."

I shook my head. "Not at all. He and I haven't been a couple since before Jackson was born. I think most of my jealousy left when I started to move on from that relationship."

Ash laughed. "Most of it, eh?" she eyed me. "I will say, always keep your heart guarded and make his ass work for you. That man is still deeply in love with you. I can see it on his face when he hears your voice from another room," her eyes widened, and she laughed, "or how he watches you when you have no idea he is. I wouldn't be surprised if he begs you back soon."

Yeah, like this afternoon when I rejected his ass.

I ignored all the stuff my heart wanted to hear about Cameron being in love with me and went back to what Avery was saying. "What happened with the rich lady at the gala?" I asked and then laughed when Avery's lips turned into a mischievous grin.

"I like how you'd rather hear the story about him suffering with another woman instead of the sweet, gushy stuff Ash was about to put out there." She pointed her thumb at Ash and chuckled, "If there's anyone who believes in the Universe and fate, it's this cute little hippie right here."

Ash rolled her eyes. "It's all true. And yes," she looked at me, "the Universe gave Cameron a good, karmic kick in the ass with the woman he boldly brought to that event."

She covered her smile and closed her eyes, trying not to laugh at the memory.

"All right," Avery said, sitting up in her chair as if to brace herself for this story. "So, we're all in the whole black-tie wardrobe—dress like a billionaire, act like a billionaire ensemble, if you follow?" she said with a roll of her eyes and a smile that teased me into wanting to know what the hell went down between Cameron and this girl.

"Yes," I nodded.

"Okay. So, we're all wearing designers and feeling super fancy, of course, but this chick is looking at us like we're a couple of gold-digging street rats because, unlike her, we weren't born into this billionaire lifestyle."

"Her dad was Peter Benjamin. I don't know if you've heard of him, but he was a wealthy financier who lost everything when the market crashed," Ash interjected. "Sorry, sorry. I interrupted. Go on."

"Peter Benjamin?" I questioned. "That guy was thrown in a federal prison for fraud or whatever, right?"

"Right. Jim has some stories about that fucker, but that's for a different day. Anyhoo," Avery practically whistled, "this woman shows up with Cam, and he's all giddy that he's got this babe on his arm."

Ash laughed and shook her head. "Little did he know, she'd taken a few bars of Xanax, along with something else, and after she downed her first glass of champagne, all bets were off."

"The guys were sitting around talking, and that's when this broad stands up on our table and begins to strip off her vintage Dior gown while singing Happy Birthday to Jim, whom she'd had a thing for since they were young."

"Oh, shit," I said.

These galas were something else to begin with, but in all the ones I'd attended when I'd dated Cam, I'd never seen such a thing. However, we'd attended those events at Cam's father's behest, and when Henry Brandt was in attendance, no one dared to fuck around.

"So, while she's singing to Jim like she's Marilyn Monroe on the President's birthday, Cameron ditches all decorum and proceeds to pull her off the table," Ash added. "Mind you, even Jake and Collin were stunned into silence, and they're the biggest pranksters of all."

"I could imagine how mortified Jim must've been," I answered. "A stunt like that could've cost him his reputation in a room full of influential people like that."

"Cam was horrified," Avery continued, "and it took Collin and Jacob to calm his ass down and get him to show his face around us the next day. Poor guy couldn't apologize enough for something he didn't do."

"His dad would've kicked his ass for embarrassing the family like that," I said.

Ash laughed. "Those men are a bunch of kids, playing on the playground. They came up with some silly apology video and somehow made that thing funny as hell. Instead of being a bad mark on everyone at our table, it was good publicity for Mitchell and Associates."

"What happened to the woman?" I asked.

"She pissed Cameron off so bad that I don't think the name Gabriella Benjamin can come up in his company without the man turning fifty shades of pissed off," Avery said. "All of that said, he's alluded to how he's never been fully happy in one of his flings or in the few relationships he's had since he left you. Based on everything he's said, he's feeling a Jess and Jacks-sized hole in his life since reuniting with you."

I exhaled and twisted my lips up. I believed Avery was telling the truth, but I wasn't convinced that Cameron would be up for the job of committing to Jacks and me. I hadn't seen this look Cam had for me that lit up the two women's faces when they referred to it, either. Maybe I just wasn't paying attention enough even to consider listening to what Cam had to say earlier.

I was attracted to him like a magnet, and I knew he was the love of my life too. But I also knew how it felt when he said he loved you above everything and then disconnected entirely to pursue something he deemed more important.

Fuck.

I'd felt like shit since I turned up my nose at the idea of giving him a second chance. In fact, this was the saddest I'd felt in years. Maybe this whole Universe thing was trying to get my attention, and my soul knew it was wrong to reject him.

I wasn't going to dwell on those things right now, and I wasn't going to keep this hard line in the sand that I'd drawn, forcing Cameron to stay on his side.

Perhaps I could let the ice wall thaw just a little and stay open. Avery and Ash seemed like two women who would've warned me off Cameron if he was still doing the *new girl weekly* thing. So maybe I would chill out a little and let Cam prove himself to me.

God, this better not be a mistake.

Chapter Twenty-Seven

Cam

Jake's yacht, *Sea Angel*, dropped anchor in Monterey Bay last night. The ladies and the kids all seemed very excited to know it was here this morning, and they wasted no time getting ready and gathering their things.

I was in charge of flying everyone to the yacht in the helicopter, something I'd been excited about doing since we got here. But sadly, nothing appealed to me at the moment.

As much as I enjoyed watching the game with Jacks, it felt bittersweet. I wanted so badly to connect meaningfully with my son, and I was struggling with how to do that after what Jessa said yesterday on the beach.

I had no idea how to get her back. The worst part was the aching, longing feeling inside. Even though she and I were physically near each other, it felt like she was a world away.

I didn't want to wallow. Instead, I needed to get over myself, accept that I'd lost the best thing in my life by not cherishing it while I had it, and move forward.

So why couldn't I? Why the fuck did I feel sick when I looked at her, knowing I could never have this woman again?

I hadn't said much to anyone since waking up this morning at four and up to now as I landed the chopper, which was filled with the last half of the gang on the bow of Jake's superyacht.

This goddamn boat was ridiculous, and if these floating five-star hotel walls could talk, we'd be entertained for days. I'd only been on this yacht a few times in the last three or four years, and even though I'd always enjoyed myself, I struggled to understand why these assholes felt the need to own such insanely opulent boats. They were like small fucking cruise ships.

"What the fuck is up with your mood this morning, man?" Collin asked after I shut down the helicopter and nodded toward the deckhands, prompting them to secure the chopper on the helipad.

"Nothing," I said, knowing everyone assumed I was in a bad mood when I got quiet. This time, they wouldn't be wrong. "All right. Let Jake know that once this bird is locked on deck, we're good to pull anchor and check out whales or whatever the fuck we're doing today."

"For fuck's sake," Jake said, approaching where I'd just stepped out of the helicopter, "I'm right here, asshole. Tell me yourself."

I rubbed my forehead. "Sorry, man."

"Now, say what's on your mind," Jim said.

"I'm not talking about my personal shit," I said. "Seriously."

"Are you concerned about Jackson and the surgery?" Collin questioned, knowing that on the rare occasion I wasn't in a light-hearted mood, it was because of a patient.

I wanted to lie and say yes.

"Nah, man," I said, then forced a fake smile. "I just slept like shit last night."

"Well, you flew that chopper like the dreamboat pilot you are," Jake said, always acting like a dipshit to lighten the mood."

"Totally dreamy," Collin said, with the same dipshit humor as Jake's.

"Why don't you two idiots make sure the ladies and kids are settled while I help Cam finish up?" Jim said, casting them a knowing glance.

I remembered the days when I was as much of a fuck-off as these two, but those days seemed to slip away as soon as I saw Jessa again. Since then, I'd been struggling with the guilt of leaving her *and* beating myself up over letting her go.

I was dealing with all that fallout, and I hated it. I wanted to get the fuck off this vacation, walk back into my hospital, and bury myself in work to avoid seeing Jessa and Jackson until they decided on this surgery. Then, I could perform the operation, help Jackson during his recovery, and then we'd move on with our lives. It would be precisely what Jessa fucking wanted it to be; me as the surgeon, and that was it. What else could I do at this junction without detrimentally affecting my son?

"I'm finished here, man. You can go with the guys," I said, looking around and wondering why Jim was hanging back.

"Seriously, dude. Are you okay? You don't look right," Jim said, tilting his head as if examining me.

Ah, shit. What was it about Jim? All he had to do was flash his goddamn CEO expression to make us all feel like we had no choice but to spill our guts. There was no use in playing coy. He was like a human lie detector.

"It's Jessa," I admitted. If there ever was someone to air out your problems to, Jim was the man. Might as well rip off the band-aid and get some advice, wanted or unwanted.

Jim's emerald green eyes looked like jewels when he pulled off his aviators and smiled with a knowing grin.

"I know," he said.

"And how would you know that?"

"If the problem were that you couldn't perform surgery on the boy, you would've mentioned something about that this morning when you sat silently next to me, drinking your coffee."

"So what makes you think Jessa has anything to do with it?" I asked, irritated this fucker could read all of us like books.

"Because neither one of you could so much as look in the other's direction when she came in to get coffee for herself. And once she left, you looked like a boy who'd just lost his balloon."

I turned to walk toward the door that admitted us into the staff corridors of the yacht.

Jim was one observant son of a bitch. That's why he was so fucking successful in business. The man was forever reading the room and quietly observing things on a much deeper level than the rest of us.

"You know, one day, you'll give yourself a day off and stop worrying about everyone who crosses a room that you're in," I said, smiling at a brunette waitress who was part of the staff.

"Good morning, gentlemen," she said, holding a tray filled with different fruits and giant muffins. "Can I get you anything?"

"We're all good. Thank you," Jim said.

"I need to shake this fucking mood or get off the damn yacht," I said. "I have no idea why I'm feeling like this."

Jim smirked, "Let me guess. You tried to sneak into her room last night to get laid, and she nailed you in the balls before kicking you out. Am I close?"

"Ha, ha," I said dryly, following the winding stairs to the next floor. "Finally, your ass is stumped. I should leave you to wonder as payback for being so observant."

"Cam," he said with a laugh I knew he tried to hold in, "what the hell happened? I've never seen you in such a shitty mood in all the years I've known you."

"I fucked everything up," I said in defeat. "I walked away from the only person I've ever loved, and now, here she is, back in my life as punishment. I can't live like this."

"Live like what? I'm confused."

"See," I opened my arms and widened my eyes, "I can't even make sense of how I feel. I can't fucking do this. If she doesn't want me back, then fine, but Jesus." I started walking through the grand atrium of this insanely beautiful yacht. "Shit," I said, seeing that Jim was back where I left him, wondering what I was doing.

We were all lucky I successfully flew the helicopter here because, as of right now, my brain was shutting down on every level. I was consumed with the loss of this woman, and it was the most painful fucking thing I'd ever felt.

"Where are the damn stairs on this thing?" I asked, frustrated.

"Over here," Jim said, punching the buttons on the wall with the side of his fist. "And you aren't going anywhere near everyone else until we work this craziness out of you."

"I'm heading to my room," I said. "I need to calm down."

"Yeah, your flushed cheeks clearly indicate that your blood pressure is about to pop a brain cell or two in that genius surgeon's mind of yours. So let's get a drink while Jake and Collin entertain everyone when the boat comes to pick them up for whale watching."

"I'm fine, Jim," I insisted. "I just need to do some push-ups or run the track on this yacht to get this shitty energy out of my system."

"Good idea. The track is on the lower deck. I'll meet you down there in ten," he said after we stepped out of the elevator that led to the living quarters on the top section of this yacht. "Let me tell Avery, then you and I can work out our frustration together."

"Frustration? You? You're the calmest mother fucker on the planet."

He chuckled. "Thanks for the compliment. See you down there."

After Jim and I sprinted this massive ass yacht for nearly thirty minutes, I felt renewed after all that rotten energy was out of my system. Jim and I had gone to our rooms to shower before meeting up on one of the party decks. I grabbed a juicy chunk of watermelon and sat on a lounge chair while waiting for my friend.

"All good?" Jim questioned as he walked out, making his way to the bar across from me and ordering a drink. "Bourbon. Neat."

"Much better." I wiped off my hands and walked to the bar where Jim stood. "I'll take a bourbon too."

He sipped the amber liquid from his glass. "Since we're technically on some form of vacation, it's perfectly acceptable to have a drink at noon, right?"

I glanced at my watch, "Eleven-thirty, but I won't say a word to the rest if you won't."

Jim chuckled, and we walked to a table that overlooked the back of the yacht. "I can't understand my brother and that damn bar," he said. "The idiot hires staff for table service and still has a bartender." He glanced over his shoulder and waved off the young waitress approaching from out of nowhere, then he turned back and shook his head. "See what I mean? What the fuck? Why the bartender and bar if everyone is going to follow you around to wait on you hand and foot?"

"Ah, probably gives him a hard-on to have all the luxuries at his fingertips. Who knows, it's fucking Jake," I laughed.

Jim's features lightened, taking another sip of his drink. "Good to have you back, buddy," he said. "And listen, I get it. I do. I fucked shit up in the worst way possible with Avery when we were dating. I lost the best thing that'd ever walked into my world with her and Addy at the time, and I didn't think I'd get her back." He looked out at the ocean thoughtfully, "It takes challenges like these, though, to make you appreciate what you have when you get it back."

"That's the difference between you and me; you got the girl in the end. I messed this one up bad."

"Oh, yeah?" Jim grinned. "Did you fire her and act like the biggest asshole she'd ever met, all while she had a kid to feed?"

"Well, you got me there. Jesus, you *fired* her?"

"Practically had her escorted out of the building by security because she lied on a resume. The worst part was that I knew she wasn't the person I'd made her out to be." He exhaled, and his features darkened, "I should've never been so harsh to her, yet I was. I was struggling with some serious demons at the time. I know it's not an excuse, but that was why I put her in a position to be perfectly justified in never wanting to see my face again."

"And what was the trick?" I asked, taking the bait on this story which I knew had a happy ending.

He raised his glass and pointed with his index finger toward the bar, "I reintroduced myself to her right over there at some party Jake was hosting on this yacht." He looked back at me and smiled. "Got the girl back."

"That was it?"

He shrugged, "Nah, but that was what reminded her about what an amazing fuck I was when we finished the conversation in my cabin."

I laughed, "Well, if sex has anything to do with me getting Jessa back, then it looks like the story doesn't end well for me."

He frowned, "You suck in bed, huh? Fuck, if that's the case, the story will never end well for you."

"No, dipshit," I said with a laugh. "I can't even find a way to kiss the woman, much less fuck her. She seriously wants nothing to do with me. I hurt her pretty bad."

"Don't be hard on yourself. She was hurt, man. And she's got a shitload of stuff with Jackson on her plate. You have to respect that. Give her time."

"Yeah, well, fuck," I said. I felt that dark loneliness creep up on me again. "How am I supposed to prove I won't hurt her like that again? It was sixteen years ago."

"I won't sit here and tell you this will be easy. It seemed like it took me a damn lifetime to work through all my issues enough to attempt anything with Avery again. I did a lot of necessary work on myself."

"But you guys weren't broken up for sixteen years. She doesn't even know the man that I am now. I'm certainly not the same fucking idiot she dated years ago who took off on a whim, you know?"

"You know the woman better than I do, so I can't necessarily guide you in that area. But I can tell you that I know the feeling you're weighted down with, and it made my ass physically ill. After watching her storm out of my office that day, I shut down and hid behind my job. I blamed it all on her, everything. At that point, I wasn't good to anyone, especially myself. Seeing you earlier reminded me of myself. I was angry at everyone and everything, throwing a billionaire's kid, spoiled brat fit."

"The fuck I was," I said, half joking, half serious. "My dad never let me get away with that shit. Of course, your father didn't put up with that either."

"No, that's not what I mean," he said as he shook his head. "We've lived most of our adult lives believing that the names Brandt and Mitchell owe us something like we deserve material things with no effort. That's why we fucked women, no strings attached, and left them like they were inevitably always going to do whatever we wanted."

"Do you think that's what I did with Jessa?"

He shrugged. "How should I know, man? We weren't good friends then," he laughed. "But if you thought she'd be fine with you running off to pursue *your dream*, regardless of what she wanted, because your perfect life was owed to you, then yes."

"Damn, you're fucking good," I said. "I work with therapists all day, and I would've never seen it that way."

"I'm not that good," he laughed and took another sip of his drink. "I told you, I lived it with Avery. I hadn't treated her like the treasure she is because I'd always gotten what I wanted whenever I wanted it. When all you have to do is snap your fingers to get things, it makes you start to dehumanize people without realizing it."

I exhaled, "I have no idea how to get her back. I don't have the words. I have no idea what the fuck to say."

"Whatever you do, don't overthink it. She'll be out of your life before you blink if you do. Hell, that ex-fiancé may come back, thinking he has all the right words, and kick you to the curb if you're not careful."

"Warren?" I rolled my eyes, "That idiot fucked shit up for good, I think."

"Like I said, don't *think*. You need to act. Follow your gut. If you feel a desire to talk *or show* her how you feel, do it. She wouldn't be on this trip if she had no interest in you. I'm damn sure she doesn't see your sexy ass as a *good buddy*, either."

"The point of this trip is for me to come out of this with a sound opinion on Jacks," I said.

"She could've stepped back and let the boy be observed in a more controlled environment." He arched an eyebrow at me, "Trust me on this. Go where you're being led, and *know* it won't be easy. If you truly love this woman, you'll have patience with her, and you won't rush it. Respect the fact that you hurt her, and you may get hurt too."

"I don't know if I can handle this kind of fucking pain."

"I'm sure she felt the same way when you left her," he said. "And then she found out she was pregnant."

"Shit." My heart sank. I was acting like a little bitch. There was no way I could waltz back into Jessa's life, thinking this second chance was owed to me. I was going about this wrong, and it all made more sense now.

"I heard a therapist once say that *hurt people hurt people*," I said, staring down at my bourbon. "She's going to hurt me, or I'm going to hurt her."

"As I said, stop fucking *thinking*. If you think about all the ways to go about this, you'll miss this door while it's open. Appreciate the opportunity to be in each other's lives again. Let the past stay where it fucking belongs, in the past. Move from there, and you'll be fine. Be the boy's doctor; until she permits you to be more to her, be her friend. Don't be the ex, and don't you dare try to make a cheap move and be her man."

"Cheap move?"

"Yes, it's cheap because you're asking her to trust you the way we entitled assholes think we deserve. Getting another shot isn't owed to you because you were careless the first time. She's a human being who trusted you with her heart once already. Jessa has every right to reject you from now until forever for what you've done, so ease up." Jim laughed. "Trust me. I've been where you're at, and I know that void you're feeling."

"Funny, I hadn't felt *this void* until yesterday. I was fucking content until now."

Jim grinned, "It's because your sorry ass figured out that everything is meaningless without love." He stood when a staff member approached. "At least you've discovered that you have a fucking heart."

My eyebrows rose as I sighed. I thought becoming a pediatric neurosurgeon was fucking hard, but I had a feeling that if I wanted Jessa's heart back, it would take patience and time. Lucky for me, patience was my middle name.

"They're arriving, sir. Lunch will be served inside due to the storm heading our way. The captain said the ship will be fine where we're anchored in this part of the bay if you or Dr. Mitchell would like to remain aboard."

"I'll speak with Dr. Mitchell and the rest of the group. If we aren't looking at rough seas in the bay, I believe the plans were to stay aboard for the night," Jim answered and turned to me. "You good with that?"

"I'll see what Jessa wants to do."

I didn't know how to approach Jessa after what Jim had said to me. His words sank in, but they also put me into a bit of a tailspin. Had I been treating people like a revolving door my whole life, taking everyone for granted? I'm not sure I wanted the answer to that question.

Chapter Twenty-Eight

Jessa

Being on the whale-watching excursion was nothing short of exhilarating. However, I was still shocked that Cameron, adrenaline junkie that he was, didn't come along. Something was up with the helicopter, so he stayed on the yacht with Jim, who needed to handle some business for his London office.

Nevertheless, both men certainly missed out on quite the experience. We took a boat that had been lowered from the side of Jake's superyacht, which seemed the size of a regular goddamn yacht. Such was the life for billionaires, I guess.

Speaking of enjoyable, private, billionaire-chartered whale-watching tours, Jake had brought along a couple of Marine Biology students from the local university. The boy and girl were in their senior year at California State University, Monterey Bay, and they were the politest and coolest young adults you could ask for. They certainly made an impression on all of us.

They guided the driver of Jake's mini yacht to where the whales played and fed in the bay. At first, it was rather dull, but the nent came the closer we got to spot the whales. The students pointed to where the seagulls swarmed over the white caps of the ocean, stating we might see a fin or a tail.

There were about a hundred false alarms and non-stop laughter before Jake's son, John, spotted our first whale. Then it got crazy fun. We were all acting like silly kids—Jake and Collin more so than the rest of us—running from port to starboard, looking for the next whale.

Suddenly, a huge whale was heading straight for us.

"Holy fuck!" Jake said, covering his son's ears so he could nail the f-word with the sincerity he felt. "Jesus!"

My eyes must've been the size of silver dollars when the massive-ass whale started to get too damn close to the boat. The mini yacht felt the size of a canoe compared to the creature approaching where we floated helplessly.

"My God," Ash said in awe.

The giant humpback whale was the most majestic creature I'd ever seen. I stood there, gaping in wonder, before I walked to the ledge, held onto the railing, and watched it glide through the water, dangerously close to us. It wouldn't have taken much for the whale to breach the hull of this boat, but as I watched it move by, everything seemed so peaceful.

I smiled when I turned and looked at Jacks, standing next to Addy between Jake and Collin. Everyone was silenced by the magnificent creature swimming gracefully below our boat.

"That was the most insane feeling in the world," Jacks said.

"No shit," Collin said. "I swear, my balls are in my throat right now."

"In your throat?" Jake laughed. "I'm not sure if I even have my balls anymore."

Jacks laughed, and I just rolled my eyes.

"If you all look to the port side, you can see that the whales are starting to hunt for food," the young man named Ryan said. "Over there." He pointed to a sudden disturbance in the water. "They're doing what we call *bubble-net* feeding."

Sarah, his college companion, looked down at Addy, who was really trying to be her friend. "They're blowing water below a school of fish right now," she said. "It forces the fish up, and then the whales will swim up and catch the fish in their mouth."

As soon as the guide said it, Addy and the kids squealed when the ocean opened, and the large whales' mouths appeared and swallowed the fish.

Whales began shooting out of the water in the distance, and that's when the curse words started flying—I even got a raised eyebrow and a laugh from Jacks when I said *holy shit* more times than I could count on one hand.

My heart was pounding with excitement as I watched this show. I could only compare it to watching the grand finale of a firework show that exceeded your expectations.

We'd watched the whales for a good two hours until the captain of the yacht notified the driver of our boat that bad weather was approaching, and the trip would need to be cut short.

Leaving was a bummer, but I couldn't have been more grateful for the experience. I felt exhilarated by the majesty of nature, but I still felt the lingering sorrow from pushing Cameron away yesterday.

He'd gone on about how right things felt when we were together and about a feeling of missing family, and if I was honest, I was feeling that way right now without having him here. I wished I could see Cam next to Jacks, admiring the whales and having fun together. It was like a piece was missing from this enjoyment because he was gone.

I'd never been so goddamn fickle in all my life. Was fighting these feelings like swimming upstream, or was I doing the right thing by keeping Cam away? If it was right, why did it hurt so bad?

I tried to shake off my thoughts as we boarded the yacht again. I didn't want to be in my head all day, and I didn't want to be in another shitty mood like yesterday.

"They have lunch ready in the dining room. The kids opted to take theirs on the bottom deck," Ash said. "Did you have a good time?"

"The best. That was better than I could've ever imagined. Thank you," I said, knowing it was her and Jake's yacht and the mini yacht that allowed us to have such a wonderful time today.

"Listen," Avery said as we all walked through the luxurious boat toward the dining area, "the guys are heading back on the helicopter tomorrow, and Ash took the week off. Jake informed the captain that the yacht is ours for the week if you and Jacks want to take a fun little cruise down to Southern California with us."

"Oh, wow. That sounds incredible," I said, loving the idea of spending more time with my new friends. "Let me check with Cam, though. I think he has an appointment for Jacks to do some more scans on Thursday, but I'm not sure."

We walked into the dining room to find an elegant spread of fruits, vegetables, roasted turkey, ham, and even a prime rib roast sitting in the center of a large, polished wooden table. It looked like a Medieval feast.

"Wow," I said, sitting next to Cameron and smiling at him. "This is quite the spread."

His mood hadn't changed since this morning. I'd had the feeling earlier that the helicopter issue was an excuse for him to avoid whale watching, and now, I knew it was.

I kept replaying the sincerity in Cam's sapphire blue eyes when he talked about us being a family and the look of devastation when I basically told him to fuck off. Of course, I'd treated him as if he were still the Cameron I remembered from high school, the man who could say one thing, then crush me while doing another immediately afterward. I didn't want to take a chance and risk that kind of heartbreak again. The stakes were higher now.

But my mind wouldn't let it go last night. I tossed and turned, thinking about how Cam helped Jacks through that seizure the way he did and how he talked to Jacks like a he was his son, not his patient.

I was aware that my cold exterior was unhealthy and that after all these years, my reaction was possibly unfair, but what difference did it make now that I'd iced him out? He was pissed, and I was confused.

"Tomorrow, I'm flying the guys back to Southern California because they've got to work. Jake has left the captain orders to bring the yacht down the coastline to Long Beach this week with the ladies and kids."

"Okay," I said, trying to keep my spirits up. "What should Jacks and I do?"

I was confused by the tone of his voice and not being direct with his point.

He swallowed a bite of meat and wiped his mouth with a cloth napkin. "I wasn't sure if you and Jacks wanted to spend the rest of the week with the ladies and the children or go back in the chopper."

I swallowed a bite of the ham I'd sliced into. "Didn't you have plans to run more tests on Jacks?"

"I will proceed with ordering more tests once the surgery is decided upon," he said.

Guess I can't get mad when he does what I tell him to do and act like the surgeon instead of a boyfriend, I thought, completely uncomfortable with this conversation.

"We'll probably just go home with everyone. I need to stay focused on our next steps, anyway. I need to find a place to rent, find a car, and —" I stopped when I felt my heart rate pick up a little at the thought of the responsibilities I'd been neglecting. Getting caught up in this billionaire wonderland was effortless, but I needed to start prioritizing things.

"Jessa," Ash said from across the table, "you're staying in Malibu, right?"

"Yeah, we are for now," I responded more calmly than I felt.

"Jake and I have a beach home there, and we rarely use it." She pursed her lips and looked at Jake, who was nodding along with her, "You're most welcome to it if that helps ease the burden of everything that's going on."

"I couldn't," I said. "I can't thank you enough for the kind offer, but I really couldn't."

"Why the hell not?" Jake asked, sitting back and sipping a beer after inhaling his lunch. "We've got no use for the place. We always rent it out during fall and winter; what's one month early? The place is yours for as long as you need it. No strings attached, of course. Use it before the cobwebs take over."

"And don't say no because you think it's rude to say yes," Ash insisted. "We wouldn't offer if we didn't want to help make your life easier. You aren't putting anybody out or anything."

I felt tears pool in my eyes at their generosity, and the relief that washed over me was bigger than I expected. "Okay, yes. I really can't thank you enough," I said. I laughed and smiled at Cameron.

"He's got a pretty badass Bugatti parked there, too," Cam said, grinning at Jake. "I'm sure he'd be happy to let you run that sucker back and forth between appointments."

"I'm afraid that's where the charity dies on my behalf," Jake laughed. "You can, however, use Ash's Land Rover. I'm sick of acting like we're the Brady Bunch in that thing anyway."

Ash rolled her eyes. "Is that what you think about it?"

"It's a Land Rover, not a minivan," Jim said. "Don't be such a whiny bitch about it, Jake."

Because the children were eating in another area of the yacht, I finally heard Jim speak up more. The striking man, who could've been Jake's twin, had previously seemed stiff and reserved. I liked this side of him.

"*I'm* the bitch?" Jake questioned in a funny high-pitched voice as if he were astonished at what Jim had said. "Shall we address *your* bitchiness with the fact that you insist on being chauffeured in a Bentley everywhere you go?"

"Oh, fuck that," Jim said, rolling his eyes.

"Nah," Cameron jumped in with a laugh. "Addy told me she thought you didn't know how to drive the first time you rolled up to McDonald's in that Bentley."

"Hey, assholes, would you please stop bickering for half a second?" Collin interrupted and looked at me. "Elena and I have a Range Rover that we hardly ever drive. It's yours."

"Collin," I went to speak but stopped when he put his hand up.

"If Elena didn't have to leave for work last night, she would be sitting here and insisting on it." He leaned forward and rested his elbows on the table, exhaling as he looked at me seriously. "Please don't make me go home to my gorgeous, fiery Cubanita goddess and explain why I allowed her new friend to stress out about transportation when we have cars at home collecting dust." Collin raised his eyebrows at me expectantly. "She wouldn't hear of it, and everyone knows what my goddess wants, my goddess gets."

"He ain't lying about that," Jake teased his friend as everyone laughed.

"Seriously, though," Collin continued, leaning back in his chair. "We're all here to help, and we *want* to help. So, take the week and enjoy the Pacific Ocean while we dummies get back to work."

"Speaking of work, I work remotely, so I probably need to get back too," I said.

"Every mother electronic device you might need for business is on this yacht. There are even four meeting rooms if you need to do a video conference or something," Jake said.

"Really?" I questioned. I shouldn't have been surprised. This yacht was insane.

He chuckled. "If I want Jim or Alex and Spencer to get on this boat, they can't be cut off from their empires, you know. God forbid the Wi-Fi not work; they'd probably jump overboard and swim to shore if that happened."

"Very funny," Jim said as Avery laughed and knowingly nudged him on his side.

"Wow, okay. Well, let me think about it. It just makes me feel a little irresponsible, like it shouldn't be this easy."

"Life is hard enough, Jessa," Collin said. "Take help when offered because not all problems have such an easy solution. No need to drown when everyone is throwing a life preserver; you feel me?"

He was right. I didn't have to decline their offers because my ego or sense of decorum told me to. I had a lot of issues to tackle, and now, because they were so generous, worrying about a place to stay and a way to get around wouldn't be on that list.

"You're right," I said with a smile of relief and gratitude. "You should be a therapist."

"I'm married to one," he chuckled. "And when I forget to stay positive, she handles that shit with a quickness."

"I appreciate all of this, thank you all," I said with as much gratitude as I felt.

Cam rose and glanced over at me. "So, you'll be staying aboard, then?" He smiled, but his eyes were sad, and I felt that in my heart.

"I just might," I said with a smile.

He looked at the others at the table, "I'm going to head to my room for a bit. I'll see you all on deck after the storm passes." He waved his hand in the air as he quickly went away.

I knew something deeper was going on with Cameron, and I was the cause of his sadness. I could tell he was grateful for the generosity of his friends, but something wasn't right with him.

"Would you all excuse me?" I said, standing up.

"Absolutely," Jake said too quickly.

"No worries," Jim said, staring curiously in the direction where Cameron disappeared.

"Relax," Collin added. "The kids are with the activity coordinator, and, trust me, they're having a shit-ton more fun than we will for the rest of the day."

"Activity coordinator?" I questioned.

"Yep," Jake grinned. "Best damn hire I've ever made on this yacht. It's practically like dropping them off at Disneyland. The only bad part is that Jacks may never want to get off this thing once it reaches Long Beach."

Jim laughed. "No shit. Addy would rather be on this yacht than my company one, and she named the goddamn thing."

The rest of the gang continued talking while I went hunting for Cameron's room.

This place was like a floating palace, and I should've known better than to go roaming these halls alone without a freaking map. I could tell the bad weather had arrived because I felt it moving a bit for the first time being on this yacht. It wasn't much, but it was enough to notice.

"May I guide you to your stateroom?" a woman asked behind me.

"I'm looking for my friend, Cameron Brandt?" I said when I turned back to find a beautiful young lady.

She nodded. "Dr. Brandt is on the upper deck. Follow me, and I'll take you to him."

I followed the woman until we reached the door that led to the outside deck of the ship, and she opened it for me.

"Thank you," I softly said.

The door opened and closed during a loud grumble of thunder, so Cam had no idea I was standing out here. He leaned against the railing on his forearms, his hands clasped together, as the rain fell into the choppy gray water below. He had one foot propped up on the bottom rail, but his attention seemed to be focused on his hands.

He was so unbelievably handsome, and I knew what I was about to do.

Skydiving in this weather would've probably been safer than trusting this man with my heart again, but here I stood. I felt years of heartache and grief fall off me like scales when I allowed myself to open my heart again to the tall, dark, and handsome man resting against this boat's rail.

Everything inside of me told me this was a good thing. This is why fate brought this man back into my life. I needed him more than I would've ever allowed myself to admit.

And, somehow, I wasn't scared.

Chapter Twenty-Nine

Cam

I loved the rain; it reminded me of the trips my parents and I took to Europe. My father always had the most exciting plans for us when we arrived, and then it seemed to rain the entire time we were there.

Not even money could ensure that my father's plans didn't fall through, and he had more money than he or generations to come could spend in their lifetimes. Even so, the rain forced a change in our plans every time.

My father never allowed the weather to ruin his mood, though. Instead, he found a way to do something entertaining, even if it was playing cards around the kitchen table as a family. And we loved it because even though daily life seemed to keep us busy and apart, little things brought us back together.

Even though my father raised me not to depend on money for happiness but to appreciate the freedom it gave, I somehow wound up doing the opposite. I'd somehow lost myself along the way, and, as Jim said earlier, I'd started to believe everything was owed to my spoiled ass.

What this boiled down to was that I always assumed I would inevitably get what I wanted because, so far, I had. I'd never met any resistance in my rise to success. Granted, it took hard work to get where I was.

Nothing had been handed to me, but I'd also stomped on people without realizing it to get there. I'd had the perfect girlfriend—total wife material—and I'd walked away because what I wanted was more important. Now that fate had brought us back together, I'd just assumed that it'd be water under the bridge and my big, heartfelt declaration of love would be enough to get what I wanted. I was wrong.

I knew I'd been selfish with Jessa, and I always felt bad about it, but I understood now that saying sorry and expecting things to work out just because I wanted them to wasn't how the world worked.

I was a piece of shit who'd walked away from a treasure, and I didn't deserve that woman one bit.

I wanted to believe that fate brought Jessa and me together again so I could make everything right and be a father to my son, but why did I think a chance at a family was owed to me?

All I could do was look out at the rain and wonder how to make the best of a bad situation like my father used to. How did people get through stuff like this and come out happy on the other side?

Maybe I needed to let it all rest. Let it go, and deal with the decision I made sixteen years ago. That led me to become an accomplished pediatric neurosurgeon, and I couldn't have any regrets about it. I made my choice a long time ago, and it came with consequences.

Fuck, I messed this shit up! I thought, standing up straight from where I'd leaned against the railing, wishing I had the courage to rejoin everyone for lunch just to be near Jessa again.

"Cam?"

My head snapped to my left, and I lost myself in her crystal blue eyes.

"Hey, Jess," I said, and I could hear the sadness in my voice.

Fantastic, Cam, be a little bitch because that's attractive, I thought, hearing how pathetic I sounded.

"Am I not Jessa to you anymore?"

Where was *this* coming from?

"You'll always be my Jessa," I said with more confidence than I'd displayed a second ago. "Always."

She faintly smiled in return, which made me nervous. Did that statement make her uncomfortable? Jesus. What was wrong with me? I was anxious, vulnerable, and insecure. I needed to pull myself together. There were way too many thoughts floating around my skull about right and wrong, and I didn't operate in these gray areas.

"That's good to know," she said.

Every ounce of nervous energy in my system faded when she spoke.

Okay, there's some balance here. Let's go with that.

The crisp, cool air cracked with the energy that suddenly radiated between us. I had no idea what'd changed with Jessa's attitude, and I didn't want to jinx anything by asking.

"Was there a change in your plans?" I questioned, wondering what brought her out here.

"Yeah," she smiled, that cute smile I remembered from long ago. "My plans to not give you a second chance have changed."

Was not expecting that. At all.

I had no idea what my expression was because I was numb with shock everywhere but my dick.

She chuckled as if she read my mind, and I was face-to-face with the boldest, most confident, and charming woman I'd ever met.

"You are so beautiful," I said, leaning against the rail, trying to pull my shit together.

She rolled her eyes because anyone who knew me knew *that* was cheesy as fuck.

"And you're so handsome."

"Are you coming on to me?"

"Maybe."

Her chin lifted, and she had a look that teased every nerve in my body. I was at her mercy, and it seemed she knew it.

"Let me guess, the whales were getting a little wild out there, and it reminded you of better times with me?"

Still cheesy, but at least I sound more like myself.

"Oh," she gave a goofy look, "that's exactly what happened."

I laughed. "Listen, I meant what I said yesterday on the beach, but I need to tell you that I know I don't deserve everything I proposed to you. The family, the happiness, all that. It was foolish of me even to consider you'd give me another opportunity when I took you for granted the first time."

"Thank you for saying that, and thank you for not pressuring me," she said, turning to lean on the rail of the ship as I'd done. "We were young then and so dumb," she laughed and shook her head, "but we did start a life together that we didn't get to finish."

"What are you saying?" I asked, knowing what she was saying but needing to hear it spelled out.

"I want to give it a shot and see what's possible between us." She turned and looked at where I stood in shock, staring down at the wind blowing through her hair. "Slowly, though. I guess I'm trying to say that I'm sorry I pushed you away so quickly. I just wasn't expecting you to say anything like you did, and it took me by surprise. It scared me."

"When has the fearless Jessica Stein *ever* been afraid of anything?" I smiled and felt the barrier drop between us.

I stepped closer to her and moved a strand of hair from her neck, letting my fingertips gently caress along her décolletage. I'd give anything to have my lips running along this warmth of her skin, to taste the sweet fragrance of her perfume.

Slow the fuck down, Cam.

Jessa's eyes never left mine, and I could see how different a woman she was from when I knew her in college. The woman who stood before me now shook me to my core. I felt her confidence and beauty, and my desire for her rose with every breath I took.

"I never stopped loving you," I said in a low voice.

Before she could answer and I could make the next move, the wind picked up and blew the moisture from the rain onto the balcony of the yacht where we stood.

Jessa squealed, and I made my move. I swept her off her feet, literally, and my next plan was to sweep her off her feet in every other sense. I had my Jessa back. I knew it, I felt it, and I was never letting her go.

That was the last thing I thought before my lips met hers.

Chapter Thirty

Jessa

I intended to talk to Cameron, not end up in his arms. My mind was begging me to stop this, but my heart spurred me on.

Cameron walked briskly into the ship to get out of the rain, which had switched directions and was blowing in on us under the covered deck. As he walked, my lips moved to his neck. He smelled goddamn good, like if you could bottle a sunrise and mix it with morning coffee on a perfect autumn day.

"Holy shit, this is *your* room?" I questioned after we'd stumbled in, all the instant love and romance out the window, taken away by the storm that howled around the yacht.

"We can discuss sleeping quarters later," he said, grabbing my hand, his eyes pleading with me to stay in the moment.

I pulled my hand from his as I checked out this stately room fit for a real-life king. "This is amazing. So, is this the part where you tell me that you're the *real* yacht owner?"

He smirked and slid his hands into his trousers as his eyes roamed around the large room.

Mine did too. This place was made up of windows, an elegant balcony with a built-in spa, a super-sized king bed, a sofa, and the hallway I'd just walked through to get here.

"This is wildly beautiful."

"You're welcome to stay and enjoy the luxury it has to offer," he grinned, watching me with a look that sent a chill up my spine.

This man was the epitome of sexy.

"Jackson," I said, stopping the forward progression of where Cam and I were headed. "I can't just run off like this."

"The kids are with the activity directors," he said with a confused yet humorous expression.

"Yes, I know that," I said, feeling unnerved by the dark expression he wore, standing across the room from me. "I can't just disappear, though. What if he has a seizure, and they're looking for me?"

While I was trying to shake the sudden nerves, Cam kept his expression as serious as it was when we were talking outside.

"First off," Cameron started.

"First off?" I said, trying to keep the conversation moving forward.

"I've already discussed Jackson's epilepsy with the staff. All safety measures were implemented for him long before we arrived yesterday."

I cocked my head to the side and smiled, "Well, thank you for that."

"I wanted you and Jacks to be comfortable. Since I specialize in epilepsy, I've got all precautions in order. And while on a yacht," he smiled and waved his hand around the room, "it's nice to have medical aid close by, if for nothing else than to feel more comfortable while knowing the hospital is not right around the corner."

"And to have a pediatric surgeon aboard as well," I teased, feeling my sudden nervousness dissipate.

"Always nice to have a doctor who specializes in the field of your medical condition aboard a yacht." His forehead creased in humor.

He crossed the room to where I stood. "Everyone on the boat has our cell numbers in case something happens." He took my hands into his strong ones, "Is this how you've been living with Jackson?"

"Living like what, not able to do anything without worrying my son will have a seizure around people who have no idea what to do?"

"Yes," he sighed. "My God." He paused and looked toward the windows where this storm didn't feel like the romantic moment of moments ago.

"Sorry. I sort of killed the moment."

"You didn't kill anything." He looked at me with touching sincerity. "I am so damn sorry you've been doing this for so long, and I had no idea. I feel guilty that I went on living a carefree life, you know. It's so unfair to you," he said before he took a deep breath and continued. "I don't want to dredge up old things, but for the sake of moving forward, I just need to say that I wish you would've told me—you absolutely could've told me at any point—that you were pregnant. We were so close, Jessa. We weren't just your average couple in college, you know?"

I shook my head. "No, we weren't. A lot of it was on me, Cam. I respected that you wanted to create this life for yourself, and I didn't want to hold you back. I guess, anyway. I didn't feel right calling you up and dropping that on you. I figured you moved on for a reason, and I didn't want anyone who didn't want me."

"Oh, Jess," he said in a sad voice. "I'm so sorry I put you through that."

I reached up to the dark stubble that defined the handsome features of his perfect face, "Let's keep the past in the past."

Everything but the ship slowly swaying in the choppy waves seemed to have stopped. Cameron's eyes were so piercing that my breath hitched in response to his expression.

"Until yesterday, I didn't realize that I'd been chasing selfish desires that would never fulfill me," he said, his thumb coming up to trace over my bottom lip. "I've never loved anything more than I've loved you, Jessa."

"Prove it," I said boldly.

His hands came up and rested on each side of my jaw, and his thumbs gently caressed my cheekbones while my heart kept a cool, steady rhythm. Thank God because I was scared for a moment that my nerves would completely ruin things.

Everything felt like it was in slow motion, though the energy between us in this room was far from that.

Cam's lips were on mine, and chills covered my entire body when our lips touched.

In hunger, I pulled his bottom lip between mine, his arms pulling me closer. Cam tasted as good as he looked, but he was not the wild man from my youth. He stood as still as a statue, allowing my lips to move from his and run along his neatly trimmed beard. I ran my hands around his taut waist and along his back, wanting more of him.

"I want you, Cam," I softly whispered when my lips reached his ear.

"I love you," was all he said, and then I was pulled into his arms, and his kiss became consuming.

This kiss was raw and explosive, and it awoke sensations I hadn't felt in my body for far too long. Years ago, I figured my sex drive had abandoned my ass for good. It may have. I knew now that it was back in full force, responding to this specimen of a man I'd missed desperately.

Our tongues met with fervent purpose, reuniting in a way that made me acknowledge how long it'd been since I'd been kissed like this as if he were memorizing me, and I found myself needing air.

I pulled my mouth from his, inhaling his masculine scent deeply and filling my lungs with oxygen. Cam seized the opportunity to bring me back into his arms and lay me gently on the large bed.

He moved his body gently to cover mine, and while I searched for air, feeling overwhelmed by sensuality, his hands carefully removed my shirt.

Thank God I wore the lace bra, I thought with sudden insecurity.

I'd long had stretch marks and hadn't made it to a gym in the past decade, which made me twinge with insecurity, knowing I was not the perfectly toned twenty-something girl he knew intimately so long ago. I even had the incision from the C-section to prove it. I didn't like to think of myself as insecure, but I was human, and the thought of being compared to my younger self was starting to freak me out.

"Jess?" he questioned. He sensed my brief disconnection, and he looked at me with curiosity.

I reflexively made an X with my arms over my chest, hiding my saggier-than-he-remembered breasts. A lot had changed in my body since I'd had our son, and I was ashamed that I didn't have the confidence not to care.

Cameron seemed to have read my mind, and with a gentle smile, he moved one of my arms from covering myself.

He removed my other hand and smoothed his thumb over my nipple, hardening it. I watched as he licked his lips, his eyes studying my hard nipple, then he gently placed a kiss on it through my bra. Finally, his lips gently glided over my bra and across my chest to my other nipple.

After placing a tender kiss on it, he smiled at me, "You do not need to hide your body from me, baby," he said in a low voice. "You are perfect in every way."

I licked my dry lips and smiled. I didn't know what to say, and the pulsating situation between my legs made me not want to say anything that might end this.

Cameron's lips returned to my neck, and I relaxed beneath him again. All it took was Cameron's lips to run down the center of my neck in hunger to let the ecstasy take over.

Cameron's hands went possessively up my arms, bringing them up and into the pillows above my head. He settled his body between my legs, and I felt his hard cock against my aching sensitive parts. I softly moaned as Cameron's lips moved down the center of my chest.

His kisses became greedier as his lips claimed my body, blazing a fiery trail down to my abdomen.

His lips reached my incision scar. "Fucking perfection. God, I love you," he whispered, his hot breath kindling the fire his tongue created while tasting my body.

All I could do was moan and writhe beneath the man as he confirmed that no matter what changes my body had gone through over the years, he still craved me as he once did.

My legs fell open as my ass pressed into the bed, my stomach arching up, my entire body wanting more of this.

All the dormant sexual energy was returning to life in me at full speed, and it felt like I could orgasm without help.

Cameron gently removed my panties, then his mouth went to my inner thigh, prompting a slight current to jolt inside me in anticipation of what he was building up in me.

I moaned softly, and Cam took that as permission to cover my clit with his mouth.

Holy fuck! It was so sensitive that one would think I'd never experienced this before. I chewed on the corner of my bottom lip while Cameron's mouth and teeth gently worked the sensitive area between my legs.

I was dripping wet and coming undone as Cameron satiated his hunger.

I need him inside me, I thought, reaching down and grabbing a fist full of his thick black hair.

Cameron groaned and the subtle vibration escaping the man's mouth covering my pussy sent me over the edge.

My heels dug into the surface of the bed while my hips moved off the bed in pleasure. Cameron's tongue moved away from my clit and into my opening. I gripped the comforter of the bed, holding on for dear life while Cameron slid his tongue in and out of my sex.

I hadn't come like *that* ever.

Once the violent ripples of my orgasm subsided, I reached for his head and forced his eyes to meet mine.

"I need you inside me," I nearly growled.

Cameron and I smiled at each other. Our souls had been apart too long and were finally reunited as they should be. This was my man; *this* is what I'd needed, this closeness and security.

I felt loved, beautiful, and glorious, and it wasn't just from the orgasm. It was because I felt treasured.

Without another word, Cameron's body was now covering mine. I braced myself, knowing this was just the start of a new beginning with the man I loved so desperately.

Chapter Thirty-One

Cam

Jessa's eyes were glossy and so riddled with the ecstasy that I'd nearly come after watching the pleasure rip through her. The taste of her sex on my mouth drove me to seek more, and my cock ached with the need to feel her.

Her legs fell open while she moaned and licked her perfectly plump lips. I needed more, I wanted more, and my desire fueled a wilder side of me that began taking over.

I positioned my cock to line up at her slick entrance, all while my eyes focused on her tranced ones. I slid my fingers into her opening, and feeling her slippery wetness forced a spark of energy throughout my chest and into my balls.

I've never felt this fucking turned on before, I thought as I managed to rein in my sensual appetite so I could last beyond entering her. After all these years apart, there was no way I would ruin this.

I rolled my slick fingers up and down my shaft, my dick sensitive as fuck, and Jessa consumed everything in my mind as she panted while coming down from her orgasm. I dipped my head and took one of her full breasts into my mouth, rolling the tip of my tongue around her hard nipple.

She's perfect.

My dick was pulsating and dripping when I lined it up to her hot sex. I lifted my head, her hands bracing herself and holding onto my hair while she smiled, luring me in. I licked my now dry lips and moved my hips forward.

Jessa's hands went under my shoulders, and her fingertips pressed hard into my back as I gently pushed my cock in further.

Oh, fuck yes. Yes. I was so fucking sensitive that it was taking everything in me to hold back now. I didn't want to take my thoughts elsewhere, though. I wanted my eyes on hers while our bodies molded into one, ending the years of separation that should have never happened.

I licked along the center over her chest, pushed further in, and was doing great until her tight pussy clenched hard around me. I was in deep, but not deep enough.

"God, I love you," she whimpered as I slowly moved in.

This felt too good.

My breath caught, every muscle in my fucking body tensed, and I felt an orgasm creeping up, trying to bring me over the edge before I could even enjoy a second of this.

"Fuck, fuck," I spoke.

Jessa groaned while I gripped the base of my dick, stopping everything right then and there. My forehead collapsed on her shoulder, and my eyes rolled into the back of my head; I had to take a knee and reset, or it would be over before it started.

Once things were mildly under control with no threat of a pre-ejaculation incident, I gently kissed along her shoulder, moving slowly inside her.

"Cam," she breathlessly said, her voice so tantalizing that all it made me want to do was love her like this for the rest of my life. "Look at me, handsome."

I licked my lips, fully in control now, and brought my eyes to meet hers. "I love you so much," I said, so damn serious I shocked myself.

"I love you," she said, her eyes filled with more ardor than I'd ever seen in them.

My lips captured hers, tasting the sweetness of the kiss I'd missed for too long. Once I'd pulled my shit together and got it all back under control, things progressed to the next level.

Jessa moaned a throaty yes when I moved in and out of her more fluidly than the virgin-like movements I'd started with.

The sensations of her warm pussy clenching and releasing my cock pulled me under a spell of sheer ecstasy and desire. My mouth captured hers, my tongue forcefully exploring while I continued to claim this beautiful woman with everything I was.

Jessa whimpered, panted, and sighed blissfully while she clung to my back. I slid my knee under her leg, my lips sucking onto her bottom one as I thrust in and out in faster movements.

"I want you deeper, baby," I said, pumping harder.

"Fuck," she moaned as she clenched her hands over my ass.

I watched as her head fell back and her arms went up over her head. My tip found her deep spot, and I smiled with the pleasure it gave me.

Jessa was wet and writhing beneath me while her mouth fell open, gasping for air. I massaged my dick against the hard surface of her deep spot, forcing curse words from her lips. I was stoned as fuck, watching her claw the pillows above her head.

My eyes were fixed on her breasts as they bounced with each movement I made, but I wanted to see that look on her face again. The look that told me this was the only place she wanted to be for the rest of her life.

Fuck yes, baby, I thought, pumping harder in, knowing her pussy was clenching and begging me for more.

My eyes felt heavy with desire. My cock was locked and loaded, ready to end this the right way and fulfill my only aching desire since I saw her beautiful body for the first time in too long.

"Give it to me, Jessa," I urged, needing her to let it go so I could follow.

The buildup was getting painful, even though I didn't want this to end. But I knew I had the rest of the night ahead of me, back-to-back sessions, with the current desire I felt.

"Oh," she said, then bit down on her bottom lip. "Cam." She thrust her hands back in my hair, nearly pulling it out and bringing a sliver of pain that forced a spasm through my balls and into the base of my cock.

My dick started pulsating, and I hung onto this incredible feeling. Holy fuck, this felt amazing. A vibration radiated throughout my body, tightening my abdomen as I worked Jessa's pussy into a spasm.

"Deeper, Cam. Deep." Her lips pinched together, and then she gripped my face.

The eyes of the woman I was hopelessly in love with met with mine. They were severe but desirous. I felt a chill run down my spine, an electric current flowing throughout my body as I pulled the orgasm out of Jessa to meet with me.

I pumped harder, and my balls tightened. Finally, I groaned as I captured her mouth and threw my ecstasy and release into our kiss and her perfect body.

We moaned and moved together, riding out this pleasure and rekindling a romance that was put out by the bullshit of my selfishness.

Never again, I thought, feeling cum explode out of me and into my girl.

I growled into Jessa's mouth, my tongue massaging against hers, imagining it being her clit. I grew wild with a hunger for more. I wasn't stopping here. I wasn't done reminding Jessa who the only man in her life should've been.

God, I loved her...I really did. And more than I ever thought possible. But this was just the prelude to what I would do to show her I would never again take my treasured gift for granted.

Chapter Thirty-Two

Jessa

My body was covered in chills as I felt the last of the most powerful orgasm yet rip through me. Everything was throbbing, awake, and alive.

It seemed apparent that I hadn't lost my drive; I'd just been with the wrong man. Women were emotional creatures, and the emotional connection that Warren and I once had was long gone, so all the hormone supplements I'd been taking to regain my libido were a waste of time.

I felt now, more than ever, that my love for Cameron had never subsided. It just faded into a black abyss, where all my hope for ever having a future with the man had gone after he left me. But our souls apparently saw it differently. After having this man inside me, seeing his transfixed eyes as he went over the edge in absolute ecstasy, it told me that this was right, we were right. And as Cam's lips kissed tenderly along my neck and over the base of my throat, I felt complete.

"I love you," Cam whispered, his lips on my chin as he continued to move his softening dick slowly inside of me. "You feel amazing."

I ran my fingertips over his shoulders and the lines of his muscular arms. "You don't feel too bad yourself," I teased with a lazy laugh.

His body shuddered when my fingernails ran down his sides, exploring the man's perfect body.

The rain was pounding outside, and everything felt so cozy and right. There were no regrets, no worries, and no concerns. It was just Cam and me, renewing a love that was once dead and gone.

"Fuck!" Cam moved away as if my body had electrocuted him. "God, I am so sorry," he said, rolling onto his back and covering his eyes with his hand.

"Did I miss something?" I questioned, perplexed.

"No condom," he said as he held both hands over his face.

"Well, you promised to love me, and I think you might have even proposed marriage at one point while you reached the second orgasm." I frowned in concentration as his shocked eyes met mine, "Yeah, that was it. It was the second time you came. That's when the proposal happened."

"Jessa," he said, exhaling, "you're not freaked out by that?"

"I should be," I shrugged. Maybe I was high from having so many orgasms in a row. I didn't know, but I was giddy as fuck. "I think you're freaking out enough for the both of us, though."

He rubbed his forehead, staring up at the ceiling. "If you get pregnant again..." He closed his eyes and pinched his lips.

"What's the matter, Dr. Brandt? Are you scared?" I teased.

I'd taken birth control pills religiously since Jackson was born, and I had no reason to believe they'd fail me now. Besides, I didn't have the emotional capacity to worry about something that wasn't a guaranteed issue. I had enough real problems without inventing problematic scenarios and worrying about them.

I felt happy for the first time in a long time, and I loved this feeling. I loved feeling unafraid and just fucking delighted. I had to hang onto this for as long as the feeling stayed with me.

He looked at me, and a smile turned on one corner of his mouth. "Far from scared, beautiful," he said as he turned on his side to face me, his cock becoming firm with the movement alone.

I bit down on my bottom lip, seeing the length of his beautiful dick, the one thing that rocked me right over the edge without help from anything else. Yes, I'd been with a few men before and after Cameron, and no, they couldn't bring me to orgasm like he could.

His fingers ran over my hips as I lay there, facing him. My sex spasmed, and I smiled, watching his cock return to attention.

"Miss him?" Cam said, having always referred to his dick as another person.

I nodded, and my eyes met his. "More than I knew," I said, arching an eyebrow at him, feeling his hand move over my ass and pulling me closer to him.

"That's not surprising. I'm fairly confident nothing has been able to take his place," he said with a laugh and a lingering kiss on my nose.

"Well, I wouldn't say that." Hell no. I wasn't giving him *this* much this fast.

"Oh?"

"Oh, is right. Mr. Lucky-Dick has had some stiff competition," I said, widening my eyes in humor.

Cameron's eyes narrowed. "Then I suppose you and I will be on this yacht an entire week, not leaving this room until I'm assured all this competition, which I was foolish enough to allow, has been erased from your memory, and you become obsessed with me again."

Cam and I always had fun together, doing the stupidest shit, laughing, and not taking everything seriously. I always felt young and fearless with him, and I loved having these feelings returning to me again.

Most couples' post-coital pillow talk wouldn't consist of their previous sexual dalliances, but this was Cam and me. The best part was wondering if the other was being serious or just fucking around, and with Cam, he was always fucking around.

I laughed at his eyes as they studied mine. "I don't know," I said, my eyes wandering to the corner of the room, "I got pretty creative after you left for that other college."

He propped his hand up and rested his head against his palm. "Pretty creative, eh?"

"Yup," I said with a smack of my lips, "I had an orgasm so wild, I was seeing stars." I laughed at how stupid that sounded.

Cameron licked his lips. "Really?" His eyes grew hungry. His dick was at full attention as he settled himself between my legs again. "Time to up that game, baby," he said, his eyes fixed with purpose.

At some point, we were going to have to discuss where the fuck we were going to take everything from here, but right now, I just wanted to feel these feelings with my Cam again. And with Cam, more rounds *always* equaled better sex.

The sound of a phone buzzing in the room made my body jerk awake.

"Oh shit!" I said, my heart pounding, having absolutely no sense of time. "No, no, no," I chanted as I shot out of bed, nearly running into the sliding glass doors to my right.

"Jessa," Cam said, coming out from nowhere. I covered my heart and jumped back in my panicked state.

"Jesus! Say something before you just manifest from thin air." I ran a clammy palm over my forehead. "How long have we been here?"

He'd just taken a shower. His hair was wet, and a white towel was wrapped perfectly around his waist.

Damn, you're so fucking hot! I thought.

"Nope, not going there." I held my finger up. "We're not having another round. I have to find Jacks, and I need to find my goddamn phone," I said in frustration, totally fucking out of it.

Cameron pinched his lips, then licked them in the Cameron-style of maintaining his composure while I was losing my shit. Jacks was most likely looking for me, and, of course, he would find me with his *doctor*.

Shit, this is not good.

Cam walked over to show me it was his phone that was blowing up. He waved the phone at me. "I'm on a group chat with the dipshits on this yacht," he said, looking at his phone. "They're blowing it up because you and I went missing about two hours ago." Then, he laughed, "Collin and Jake have bets going like the dumbasses they are."

I knew my eyes were bulging out of my head. "Well, isn't this just super?" I said, finding my shirt had fallen to the floor. I picked it up and pulled it back on, "Where are the rest of my damn clothes?"

Cameron let out another laugh.

"You think this is funny?" I questioned, angrier than a wet hornet.

"I think you're the most adorable, sexy woman I have ever known." He leaned against the desk that was situated across the room. His arms were crossed as he watched me fidget with my jeans, struggling to think. "Jacks texted," he said casually, and I froze. "It's what woke me up after I dozed off, holding you in my arms."

"What did he say? He's probably blowing my phone up."

"He mentioned he wanted flying lessons or something like that." Cameron shrugged, "I texted him back and said it was up to you. Then we went back and forth." He tilted his head to the side while all my panicked movements stopped, and I suddenly felt like I could dress without hurting myself.

"You went back and forth?" I said with a half-smile.

I loved to see this look on his face. He looked so youthful—happy—like everything was right in his world.

He nodded. "Uh, huh," he said, putting his phone on the desk and crossing his arms. "We got to texting about some plays that badass quarterbacks such as ourselves, make in the game."

I smiled, "I find it lovely that the two of you hit it off like you did, you know?"

He rose from where he leaned against the desk. He crossed the room, and then I was in his arms, and he kissed my forehead. Then, he pulled back to where his eyes could meet mine, "I find it astounding that he pulled off a quarterback sneak play that I thought only *I* knew."

"Which is?" I asked. Cameron's eyes were focused on me, but I could tell his mind and heart were with the conversation he and Jacks had on text.

"It's the one where the defense is ready to blitz after the snap, and instead of me trying to jump on the line and get the extra yard for the touchdown, I took the snap, flipped it to the running back, and he ran it in for the first down or touchdown."

I laughed. "I know which one you're talking about. He ran that in double overtime last season. They scored and won the game."

"Absolutely inspiring," he said with a laugh. "Unfortunately, I had to crush the kid's ego by mentioning I'd run the same damn play."

I chuckled, "Yeah, I think Jacks figured he made that play up."

He looked at me, his striking blue eyes glittering with excitement. "So strange how genetics work. You know?"

"I agree," I said. "There have been many times where I've seen you in him out on that field."

His face grew sad. "I hate that I've missed so much." He shook his head as soon as my mouth dropped open to protest, "No, I understand why, but I still hate it. And I hate that I walked away from you." His hand tenderly ran along my jawline, "I fucking walked away, allowing who knows how many men to come into your life and pretend that they could love you as much as I did and will."

"I think we can make up for that," I smiled at him. "We will."

He grinned. "You bet your sexy little ass we will." He kissed my nose, "As much as I want you and Jacks to enjoy the rest of your time on this yacht over the next week, I'd think it would be nice if you both came back with me tomorrow. No pressure, but I wanted you to know how I feel."

"Well, I hadn't decided what we would do yet." I covered my eyes, "Shit! How are we supposed to tell Jacks any of this?"

"What, that I'm his father, and I'm the reason he's a little badass?" He ran his hands up my back reassuringly, "Or that his mother is fucking his brain surgeon?"

I rolled my eyes, "Turns out, both things may need to be discussed since they equally relate and hold significant value in his life."

"Why don't we go with the flow?" he suggested. "There's a lot to consider with the surgery. His rehab will be a process as it is, and we need him in high spirits, with no distractions. I would suggest not giving him any added concerns regarding his doctor being his biological father and his mother giving his dad second chances after he fucked it up the first time."

"You don't know Jacks, though, Cam," I argued. "This kid has a hopeful heart of gold. He's the most selfless kid I know. He's so positive about everything."

I brushed his finger over the top of my nose and smiled. "Like his mother," he bent and kissed my forehead, "however, I see a lot of myself in that boy, and when it came to my mother, I was extremely protective."

"Yeah, well, as you just said, Jacks has my blood running through his veins, too," I said with a smile.

He shook his head. "I see how he is with you," he smiled. "He loves his mother very much, and if he learns I hurt you, he may not trust me with the surgery, Jessa. I'm not sure I want to take that chance."

I stepped back away from Cameron, suddenly stressed about this predicament.

"Why can't things just be normal? For Jacks? For me?" I said mainly to myself, walking towards the sliding glass windows.

I folded my arms and leaned my forehead against the window, staring out at the vast ocean. Why couldn't anything in my life be fucking easy? I got a taste of living carefree and happy for a couple of hours with Cameron. It was heavenly and blissful, probably the only reason I dozed off and woke up, forgetting where I was.

I needed that. I needed to let go and live dangerously, and for the first time in sixteen years, I needed to feel this man's loving attention.

And now, there was another fucking mountain I did not want to climb.

Cam's arms went around my waist, and I felt the warmth of his bare chest against my back as he leaned over me, his lips pressed onto the top of my head. "We'll manage this together, Jessa, but I don't want to stress out Jacks about anything. I may be wrong in my assumption of his reactions to our history and present situation, but if I'm not—I don't want to find out what happens if I'm right."

"I understand," I answered, letting my head fall back against his chest. "One thing at a time." I let out a breath, thankful I was in his strong arms and feeling the love he kept professing to me. "I'm glad I have you back. I've missed you more than I knew."

His embrace was tighter around me. "I will never hurt you again. Let's work together to get our son healthy, and we'll worry about making announcements later."

I inhaled deeply. "I love hearing you say *our son*," I said, rubbing my hands over his forearms.

"I love saying it," he said. "I know this will sound cheesy as fuck, but the truth is that I feel like I'm whole now. I have my family. This is the most unexplainable feeling in the entire world."

I wanted to add to what Cam said but staying silent felt right. I knew exactly what he was saying. I probably felt it more than he did. Many nights I'd cried myself to sleep, wishing I'd had him in my and Jackson's life. One of them being the night Jacks was born. I would've given anything to see the look on Cam's face when his newborn son was placed in his arms.

There were many things I'd found myself wanting Cam to be there for, but I permanently moved away from those thoughts because they were too painful. I'd moved forward, and when those thoughts hit me, it was like taking ten steps back.

I wanted to tell Jacks everything, but I was all for following Cam's advice and keeping away from all stressful situations. Learning his doctor was his bio father would certainly trip him out, and of course, Cam was right. Jacks was very protective of me, but I knew in my heart that my boy wanted his mom to be happy.

Chapter Thirty-Three

Cam

I'd love to say that having my lady back in my arms felt like I'd never lost her, but I could sense the change that time had caused. It wasn't a bad thing, but something haunted me, knowing I'd missed so much.

A week ago, I wouldn't have given a fuck about the time and distance between us. I would've just been grateful that this beautiful woman and my son were in my life, and I would do everything in my power to keep them happy until the day I checked out of this life. However, now I was having a strange download of emotions, filling the void I'd never known existed without them in my life.

"Hey, man," Collin said as he joined me, eating lunch alone in the hospital cafeteria.

"Sup?" I said, bringing my napkin in both hands to brush over my mouth while I swallowed a bite of pizza.

"Jake would kick your ass for eating that pizza, you know?" he laughed, sitting in the chair across the table from me.

He opened a plastic container of fruit, and then my eyes moved to his salad and a plate of chicken and broccoli.

"Jake isn't *my* best friend, though," I rose my eyebrows at the healthy food he arranged in front of him, "and unlike your ass, I'm not looking to fuck him, or impress him, or whatever the hell you're trying to prove with all of that healthy shit you're eating."

Collin laughed as he forked a cherry tomato and popped it in his mouth with his usual shit-eating grin. "Don't you worry about what Jakey and I have going on behind the scenes," he shook his head.

Jake was anal about the food we ate, but no one ever argued with him. He was cutting people open and working on hearts all day, and ninety percent of his patients had issues due to their unhealthy eating and lifestyle habits. That was his life. My life and focus were on fixing brains, but I'm sure if I knew there were lifestyle changes we could take to prevent brain tumors, or anything else, I'd ensure everyone I knew took the proper precautions.

"So, Jessa returned with you and left her boy on the yacht, eh?" Collin questioned with a knowing grin. "What happened when you both disappeared for those few afternoon hours during that rainstorm?"

"Nothing," I shrugged. "We were just catching up and going over details about Jackson's surgery."

"Bull-fucking-shit," Collin said, poking his fork into his fruit bowl. "I'm not an idiot, nor are the rest of us. You walked off from lunch like a little bitch, and Jessa was hot on your heels soon after." He took another bite of salad, nearly inhaled it, then arched an eyebrow at me, "Do *not* tell me she felt sorry for your ass and took you back."

I chuckled, "And if she did?"

"I would probably kick your ass because it was too easy for you. I walked through hell and back—my balls singed by the flames—to get my girl. Jim slept in the lake of fire to get Avery back, and Jake—well, that fucker lived in hell for quite some time, praying for a lifeline to get Ash back. But you?" he waved his fork in circles in front of my face, "nothing."

I took another bite of pizza and held my hands up, "Maybe because I'm better looking than you assholes?"

"Funny. Now, spill it. What's up with you two? Is everything cool?

Does the kid know you're his dad?" Collin's pager went off, and I laughed. "Fuck! I have to go. Goddammit, you're not getting out of this so easily. Tonight," he pointed at me, "we're all going to Darcy's, and you'll be there too."

"Can't," I said, standing with him. "Jessa and I are heading out in my Cessna."

Collin held his tray, his eyes studying mine. "Damn you, Brandt," he laughed.

"Me?" I said, walking with him to dump our trash in the bin.

"Yeah, you. Always a fucking mystery. It makes me want to kiss you sometimes."

I rolled my eyes. "Get in line," I said, laughing and following Collin out of the cafeteria. The rest of the guys knew something was up between Jessa and me, but I wasn't ready to talk about it or confide in anyone yet.

I just wanted to enjoy this time. Jacks begged his mom for permission to stay aboard the yacht, so we had precious alone time that we wouldn't have otherwise, and I didn't want to squander it.

I'd planned to take her on my plane to somewhere unique and special. All I wanted was to hold her and smell the rich fragrance of the floral perfume she wore. Now I was second-guessing the whole plane idea. She'd be in the seat behind me, and I wouldn't have her eyes to stare into. Her neck to kiss.

I missed her already. I didn't want to spend another second away from her because I'd wasted too much time already.

* * *

"You've got to be kidding me," Jessa said as I rolled up to the private airport. "It's like you're trying to get dumped by *thumbs-up emoji* or something."

I grinned, bringing the back of her hand to my lips. "Shall we not revisit that damn emoji breakup scenario? I already feel like I've sorta got one foot dangling in hell while I'm back with you, if I'm honest."

Shit! That didn't come out right.

"Oh?" she laughed and then became quiet when I rolled up in front of the massive private hangar where I kept my airplanes. "I'm sorry. I had no idea that being back together—"

"Not what I meant," I smoothly cut her off, knowing what she was going to say. I twisted in my seat and placed my hand on her headrest. "It's just that *my previously normal* routine at work *never* consisted of pining away like some bitch all day at work. It took a lot of monumental effort to stay focused and not just think of wanting you in my arms," I said.

She arched an eyebrow at me. "Nice, try," she said with a shake of her head. "Jacks tries to lie his way out of saying stupid shit all the time. So, you'll have to come up with something better than that."

I met her adorable challenging expression with one of my own. "I'm not bullshitting you. You've consumed my thoughts all day. All I've thought about was wanting to get the fuck out of there so we could be in this moment now. It's hell because I have you back in my life, but when I'm away from you, you're all I can think about. You, of all people, should know that is out of character for me."

"And you, of all people, should know it's out of character for me to go flying in some private aircraft." She exhaled, seeing the blue and white Cessna parked front and center in the hangar. She fanned her hand out in front of her. "Tell me, have I *ever* given you the impression that I would enjoy flying in an aircraft that most likely has a high death percentage?"

"No," I shrugged, looking into the hangar, and admiring my favorite aircraft. "However, the Jessa I remember was daring and bold. I wouldn't think you'd mind it. And they don't have a high death percentage."

She narrowed her eyes at me. "One death is enough for me. Shit, Cam. I seriously don't want to do this. I'm already stressed about leaving Jacks on that yacht, knowing I'm lying to him about working. In reality, here I am *with his father*, whom I haven't told him about, on some death-wish date. Why can't we be a normal couple and go get an In-N-Out burger and watch a movie or something?"

I laughed. "God, I love you." I shook my head, trying to get serious because Jessa could level my ass with a stare alone, and I didn't want to upset her.

"That's why we're going up in a tiny death trap? If I'm honest, what is scaring the shit out of me is seeing that look on your face and knowing that somehow, I'm going to give in."

"Listen," I said, remembering there was a good reason I wanted to take her up in the aircraft, "I'm not trying to scare the shit out of you. If you don't want to go up, we don't have to. I get that. But I also know that with the difficult decisions coming up, fear is most likely taking over your mind, and I want you to be unafraid, no matter what happens. You can face your fears and have no regrets. You and I can face scary shit together and know that we're going to be okay." I looked back at the plane, "besides, I have a feeling you will certainly thank me later for this."

"You're not getting laid, and that's a fact. So," she opened her door, "if this is a challenge for me, *Dr. Brandt*, I'll take it. I've thought a lot about Jackson's surgery today after having time alone for the first time in a while, and yes, it scares me. I can safely say it scares me more than this plane ride."

"You'll want to fuck me after this," I grinned at her. "Who doesn't find a pilot sexy?"

"Oh, God," she said dryly and rolled her eyes, prompting me to laugh. She swung her door open with agitation, and I followed. "Isn't this just lovely?" she said, planting her hands on her hips and staring at me through her dark sunglasses. "Not only am I risking my life by going up in this thing, but I'm going up with a pilot who's a douche."

I chuckled. "Trust me, it's a turn-on," I said, thinking I'd play with her a little.

"Maybe for some brainless broad who thinks looks and skill make up the qualities of a good man," she arched an eyebrow at me, holding some sassy pose. "I, on the other hand, am *not* that woman. It takes a lot more than this shit to impress me."

I pinched my lips together in humor, "Well, we will just have to see about that, won't we."

"Fuck it," she seethed, and I could hear the trepidation in her voice as she stopped following behind where I walked to the aircraft.

"Stop stopping, gorgeous," I said, walking toward where I would prep the plane and get her up in the air before she changed her mind and all the plans I'd made for us tonight. "I think you'll enjoy just being together the next day or two, but I need you to get into this plane."

"Next two days?" she questioned. "How did you manage that?"

I turned back to her. "Long story short, I have a light workweek. The *one* surgery I'm most concerned about relates to the woman I love more than anything in this world, and I want to spend some time with her and help her decide with a clearer mindset."

"So, you just took the week off work?" she questioned.

"No," I said, "I took the next three days off work. I've got a couple of doctors who switch shifts with me all the time. Trust me, I've taken on a shitload of extra hours for those chumps. They owe me."

"Good grief, Cam," she finally smiled. "What the hell am I going to do with you?"

"Fuck me like I know you will after I take your cute little ass up in this plane," I taunted her. "Come here, beautiful." I walked toward her and pulled her into my arms. "If I'm wrong, and you hate me after this is all over, kiss me now, so I at least have that."

She stepped back, keeping me at arm's length, "If I enjoy the ride—and that's a pretty big fucking *if*—I may or may not kiss you then." Her face fell again, and she looked at the plane, shaking her head, "I can't believe I'm even entertaining this shit," she said to herself. "Just keep us alive. I really do love living life, and I never really saw myself going out in a fucking plane crash."

"Yeah, we need to get this up in the air," he said. "The more you keep telling yourself that's what's going to happen, the higher the chances are that it will."

"Let's just get this over with," she said.

I couldn't resist the woman any longer. I took two steps, and Jessa was in my arms before she could react.

This is precisely how I preferred to start this trip. My lady in my arms, her kiss as fierce as mine, on our way to one of the most beautiful places in the state.

Chapter Thirty-Four

Jessa

It wasn't until about an hour into this beautiful flight that I finally relaxed. Cam joked and played *tour guide* while flying over the farmland beneath us, and of course, with his usual sense of humor, it cracked me up and loosened me up some.

The plane flew smoothly, and when Cam wasn't teasing me, I could sense he was lost in the soothing feeling of gliding over everything. It also helped when I heard him do all his pilot talking with air traffic control, proving even more that he knew what he was doing and took it very seriously.

I felt a deep love for him after I allowed him back in again and a sense of safety in knowing everything would be okay. One of the things I loved about Cameron was that regardless of how stressful the situation was, he always found a way not to let it get to him. He was so positive about everything, and when things became overwhelming, he got out of his head about it. The man never dwelled on anything; he thought about it, gave it some airtime, then moved on.

It's also probably why the guy would never go gray, either. Shit like this was par for the course with Cam, flying to God knows where on a whim to face a fear and have a little fun while doing it. I had to give him credit, though. Getting off your butt and doing something was better than sitting around all day thinking and worrying. And, of course, when you *did something*, it had to be out of your comfort zone, or what was the point? That's how Cameron Brandt saw the world, and it's why I was falling harder and harder for him while doing the one thing that'd made me angry earlier.

He got me out of my comfort zone and out of my head. It was insane how much lighter and brighter the world seemed when you took your challenges head-on.

We landed smoothly on what seemed like a runway in a residential neighborhood, and I was confused.

"Where are we?" I questioned, trying to figure out how an airport could fit into a neighborhood.

"My buddy's hangar is just up here," he said, turning the plane to drive up some street.

"No, *where* the hell are we? This makes no sense," I said with a laugh as we passed by homes with driveways with planes.

"Fresno," he said. "Remember we always wanted to go hike Yosemite? Where the rock climbers climb up—"

"No," I said flatly. "I know the place you're talking about. I've already watched that *Free Solo* movie, and my ass is not scaling the face of a giant granite rock. I've faced enough fears for a lifetime by flying up here, and there's no goddamn way I'm doing something like that."

"Good because I, too, have no plans to plummet to my death from the face of El Capitan," he said, his voice reflecting that he was focused more on driving this plane up a driveway than convincing me to go rock climbing.

"I never know with you. So, I'm just making that clear."

"Nah," he said with a laugh. "I think the hiking trails up to the waterfalls would be incredible. Leisure shit like that is a healthy way to shake off stress. I mean, I'm not in the mood to kick my own ass over the next couple of days."

I rolled my eyes. This was life with Cameron—no one ever knew what this guy was up to. He could be tricking my ass into believing he's serious about not scaling the faces of rocks until we got there, and then the next thing I know, I'd be in a harness.

Cam and I were always balanced like this. I was the reasonable one who had to keep his feet on the ground, and he was the wild one who had to get me to try new things now and then.

After Jacks had surgery, I was sure that having Cam around would be good for our son.

"I need to call Jacks," I said as Cam helped me out of the plane. "Are we leaving right now?"

"Yeah. We're just here to get my buddy's H2. It's in his garage. So let me get the plane strapped down and squared away, and we'll head out. It's about a two-hour drive from here."

"Ah," I smiled at him, "looks like you're not getting laid after being a sexy little pilot after all, eh?"

"We're not at the hotel yet, gorgeous," he teased. "I'm ensuring that you make the phone call to Jacks now, so you can sleep for the two-hour drive because you'll need your rest when we get to the hotel I reserved."

"Ah, now I know why we're not hiking tomorrow."

"Duh," Cameron said in a goofy voice, with a wink. "All right, be back in a sec. My buddy left the keys over here. He's in New York now, so if they're not here, I need to call him."

"Got it," I said.

I turned to check out the lovely neighborhood we were in. What an interesting way for people who loved aviation to live. There was always something for somebody; you just had to pick your flavor.

Three hours later, Cameron and I walked under a canopy of stars in the inky black sky above us. I clenched his hand tighter, losing myself in the scent of pine and fresh air.

"Wow," I said. "It feels like a planetarium with all these stars. I don't think I've ever felt this close to heaven before."

Cam's arm came up around me, and then he kissed my temple. "I'm insulted," he said, his lips at my ear and his warm breath sending a shiver down my spine. "And here I thought I took you to heaven more than once last night and this morning before I left for work."

"Yeah, well, the stars," I trailed off, ignoring Cam's sexual references.

"Exactly, the stars," he said as we rounded the corner and walked under large round wooden beams toward the entrance of this beautiful hotel. "You were definitely seeing stars on every round."

"Would you stop?" I teased, playfully running my hands over the hard ridges of his abdomen.

"Okay. I will handle the reservations and get our bags up to the room. I hope you brought that sexy lingerie I sent to your beach house this afternoon?"

"When you told me to pack for colder weather, I didn't assume that piece of lace was what you meant?"

He arched an eyebrow at me as we reached the front desk. "Good," he flashed a sexy look, "because I'd prefer you wear nothing at all." He looked proudly at the hotel attendant taking his card.

My mouth dropped open, and hers pulled up into a grin. I'd love to think that the poor young woman would have been used to men like Cam blurting out shit like this all the time, but this wasn't your average hotel. This place was elegant and beautiful, like the fancy part of the Titanic, and it also looked to fit that era. Circular chandeliers held candles that flickered all around. The wall to our left was lined with glass paneling, and I could only imagine what the beauty of the scenery would look like when the sun rose in this park.

"Thank you, Mr. Brandt," the woman said, handing Cam two old-fashioned skeleton keys that seemed to fit our surroundings.

Cam snatched my hand while I continued to stare in awe at the lodge-like atmosphere of this hotel. We walked by a stone fireplace you could practically fit a car in, the flames dancing and climbing up around the pile of logs placed neatly into it.

The smell of the fireplace suddenly made me feel as though we were in some grand lodge in the middle of Montana, and while I thought the plane ride felt like an escape from the stresses of the world, this was what took me away from it all completely.

"I could wrap up in a blanket and sit in one of those huge chairs in front of that fireplace all day," I told Cam.

He looked back at me and smiled as we stepped out of the elevator onto the second floor. "Thank God I ensured we had a room with a fireplace in it, then, because I don't plan on you sitting alone in a chair. You'll be in my arms tonight," he said, his voice lower.

"Perfect. At least that stops me from getting weird looks from other hotel guests," I said as I nudged his side.

When we reached our room, Cam plugged in the old-fashioned key and opened the door, moving to the side and motioning for me to enter before he did.

"Just so you know, this is *not* called the presidential suite because the name sounds fancy," Cam said as he watched me look around. "JFK and Queen Elizabeth have even stayed in this exact room."

"Not at the same time, I'm assuming," I said, soaking up the grandeur of the suite.

"When it comes to JFK, I guess you can never be too sure," Cam laughed. "Hopefully, you approve. I wanted to ensure my lady stayed in a room fit for a queen."

When I walked in, I felt like I'd been swept away into a Jane Austen novel. Cameron could've passed for my literary hero, Fitzwilliam Darcy, and I felt like Elizabeth Bennet.

"Well?" Cam questioned.

I turned around, finding the man dreamier than before. His coal black hair gave a beautiful depth to the sharp features of his face, and his piercing blue eyes were so deep that a warm sensation swarmed deep inside of me, knowing that I wanted and *needed* more.

"You're so handsome," I said, honestly and completely caught up in this fairytale moment I'd been transported into. "Thank you. Thank you for all of this."

He crossed the room to where I stood with tears in my eyes, "You are very welcome indeed."

I reached up to his face, "This all feels like a dream, you know?"

"Oh, do I ever know," he said with a smile and a kiss on my nose. "I have no idea how we managed to find our way back to each other, but I know this was meant to be. It's not a coincidence."

"You believe there was a reason aside from Jacks for us finding our way back together?"

"I know there was a reason," he answered. "We were never meant to be apart."

"I'm proud of you, though, for everything that you've accomplished in your life while we weren't together."

"Thank you, baby," he said, kissing me and laying me back on the bed as he began removing my clothes.

I didn't expect us to move *this* fast and for me to forgive him so easily. In fact, I never saw myself back in Cam's arms like this again. I guess it was all part of the fairytale, though. Everything was so perfect and so right. My anger and resentment had faded entirely, and I felt complete.

Would everyone I knew and loved call me insane for taking Cameron back so quickly? Absolutely. My parents hated him for walking out of my life the way he did, and they'd never agreed with how I handled things on my side, either. They thought Cam needed to know he was a father and he needed to help. Instead of heeding their advice, I gave up the opportunities I'd worked so hard to get, allowing him to pursue his goals. Needless to say, that didn't sit right with Mom and Dad.

My decisions were my own, though, and I didn't give a shit what anyone thought about how I handled things.

What mattered now was that we were together again, and I felt fulfilled. It felt so right that I couldn't help but become overwhelmed with emotion.

Naturally, I started crying at the exact moment Cameron was kissing along my inner thigh, his lips massaging toward my entrance where his fingers had just slid into me.

Why now?

I covered my face with my hands as the sob erupted through me. Tears that had been bottled up broke free and feeling stupid for crying made the tears fall that much harder.

"Hey?" Cam said, rightfully confused by my sudden turn in emotion. "Baby?"

I couldn't respond, but I felt Cameron at my side, pulling my naked body against his bare chest.

It took a bit for me to control the sobbing and settle into the warmth of his side before I could start taking some cleansing breaths.

"You don't have to talk about it, sweetheart," he said, his hands running through my hair as I clung to his side.

I sniffed and stared into the fireplace across the room from where we lay on the bed. Everything was quiet, relaxing, and comforting now. I needed this peace and didn't feel bad I was taking it.

I'd been strong for so long, living in this nightmare of uncertainty with Jackson's medical condition. I'd tried to navigate everything correctly, making the smart decisions—the right ones—for myself and my son.

The hardest and most troublesome decision was coming up, but strangely, I wasn't so fearful of that right now. Instead, I knew the right answer was to trust the man holding me with our son's life. I knew the mountain we would climb for Jackson's recovery was steep, but at least I finally felt like we could climb it.

Chapter Thirty-Five

Cam

Holy shit, this better not be a dream, I thought when I felt her lips around my cock. The gentle motions of my dick being pulled in and out of firm, yet soft lips, had my groin in a spasm—in a very good fucking way.

I groaned and turned from my back onto my side. I reached my hands down into Jessa's soft hair, listening to her moan, seemingly wanting me to fuck her mouth. It took a lot of restraint not to grab a hand full of hair and pump deep into her throat, but it wasn't too hard since her tongue, hand, and mouth were working together to build up these constant glorious sensations pulsating from my dick, and up to my stomach.

"Fuck, this feels amazing," I managed, thrusting gently through the tight opening she'd made for my cock to find the most pleasure.

I was half asleep and half awake, taking the utmost pleasure at this moment.

Her free hand went over my hip, and then she clenched my ass while I lay there, gently moving my body in slow motions, appreciating every sensation of wanting to come but still holding back.

I reached up into the pillow behind me, feeling euphoria consuming me in this dark room.

"You like that, baby?" Jessa asked after she'd run her tongue from the base of my shaft to underneath my tip, where my precum was dripping out.

I used more mental strength than I knew I possessed to tighten and restrain myself in response to Jessa as she began sucking and alternating that sensation with licking all around my sensitive tip.

"Hell, yes," I barely managed to breathe out between almost whimpering in pleasure and groaning through each spark of energy that jolted through me, nearly sending my ass over the edge in that instant.

Jessa used the moisture from my dick to run her hand in a tight grip up and down my shaft, and holding back was now becoming torture.

I rolled onto my back to lay flat, dropping my knee to the side and giving Jessa all the access she wanted. She followed my movement in a graceful motion and settled herself between my legs.

"Shit," I gritted out when her hand pumped my cock in perfect movements, and her tongue and mouth went to work on my balls.

Her moaning, licking, and tight grip on my slick cock sent waves of energy pulsating up my back, and I knew I wouldn't be able to hold on for much longer.

"Come in my mouth, Cam," her voice was sultry and sexy, and her suggestion was all I needed.

"Fuck, yes. I want you to take all of me," I suggested, hoping I could watch her perfect lips swallow my cock, and then my cum.

"Mm," she moaned, her lips following her tongue, covering my dick again.

Thank goodness I'd left the hall light on, so I could see a hint of her sparkling yet daring eyes as she took me with what seemed to be a hunger I could only beg for a woman to have while swallowing my cum.

The curse words that erupted from my chest while I filled her mouth with my fluid were not audible. I gripped Jessa's hair tightly as my ass nearly shot off the bed in the electric spasm that jolted from deep inside me, sending my climax deep into her throat and mouth. I'd locked eyes with her just as I let go and hadn't stopped staring into the beautiful gems the entire time.

My mouth dropped open as I moaned with each spasm. While riding out the last of this, I finally started to come down off this high. I gently moved my hips, letting Jessa continue to suck the last cum from my cock, knowing that I would properly thank her for this as soon as I got my bearings.

"How was that?" Jessa asked with an adorable giggle.

I had my hand over my forehead, trying to get the damn stars out of my head as if this was the first blow job I'd ever received.

"It was almost too good," I said when she climbed up, and I felt her naked, warm body molded against mine. I looked down, my eyes meeting hers, and arched an eyebrow at her. "I'd like to think that you perfected the art of a blow job on *me* and me alone, just now," I smirked.

She gave me a sassy look. "I didn't realize blow jobs were considered an art form that needed perfecting?"

"Smart ass," I said, smiling at her. "And yes, they are. A relationship can easily be fucked up if a partner doesn't know how to handle their teeth around a dick."

She kept a straight face, but I felt the subtle movements of her laughter where her full breasts were pressed against my chest.

"Well, then," she said, trying to be serious in response to my stupid words—words that I was spewing out while I impatiently waited for my dick to get its act together so I could enjoy this woman in every sense of the word. "I'm glad that I perfected the art. I can't imagine destroying a relationship that fate worked so hard to bring back together and ruining it," she snapped her fingers in the air, "just like that, you know?"

"Oh, do I ever know. But, I mean, if we're going to get real about what fate had to go through with *you* in all this, then, yeah, don't want to fuck that up."

"Me?" she said, sitting up and straddling my waist.

So fucking perfect, I thought, bringing my hands up to clasp around her waist, staring at her hardened nipples that highlighted her full breasts.

"Yes, *you*," I said, smiling. "Your cute little ass fought shit, but I accepted it immediately."

"Really?" she said, smiling at me. "And when would *immediately* have been for you?"

"When I first saw you at that resort," I proudly proclaimed, believing I was ahead in this game of following my heart after seeing Jessa again.

Her face twisted up adorably. "Interesting," she said, "because I remember having to hunt your ass down for you to see Jackson, and I wouldn't have had to do that if I had your number after seeing you at that resort. So, I'm assuming you're," she paused, and her eyes widened in humor, "wrong!" She leaned forward and pressed her finger against the tip of my nose.

"Bullshit," I said with a laugh. "I listened to fate, and because you didn't, I felt karma kick me in the balls."

She shook her head, and her closed lips pulled up into a smile. "You silly man," she said with a soft laugh, "but I guess you're right."

"I am right," I said. "I felt it from the first moment we reconnected."

"That, and if you gave me your number, I probably would've never called you. And I *know* I wouldn't have reached out to you *that way* for help for Jacks."

That confused me. "Why the hell not? I wished I was braver and gave you my number so you had it for that reason alone."

"Nah," she said, shaking her head. "I would've felt like I was using you for help or something."

I let out a breath, sad that I even put Jessa in a position to ever feel this way about me. I had to eat it, though. She needed to learn to trust me again after hurting her in such a selfish way.

"I understand, but the woman I met at that resort and in my office that day—desperately seeking help for her son—was bold and fearless. And in that mindset, you wouldn't have given a damn whether it seemed like you were using me or not."

She shrugged, "Yeah, that's accurate."

I smiled. "And now that fate has seen to it that we are happily together forever in each other's arms," I rolled over, bringing Jessa to lie beneath me, "I think we should show our gratitude by fucking until the sun rises and sets again."

She ran her hands through my hair, her eyes raptly looking into mine. "I love you," she softly said, and my heart nearly stopped at the sincerity of her words.

I framed her face with my hands, tilted her chin up, and pressed my lips into the center of her neck. Her fingers ran tenderly through my hair, exciting my dick about where this was going.

As I continued to kiss along her neck, inhaling the sweet aroma of her delicious skin, Jessa's legs fell open, allowing me full access to what my greedy ass wanted.

"I won't be gentle this time," I warned, needing her more now than ever.

"Mm," she licked her lips. "I was hoping you'd say that.

My lips captured her bottom one, my teeth gently tugging and pulling on it as I lined up my hard cock to her slick entrance. As I moved my hips forward, pushing into her, I watched Jessa's eyes roll back as she moaned and nearly ripped my hair out.

Fuck, that was a little too hard, I thought, sliding in and out of her in a much softer motion. I wanted to bury myself in her, to hear her cry out my name. Hell, I'd even dig the claw marks on my back. I needed to feel this woman's enjoyment of the pleasure only I could give her, but I also didn't want to pound the shit out of her and fuck up our waterfall-hiking day, either.

Jessa moaned as her legs wrapped around me, crossing at my back.

"You like that, baby?" I said in a hoarse voice, feeling a spasm rock through my entire being in response to the sensual moans this stunning woman was making.

She took my face into her hands and nipped at my chin. "Don't hold back on me. I know what you've got, Cam," she said in some erotic voice that nearly made me come right then and there. "Fuck me."

Damn, this woman would be my undoing. But she already was, if I was honest. And fuck hiking waterfalls; I was about to spend this entire day in bed, making up for sixteen years spent apart and believing I could ever find happiness in any other woman's arms.

• • •

By the time I'd come deep in Jessa, fucking her from behind in the shower, I was shocked I could still feel my legs. We'd done it all and enjoyed it with the stamina of our younger years.

I held onto Jessa's breasts, gently covering them with my hands, moving myself in and out, riding out the last of this orgasm.

Her head fell back against my chest as she stood erect, and my cock slipped out of her.

"Damn, we're crazy," she said.

I laughed, kissed her forehead, and slid my hands around her waistline to hold her. "That's what was always so good about us," I said.

"Right, and your crazy ass is playing it dangerous too, Cam," she said, turning around in the tight little shower, wrapping her arms around my neck.

"How so?" I questioned. "If you're speaking of putting my heart out there for you to crush, then, yeah. I guess maybe I am."

She smirked and ran her hands over my soft dick. "No protection?"

My eyes widened in horror. "What the *fuck!*" I hung onto that word for what felt like thirty seconds. I didn't know what to say.

"Lucky for you, I've been on the pill since Jackson was born," she said with a laugh. "I'm just messing with you."

"Jesus, don't leave a man hanging like that," I said. "You know, this whole fate and karma thing?"

"You sound a lot like Ash with all that, you know?"

"Well, I learned about that shit from her."

"About fate and karma?" she said, grabbing the soap and lathering my balls and dick up like she owned them, which she did.

"Let's hope we play it smart and not piss them off," I said, taking the soap from her hands and repaying the favor.

"It's not a problem. At least this time, if you run off on me, I know to hunt you down if I find out I'm pregnant," she said and then slapped my ass.

"Don't tease me, beautiful," I said with a smirk.

"Oh, I'm not teasing," she laughed. "Fool me once, am I right?"

I ran the soap between my hands, preparing to soap up my face, and arched an eyebrow at her. "I like this side of you. It's almost like you're my favorite little sex addict."

She laughed and playfully pulled her bottom lip bashfully between her teeth. "I think I might have a problem," she softly laughed.

"No," I answered her, then proceeded to scrub my face. I turned and rinsed, then ducked my head under the water, "there is never a problem when a woman wants my ass so much she acts like she's addicted to it—and the woman I'm referring to is you, of course."

"It better be," she said with a smile before she stepped out of the shower.

Our reunion was better than I could've dreamed, and even though I was enjoying fucking nonstop, it hadn't slipped my mind that she'd broken down directly after we'd walked into the room. I had no idea what made her sob uncontrollably until she lay staring at the fire and fell asleep.

After I'd tucked her comfortably into bed, she'd turned on her side, away from me, leaving me to wonder. My insecure and vulnerable side assumed she regretted being with me like this. I mean, why else would she be perfectly fine until we walked into this room? I seriously had no idea. Jessa was a strong woman, so I wasn't sure what provoked the tears, and I certainly didn't expect to wake up as I did, with her mouth around my cock.

I knew I should talk to her about it, and perhaps I would do just that with some room service on our balcony, staring at the majestic view of Half Dome.

That's what we would do, have some mother fucking champagne and stare at the rocks I paid good fucking money to see from the balcony of this room. Hiking waterfalls was overrated if I put it up against having these moments with Jessa. We might not find many of these moments again once we were back to reality with Jackson.

I wanted to tell Jacks about us, especially about me being his father, but I also needed that boy to be strong and ready for surgery. *By the way, I'm your dad, and your mom and I are back together* was a bomb that was entirely out of the question to drop, both in my lover man mindset and my surgeon's mindset.

In all honesty, I wanted to selfishly tell him the truth about everything. I wanted to be a family. I wanted to make up for lost time, and I wanted him to know that I, as his father, would take care of him and his mother until the end of fucking time. But that was what *I wanted*, and this wasn't about me.

All I could do now was enjoy this time with Jessa, and we would figure out the rest as it came.

Chapter Thirty-Six

Jessa

Although Cam didn't believe I'd cried my eyes out on the Yosemite trip because I felt *happy*, it was true. He didn't press me for more information, though, and I was grateful for that because I honestly had no other explanation for the tears.

Being in a place of total happiness, relief, and, I guess, just feeling like everything was right and good brought me emotionally to my knees in gratitude for where I was in life.

I was so thankful that I took this chance with Cameron. For the last month, all we'd done was enjoy our time together. Whether riding bikes on trails up the coast, watching Jacks and Cam throw the football around in front of the beach house, or sitting around the living room and watching basketball, it was refreshing and soothing to my once overwhelmed and exhausted soul.

Jacks had caught on to the fact that his doctor and I were an item, and though I expected him to flare up a little about it, the kid adored

Cameron so damn much that he was practically planning our wedding day.

I'd come very close to telling Jacks that Cam was his father because I was beginning to feel like we were lying to him these days by not doing so. I didn't, though, because I trusted Cam when he said that Jacks needed to be mentally strong to recover from surgery. He didn't need to think about anything other than working his ass off to get his life back.

"So, you guys will be gone for a week?" Jacks asked, taking my bag from the trunk and placing it on my suitcase. "You sure you're not going to Mexico to get married?"

I rolled my eyes, still unsure of leaving Jacks, but I trusted that he was in excellent care with Jake and Ash. I think Jacks was going to bounce around and visit everyone he'd simply adopted as his own—either as aunt or uncle—since Cam and I got close. We'd spent a lot of evenings during this last month being around all of them, and it brought me joy to see him develop those relationships so quickly.

"Right, because everyone goes to Mexico to get married on a whim?" I said, grabbing him and hugging him tightly. "You know you'd be the *first* to know if I was going to get married."

"What if he proposes?" Jacks said, his thumb pointing back at where Cam was discussing something with the pilot of the private aircraft.

My eyes widened at that thought. "Um," was all I could say.

"Ha," Jacks said, hugging me tightly again.

"Hey," I stepped back, "I know that for this last month, I've probably not seemed like your *normal mother,* and even though I've done some fun and crazy stuff with Cam, nobody is pushing it on the marriage stuff. I just called *off* an engagement, if you don't remember?"

Jackson laughed, "*That* was because you were marrying the wrong man."

"You just like Cam because he's fun and spontaneous and makes you feel like there are no problems in the world."

"Isn't that why you like him?" Jacks said.

More like why I love him.

"True," I answered.

"Well, I love the new side of you that he brings out. You're finally smiling all the time and enjoying your life. You're not as worried about me as you always were."

"I love this side of your mother, too," Cam said, turning back to us. "What are we talking about anyway?"

"Mom has changed because of you. She's happier, gets out more, and has fun," Jacks finished with a cheesy grin.

Cameron draped his arm around Jacks. "I agree. She seemed to be so, I don't know, serious and, dare I say, *boring* before I came into her life, don't you think?"

"Can we please go? What did the pilot say?" I asked, searching for a new subject.

"Damn, well, I guess this is goodbye?" Jacks said, his cursing taking on a whole new level since hanging around Cam's buddies.

"Shoot," I said. "Come here. Okay, Edmond will drive you to Jake and Ash's house, right?"

"Yes, and they have all my emergency contact information. I'm staying with them for the week since Jake is working in the place of that doctor who's out on paternity leave."

"Give them hell," Cam said, ruffling the top of Jackson's hair. "You can still come with us if you want. I have a lovely villa I reserved for the week."

Jacks shook his head, "You two go and have fun. Jake mentioned something about courtside tickets to a basketball game this week."

"Really?" Cam said, turning to face Jacks. "Where'd that asshole get the tickets?"

"I have no idea, but I'm not turning that shit down."

"That's my little buddy. See, I've got it all worked out so that by the time I get home, you'll be the biggest Lakers fan I know."

"Dream on," Jacks joked back.

"I'll bet you one of my surfboards and surfing lessons that you *will* love the mother fucken Lakers by the time I step off that jet," Cam said, pointing at the plane waiting for us to board whenever we finished this brilliant conversation.

"Language?" I said, staring at Cam.

"Yeah," Jacks said, punching Cameron in the arm, "watch your language!"

Cam looked at me, and I had to cover my smile.

"You realize he's staying with *Jacob Mitchell*, right?"

"Yeah, and Ash, and more importantly, little John, who will not allow vulgarity," I added.

"Do you really believe that?" Cam said, turning back to Jacks. "Enjoy letting the curse words fly in support of the Lakers when you go with Jake. I wish I could be there to enjoy a beer and the game with you."

"Unfortunately, you have to go on vacation with Mom."

"And he can't even cuss," I said.

"Whatever will I do?" Cam said, and then he patted Jacks on the arm. "Remember, Ash is bringing you in for that scan I ordered. I'll be looking at it when I get back, and you better believe your ass that I'm going to start putting some heavy pressure on you to decide on this surgery then."

"Got it," Jacks said, more deflated.

"I know it's hard, but I want you to focus on this last month. Look at the support group you have surrounding you now. We're all in this with you, kiddo," Cam said, and I could see Jackson's eyes light up a little.

"It is good to have all of you," he said.

"Jackson, are you sure you don't want to come with us?" I asked, starting to feel uneasy about leaving my son.

"Mom, like Cam said, sometimes you have to let them grow up a little."

"Yeah, Cam did say that, but that was before I remembered that I was sending you to stay an entire week with Jake."

He smiled, "I'm leaving before Mom insists I go with you guys." Jackson leaned in and gave me another quick hug before turning and walking off. "Love you."

"Love you too, Jacks," I said.

Cam brought his arm around me. "Ready to do this?"

I looked around for the luggage. "Um, what the hell happened to our bags?"

"The captain is loading it for us," he said, walking me toward the plane. "And the flight attendant already has your favorite pasta ready to serve once we're in the air."

"Holy shit, is that how these private jets work?"

"Yeah, Jim pays these guys the big bucks to ensure every need is met while we fly the friendly skies."

"Now you're just being an ass," I said.

"True," he kissed my temple. "Let's get away and have some fun."

It seemed like all I did these days was have fun, and part of me questioned whether I should. Don't get me wrong; it was an enjoyable escape from the stresses of everything—one I told myself repeatedly that I deserved—but I could sense that I wasn't very grounded.

I was out here, living my best life, but I wasn't as attentive as usual with Jackson. I think he enjoyed that part, actually, but it was a foreign feeling to me.

Regardless, I planned to find balance in my new life with Cam when we returned from Mexico. As Cam said, it was time to start putting more pressure on Jacks for this surgery. The seizures were coming regularly, which was why Cameron ordered the scans, and therefore, we needed to make a decision.

"We do need to focus more on getting Jacks more confident in this surgery," Cam said once we were on our way, climbing altitudes in the jet.

"Yeah, I one-hundred percent agree with you on that." I turned to face him on the leather couch we sat on. "Although, we're on our way to Mexico. Not quite sure how that helps Jacks to become more confident about surgery."

Cam sipped his beer. "Don't you worry your sexy little ass about *that*," he said proudly. "I've got Jake and Collin on the case in our absence."

"I will say that's an excellent idea," I smiled at him, casually sitting back and reclining, "but I'm not so sure those two aren't just going to screw off and play with Jacks, instead of talking him into losing half his brain in surgery."

He shook his head. "Those two might fuck around a lot, but they know what's at stake, and they'll do anything to get Jacks better. Trust me on that."

"How are you managing all of this time off work anyway?"

"I've only taken two weeks off in the last two months."

"And if I took two weeks off in the last two months at my previous job, they'd fire my ass."

"Allow me to correct myself since you just re-entered my life close to three months ago or so."

"I'm listening," I said, sipping my champagne.

"I planned this week to Mexico a year ago. I've only taken maybe a couple of weeks off this entire year. But taking a solid seven days in a row is unheard of with me. I was owed this. That's why I planned it a year ago when everyone was up my ass to take more than a couple of days off at a time."

"What about your trip to the resort in Jamaica?"

His eyes widened before he rolled them. "Not even a week off, but I felt like I was at that resort for a year with those morons."

"Strange."

"What's so strange about it?" he said, confused and laughing. "Most people take the vacations they earn. I usually don't, but you've been around me the few times I have."

"I guess I always expected—" I put my hand on his knee and smiled. "Don't take offense when I say this."

"I'll be offended if you don't tell me," he said, studying me with a slight smile.

I laughed. "When we were dating in college, I always wondered if I'd be some lonely wife of a surgeon who lived at the hospital. Sort of like your career would be the third person in our relationship, taking you away from me."

"Well, that would've definitely been the case," he stated factually. "And I'm glad, for that reason only, that we didn't marry young. Perhaps we split for all that time so we could truly appreciate each other when we were blessed to be together again."

"Yes," I leaned over and met his perfect lips with a tiny peck. "I think you're right. We could've been a real mess if we married young."

"Shit," his eyes widened, and he took another sip of beer. "You'd be screwing the pool boy—"

"And you'd be screwing some intern or nurse."

"And—" He went to continue our lame accusations but stopped. "Hell, no. I wouldn't be screwing anyone at the hospital. No one in the world is better than you, whether I'm a doctor who works around the clock or not. No way I would have ever cheated on you."

"I disagree," I answered, remembering when we went through a rough patch, and my friends reported that my man was spotted with a university cheerleader.

"No," he shook his head. "Brandy Hightower set my ass up. You *know* that shit, too."

"Nothing ever happened between you two?" I questioned.

"Legs," he chuckled. "That's what everyone on the team called her. That one wished she could've taken advantage of my broken heart. And yes, she tried."

"The picture the girls took didn't show you pushing her off you when she was kissing you topless."

He rolled his eyes. "Well, I was an idiot boy whose girl dumped him days before, trying to move on. So, yeah. I guess I enjoyed her tits and a kiss."

"Look at us," I stopped, took another sip of the champagne, and shook my head. "We're talking like we are back in college, and I'm the jealous girlfriend."

He put his hand on my knee. "So long as you're my girl again, I'll gladly talk drama from years past. I don't give a shit."

"Oh, trust me, it'll get old fast, and you *would* give a shit."

Let's just enjoy this vacation because once we get back, shit will get real with this surgery. Even though I plan to be involved in every part of this recovery, you will see why it was lovely to have me away from that hospital for a week."

"That bad, eh?"

"Damn place holds me prisoner sometimes. At least it feels that way."

"I'm excited to do this, you know? Just like the hospital holds you prisoner, I feel like my stress and worrying about Jacks has been holding me hostage as well."

"It's perfect, then. You and me getting a fresh start."

"By playing around?" I said, referring to our carefree lifestyle these days.

"If that's what you want to call it. Yes, beautiful," he leaned over, slid his hand over the back of my neck, and kissed me, "let's play around a little."

Chapter Thirty-Seven

Jessa

Cameron and I were on day three of our vacation, and this place was nothing short of paradise in every sense. Punta Mita was mind-blowing, to say the very least. The tropical area felt like an island of its own.

From the white sand beaches to our fantastic villa, I woke up every morning content to my core.

"What's on the list today?" Cam asked, walking out of the shower naked, knowing I would appreciate the chance to ogle him.

I pulled my hands up behind my head and into my pillows, allowing the blankets to slide down from where they covered my breasts, offering him a little something too.

His eyes sparkled like the cobalt blue color of the ocean water just beyond our master suite.

"I'll take this as my invitation," he said as he climbed onto the bed, crawled over my body, and his deliciously hard cock rubbed against my abdomen. "God, I want you, baby."

I ran my hands up his back, knowing we'd start the day like this as we had every other day since we'd arrived.

"What are you thinking about?" Cam asked as I sipped my fruity cocktail.

I pushed my hair from my face as the wind blew it around. "About how happy and relaxed I am," I said, smiling at him.

"That's because you're finally living a little, and you're not strapped down by worry and stress." He leaned over and kissed my forehead before he stood. "I'm happy that you're enjoying yourself." He shook his empty beer bottle. "I'm getting another. Do you want the bartender to make you another cocktail?"

"I think I'll switch to water. It's only two in the afternoon, and I'll be too drunk to eat dinner tonight if I keep this going," I laughed.

"Back in a sec," he said, then walked back into the villa where, for some ridiculous reason, we had a chef and bartender at our beck and call.

I brought my attention back to the ocean, watching it sparkle in so many iridescent ways, and genuinely proud of myself for not bugging Jacks this entire vacation.

The rustling of the palm trees in the breeze, and the waves crashing into the shore, were hypnotic, and I was so thoroughly relaxed that I could've fallen asleep.

"Jessica," Cameron said softly, most likely not wanting to startle me.

"Mm?" I said, stretching a little, realizing I was about to doze off from the combination of the alcohol and the soft, warm breeze.

He ran his hand over the top of my head. "Baby," he said, and my eyes widened when I saw him kneeling at my side.

Holy shit. Was Jackson right? Is Cam going to propose?

"Cam?" I said with a laugh and a smile. I was more nervous than excited at the thoughts running through my head. I wasn't sure I was ready to take this step. This careless lifestyle had agreed with me so far, but I wasn't sure I should jump right back into an engagement. "Umm, what are you doing?"

I smiled bashfully, knowing precisely what he was doing. This was Cameron, and spontaneous was his middle name.

But his expression didn't change with my smile, and it confused me. Something wasn't right; I could sense that now.

"I've arranged for the jet to be prepared to take off within the hour. The captain assured me that he would be at the airport in thirty minutes and the plane would be ready. We can't waste any time."

"Oh my God! Is it Jackson?" I screeched. It felt like a building had landed on top of me. I couldn't feel anything but pain, stabbing my heart and taking the oxygen from my lungs.

I should've known something bad would happen while I was off living in some euphoric fantasyland with Cameron. God help me! What have I done?

Calm the fuck down, and get ahold of yourself, Jessa!

"Tell me what happened," I demanded, my voice grave but controlled.

I stood up, still bracing myself for the worst.

Cameron was as solemn as I was. "We need to get to the hospital. I need you to sit down. I need to tell you about our son's condition."

"Holy shit," I cried, starting to crack.

No, no, no!

I sat down, and Cam knelt in front of me. My heart was racing, my palms were sweaty, and my legs trembled as a numbing sensation fell over me.

"No," I shot up again, practically knocking Cameron back on his ass, feeling like I had to run to get to my son but had no clue which way to go. Where was he? Was he okay? Did...did the worst happen?

"Goddammit! What happened to my son? Is he dead? Tell me right fucking now! Is Jackson dead, Cameron?" I screamed at him like a lunatic and felt completely disconnected from my body. "Where is he?"

"He's not dead, Jessica." Cameron's voice was deep, smooth, stern, and precisely what I needed to stop hyperventilating and take a deep breath.

He put his arms around me as I stood shaking and lightheaded, feeling I might faint at any second from the loud ringing in my ears.

Cameron pulled me back, steadying me and holding tightly onto me. "He is in a coma. It is *not* deadly," he continued before I could utter a word, "but I need more answers than the vitals Jake relayed. I need more information, and I need to help our son."

My brain must've confused what Cam had told me. There was no way Jacks was in a fucking coma. No way.

I stepped back into my body with a vengeance and took control. I couldn't listen to this nonsense. I needed to hear something that made sense, and this wasn't it.

"No, he's not. He's with Jake and Ash," I said. This could've easily been some crazy nightmare I'd conjured out of guilt for leaving Jacks in the first place.

"Jessa, listen to me," Cameron's voice was authoritative. "The housemaids are packing our things," he pulled his phone out of his front pocket and stared at it, "and the car is here to pick us up. We need to leave now."

"This isn't a nightmare?" I asked, feeling the weight of the truth from underneath my cloak of instant denial.

"No," he said, his voice calm and steady. "But we need to get to Jacks immediately so I can assess his condition and decide my next steps to save him."

You can't help Jacks if you are freaking out, Jessa! Help or get out of the way! My internal demands felt like they came from another person. Maybe it was my fucking guardian angel; who knows? But I *do* know that something washed over me, abating my panic and turning it into laser focus.

"Do the doctors know what happened?"

"I'm waiting on a call back from Dr. Fremont. He's the physician caring for Jackson until I return. They're running scans on him, and we'll have those results within the hour. I've already called ahead to my medical team, and they are calling in the ones I specifically requested for surgery if that is my decision. Unfortunately, I won't know more until we arrive at the hospital, so we desperately need to leave." He took my elbow in his hand, "Are you able to walk? Your legs seem a bit shaky."

"Yes, I'm fine," I said. "We need to go."

"Please, have the luggage transported to the airport. I'll ensure the next commercial flight brings them to LAX, where they will be received," Cam said to one of the housemaids frantically running around, gathering our items that were strewn all over the place.

Ring! Ring!

The sound of Cam's phone as we sat silently in the car nearly made me jump out of my skin.

"Yeah, you're on speaker, Collin," Cam said, looking at me.

"Jessa is next to you, I'm assuming?" Collin questioned seriously.

"She's right here and can hear you," Cam said.

"Okay, good," Collin said.

"Where's Jake? Was he with him?" Cam interjected.

"Jake is still with him. He told me to call you both and run interference while he stayed with Jackson and Dr. Fremont."

"I barely got vitals from Jake before I had to take the call from the hospital," Cameron said. He looked at me, "I told them to bypass calling you since you were with me."

"Fine," I answered, not caring about these details. "What happened, Collin? I need to know exactly what happened to my son."

"Apparently, he went into a seizure, and as he began coming slowly out of it, another seizure followed, and then another. His seizures were back-to-back, not even five minutes apart," Collin said. "Jake says Jackson had maybe four seizures before he fell into this comatose state. With the vitals Jake gave me, I can confirm he's scoring a five GCS."

"What the hell is that?" I snapped.

"Sorry, Jessa," Collin said. "It's the Glasgow Coma Scale."

"It's how we rate the extent of impaired consciousness in patients who may suffer any form of acute medical or trauma-like situations," Cam explained.

"Being rated a five on that scale," Collin interjected, "while not great, it simply means that yes, he's in a coma. And Cam, I'm only confirming what he's already been assessed at, given pupil dilation and his responses to sensory."

"I'll know more when I arrive," Cam said. "I'm just perplexed, trying to piece together why he went into a coma in the first place. I'm more concerned about the back-to-back seizures in a short period."

"Right and with no recovery before the next," Collin added while I felt myself growing numb again.

I couldn't believe this was *my son* we were discussing.

"It sounds like status epilepticus," Cameron said, leaning forward and pinching the bridge of his nose.

"I think that may be what occurred," Collin agreed.

Cameron looked at my confused expression. "Status epilepticus is when either a seizure lasts longer than five minutes or more than one seizure happens in under five minutes."

"How did this happen? How could *that* happen?" I questioned, dropping my face into my hands, wishing I'd been there for my son when the seizures had taken a turn for the worse.

You should've expected this instead of running off like a fucking schoolgirl with no responsibilities! I scolded myself. *You knew his seizures were worsening, and you still let him stay behind.*

The guilt echoing in my brain was deafening, but I needed to concentrate.

"His seizures had advanced and progressed, but not to the point that I thought SE would be something he'd be facing in the near future," I heard Cam say to Collin and me.

"And that was why you ordered more scans because it seemed the seizures were becoming more frequent?"

And why we should have never left him until we knew more, I thought, crying into my hands.

I felt Cam's hand running calmly over my back.

"Right," Cameron answered Collin. "The seizures were occurring more often, but definitely *not* at a rate that they would potentially consume him like this."

"After working with adult patients with Jackson's medical condition for so long, I agree with your assessment. I wouldn't have imagined SE would become an issue for him."

"But it has," Cameron answered. "I just need to determine the next steps to help him and bring him out of this comatose state."

"Do you think you may move forward with the surgery with him in the coma?" Collin questioned.

"Not sure," Cameron said. "I need to see the scans and go over labs and bloodwork. Fuck, I hate that I'm not there!" Cameron growled.

I pulled my face out of my hands, my rage matching Cameron's.

"What the fuck were we thinking to leave the country with my son sick like this?" I questioned Cameron accusingly.

"Because he wasn't sick *like this*," Cam seethed. "If I saw this shit coming, I would've pressured you both to go through with surgery after I saw his first scans."

"Bullshit," I snapped back.

"Jessa," Collin interrupted us as we escalated the conversation in the back of this SUV. "If Cameron were God, he would've known. Honestly, this happened, and it *will* be fixed. You have every right to be pissed, but please understand that the brain is a mysterious entity. We can't predict everything that will happen. We just can't. We can only control what we can control."

"If I saw Jackson's left hemisphere acting out of character and could have predicted an anomaly with his epilepsy, yes, you damn well better believe I would have mandated this surgery as his physician *and* as his father who loves him."

"I just don't understand," I answered, furious at myself and becoming angrier at the world by the second.

Cameron's hand covered my fidgeting ones. "I understand that more than you know," he said to me. "I need to see why he took such a harsh turn so suddenly," he returned his attention to Collin. "But, to answer your question, Col, I don't know if I'll operate on him and perform the surgery at this point. I can't be sure."

"I have operated on comatose epileptic patients before," Collin said, "and my surgeries were successful. If you need my input on *anything*, please know that I will happily advise."

"I appreciate that," Cam answered. "I've assisted on two other surgeries in such conditions, but the patients were stable. I need to see those scans."

"All right. If I hear anything, I'll call, but I'm sure you'll hear from Jakey first. Both of you stay strong. We're all in this together for Jacks."

"We're just arriving at the airport," Cam said. "We'll be there soon."

"I'm calling Warren, and I need to call my parents," I finally said, having had enough of hearing about this shit and knowing we had a minimum two-hour flight before we got to my comatose son.

This was an absolute worst-case scenario, and half the reason we hadn't put any stress on Jacks for the surgery was that I'd been fucking around with Cameron.

It was the entire fucking reason, actually. Cam and I were out here living it up billionaire-style, high on life without a care in the world, and that was why my son was in a coma instead of recovering from a surgery he should've had a month ago.

All this happened because I started screwing off and letting my responsibilities to my son slide. I'd permitted myself to let go of my burdens and unwind while my son's condition progressively worsened. What kind of mother does that? And what kind of a man lets her?

This was all the product of me acting irresponsibly. I was ashamed of myself and took full responsibility for my son's condition.

When my son needed me most, I was gone, and I'd never forgive myself for that.

Chapter Thirty-Eight

Cam

I could tell Jessa internally cursed the ground I walked on, but no more than I did now. Regardless, I wouldn't allow her or my emotions to interfere with the medical emergency facing us.

Although these jets flew higher and faster than a commercial airliner, the fucking thing couldn't get to LAX fast enough for me.

"Fuck, Fremont," I growled at my phone, wanting to know Jackson's official Glasgow score and what was being displayed on his scans.

Jessa remained quiet while I went through a hundred different scenarios in my mind of how this might play out, but once we were at flying altitude, she'd gone to the back bedroom of the plane and hadn't emerged since.

Ring!

"Dr. Nguni," I said, answering the Chief of Pediatrics' call before the second ring. "I'm on my way. The captain said we're thirty minutes from descending into LAX."

"Very good. I need to know where things stand with this patient," he said.

From the tone of his voice, I could tell he was referring to my relationship with Jackson. I felt a jolt of fear strike me like a lightning bolt. How could I fix Jacks if I couldn't be his physician?

"Doctor," I started, hoping to God this man would allow me to assess my son's condition and let me get straight to work.

"Dr. Brandt," he said, his voice leveling me. If there was anyone who could put my ass into the mindset it needed to be, it was Chief. He was a seventy-two-year-old veteran surgeon with nerves of steel, and I respected him immensely. "You will not land and immediately go to work. Dr. Fremont confirmed that this boy is your biological son, and you and I discussed your paternity briefly after his initial evaluation with you."

"Yes, that is all true."

"Then you understand that while your son is stable, I need you to determine the proper protocols and decide if you can make the appropriate judgment calls as his surgeon and not his father."

"Chief," I said, "he's my biological son. I do not—"

"Cam," he interrupted. I could tell from his tone that I would not like where this was headed. "I *also* understand that you have recently spent significant time with him and his mother. Word gets around in this place, as you know, and I've been informed that there may be a deeper bond than a biological one."

Most chiefs didn't speak to their staff so candidly, nor did they give subordinates the chance to voice their beliefs about how situations, such as this unique one, should go. So sometimes—and I mean sometimes—Dr. Nguni allowed us some freedom to make judgment calls on our own.

I'd had at least an hour and a half to process this situation, and I could sense that Nguni was allowing me to argue my case about how and why Jacks would be safe under my care—whether he was my son or not.

I also understood that Chief was my voice of reason right now because my patient had fallen into a coma after I'd not pushed him hard enough to have surgery. It was my duty to Jacks not to beat myself up for not putting more pressure on him and his mother to make this decision.

But the God's honest truth was that none of the scans or tests had revealed that Jacks could crash this hard and fast. There was no indication he was in such danger. I wouldn't have let him out of our sight if there were.

Although this was a rare case, with the brain, anything was possible, and I should've expected the worst instead of hoping for the best.

"Sir, I am proud to say that Jackson and I have grown closer over the last month. Perhaps that is why I am driven to help save my son."

"And why was there no encouragement for this surgery before your vacation?"

"Chief, you know that I would've canceled my vacation in a heartbeat if my patient wanted to go ahead with the surgery. I plan to follow every protocol, knowing that my Hippocratic oath will drive me to make all my decisions, not the fact that this is my son. I plan to assess him myself while working with my colleagues and the other professionals who may or may—"

"All right," he interrupted me, half chuckling. "You don't need to bullshit me with all that stuff. I know you're a fine surgeon, Brandt. I just need to know where your mind is at. You know that we do not advise doing surgery on our loved ones. You understand this, yes?"

"More than you know, and I will ensure that it is not taken for granted that you've allowed me this opportunity, sir."

"I just want to know that when you storm into this hospital, your head is in the right place."

"I understand that, thank you. And thank you for calling on my patient's behalf," I responded.

"Fremont is still with him, and I will be at Fremont's side until you arrive. It's my day off, but I want to be here for you, the family, and our staff, as I know this will be felt personally. You have family behind you, Dr. Brandt. That is what makes us a unique medical team. So do not let your mind *go there* and feel alone in any decision you make moving forward."

"I appreciate and understand that. Thanks, Chief," I said, then hung up the phone and began to center myself.

There was no more room for emotions, and I fucking knew that.

Ring!

I picked up Jake's call immediately.

"Hey, buddy. How far out is the jet?" Jake asked. "How are you and Jessa doing?"

"I'm pulling it together. Jessa is in the back and hasn't said a word to me since we boarded, and she went into the private bedroom."

"As to be expected," Jake answered, cool as a cucumber always. "So, I'm not sure where your head is in all of this? Do you want me to run you down on what happened, or would you rather wait until—is it Dr. Fremont?"

"Yeah, Fremont is the attending physician until I arrive. Chief just called too."

"Yes," Jake answered, "I looped in Chief before he called. I hope the call went well?"

"It's a good thing Nguni is as badass a chief surgeon as you are."

Jake laughed, "Now you're just fucking delusional, though I'll take the compliment since everyone tells me I'm too young to be chief and that I'm lucky I even have hair on my balls."

I wanted to laugh, but my head just wasn't fucking there. "Tell me what happened. I'm sure Jessa is either talking to Ash about it, or she just fucking hates all of us for this."

"Get out of your head, man," Jake said. "Seriously, I don't want to say who gives a fuck if she hates everyone or not, but I fucking will. You are no good to her or your son if you start with that. You wouldn't allow angry parents to make your decisions any other time, so don't start now. Do *not* let emotions take over. We'll all take care of Jessa while you make the decisions that need to be made for your son."

"Right," I said, closing my eyes. Jessa would be fine. She was just processing this fluke occurrence as best she could. "Nothing indicated to me that something like this could happen, even after his seizures became more frequent."

"Of course not. You couldn't have known this would happen any more than I could know one of my patients would have a spontaneous heart attack. We do the best we can with the information given to us. We can't predict whether an anomaly will occur. We're not God, and you know that. Do not do this to yourself."

"Yeah, well, I don't know," I said, sighing.

"You know Collin has your back on this too. That fucker had to hold his wife's brain in his hands and cut. He also didn't ask to be in the position you will likely be in soon, and you better not push him away if he offers advice."

That pissed me off. "Why would I push away one of my best friends?"

"Because I can hear it in your voice, Cam. You're fucking scared, and you're spinning. That mindset will fuck you, and the next thing you know, you've pushed everyone away," Jake said. "Now, let's get back to why you're blaming yourself for going on vacation before you talked this kid into having this surgery."

Jake wasn't wrong. I could already feel myself wanting to isolate, which wouldn't be in my or Jackson's best interest.

"I get it, Jake. There was no stopping this from happening, and vacation or not, Jessa and Jacks were not ready to go through with this surgery."

"Which is why Collin and I were working on Jacks while you were gone," Jake said. "Now, would you like to hear something positive?"

"Yes," I said.

"That boy of yours is just as crazy as you are. On a fucking bet, he told Collin and me that he would be having surgery to prove he could throw a ball with his left hand if he had to."

"You're shitting me. Was he serious, or was he just fucking with you two?"

"Collin told him stories about his patients who should have had this surgery but couldn't because of their age. Sad fucking stories, but they made Jacks want to seize the opportunity instead of squandering it through indecision."

I felt tears fill my eyes, wishing I'd gone to Collin before. "I should've thought about doing that sooner," I said, feeling my voice crack.

"Should've thought of what, having me and Col use our genius minds to help your sorry ass out?" Jake said, trying to change the tone of this conversation. "Shoulda, woulda, coulda, Cam. You know better than that."

I chuckled. "Yeah, I know. I know," I said, leaning back in my leather chair. "I need to get my head straight and drill down how I will proceed now that he's in a coma."

"Yeah, he dropped right before we got in the car to go to his appointment. By the time the ambulance arrived, and after his third seizure in under six minutes had rendered him unconscious, I feared the worst."

"Fuck, man. Never in a million fucking years would I have imagined such a massive electrical storm."

"I did the Glasgow with Collin over the phone while waiting for EMS to arrive, and Collin rated him a five due to pupil dilation and his unresponsiveness. EMS got him on oxygen, though, and even though they were shallow breaths, I sensed he was breathing well enough for oxygen to enter his brain."

"I'm praying that I don't find any damage when the tests come back," I said, feeling nauseated by this nightmare.

Maybe I wasn't cut out for this? Perhaps I'd grown too attached to Jackson, and I didn't have what it took to be his surgeon. I sure as fuck wouldn't ordinarily be *this* emotional with such a small amount of information on a patient. And that scared the shit out of me.

"Just get your ass down here. Word is buzzing through all the residents and surgeons, so you'll have plenty of help at your disposal should you need it. Collin is on call tonight, and you know he'll sneak down to the pediatric ward to lend you some of his wisdom."

"Got it. We're landing soon, so I'll get off the phone and get my head straight."

"We're all here for you and Jessa, brother. You better fucking know that."

"I know, and thank you," I said.

I needed to check on Jessa. I nearly came undone when she said she was going to call her ex. Did I screw things up that bad? I needed her to know that these occurrences were uncommon. I would've pressed harder for the surgery if I knew *this* would happen. I would've scared the fuck out of her and Jacks with this specific nightmare scenario if I thought it was a possibility.

I couldn't let myself feel guilty. I would not allow a freak incident to force a very frightened Jessa into making me believe this was my fault.

The worst part was that I was putting thoughts and words into Jessa's mouth that she hadn't relayed to me.

I was projecting my insecurities, and I needed to get over it, or I was no good to anyone.

I had to fix my son, and I was on my way to do precisely that.

Chapter Thirty-Nine

Jessa

The last thing I remembered was getting confirmation from my parents and Warren that they'd all be on the next flights to Los Angeles. After that, I was stuck in my head about everything that'd gone wrong since I left Jacks to go on vacation with Cameron.

I couldn't think of anything but my guilt for this happening to Jacks while I was enjoying living the life of an adventurous billionaire's girlfriend.

Everything that happened from when I hung up the phone and walked out of the plane's private bedroom until now was a blur. I vaguely remembered the plane landing and the car ushering us to the hospital, but that was it. I recalled loud ringing in my ears, and now, I was reclined on a sofa in a small, immaculate room with pictures of biplanes hanging on the wall.

How did I get here? I thought, feeling completely strange. I had to be in the hospital because I heard doctors being paged over the intercom, but I couldn't have traced my steps if my life depended on it.

"Jess," Cam said, shocking me by entering the room, wearing dark blue hospital scrubs and a white lab coat.

I sat up, getting my bearings, knowing I'd been a crazy zombie since I learned my son had gone into a coma.

"Jessica?" Cam said, his voice and demeanor changed entirely. He was gravely serious, and I realized then that I'd never met this side of Cameron.

"Cameron," I answered, unsure what to say.

"How are you feeling?" he asked.

"Me?" I questioned him, more confused than irritated that we were talking about me instead of my son.

I smeared my hand over my forehead. It was sweaty, and my palms were clammy. "How'd I get here?" I asked, knowing I'd lost important time somewhere along the line. "I can't remember anything."

"It's because you fainted," he said, answered.

"Fainted?"

"Yes, how are you feeling?"

"Jesus, Cameron, who cares how I'm feeling—"

"I do," he answered stiffly. "My son is in ICU, and the woman I love fainted after seeing him in that state. I need to ensure you're feeling better after waking up from that?"

"I'm confused," I answered honestly. "Did I see Jacks? I fainted? I don't—I've never—"

"It can happen to anyone in overwhelming situations, Jess."

I felt so damn tired. "What have I missed?"

"You fainted when we walked in to see Jackson. Thank God I was behind you when it happened. I caught you, and you didn't injure yourself."

"Thank you," I said, my mouth dry as the desert. "I need some water, though, and I need to see my son." I took the water bottle Cameron pulled out of a fridge in the corner of the room and started crying. "All I've wanted since I learned my baby was hurt was to hold him in my arms, and once I get the chance, I fucking faint?" I growled the last word, feeling hopeless and worthless.

"Don't do that to yourself," he said. "This whole situation has caught all of us off guard. It's helped me to see the images of his brain and go over them with my team," he sat next to me.

"And what did you find?"

"The scans are showing positive outcomes for what I feared most. I was afraid he may have suffered brain damage from lack of oxygen, but that is not the case. It was as if all that activity firing off at once made his brain protect itself, and it shut itself down. It's the closest thing to a miracle that could've happened to him, but time is of the essence. I *must* perform this surgery now to remove the diseased portion of his left hemisphere and allow the right hemisphere to take over."

"So, this is it? It's like his brain is giving us no other option?"

"He may wake from this in a week or so," he said, placing his hand over mine, "or it may take longer. Having viewed all the scans, I'm confident that he *will* wake. However, I am not confident this won't continue to happen. I am in a place as a surgeon and as his father where I don't want to take any chances."

I closed my eyes, grateful that Jacks would wake up again but scared about what would happen if we didn't do the surgery *and* if we did. I felt like I was backed into a corner. "What if we do this?" I stopped myself. "What if I tell you to do the surgery, and he wakes up paralyzed and never forgives us for taking out half of his brain without permission?"

I saw the faintest look of relief wash over his face. "I talked to Jake while you were in the back room on the plane," he said. "Jake told me that he and Collin spent some time working out some details of what life would be like if he opted out of the surgery."

"Working out some details? How?"

"Well, you know that Collin is a neurosurgeon, and though pediatrics is not his specialty, he also deals with epileptic patients. He shared a few stories with Jacks, making it more real for the kid. Jacks realized that he'd be foolish not to have it. He agreed—" he paused, and I could see tears in his eyes.

I watched as a tear slipped out of the corner of his eye, running down to the dark stubble of his cheek. "So, he was willing to have the surgery?"

"Yes. Fuck, I can't let these emotions get into my head. I'm doing a good job keeping them pushed down." He sniffed, then shook his head and frowned. Finally, he looked at me with glaring sincerity. "I'm so sorry I didn't see this coming. I'm sorry to you and Jacks, but I promise I will make this right and fix him. I will bring him back to us with a healthier brain."

"Stop apologizing, and just fix our son, Cameron," I said. I was feeling a million emotions but holding onto one—determination.

I knew Jackson would get better, and he would beat the odds.

"I have more blood work, labs, and scans coming back. If I feel confident in what I see and that he will do well in this state and surgery, I want to schedule it for the morning after tomorrow."

"Isn't that a bit soon?" I questioned, then saw the severity in Cam's eyes and nodded. "I understand you probably know more about all of this than I do but are you sure you're ready for this?"

"I wouldn't consider this surgery if I wasn't," he said.

"I need to be sure you're doing this prepared, ready, and not just *doing* this because we screwed up by taking a vacation and shirking our responsibilities to our son, not pushing him to have surgery earlier."

Cameron's face grew dark, "I understand why you might believe I couldn't perform a surgery because—"

"Stop," I said, crying again and then hugging him. "I'm sorry. I didn't mean that."

"Jessa," he pulled me back and stared intently into my eyes, "I understand your fears and concerns. I have not given you much to go off while being Jackson's doctor by only doing *fun things* while bonding and enjoying our time together."

I nodded because it was true; deep down, that's how I felt about Cameron. *Was* he the responsible doctor he said he was? He sure hadn't been acting like it.

"I need you to push all of that away, though, and trust that I've been watching him even when I was *enjoying* my time with you both. I've mentally processed how he behaves in and out of the seizures and how he behaves coming out of them. This *is* my field of expertise, so while you may think I've been screwing off, I've been paying close attention. I needed to know *if* he was a strong enough candidate for this surgery, and I can confidently say that he will most likely surprise us *in time* with how well he does in recovery. On the surface, perhaps I made it appear like I was just messing around with him, but that couldn't be farther from what I was doing."

"I just need to be certain you're doing this for the right reasons," I said. "I need to be sure that his doctor is making the decisions and not his dad, who could possibly feel guilt that this even happened."

It was harsh, and I knew it. But my son was facing brain surgery while in a coma performed by a man who just happened to be his newfound dad. So, I needed reassurance that Cameron wasn't trying to make up for anything—like I could see myself doing.

His features darkened even more; now, he was the cold, handsome surgeon I saw when he walked into this room a few minutes ago.

"I would never cut into a child because I felt guilt or remorse for lack of judgment," his tone matched his grave expression. "That is how mistakes, botched surgeries, and even death happen on the surgical table. I pride myself on putting my patients and their good before my own. I will never get greedy in the surgical room, and I ask that you trust me on that."

I pinched my lips together, feeling somewhat intimidated by the tall man standing before me. I didn't know this man, and I thanked God he finally introduced himself to me. I needed to believe my son was in good hands and not in the hands of the man who had swept me off my feet for an entire month. I didn't want the crazy, wild, and goofy Cameron anywhere near my son, and I sure as hell didn't want a remorseful Cameron operating on him.

I wanted this asshole—the arrogant surgeon who knew his shit—to save my son from the hell I allowed him to go through because I was too busy believing that life owed *me* for a change.

"Before I came in to get you, Jake told me that the girls have been trying to contact you. I informed them about what happened when you saw Jacks in the room and that you were lying down."

"I can check my phone later," I said coldly. I didn't care who was trying to get ahold of me. I needed to see my son. "Take me to Jacks. I want to be with him. I think I've spent enough time this month putting myself first."

"I just wanted to let you know that the ladies are here at the hospital if you'd like the company. I will be going over many things to assure that Jacks will do well in surgery."

"While I appreciate that, I don't plan on leaving his side until he's taken into surgery," I said. "Warren and my parents should be here tonight, so I'll have his support when he gets here."

"Warren?" Cam's expression darkened.

"Don't start," I said. "You need to let me deal with this my way, Cam. Warren has been a huge part of Jackson's life. In fact—"

I paused.

Don't fucking say it.

"In fact?" Cameron urged, and his irritation fed mine.

"I just know if I were with Warren, I wouldn't have spent the last month living in a fantasy world, and I would've been there for my son."

"Is that what you feel this last month was, a fantasy world?"

"Wasn't it? Living some idea, focused on our perfect little family, while we should've been focused on fixing Jackson and not our relationship? Instead, we were careless and foolish, and now my son lies helpless in an ICU bed. And for what, so I could have a little fun, right? Put myself first for once, yeah? Isn't that what you've been telling me this entire time?"

I covered my mouth, forcing myself to shut up. I saw the pain in Cameron's eyes, and I knew it wasn't fair. I wasn't mad at him. I didn't think I was, anyway. I was mad at myself. Mad at the world. I was just fucking mad.

"Instead, you were with me, living a life with your son that you *both* deserved. A fucking fluke incident happened, and now you're blaming your lack of judgment for taking me back?"

"That's not what I'm doing, Cameron."

"It doesn't matter at this point. I cannot worry about how this affects our relationship. I can't worry about anything. I must focus on Jackson and helping him."

"I couldn't agree more," I answered. "I need to be with him. Have you decided how you'll move forward?"

"As I said, I'm still waiting on more labs. I'll meet with my surgical team after I bring you to his room, and there, we will go over everything, including the safest way to proceed."

"Do you believe you'll do the hemispherectomy?" I asked.

"Yes," he answered. "With everything I've gone over, I can safely say that is the best option. I just need more results back before we make the final decision."

"Okay," I answered, my emotions stable.

I needed to be with Jacks and wait for Cameron to get his answers, and then we'd go from there. My parents and Warren couldn't get here fast enough.

I had no idea why, but Cameron brought me no comfort right now. I desperately wanted and needed someone familiar, and Warren had always been an anchor. I knew he would ground me, and I needed that comfort more than ever.

Chapter Forty

Jessa

I hadn't seen Cameron much since my parents and Warren arrived, but it wasn't because he was upset they were here. Cameron had been in *Dr. Brandt* mode since I woke up in his on-call room four days ago after I fainted.

He'd been relentlessly going over lab work, ordering more and more scans of Jackson's brain activity, and while he was in that mode, I would talk to my sleeping son, doing everything I could to bring him back to me.

I pulled my fingers through the top of Jacks's silky-soft onyx hair. There was a terrible hole in my heart and soul that I could never describe, and now and then, the pain caused a spasm to rip through me when I took a breath. I was exhausted and wanted my son back, but all I could do was keep pushing through each moment, hoping for a miracle.

Today, a pediatric neurosurgeon from Stanford joined Cameron's team at Cam's request. The physician was a friend of Cam's from college, and Cam said he wanted the man's second opinion as things were leaning toward a better outlook if the surgery was performed.

I trusted Cam and his team explicitly after living in this hospital twenty-four hours a day, all week. Still, I wanted Cameron to feel one hundred percent sure about everything, so whatever that man needed, I was behind it. I wasn't arguing with anyone at this point.

"Jacks, you've officially missed the playoffs. You and I know that Cam and his buddies would've made sure you saw it in person if you would've just woken up," I said.

Then a thought hit me, and I walked out of the room to find a nurse.

"Ms. Stein," the older woman greeted me. "Is everything okay?"

"I have a silly question," I said. At this time of night, the only thing that could be heard in this hospital wing was the beeping of monitors and the shuffling of nurses when they got up from their desks to check on patients every so often. It might've even been considered peaceful under any other circumstances.

"Nothing is silly," she smirked. "I'm Polly, by the way. I see that Laticia is assigned to your son, Jackson. Would you rather ask her? She's just with another patient."

"No, I'm good," I answered her smile with a tired one of my own. "I just had a question about patients in a coma."

"You want to know if they can hear you while they sleep?" she said inquisitively, and after I nodded in response, she continued. "There are many schools of thought on the topic, but I believe they can. Call me eternally optimistic, but I think there is too much evidence to suggest they don't. We've had a handful of reports from patients who had certain recollections from their time in a coma, so who am I to dispute that?"

"Really?" I might not have been an *eternal optimist,* but I needed to hear that. "I read about it online, but there are so many conflicting stories."

"I think it depends on what state their brain may be in, but I believe the subconscious mind picks up everything."

"I think so, too. I hope so, anyway."

"Just keep talking to him, Mama," she said. "If anything, he will find comfort in your voice."

"Thank you, Polly."

I walked back into Jackson's room, seeing my handsome son resting peacefully, and I took his hand in mine. "This better work," I muttered, feeling my anxiety climb. "The nurse says that you might be able to hear me, Jacks, and I hope you can. Maybe if I keep talking, you'll want to wake up just to shut me up." I laughed nervously as I rubbed his limp hand. *Here goes.* "So, I'm going to tell you something about Dr. Brandt. Remember when you told me that you two had so much in common and that it was freaky?" Jacks and Cam had taken on Jake and Collin in a game of tag football on the beach that day, and Jacks noticed how Cam threw the ball *exactly* the way he did. "I almost told you then, but Cameron and I decided to wait until after your surgery, so you weren't stressed or anything, but—" I inhaled, paused, and then continued with a big sigh. "Cameron's your dad, honey." I sniffed and wiped a tear from my cheek, wishing I could look into his beautiful eyes as I revealed this. "Imagine that. Your best buddy—and doctor—is actually your father. We were very young when it happened, but it happened nonetheless, and we really need you to come back to us now, Jackson."

I exhaled. The last of my nerves that'd spiked had dissipated along with all my hope and excitement, believing that revelation would snap my son awake. I would've dealt with any kind of fallout later, and when nothing happened after my life-changing reveal, I would have begged for any type of fallout to happen just to get him to wake up. I was desperate.

"Come back to me, Jackson. Please wake up and talk to me, yell at me, or tell me you want me to leave you alone!" I was pleading, begging, and crying with the desolation I felt. "Tell me anything, baby. Just please wake up. Please, please, wake up, Jacks."

I let the tears erupt from deep inside and laid my head on his chest, holding him and wishing he was awake to shove me off him. I felt like I would go mad if Cameron didn't have a solution by tomorrow. I needed something. Right now, all I could do was sob and be as close to my sleeping, handsome man as I could be.

. . .

"Come here, Jess," Cam said, rousing me awake after falling asleep on Jacks.

He positioned me to turn and face where he knelt in front of me. I reached for his face and studied his eyes. "I need him back, Cam," I said, running my thumb underneath Cam's brilliant eyes. "Please do something."

I started crying again and leaned into his embrace. I felt Cam soften and hold me for the first time since meeting the solemn surgeon who'd taken over. His arms ran up my back, bringing a warm and soothing comfort to my aching soul.

"I'm going to, Jessa," he said. "I'm going through with the surgery."

I snapped my head up to look at him. "You're confident?"

As he nodded, I could see he was sure. "If I weren't confident, I wouldn't consider it as I've told you. But, yes, this is going to take care of a lot of issues. After surgery, he may wake up within hours, or it might take days, at the most. I need you to understand there can and may be complications, though, as with any surgery."

"I understand. I think I do, anyway." I sniffed and ran my hands over my eyes. "Please tell me you're saying this because of protocol or something?"

"Yes, protocol, but I also want you to be prepared for anything," he continued. "I know this has been quite a journey for you and our son, and this will be the steepest mountain to climb. However, this past month has shown me that you and Jacks have what it takes to get to the top."

I hugged him tightly, and for the first time since this happened, my inward resentment of Cam subsided. Maybe it wasn't fair of me to loop him into my self-loathing, but I did. He was my accomplice in selfishly neglecting our child, and even though I couldn't forgive either one of us for our actions, it felt good to know he was able to help turn this situation around. At least one of us had the power to redeem ourselves; it sure wasn't me, though, and I wouldn't let myself off the hook that quickly anyway.

I pulled away as the ICU nurse admitted Warren. "Dr. Brandt, there's a call for you."

"Thanks, Laticia." Cam stood and faced me as Warren stood next to me. "It's good that you're here," he acknowledged Warren. "The phone call is from the lab. They've got the results I've been expecting to show that Jackson is a candidate for surgery, and so, I plan on surgery at four in the morning."

"Don't you think that is a bit fast?" Warren questioned Cameron.

Cam eyed me, then Warren. "Actually, I believe the surgery could have taken place yesterday; however, I wanted Dr. Astor's opinion. You are aware of that, are you not?"

Cameron was that hard-faced and stiff-talking surgeon again, and Warren was face-to-face with a man who would bury him with words if he wasn't careful.

"I understand that, Cameron—"

"Thank you, Dr. Brandt," I acknowledged Cameron professionally since his current demeanor demanded it, and Warren knew that.

Warren was being a prick, and I knew it. I wasn't in the mood for games, though. I wanted my son to be well and for Cameron to be confident in this surgery. I didn't have time for cockfights between two grown men who hated each other.

"I am very confident performing this, like I was telling you, Jessa," Cam said. "It will be roughly a six-hour surgery, and I expect a full recovery after that. We will have our neuropsychology team ready to aid you with any further questions, but that will come after surgery. This can take a toll on you, but you've already been through hell, so this is just one more thing to push through."

"I understand," I said.

"Once Jackson is awake," he looked between Warren and me, "which I expect to happen within hours after surgery, our rehab center will begin working with him immediately. I want him to be challenged, and I will not back down."

"Do you think that is necessary so quickly after surgery?" Warren asked, speaking before I could.

"If I didn't, I wouldn't demand it," he answered, then looked at me. "After spending a fair enough time with Jacks, I'm confident that challenging him immediately—starting small, of course—is what he'll need and where he'll thrive. The teams will go over all of this in further detail."

"Thanks, Cam," I said, forgetting about Warren and hugging Cameron with the sincerity and relief I felt.

"He's going to surprise all of us," Cameron said with a smirk, his deep blue eyes sparkling as they stared into mine. "I promise you that, Mom."

With only a fraction of a second to feel that spark that made me come alive from the inside out, he half-smiled, then pulled away. "Both of you should get your rest. Starting tomorrow, you'll face many mental and physical demands. And when Jacks is awake, he will need you to be rested and ready to go to work with him."

"I'll get her to the hotel," Warren slid his arm around me and looked at me. "Your parents need to know what's going on as well."

"I can speak with them. Where are they?" Cameron asked.

"I don't think that's a very good idea," Warren said, and I pulled away from him the minute I sensed his enjoyment at relaying that information.

I would've been shocked if anyone despised Cameron more than my parents. They were also the most passive-aggressive people I knew. I loved my parents, but they stopped talking to me for a time because I didn't nail Cameron to the wall for knocking me up and taking off. They didn't appreciate when I didn't take their advice, and, as certain people love to do, they got their feelings hurt and made it about them.

I put up with it because I wanted Jackson to know his grandparents, and I hated the thought that my parents were upset with me. It killed me to have that contention, so we worked through it eventually. Once Warren came along, my mother and father adored him for *taking on another man's burden* by caring for his child and the woman he'd selfishly left behind.

I avoided the *Cameron Brandt* discussion with my parents like the plague. And now, here Cameron was, wanting to speak with them. And why shouldn't he? He was their grandson's doctor. I just didn't know how it would play out.

"You may not think that's a good idea, Warren," Cameron said, after studying him for a moment, "but they are the maternal grandparents. If they have any questions, I would like to answer them."

Warren looked at me. "Your parents don't need to be put in an awkward situation. They're as stressed as we are, and, as you know, their opinions aren't very high of Cameron."

"I'm standing right here, Warren," Cameron seethed. "And I understand if Rod and Patty don't want to have the stress of their grandson's—"

"Is it absolutely necessary?" I cut Cameron off, not wanting the added stress of this. "I can relay the info to them. And honestly, if you're doing the surgery at four in the morning, maybe it's best if you get some rest. Focus on Jackson, and I'll deal with my parents."

Cameron eyed me, and I didn't want to know what the man was thinking from his expression. I hadn't meant to insult him, but I did not need the added bullshit of my parents hating him right now. I couldn't do it. It would hurt Cam, and it would hurt them. It was just too fucking much.

"If you feel more comfortable giving your mom and dad the information, then fine. I'll head out since I'll be back here first thing tomorrow." He spun around and then was gone.

"Shit," I said, feeling horrible that I'd inadvertently chosen my parents over Cameron. "I feel awful."

"Don't," Warren answered. "Cameron should know this isn't the time to be the hotshot doctor and make amends with your parents that way. It's absolute nonsense, and I, for one, would like to respect your parents' wishes of never being in his presence again."

"Jesus Christ, Warren," I looked at him. "That's a bit harsh. What they don't like about Cameron happened sixteen years ago. My parents should be over it by now."

Warren took my hand and gently guided us out of the room. "Jessa," he said once we were walking through the hallways and weren't in earshot of anyone, "your parents love you very much."

"I know that," I said, rolling my eyes.

"So, you know their current disdain was renewed after learning that he was apparently flying you everywhere in private jets and playing on the beach when he should have been focused on healing your son," Warren said, repeating everything I was ashamed of myself for.

"This is bullshit," I said. My world seemed to be spinning out of control, and I didn't feel like it was a good idea for me to leave my son. "I can't leave the hospital. I won't."

"You need to get some proper rest, and staying here isn't going to give you that," he answered.

"I can make my own decisions, Warren. Thank you."

"Don't take this the wrong way, but the last time I left you to make your own decisions, Jacks ended up in a coma while you were in Mexico."

I glared at him. "Fuck you," I growled. "You don't think I already blame myself for this?"

"I just don't understand where your mind is anymore, Jessica. None of this has made sense since you flew out here and hunted that man down for help."

"After the surgery, and when Jacks is recovered, you'll understand," I said, suddenly feeling weak from arguing with Warren.

Weak and stupid.

"Then why wasn't the surgery decided on in the beginning, Jessica? Why is he *suddenly* the heroic doctor? I don't want to insult you, but you should understand that this whole thing makes people question you and your relationship with Cameron. It's not a good look for a mother who says she wanted help for her son and ends up in bed with his doctor."

"I'm not doing this," I said, walking briskly away from him.

"Doing what?" he questioned, stepping up to keep up with me. "Listening to the truth? People talk, you know?"

I was stopped when he tugged my arm and placed his arms around me.

"I just want him better," I said.

That was the end of my fight for my own happiness.

Somehow, I'd given Warren and my parents power over me, and I was too weak to fight for it back. I didn't even know if I wanted it back. I clearly wasn't responsible enough to keep my son from nearly dying. I deserved this shame for what I'd done to Jackson. It was painfully obvious that my decision-making couldn't be trusted.

I hated that I felt so weak. I hated that everything Warren was saying was right. And I hated that I agreed with him.

Chapter Forty-One

Cameron

I began surgery on Jackson at 0400 hours. After seven hours of supreme focus, communicating with my surgical team about what I was finding and where I was disconnecting the damaged hemisphere of his brain, Jackson was safely out of surgery and in the pediatric ICU.

"I spoke with the family," Dr. Fremont said with Dr. Palmer at his side. "They're happy to know the surgery was successful, but they're still waiting on you."

I nodded. I didn't walk into that room directly after surgery as I would've done with any other case, and it wasn't because of the emotional storm I'd been through over the last seventy-two hours either. It was because I wanted to stay by Jackson's side from the moment that I made that first incision to the point that he was safely and intensively being monitored in the ICU.

"Thank you. I trust they are grateful to hear the good news," I said, smiling for the first time since walking into the hospital at three this morning. "I'm on my way to see them now."

"Fine job today as usual," Dr. Palmer said, her eyes bright.

"Thanks, Palmer," I said. "I'm glad everything went smoothly. Sometimes you get lucky, and we sure as hell did today with Jackson."

"Some might call it luck," she said. "But I don't."

"Oh?" I said, smiling over at her as we walked to the family waiting room, "what would you call it?"

"Talent," she laughed. "How can you say *luck* played a role in that?"

"What else would I call it? Maybe luck makes it sound like I was in there rolling the dice, but when it comes down to it, isn't that what we're doing? We never know what's going to happen despite all our training."

"Yes, but I believe there are angels in that room," she nudged me in the side, "and on your shoulder to help guide you. You didn't just get *lucky*. You're skilled enough to make all of that happen with diligence."

"Well, if I viewed it that way," I smirked at her, my mood lightening up some more, "then I'd be one arrogant son of a bitch."

"Neurosurgeon and arrogance; I think those words go together, right?" she chuckled. "Douchebag? It's all the same."

I laughed. "Easy, Dr. Palmer," I said. "Let's just agree that I won't pretend luck played a part in this brain surgery. No one wants to think the person holding their loved one's life in their hands is a gambler."

"You're a piece of work, sometimes, Dr. Brandt. Just take credit where credit is due."

We approached the family waiting room, and I felt that darker emotional state wash over me again. The state I was in when I'd watched Jessa lean on Warren for support.

Fuck luck, I thought. Lucky was the last thing I was when it came to Jessa. That couldn't have been made more evident these past few days.

"They're all extremely excited to see Jackson, especially Ms. Stein, of course," Dr. Palmer said.

"Very good," I said, shrugging off the look of concern she shot me.

The entire pediatric ward knew that Jessa was my college love, and they loved how fate had brought Jessa and my son back to me. However, a little-known, important fact was that somehow, I lost her in the whirlwind.

Fuck. I couldn't think about that now.

I walked in and saw that Jessa, Ash, and Elena were hugging, laughing, and crying. And Warren was with Alex, Spencer, and Jim.

Wow, this bastard thinks he's in the same league as my friends because he's also a businessman? I thought. Maybe it was a childish response, but I was irritated that the fucker was anywhere near my friends after Jessa had decided to lean on him instead of me.

What a surprise. Her parents aren't here. They hated me, which was fine with me, but I couldn't understand why they were such cowards, running away every time I came around when we were dealing with something so vital. I had no headspace to consider them right now, though. I'd lost Jessa again, and I felt that acutely. They were probably part of the reason for that, and Warren was the other.

I still hadn't a fucking clue where it'd spun out of control between Jessa and me. All I knew was that, even though she told me not to apologize to her or blame myself for Jackson's freak accident, she sure as fuck made me feel like it was all my fault. Hell, if she trusted Warren so fucking much, why didn't she have that useless prick perform our son's lifesaving surgery?

I rubbed my forehead and removed my surgical cap, forcing myself to get away from these stupid feelings, being jealous and acting like a victim.

"You okay, Doc?" Warren asked.

I straightened up. I wasn't about to engage this fucker in a conversation while feeling how I did, especially when the guy's stupid cocky expression made me want to bitch slap him.

"He just performed surgery on his son," Spencer Monroe said, looking at Warren as if he'd said the stupidest thing possible. One thing about Spencer, he was always the biggest dick in any room, and if Warren thought he was going to take a jab at me, Spencer would make him look a fool with no help from me.

"Yeah, well, he looks a bit exhausted. I was simply just asking—" Warren started to defend himself.

"That's a stupid fucking question for a surgeon who just saved a child's life by performing *actual brain surgery*," Spencer said, not letting up.

Spencer could sniff out a weasel from the deepest underground burrow, and he had no qualms about putting an asshole in his place.

"It's all good," I said, feeling the temperature of the room rise. I looked at Jessa. "As you were informed, Jacks is in recovery. I hope you'll forgive me for not joining my team earlier to fill you in about surgery, but I wanted to see that our son was settled in his recovery room and the ICU staff were brought up to speed with my specific orders."

To my shock, Jessa crossed the room and wrapped her arms tightly around my waist. "Thank you, Cameron. Thank you for taking care of him," she sniffed, and her hug grew tighter.

I was afraid to hug her back or show any emotion because I was scared to death that this would never happen again. I had no idea where she and I were, but emotions ran high after surgeries, and the gratitude that was born from successful surgery made them run even higher. So, whatever affection Jessa was giving me now, chances were that it came more as a flood of relief than a desire to be close to me.

I hugged her back, but I was rigid. My guard was up, no doubt, but I would be a fool if I didn't protect myself emotionally.

I stepped back a little and smiled into her tear-filled eyes. "I'm here to take you to him, but you need to understand that the real work will begin in recovery. I believe that he will wake up soon, and when he does, I need you to keep a positive outlook for him."

"The neuropsychologist was here and spoke about that too, what to expect and everything." Jessa looked back at Elena, who was also a neuropsychologist, and then back at me, "Elena's said she would be there for both of us too, Cam."

"Thank you, Laney," I said, smiling at Collin's wife, who was always the freaking light in the darkness due to her expertise in matters of the brain *and heart*. "So, you're ready to go see him?" I asked Jessa with an excited smile.

"I won't leave his side."

I grinned. "You haven't left his side since all of this happened. I'm shocked you allowed him in my care for the surgery."

She chuckled, "Take me to him. I might lose my mind if he wakes up before I get to him.

. . .

Jacks woke up later that night while Jessa sat next to him, holding his hand and doing a damn fine job of not crying or appearing to be stressed—all the emotions we didn't want around him.

I was in and out, ensuring that Jacks responded well to waking up. It was my expectation that he would not be able to speak when he woke up, which was common after disconnecting the left hemisphere of his brain. The right side of his body was not responding as it would have with the left hemisphere doing that job, but there was still some good news.

Jackson's troubled hemisphere did not require me to remove it entirely; because of that, his brain was still intact, and I was able to disconnect the pathways for this hemisphere to send signals to the body that would result in a seizure. Even so, I would keep him on a mild epilepsy medication for at least two years to ensure we'd successfully silenced the brain.

It was now up to the right hemisphere to do the job of the left. At his age, with his brain nearly fully developed, there was concern that his right hemisphere would not learn, but I knew my son would fight back. And with grueling physical and mental work, I knew we would all be impressed with his comeback.

"You've slept for long enough, kid," I said, seeing that the left portion of Jackson's face pulled up, but the right did nothing. "I'll give you a day or so of rest before we turn this into a spring training situation."

I watched him, as I'd been doing since he woke up, and my mind went straight to helping him with a speedy recovery. He was a lot like me, competitive and determined. Things needed to be a challenge and move fast. It's how I played sports, how I drove myself straight into this career, and what I wanted to see in him. And I did.

"You've got no response to that?" I said, trying to work him up a little as I saw a certain glimmer in his eyes. "Don't tell me you're just going to lay around in bed all day."

There's my boy, I thought, seeing him become somewhat irritated.

He moved his head, and his eyes shifted toward the ceiling. This was a good start, but I knew there was more to come. Rest was number one at this point, though; after that, rehab would start. That's where we would see more improvement.

I patted Jackson's foot. "Get some rest, kiddo. You'll need it when I start kicking your butt in the morning."

"Dr. Brandt," Selena, the nurse in the room, called out. "The therapist will be in tomorrow, but she'd like to go over some details of the recovery plan with you and Ms. Stein sometime today."

"Excellent. Anything else before I make my final rounds for the night?"

"No," she smiled. "I must say, Jacks surprised me with how quickly he woke up."

"I wouldn't have performed the surgery if I thought it wouldn't have brought him back to us," I answered with a smile. "It's going to be a tough road for him, but I'm glad to hear that the rehabilitation therapists are ready to go. I requested a team, so I may have to call out and ensure that happens."

"I'm not too sure about how they'll go about it, but I'm sure if that's what you requested, it will happen."

"Thanks, Selena. I'll be back to check on him in an hour or so. His mother will be back before we all know it, though," I chuckled, wishing Jessa and I were enjoying this together. But her parents and Warren were practically acting like bodyguards to ensure it was difficult as fuck for me to be around her.

It wasn't helping that she was also avoiding me, but honestly, I didn't have time for *that* shit. I had to remain focused on Jackson, and I knew that's where Jessa's focus was.

After everything shook out, and Jacks was moving forward, I would steal her away, and hopefully, we could straighten out the things that went wrong.

Part of me understood that having her parents and Warren here would make that difficult, but they needed to understand what I already knew: I was *not* losing my Jessa or my son ever again.

Chapter Forty-Two

Jessa

A week into Jackson's therapy, I finally felt like my world had stopped spinning wildly out of control. Jacks was doing very well, and I couldn't be prouder. When he started, he could barely move his mouth, and it nearly killed me not to hear his voice. Now, he grumbled, and his expressions were also starting to improve.

The most frustrating thing beyond Jackson's rehab was dealing with my parents and their seemingly never-ending stream of demands on me.

"Jessica Ann," my mom said, her crystal blue eyes as stern as they always were when I didn't *listen* to her advice. "I just want you to follow your head and *not* your heart. I know that sounds ridiculous, but you have a son who will require a lot of your—"

"Stop, Mom. Just stop," I said, interrupting her. I'd heard enough of this crap all week. "I know the last person you want my son and me around is Cameron. For the millionth time, I know that. You've hated him since he took off in college, and yet, you *should be* thanking him for doing it because he pulled off a miracle and brought Jacks back to us.

But, instead, you and Dad still can't forgive him." My heart was racing under her fierce gaze as I dared to talk back to her. "And do you want to know the worst part?"

"Do tell me," she put her perfectly manicured hand on her hip like a sassy five-year-old. "What could be the worst part of Cameron Brandt getting you pregnant and then, with all of his *expert* knowledge, choosing to pay more attention to getting back into bed with my daughter than fixing the son he suddenly claims to love?"

My blood pressure was through the roof, and my heart was pounding in my head. "I *never told him* about the pregnancy. You and Dad judge him for actions he never got to prove and decisions he made without all the important facts."

"Judge him for actions he never got to prove?" my dad interjected, his voice booming with frustration. "He proved himself well enough to me, Jessica. He managed to convince you that his happiness was most important, and that's why you kept things a secret."

"I'm not having this conversation again," I said, worn down to my core. "He's proven he's a wonderful father. I've witnessed all of it first-hand."

"A wonderful father, eh? I struggle to imagine that," my dad scoffed. "You need to start thinking around that man. I see the nurses gawking at him. I see everyone, including my daughter, staring at him like he's God's gift. Maybe he is, and that's fine. But you are making horrible judgment calls because you are caught up with this man in the worst way."

"I'm not," I paused, tears in my eyes, frustrated as hell that my parents were piling this on. "I will not stand here and listen to this. Not anymore. You've turned an amazing week for my son into a hellish nightmare for me, and for what? To prove that I was wrong to date Cameron again?"

"We're not trying to prove anything, honey. We're trying to help you. We see the way you look at Cameron. When you were with him in Mexico, Jacks got sick. We're just concerned about your happiness. That's all," my mother added.

"I understand that I got caught up in a fantasy with Cam, Mom," I said, caving to this bullshit because I needed it to stop before I had a literal stroke from my blood pressure spike. "But I trust myself now. I just hope you'll trust me too."

"Oh, honey," my mother took me into her arms. Her floral perfume reminded me of my childhood and the constant hovering my parents did. "We just want to be sure when we get on that plane in two hours that you're doing the right thing with Warren."

I hugged her back. "Mom, please, for once in my life, just trust that I'm a good mom and love my son. I can't have you and Dad going insane from my choices," I said, pulling back and locking eyes with her. I looked at my dad, "Trust me. I'm a good daughter and mother."

My dad walked over to me, his white hair brightened by the sun as it beat on us in the parking lot of St. John's. "We're sorry," he said, hugging me, "we're just concerned." Then, he stepped back, and his brown eyes bore through me, "Be wise. I'm glad you have Warren here. If you didn't, I don't think we'd be able to leave, but now, we know you're in good hands."

"I'm going to be fine. Enjoy your flight, and please, just support me for once."

Jesus H. Christ, just go! Today was the first time in two goddamn weeks that I was leaving the hospital, and this was my sendoff?

The thought of leaving the hospital turned me into a wreck in the first place, and getting an ear load of this crap from my parents was enough to send me to the crazy house. There were no winning arguments with them, and I probably wouldn't hear from them for at least a week because I wasn't being their *obedient daughter.*

"Enjoy your evening with Warren. Tell Jacks we love him again, and we look forward to updates," my mother said, becoming her usual aloof self, and I had no energy to give a damn at this point.

"I will. Fly safe."

We gave our final goodbye hugs, and now, all I wanted to do was talk to Warren. He, of all people, understood how horrible my parents could be to me in the name of their love.

A nice evening out, a few laughs, and someone I could depend on sounded nice. Jacks was with Cam, so I knew I could get away safely. Mom and Dad were out of here, and now I could focus on Jacks without hearing about how irresponsible I'd been for running off with Cameron and taking him back after all these years.

Later that night...

"I'm telling you," Warren said, straightening his tie, "Jacks is one strong kid. Cameron said he's even impressed with Jackson's advancements in physical therapy." He looked at me through the mirror where I stood behind him before he turned around and smiled at me. "He's already in the rehab center of that hospital, so that means he's coming along well."

I forced a smile; I'd been doing that a lot lately with Warren. It was strange. Part of me needed him right now, and part of me needed him gone.

"I know," I finally answered Warren. "Are you sure we should be going out to dinner to celebrate? Maybe we should be bringing the dinner to Jacks."

"Oh, sweetheart," Warren said, smiling. "Yes, I'm sure we should be going out tonight. You need it. This afternoon you couldn't stop telling me how happy you were that your parents were gone and that getting out would do us good. Let's get away, and let your mind unwind some." He leaned forward and kissed my forehead. "Listen, I'm heading back to New York for a couple of days now that everything is settled here. It will be nice to have some one-on-one time to sort things out, you and me. There's nothing to worry about with Jackson. You said that you feel so much better now that he's in the rehab center. Stop allowing your mind to run all over the place. There is no need for that."

I couldn't deny how very *off* everything felt. Being back with Warren —if that's what anyone would call this—wasn't sexual. There'd been none of that. It was like having a roommate or a close support system, and there'd been no pressure in the romance department. And when I thought about it, that's what Warren's and my relationship had been like for quite some time before I even called off the engagement.

I smiled. "Well, you and I are not officially back together," I said, hoping he was assured we weren't a couple. "But I appreciate you being here for Jackson and me."

"Let's just go get dinner," he said, dismissing me as he always had. "I have reservations, and then I'm leaving on a red-eye flight tonight. So, let's stop talking about all this stuff that stresses us out and focus on how we will work together to support Jackson once he's released from the hospital."

"That sounds nice," I said.

After a delicious yet exhausting meal with Warren, I was glad to be back at the hospital. I felt good after having eaten, but all I wanted was to see my son. I didn't want to think about relationships; more than that, I was sick of everyone telling me what I should and shouldn't be doing. Or how I should or shouldn't feel. I just needed to see my son.

I walked into the hospital, noticing how different this place felt at night. Strangely, it was more peaceful and more promising. At least it seemed that way since my son had awoken from his coma.

I walked into the serenity of the pediatric ward, seeing the holographic images on full display for the children. This place was unique and such a beautiful environment for the kids.

"Ms. Stein," Sally said. She was the evening receptionist at the entrance of the pediatric ward, and she knew me intimately by now. "You look well. Did you do okay, leaving for a while?"

I smiled at her. Her long chestnut hair was pulled neatly into a ponytail, and her glasses highlighted her deep brown eyes. "I wish. I honestly don't think I will have it together until I leave in a month with Jacks," I said.

"Feelings of guilt?" she questioned with a sympathetic grin.

"How'd you know? Sheesh, not even Warren could pick that up," I laughed.

"Most parents who leave for the first time come back with the same guilty expression you have. It's a normal emotion given everything you've been through."

"Very true," I said, being reminded that I wasn't the only parent going through a nightmare like this with a sick child. "I need to stop thinking I'm the only mom worried about her child like this."

"That's very common too," she said with her friendly smile. "Don't beat yourself up or you'll be no good to Jacks when you see him."

"How's he been doing?"

"Well," she looked at her Apple watch and chuckled, "since you've been gone, he's finished up with the speech therapist."

"The speech therapist came tonight?" I said, stopping her from saying another word.

"Yes," she looked at me skeptically. "Ms. Stein, all is well. The therapist said she enjoyed the progress that was made tonight."

"Thank you, Sally," I said, then pulled my purse strap in tighter and nearly speed-walked through the halls to get to the elevator.

This is why I haven't left the hospital. And this is why I shouldn't have gone out for dinner tonight. I can't believe I missed the speech therapist's visit!

Why wouldn't Cameron have called me? Oh, right, because I shoved him into the friend zone, and the 'Dr. Brandt only' category. I'm fucking everything up by thinking I'm doing the right thing...and now this?

The elevator doors opened, and I rushed out as carefully as possible, knowing this floor housed patients recovering like my son. The last thing I needed was to hurt someone else while berating myself for abandoning my son once again.

I walked briskly down the walkway that led to the numerous rooms on this floor. There was a glass half-wall to my right. Beyond the railing of the glass was an impressive sports arena. Kids in recovery would go there to throw Nerf balls, actual balls, or holographic balls while working with their therapist to improve their motor skills or just to help them stay active.

I'd previously toured this rehabilitation area with Jacks, and we found the sports arena intriguing. Unfortunately, Jacks couldn't stay in the place due to certain flashing lights possibly provoking a seizure.

Thankfully, out of this nightmare came a silver lining: my son hadn't had one seizure since Cameron operated on him.

"Where's Jackson?" I questioned, unsure of where he could be at this hour. "He's not in his room?"

"Ms. Stein, he's with Dr. Brandt and Dr. Brooks," Nurse Julia answered.

"I'm sorry, but where? And why?"

Cameron, what the hell are you doing?

I heard Cam's laugh coming from the arena.

"Jackson insisted, and Dr. Brandt thought it would be fine to go to the arena to get him out of the room for more than just the therapist appointments," Julia went on.

"Thank you," I said.

I turned and walked to the glass wall where the sounds came from below. I covered my mouth, tears stinging my eyes when I inched toward the glass railing and leaned against it, marveling at the sight below me.

"All right, Champ," Collin said, wearing his blue scrubs. His short blond, messy hair was nearly white under the arena's lighting. "Your mind thinks you're right-handed, and that's the only way you can throw a ball, right?"

"We're going to change it," Cameron added, looking strikingly handsome from this vantage point in navy scrubs that matched Collin's.

I looked at Jacks, sitting in his wheelchair, and I covered my heart when I saw his right foot move. "Oh, God," I whispered, choking back tears, finding excitement in the smallest things. This was huge.

Jacks let out a sound. His head was braced in the wheelchair because he still didn't have the ability to hold it upright for too long.

I smiled again.

"Shit," Collin said when Cam hit him in the chest with the Nerf football. He took the regular football, smiled at Cam, and rocked back on his left leg before he fired the ball back at Cameron. "That's BS, dude. You told me you couldn't throw with your left arm."

"I can't," Cameron said, laughing and looking at Jacks. "Nice, though, right?"

Jacks moved his foot again while Cameron walked over to get the dud-throw that Collin threw with his left arm.

Cam was still a great shot, but I wasn't so sure he nailed Collin in the chest by throwing that with his left arm.

"Throw that shit back to me," Collin said. I rolled my eyes at their profanity. They couldn't resist even when some kids or families had to be around, listening to doctors act like idiots.

"I just threw it at you, Jacks saw it, and I watched you cry like a little bit—" he stopped himself from finishing the word, and I noticed that Jacks seemed more animated than he had since he woke up from surgery.

He absolutely loved these two, acting like stooges.

"Throw it again, *left hand*, because I'm doubt—" Collin was hit in the gut this time, and he bent over, holding in his curse words.

A little girl squealed and laughed. "He got you, Dr. Brooks. Right in the nuts!" she declared, her cute voice echoing through the arena and up to me.

I closed my eyes, and my lips tightened as I shook my head. *Glad these two are setting great examples on the floor,* I thought in humor, unsurprised.

"Hey, Jacks!" Two other kids walked over to where Jacks sat in his wheelchair. The little boy who called his name rubbed the top of his shoulder carefully. "Feeling good?"

Jacks moved his head just enough to let me see from here that his answer was yes.

"Me too. I want to play football," the other boy said, his head wrapped in bandages.

"Not with the way Dr. Brandt throws with his left hand, kid," Collin said, still recovering from the nut-shot Cameron sent his way.

"My name's Tommy," the boy said, correcting Collin with annoyance. "I'll be just fine."

"That's what I like to hear," Cam said, walking over to where the three kids stood around Jacks. "However, having just operated on you, I'm not clearing you for the regular football yet."

"It wouldn't be fair, Dr. Brandt," Tommy said. "Jacks can't play, so we can't play."

"Don't start that. We're all here to help each other work harder." Cam smiled at Jacks and knelt. "Jacks would be pretty upset with me if I didn't let you play so you can get better faster. I'm sure of that," Cam said, looking at Jacks and reaching to rub his knee. "Right, kid?"

I could see the movement in Jacks, and it appeared he agreed with his dad.

"Listen," Collin said, stepping up to the group, "how about we all use the holographic balls to show Jacks that we can throw a football with our left arms just like he's going to. In fact, we better learn how to now because I have a feeling Jacks is going to beat us all when he gets there."

"Holographic balls? Really, Dr. Brooks?" Cameron said, standing up and laughing.

"I should like to have more kids, and your left arm is about to end all hope for Elena and me if we use a ball that can do damage," he answered.

"All right," I heard another voice, and it was Jake. "I'm off shift and ready to do this!"

"Awesome," Collin said with a devilish grin, throwing the football into Cam's chest. "Cam throws a mean ball with his left hand, Dr. Mitchell. You'll be impressed."

"Do it! Do it! Do it!" the kids said in unison.

Happiness covered me like a warm blanket on a chilly autumn afternoon. It was comforting to watch Cam and his friends give Jacks hope and encouragement for his recovery in this manner. It was heartwarming, and I needed to see it more than I knew.

Cameron wasn't giving up on Jacks in any way. He'd shown that to me in other ways, but seeing him prove that Jacks could train his brain to throw with the left arm instead of using his right arm was monumental for Jacks and me.

Even if he wouldn't regain use of his right arm, he still had his left arm to throw with. How strange that something so minor could impact my emotions in such a huge way. This was all so much more inspiring than I'd expected.

They said that I should expect miracles to happen this month, and after not speaking to Cam much since everything happened, I wondered if it would take a miracle for us to ever work again.

Chapter Forty-Three

Cameron

This month flew by faster than the hell that caused the fallout of my and Jessa's short-lived relationship. Sadly, we grew farther apart, with Warren constantly lingering around and my focus more on Jacks than anything.

I had to take partial responsibility for it dissolving to nothing, as my only priority was Jackson and my everyday busy life as a top surgeon at this hospital. I felt myself sinking into that dark void more than once but throwing myself into working and being with Jacks made those sensations go away as quickly as they came.

"Look at your pimp self," I said to Jacks, walking into the room where he was dressed and ready to leave rehab.

"I'm good, man," he said. His words were still a bit slow, but the speech therapist said he'd made excellent progress, and by next week, Jacks could be talking like he'd been before the surgery.

"I'm so damn proud of you, kid," I said, hugging my son with whom I'd formed the most wonderful bond throughout his recovery. Then, I stepped back and looked into his cheerful eyes. "Seriously, you're doing better than I expected a sixteen-year-old to do in recovering from this surgery. Insanely better, and it's just a matter of time before we get the brace," I pointed at the brace on his right arm, "off your throwing arm and get you back in the game."

Jacks smiled and unexpectedly hugged me back, "Thank you. You helped me so much."

I felt tears burn in my eyes and knew I could quickly lose my shit if I weren't careful. "You helped me too, kid."

"Oh?" Jessa chirped with excitement, walking into the room. "How's that, Doc?"

I didn't know if it was the excitement of Jackson's big day of going home, the anticipation of where it all went from here, or the realization that Jacks had got me through a month that I probably wouldn't have survived without him, but I stared into Jessa's radiant eyes, and I couldn't tolerate being back in this position with her.

I needed her back.

"The car's here. The Uber is a killer ride, Sport," Warren said, his voice slicing through the air and making me angry the moment I'd heard him.

This fucking guy again, I thought. The bastard had come back into Jessa's life and most likely manipulated her into taking him back because he knew she was vulnerable.

"All good here, Dr. Brandt?" he said. I couldn't stand this man, and that was putting it mildly.

"I just signed off on the last of his charts." I looked to where Jessa and Jackson stood together, ignoring mine and Warren's bizarre stand-off. "The therapists will meet with you tomorrow and review the outpatient rehab guidelines." I looked back at Jackson. "When you're ready, Collin and Jake have insisted on a game of beach football," I said. My friends and I worked with Jacks over the past month to ensure he kept moving forward, fighting, having fun, and never giving up.

"Don't you think football is pushing it a little bit?" Warren popped off.

"Okay," the outpatient team leader said, walking into Jackson's room, where I was ready to punch Warren in his whitened teeth.

Fucking douchebag.

"All's good here. He's officially discharged from St. John's," I said, smiling at Jacks. "I'm on-call this week, but your mom and I discussed me popping in and out to check on you if that's good?"

Jacks smiled, but it was apparent the poor kid was confused. One day he was going to Lakers games with my best friend while his doctor and mother were on vacation in Mexico, and the next thing he knew, Warren was back in his life—and now living in Southern California. He hadn't said a word about any of it, but honestly, he had more significant problems than discussing his mom's relationship patterns.

"Laguna Beach isn't exactly around the corner from here," Warren said. "Are you sure you can be that far from the hospital?"

You're a fucking prick, I thought, hating this asshole more and more by the second.

"Don't be a dick, Warren," Jacks said, shocking me. And after looking over at his annoyed expression and Jessa's wide eyes, I didn't know where to take this.

"I see you've learned some lovely foul language while under the care of Dr. Brandt," Jessa said as Warren tried to figure out how to pick his jaw up off the ground.

Jacks smiled at me. "Dr. Brandt doesn't cuss," he laughed.

God, this boy. I wanted to hug him and tell him he was a chip off the old block, but that was for a different day. It was another thing I wanted to discuss with Jessa but would do so when this gnat of a man wasn't hovering around like the annoying fucking insect he was.

"Never," I agreed. "All right. The team is here, and the rehab center usually does a fun send-off when patients leave, so don't keep them waiting."

"I'll see you soon?" Jacks said, and I nodded.

As the room filed out, Warren decided to pull a chickenshit move and glare at me like a middle schooler. I'd had about enough of his shit for the past month, and I wasn't about to let this bitch piss me off on my son's big day.

"Can I speak to you for a moment, Warren?" I said, staying back.

"It's okay," he said reassuringly to Jessa while I kept a professional expression and refrained from rolling my eyes.

"Yeah, I'm not going to kick his ass or anything," I said after she halted. "I just need to go over some stuff, ensuring Warren understands. I haven't talked to him much over this past month, and I want to ensure he's up to speed with supporting Jackson and you."

I plastered the fakest smile I could manage to get Jessa to trust that I wasn't going to level this dick standing proudly to my left, and she hesitantly left the room.

"What's the deal, Cameron?" Warren questioned.

I slid my hands into my pockets. "I intend to get my lady and my boy back. I suggest you not get too comfortable living in Southern California."

I didn't give a shit anymore. I might as well make my intentions clear with this fucker so he wouldn't be surprised when his ass was heading back to New York in less than a month.

"Oh?" Warren said, his gaze darkening. "Well, if it makes any difference, *I* wasn't the one who called and begged for me to come back into their life—that would be the woman out there who doesn't trust herself with you. So maybe you should tell her, not me."

I smiled, "She was scared, and that happens. So, I'm not surprised she'd fall back into the arms of a man who most likely made her comfortably miserable."

"Miserable, my ass," Warren said. "She's a good woman, not the type to live her life chasing adventures and thrills. I know you believe it's as easy as that," he snapped his fingers to prove some point, "but there are responsibilities in this life to attend to when you're not born with a silver spoon in your mouth."

"You insult me because my father was wealthy?"

"You insult yourself, Cameron. Take my advice: if you care about Jessica and Jacks, leave them alone. Let them live a normal life where they aren't spoiled by material things that give false hope."

"What the hell is that supposed to mean?"

"They're not grounded when they're with you. Not everything is yachts, expensive cars, and beach houses on loan by friends. That isn't the real world, and until you can see that, you'll never understand why Jessica blames herself for her son falling into that coma."

He turned and left as quickly as he could.

I didn't know what to think. What I did know was that this intimidated asshole had insulted me and my life, which he knew nothing about. The idea that I wasn't grounded was laughable. I was a top pediatric neurosurgeon at a world-famous hospital, and I didn't become so by galivanting around the world on a yacht with no responsibilities.

I certainly hoped that short-sighted prick heeded my warning because I was on a mission to take back the two most important people in my world, and none of his petty insults would stop me.

Chapter Forty-Four

Jessa

With Jacks and I living with Warren in the Laguna Beach condo, one might assume that Warren's and my relationship had been rekindled, but that couldn't have been farther from the truth.

Warren and I had picked up where we left off, minus the engagement. There was no sex, no romance, no connection...nothing. Vanilla was a spicy way to describe us. But Warren made me feel grounded, secure, and comfortable, whereas Cam made me feel wild, carefree, and, for lack of a better word, careless.

No matter how often I tried to work things out in my head, I always ended up on that fateful day in Mexico, where I was lost in bliss, debating whether to have another drink, when Cameron walked out to me. I was floating on clouds and higher than Snoop Dogg (as that joke goes), believing he was about to propose marriage to me.

Then, reality hit me like a meteor. The downside of living in a fantasy world is that the stresses of everyday life *will* hunt you down and find you, so you better be ready. Being half-buzzed and deciding whether I'd accept Cam's marriage proposal was me living in that fantasy. My son falling into a coma was life's way of telling me to keep my ass planted in reality and pay attention to my responsibilities.

Warren agreed, and the three of us moved into this lovely condo in Laguna Beach. And every morning that Jacks and I got out and walked the beach, I would look up at the incredible beachfront homes, reminded of the house Jake and Ash so generously let us use and of Cameron's place in Malibu.

"Jessa?" I heard a woman call over the sound of waves crashing onto the shore. I turned and saw Bree Grayson, a lovely woman I'd only met once. Her husband was one of Cam's close friends, and Bree was introduced to me by Ash, Avery, and Elena when we met for dinner a while ago. Her bright smile popped the cutest dimples on her cheeks, and she half-jogged over to Jacks and me. "You must be Jacks!" she said, noticing the brace on his right leg and arm. "Well, aren't you adorably handsome? You look great!"

"Jacks," I said, smiling at his confused expression, "this is Bree Grayson. Her husband is Alex. He's good friends with Cam and Cam's friends."

"I've heard them talk about him. It's nice to meet you, Bree," Jacks said, reaching out his right hand. His movements were still slow, but he was making good progress. "Sorry, it's a bit hard to shake with this hand."

"Don't you dare apologize," she said. "I've met grown businessmen who have full use of their right hand, and they don't even have the courtesy to use it to shake my hand."

"Tell me about it," another blonde woman said as she approached. She looked like she'd been transported from a Gucci runway to the beach for God knows what. She peered at Bree through her oversized sunglasses. "Those men don't offer you the courtesy of shaking your hand because they're full of themselves." She looked over at Jacks, "So, always make sure you shake a woman's hand because if you don't, chances are she will assume it's because you wore it out the night before giving *yourself* a little hand if you know what I mean?"

She took a sip of the Cosmopolitan she held unabashedly in her hand, unconcerned that any random police officer could see her and fine her for it, and I couldn't help but laugh. *Who the hell is this woman?* I thought in humor. Her large, floppy beach hat and the way she spoke made me feel like I was standing with the real-life version of Samantha from Sex and the City.

"You'll need to pardon my friend. Everything is sexual with her," Bree said, staring at her friend in shock as the woman shrugged her shoulders. Bree shot her friend a look as if to censor her, and then she looked at Jacks. "Jacks, this is Natalia; Nat, this is Cam's—" she paused, and I knew she was searching for words other than *Cam's son*, "Cam's patient. He's recovering from surgery, and he's doing remarkably well."

She pulled off her sunglasses and eyed Jackson. "Dear God, you look just like Dr. Brandt!" she said. She looked at me as I subtly shook my head, pleading with this woman to shut her mouth immediately. I must've looked like a deer in headlights because she caught on instantly and corrected herself. "I just mean, you certainly are a gorgeous young man, aren't you? Cam would love to know he's been compared to a handsome man like yourself, especially coming from me."

Jacks smiled but didn't say much because I knew he was inwardly drooling over this woman. She was one of the most beautiful women I'd ever seen, so I could only imagine what a teenage boy thought of her.

"So, you know Cameron?" I asked, wondering if Cam was dating or had dated this woman. I wouldn't have been surprised.

"Oh," she smirked at me while Bree chuckled, "that's a story for a better day when young men who have proper manners aren't around."

Now, my interest was piqued. Who was this woman?

"I'm down here checking out some real estate with Breanne," she said. "Why don't you join us for lunch later?"

"They're not in the market, Nat," Bree said. "But we're all going to Jim and Avery's house tonight for Jake's birthday. We're lowkey getting everyone together."

"I'm going to pass," I said. "Cam was over this morning, working with Jacks a little bit, and he invited as well, but I think it's best for us to hang back."

"Best for whom, dear?" Nat said. "These little bashes are where the good stories about all these crazy men are told."

"Right," I answered.

"Mom," Jacks interjected, "you need to stop hiding from everyone."

My face flushed red, irritated that Jacks would embarrass me in front of Cam's friends. He'd been a bulldog in recovery and that mentality had him smarting off every chance he got these days. I knew he was angry that we were back to living with Warren again, and that anger was pointed in my direction.

He lit up when Cam was around, but after Cameron left, my son would dismiss himself to do his treadmill, stretches, and computer therapy in his room and away from Warren and me.

I might've gained security from Warren in all of this, but I felt like I was losing everything else around me by choosing stability and comfort over being wild and carefree, starting with my son.

"I wish I could say that's what I was doing, but that's hardly what is happening."

"Could've fooled me," he said. "Nice to meet you both, ladies. Have fun tonight, and tell everyone I said hi."

"I—" I paused, pointing my thumb back toward where Jackson turned and walked away, "I need to get back. Very nice to meet you, Natalia. And it was great to see you again, Bree."

"Jessa," Bree said, stopping me, "do come tonight. If for no other reason than to hang out with us girls again. We miss you."

"Let me see if Warren is okay to stay with Jacks—"

"Hold the fuck up," Nat interrupted. "Forgive me if I'm being forward here, but is this Warren guy the *acting parent* for your son?"

"Acting parent?"

"Yes. You're not with his dad—whom I can easily assume is Cameron since your son looks exactly like that hot snack of a man—so is Warren his father figure?" Nat questioned, and her confident tone made the statement hilarious instead of intrusive.

"Yes, Warren is pretty much his father. He has been for years."

"For years?" She pulled her oversized glasses down. "Well, honey, then there's no asking. There's simply insisting that he stay with your son so you can have a girls' night."

"I don't think he'll be cool with me hanging out with a bunch of Cam's friends," I honestly said.

"So, you got back with the man and *then* allowed him to put a fucking leash on you? Nah, you need to get out. After *that* statement, I can tell you'll never know what life is outside of being a caretaker and a lonely little housewife," Nat said. "You're too good for that. Completely unacceptable."

"Nat, you're being rude," Bree said. "Sorry, she lacks the ability to give a shit. Some people love her, and some hate her."

"At least I'm black and white. There are no gray areas where I'm concerned. There's too much stress in the world not to have clarity with people. But listen, hun," she continued, and somehow, I appreciated her directness, "if you've put yourself in a position to depend on a man, and he begins to take your freedoms away, your sex drive will die first, and a vibrator won't even resurrect it. There's only one way to go from there: antidepressants, wine, and, inevitably, reality shows about housewives and bake-off challenges. Now, I know what you're thinking, and those things are all great on their own, but none of them should be binged, especially in tandem."

"Jesus, Nat. You make it sound like she's a prisoner for checking in with her partner," Bree said as the wind whipped through Natalia's pashmina.

"Losing your sex drive and not being able to live your life a little is more like a death sentence, Bree. Please, God, do *not* tell me that after a year, Alex has stripped you of your rights as well. Does the vibrator I purchased for you no longer enhance the nights when he's traveling?"

Bree and I both started laughing. "Are you in real estate or porn?" I asked, laughing. I hadn't felt this light in too long.

"The porn industry could use my help, that's for goddamn sure, but I don't dig that now."

"I swear, you can work yourself up over nothing," Bree said.

"I'm always running at an even ten out of ten, ready to go when the moment arises," she answered with a smile.

"I have to know something," I said, glancing back and seeing Jacks talking to a couple walking their Labrador on the beach. "Did you and Cam hook up?"

She smiled, "You're adorable, and I see why you and he have created such a beautiful little human in your son."

"No," Bree said immediately. "I think Cam is the only man to ever turn down an advance from Nat."

"Truth," Nat said. "That guy is one hell of a scoop of caviar on a cracker. I was working every move and angle I knew—and trust me, honey, I could write the books on seduction—anyway, he played along all night, then turned me down."

I chuckled, "That doesn't sound like the guy I dated in college."

"He mentioned something about not being the man he once was when he was younger, but who knows." She threw her hair over her shoulder, "There's plenty of other eligible men who aren't afraid of me, so it took me a good three minutes to get over the rejection, and he and I have been good friends since."

"You know what? I think I will take you up on your invitation," I said, feeling in much better spirits.

Strangely enough, I loved this Natalia character. She was a kick in the ass, and her personality had put me in the mood to be with the girls. If I saw Cameron again, who knew, maybe we'd talk.

"It's the fear of losing that sex drive that will help you make better decisions, this one being the first, of course," Nat said.

"Or she could want to have a night out with friends?" Bree said.

"Like I said, fear of losing the sex drive. Depression is the beginning, and then the meds bury it. I'm not a doctor, so don't go quoting me, but in my experience, that's usually how it goes. A controlling man controls more than he knows."

"And ruins more than he knows," I answered with a laugh. "Listen, I'm going back to the house, and I'll see you both tonight. I turned down Cameron's offer earlier, so I'm not sure he'll be—"

"Who cares?" Bree said. "Cameron's a big boy. He'll be pleased you showed up whether you came by his invitation or ours."

I shook my head and laughed. Then I noticed the mysterious smiles the two women offered each other.

"Am I missing something?" I questioned.

"Nope, we're taking off." Nat turned and hooked her arm through Bree's. "We'll see you tonight, gorgeous," she said with a laugh and a wave of her hand.

I would've loved to brush it off, but I could tell that I didn't run into these two on the beach by accident, especially in Laguna Beach, this far south from where all of Cam's billionaire friends lived.

Maybe the girls really were down here walking the beach and just randomly ran into Jacks and me. Shit like that can happen, right? A text buzzed on my phone, stopping me from overthinking.

> Jacks: *Warren and I are heading out together.*
> Jessa: *Okay. I guess I'll order in food and enjoy some alone time ;)*
> Jacks: *Go have fun with your friends, Mom. Please.*

Something was definitely up. Jacks never wanted to go anywhere with Warren. Warren was dull and dry, and when he tried to fit in and be Jackson's buddy, the awkwardness of it drove Jacks insane. The divide with Warren had only seemed to grow since Cam and Jacks had become closer, especially since Cam had spent so much time with Jacks lately to help with rehab. We owed Cameron everything. I knew Cam was the reason Jacks had worked so damn hard to get this far. Cam pushed him, and Jacks loved it and thrived.

I didn't have the mental capacity to dig into any hidden conspiracies about getting me out of the house, but I was grateful for the opportunity. And if all these outside forces were working on getting me to socialize, they'd succeeded.

Chapter Forty-Five

Cam

"How's the kid?" Spencer asked.

I looked over at the sharply dressed businessman, wishing I could be as much of a dick as he was at times. For the last couple of months, my attempts to get Jessa back had failed miserably, and I was stuck with that terrible empty feeling. Even staying busy at the hospital these days didn't do anything for me.

"Doing great," I managed, tipping back my beer and downing half the damn thing in one swallow.

"When are you two going to get your bitch-asses in this pool and help us turn up this fucking water polo game?" Jake asked, throwing the ball from inside Jim's rooftop pool to where I sat on lounge furniture with Spence.

"When we go back to the days when we were four, like you idiots," Spence answered, taking a drink of his scotch and laughing.

I eyed the hard liquor, debating if I should take my chances and pour myself one, but with the mood I was in, it probably wasn't the best idea.

"So, tell me," Spence said, leaning his elbows on his knees, "what's going on with you? You look like hell, which shouldn't be the case from everything Jim has told me about how well your son is doing in recovery."

I shrugged, and in the distinguished art of trying to go bald at a young age, I rubbed my forehead for the millionth time this month.

"Jacks is doing amazing. The kid is determined to get past the limp, and his vision and right arm are still trying to fuck with him." I smiled and stared into the firepit, "He just doesn't quit."

"A lot like you then, eh?" Spencer said.

I looked over at Collin, Jake, Alex, and Jim tossing the ball around in the pool, making up some game like we always did, and wondered how I'd somehow traded places with Jim. He was usually up here, chilling with Alex or Spence on the sidelines. They were notorious for having one of their epic business conversations while the rest of us entertained ourselves like toddlers at the park.

"Guess so," I said.

"How's Jessa?" he asked.

In being around businessmen all my life, I knew the tone that Spencer used well. It meant he was guiding this conversation in a direction that would either help me or make me angry. There was no in-between.

"Madly in love with that Warren bastard," I said, then closed my eyes when I realized I'd said it loud enough to stop the ball from being traded by my friends in the pool, bringing a mischievous and all-knowing grin to Spence's lips.

"That's fucked up," he said casually.

"Yeah, you think? Jessa and I were just getting things started, getting to know each other again, and then it's like, boom! Like it wasn't meant to be or something."

"Wasn't meant to be my ass, Cinderella," Spence said with a laugh.

"You wouldn't understand," I said with the same annoyance I felt. "Let's just end this conversation right here."

"I'd gladly let that die; however, your depressed ass just told me I wouldn't understand something. That doesn't fly with me," Spence said, acting like a cocky asshole.

"That's why your last deal made us more money than Mitchell and Associates had ever done," Jim said. He dried off and caught his daughter as she rushed to him when the women passed by with the kids. "I've got her," Jim said, waving at Avery.

It must be nice to help your lady out instead of having her kick you in the balls repeatedly with her new man.

Fuck. I was acting like the biggest bitch ever, but I was so damn defeated that I didn't know what to do.

"Mm-yeah," Izzy said, reaching her arms out toward me. She kicked her two-year-old chubby legs against Jim's in protest while I smiled. This little girl, with her pitch-black hair and icy blue eyes, was my little buddy. I adored her feisty personality and how she could give Jake's son, John, a run for his money.

Jim popped the pacifier out of Izzy's mouth. "Now you can talk, Izzy," he said.

"And here I thought little Izzy had you wrapped around her finger," I said, smiling at Izzy, who was now angry at her dad.

"She does," Jim grinned at his annoyed daughter. "But this whole pacifier thing needs to end and soon."

Izzy frowned and looked up at Jim with a lethal expression. "Well, you've officially pissed her off," I laughed.

"She looks a lot like you do these days, Cam," Spence added.

"How so? I didn't realize I looked that adorable when people pissed me off?"

"You do. Your pretty blue eyes must make you both look the same," Spence said. "However, little Izzy doesn't have a look like the world is ending when things don't go her way," he sat back in his chair and took another sip, "so that's where you're different and not as cute as her."

I rolled my eyes and had a feeling I'd be doing a lot of that tonight.

"What's going on with you, Cam? Catch me up on how things are going with Jessa. Last we spoke, you put Warren in his place and were planning to get back your son and Jessa?" Jim asked, joining the grand inquisition.

"Yeah," Spence said after I looked down, pissed that my plans weren't working out. "His bark is a lot louder than his bite."

"Fuck that noise," I said to Spence. "I've tried. It seems all I do is push them further into Warren's arms."

"Warren is the biggest fuck-knuckle I've ever met. And you *honestly* think you've lost your son and Jessa to that dipshit?" Spencer laughed while he and Jim exchanged knowing glances. "You're losing your game to a man who practically begged Jim and me to hire him to work in our advertising department that day in the hospital? He's a fucking douche. How the hell are you letting that guy beat you at *anything?*"

"He hit you both up for jobs while I was in surgery with Jacks?" I said, shocked at this revelation.

"Not shitting you," Spencer said. "The man has no dignity. If he did, he would've never asked friends of Jessa's or *Jessa's ex* for a job."

"We had to pull him over to a corner to entertain him and keep him away from Jessa because he was no good to her. I suspect his chattering was grating on her nerves, and rightfully so under the circumstances," Jim said. "I imagine she would've been mortified if she knew he was hitting us up for jobs, though. It took Alex and Spence's directness to level him down quite a lot, but if it were up to me?"

"You'd have him curled up in a ball in the corner of the room, crying like the bitch he is," Spencer said to Jim and then turned to face me. "Listen, Cam," he grew more serious, "don't let this whole thing get into your head like this."

"Spence, forgive me if I'm too forward, but *you* can't be troubled to hang onto a woman for more than a night. I'm not sure I can see this as no-big-fucking-deal as you can. She's the love of my life, and I fucked it up."

"Dat-dat-mir!" Izzy said, pointing at me.

Jim chuckled. "I'll never know what the hell she's saying, but she says this shit every time she gets pissed."

"It's pacifier talk for *stop acting like a bitch, Uncle Cam,*" Alex said, drying off, shaking his head, and joining us. Great, now I was about to get lectured by three businessmen. "Right, Izzy?"

"Wrong, Uncle Alex," Avery said, walking out to where we were. "Why are we all out here cussing up a storm in front of Izzy? It's bad enough we can't figure out what half her words are, and something tells me this *dat-dat-mir* phrase is probably a few curse words rolled up into one." She leaned down to get her daughter, who was reaching up for her. "Time for bed, little one." She looked at me, "Jessa is here. She's been talking with Laney downstairs, so dry it up, handsome." She winked in her usually sassy Avery way, "I think this may all come back together for you. The rehab might just have taken longer for your relationship malfunction than Jackson's did."

I rose, bringing smiles and humor to everyone's faces.

"Send her up here," Spence said. "Quick, Cam, jump in the pool. Let her see what she's been missing for a couple of months."

"I agree," Alex smirked.

"Anything else from the men I won't be taking advice from tonight?" I looked at Jim.

Jim sipped his bourbon and shrugged, "Dat-dat-mir?"

"Yeah. That about sums this up," I said, feeling more anxious than I should.

"You're going to be fine," Avery said, pulling Izzy tightly into her side. "But the whole bare chest in the water thing couldn't hurt your case."

"Nice, Av," I answered with a smile. "Is Jessa okay?"

"I don't think she's going to be okay until you and she work things out," Avery said. "Might be just me, but she and Warren are toxic. I think she sees that, but if *you know* that, you have an angle."

I smiled, feeling my spirits lift. Thank God for that, too, because when I got here, after Jessa and Jacks had declined my invitation to join me at Jim's house, my mood was shitty.

Now, all I could do was hope that things went well. Lately, it seemed like every time I got my hopes up with Jessa, everything always went south.

I walked through Jim's pimp as fuck Hollywood Hills home, and with each beat of my heart, my feelings of excitement faded, and the nerves took over.

Fuck, Cameron, this is what you've been praying for.

"Hey, Cam," Elena said with a bit of liveliness. "Can I talk to you for a second?"

"Haven't we had enough of your sneaky-therapy sessions, Laney?" I asked with a grin.

"We have," she said with a challenging eyebrow arch. "And thank God for my sneaky little attempts to peel you like an onion, or else you'd be a prisoner at St. John's, hiding behind work and from all of us."

"So, what is this?" I asked. "Seriously, I'm confused."

"Just come here and stop asking questions," she said, leading me to a spare room in Jim's home.

She closed the door behind us, "I'm on my way to see Jessa. I don't want to keep her waiting."

"She'll be fine. She's with Nat and the girls."

My eyes widened. "You left her alone with *Natalia*?" I asked incredulously. "Jesus Christ. Trust me, Nat is *not* her flavor."

"Nat was not *your* flavor," she said with a laugh. "Jessa likes her. In fact, I think we all have Natalia to thank for helping Jessa come to her senses about coming to talk to you tonight."

"How the fuck is that possible? The only thing that woman cares about is money and sex."

"Nat cracks all of us up, so take it easy on her. Now," Elena said, more serious, "Jessa doesn't need fifty-million questions about why and how she left you."

"Why are you telling me this?"

"Because she's been with that asshole for a month now and blowing your ass off. Anyone from the outside looking in would judge the situation harshly."

"I don't blame her for leaving me and believing she could find more stability in Warren. Unfortunately, I didn't have much time to prove myself to her before things went horribly wrong with Jacks."

"I know," she said. "Both of you needed this last month to heal with Jacks, and I feel you both have. You just need to understand that sometimes, when something is right for two people, it takes time to heal, and healing separately, to realize that you need to be together."

"You act as though I'm going to go in there and blow up on her or something."

"I know you would never do that to her or any other woman, Cam," she said. "But emotions do some crazy shit to us, and she's been with another *man* for over a month."

Her eyes locked onto mine, and we were in some standoff now. "Yeah, and that's fine. So long as she's not here to tell me she's engaged to him again and on her way back to New York, I will keep my cool. Trust me."

"Right," Elena smiled, and I sensed that more things seemed to be at work here aside from Jessa stopping by tonight.

"Right," I mirrored her, trying to pull the information out of her. "What the hell is going on, Laney?"

"There's my Diosa Cubanita. What are you doing with this old sap?" Collin said from behind me, stepping into the room where Laney and I were talking, with the door half-closed.

"Oh, you know me. I'm just psychologically intruding on a romance that I believe needs to happen," Laney answered while Collin placed his arm around her.

"What'd you tell this guy?" Collin asked, acting *fucking weird*.

"I'm going to go find Jessa," I said. My friends were acting beyond strange, and I was starting to lose patience with them.

"Good luck, buddy," Collin said.

"You'll do great," Laney said.

I turned back with a frown, studying the two standing there like the parents on a *Leave it to Beaver* episode, and I forced a smile on my face.

What the fuck was going on with those two?

Something was entirely off with Collin and Laney, and because they were dumb enough to make it obvious, I was smart enough to hang back to listen on the other side of this door, hoping I'd overhear something that might shed some light on things.

"Do you think this will work?" Collin asked, and I smiled. I *knew* these assholes were up to something because these were my friends, and only my friends would play games, believing they were bringing Jessa and me back together again.

"How was he at the pool?" Laney questioned.

"Acting like a bitch," Collin said with a laugh, and I rolled my eyes.

"Spence kept him busy while you ladies were with Jessa. How do you think she feels about all of this?"

"Oh," Elena giggled as her phone chimed, "this is Jacks. Let me tell him he did well and that our plan is going smoothly."

Jackson? Texting Elena?

"What the fuck?" I said, entirely confused now.

"What?" a female questioned from behind me, causing me to nearly jump through the door where I was eavesdropping.

I turned. "Jesus, Natalia. Announce yourself or something," I said.

Her rosy-red lips pulled up as she crossed her arms in front of her chest.

"Announce *my*self? Perhaps you should announce *your*self to whoever you're spying on, on the other side of that door." She laughed. "What's going on in there that would shock you?"

"Wouldn't you and your kinky little self love to know?" I said, slipping my hands into my pockets, a bit thankful that Nat was the one to catch me and not anyone else.

"Indeed," she said without missing.

Time to kick the ball back to these assholes for sneaking around behind my back. "It's Collin and Elena. I was on my way to see Jessa—apparently, she's here to talk—and I saw Collin sneak into that room," I said, trying to act cool.

"And why would that lead you to spy on him? Last I checked, Jim's place wasn't a murder mystery house where the guests were all suddenly disappearing?"

"Well, it sounded like he fell," I answered, trying to think of something, knowing by Nat's strong eyebrow arch that she was catching on to my lie. "So, I went to open the door, and then I heard Elena say—" I paused, searching for something that would make me spy on my two married friends.

"Say?" Nat pressed.

"God, this is embarrassing. I'm embarrassed for Collin, actually," I said.

"Then it must be bad," Nat humored me. "So, spill it, blue eyes."

"He said to go easy while shoving it up his ass like last night," I said softly, acting like I was repeating Collin's words.

Nat rolled her eyes. "*That's* what's got you spying behind the door, married people's kinky sex shit? Good God, I struggle to know what you would've thought of me in bed," she said unamused.

"Well, if a man taking it in the ass from another woman is not the least bit shocking to you, then I'm glad I never went home with you," I said, staring at this woman and wondering if *anything* embarrassed her.

"Cam, let me inform you of something," she said. "There are plenty of men in this world who take it up the ass from their wives all the time, literally and figuratively. Some like it, and some don't. It seems like Collin likes it, so what's the fun in listening unless that turns you on?"

How the fuck did this backfire in my face?

"God, no. That doesn't turn me on."

"Then why are you listening on the other side of the door like some creepy voyeur?"

"Fuck me, Nat," I answered. "That's not what I'm doing. I'm not a fucking creep."

Her eyebrows shot up, "What the hell else would you call it? Listening to your friend get pegged without anyone knowing? I say that's creepy, and I think you're probably turned on, and since you're most likely not getting any lately, you'll—"

"Stop!" I held both hands up. "I'm not creepy, I don't need a piece of ass, and I'm not turned on listening to my friend take it in the ass."

"Who's taking it in the ass this time?" Jake said, bounding down the stairs, hearing everything I told Nat after my voice rose in frustration.

"Collin," Nat said. She pointed at the door I was standing in front of protectively, praying that Collin and Elena didn't hear any of this. "Cam was standing out here with his ear pressed to the door, listening to his friends' matrimonial coitus."

Jake's expression tightened in humor while he pulled on his shirt, his hair still wet from being in the pool. "I thought Collin only liked it when—"

"The fuck are you all doing out here?" Collin said, opening the door and zipping up his pants.

Dear God, I should've known he'd prove my lie true because he and Laney could never be left alone without something happening.

Jake recovered his humored expression while Nat simply smiled.

"Was it good?" she taunted as only Nat would do.

"Always is," Collin said, not realizing he should be mortified because no one thought he'd just had a regular old quickie thanks to my lie.

"I thought I was your one and only," Jake said with a laugh. "Seriously, you're into that, though?"

"Uh, yeah. How has that not always been obvious?" Collin answered, looking at us as if we were all crazy.

"Right?" Nat said with a sexy arch of her eyebrow as Laney walked out, adjusting her dress and oblivious to the disaster I'd created out here. "You are one lucky girl."

She smiled and hugged Collin at his side. "I know." She kissed where her lips reached his upper arm. "And let this be a lesson to you, Natalia," she giggled, still glowing from her tryst, "marriage doesn't dull the sex life."

"Indeed, not," Nat said. "And that's why I'm jealous."

"I am too," Jake chimed in. "You two know no bounds, and apparently, *that's* the fucking key."

Oh, fuck me. I wouldn't be surprised if Jake went home and asked Ash to give him the old heave-ho next.

"That's always been the fucking key," Collin answered. Then he looked at me, "Speaking of fucking, why are you still here? I figured you and Jessa would be halfway to heaven by now."

All eyes were back on me, and instead of clearing up any of this, I let it all ride. Bastards always gave me hell anyway, so I might as well let Jake believe the key to keeping sex alive involved his wife strapping on a dildo now and then. Who knew? Maybe Jake and Ash were into that kind of thing, and I did everyone a favor.

"Before I take off to catch Jessa," I said, adding one last nail to the coffin, "Little John is upstairs by the pool, Nat. He was hoping to see his favorite Aunt Nat before bedtime."

"Oh, my bubs," she said and jogged off.

I smiled at what I knew awaited her and how my sweet revenge on her for backing me into a corner would come back tenfold when she walked out and saw Spence instead of little John.

"Why'd you send her up there? John's in bed," Jake said with a laugh.

"Why else?" I smirked.

"Karma is a bitch, and Nat will crack the whip on karma's ass, Cam," Collin said while Laney laughed.

"You guys go ahead," she said to Collin and Jake. "You get your handsome butt to Jessa," she told me. "I'm going to save Nat from being forced to interact with Spencer Monroe."

Elena sent us all packing, and I had to hope karma didn't get me back because I'd had enough reckonings for one lifetime.

I was ready to make everything right.

Chapter Forty-Six

Jessa

I glanced down at my watch, and even though it was nice to see the girls and visit them for the last half hour or so, this whole thing was starting to feel weird.

First, it was Jacks and his crappy mood when I didn't accept Bree and Nat's invitation to come here. Then, after I returned to the house to talk to him, he was adamant about having some *guy time* with Warren, of all people. Then, finally, as if my son's odd behavior wasn't strange enough, Elena calls and insists I come to the house because she's *worried about me*.

I bought into that one a little bit because, in truth, I was a little worried about myself. I'd been hiding behind Warren's business trousers instead of owning my shit as a strong woman would. Mom and Dad's visit didn't help me in that department, either. They only reassured me that I was weak without a strong man in my life.

They were horrible when it came to Cameron too. Almost embarrassing. Talking shit behind his back, and when they knew he was coming over to see Jacks and help rehabilitate him, they left the room. They made that shit obvious, too. Obvious that they had zero backbone and zero support for Jacks unless it went their way.

It's how my parents always were, though, and why I had no intention of moving back to Washington for their support. They still treated me like I was the reckless girl from college, and if I didn't do what they felt was suitable for me in my life, they ignored me.

They were next to impossible to get along with, yet somehow, I always managed to deal with them when they popped in and out of my life like this.

Why are you thinking about them? I thought, pacing the floor of this room, which had a spectacular view of Los Angeles. *Why are you even here? Because Jacks said it was good for me to get out? What is with that boy anyway? I know this is about Cameron.*

"Jessa?" Cam said. I whirled around, and my breath caught when I saw this man looking so damn attractive in a tight black shirt and blue jeans.

"Wow, you clean up nicely," I tried to tease, but I knew that comment was as stupid as it sounded.

"Yeah, I guess I do." He held his arms out, his biceps stretching the hem of his shirt, and my feminine parts sprang back to life with a zing I almost forgot about. "Especially after the only thing you've seen me wear over the past month are scrubs."

"Meh," I placed my hands on my hips and teased him with a smile, "you look pretty good in those too, Doc."

He smiled and pointed his thumb over his shoulder, "Avery caught me upstairs and mentioned something about you wanting to talk to me?"

I frowned. "I did?" I questioned.

"I have no idea. I'm just repeating what she said."

"Interesting," I stared past him at the open entryway. "The girls invited me over, Jacks insisted that he wanted to hang with Warren, and that was after acting like I was the worst mom in the world for turning down the invitation to come over tonight—" I paused, seeing Cam frown, most likely in response to my comment about Jacks wanting to be with Warren. "No, something's up," I said. "Jacks can't stand

Warren, and the only thing he's been excited about since leaving the hospital are the days when you come over. So, I'm not sure what's going on." I pointed at Cameron, "Did you and Jacks set this all up? I mean, the girls invited me over, but after only thirty minutes, Elena told Avery to get the kids, and then the next thing I know, I'm being told you want to talk to me, so they all took off. But not before Nat gave me some pointers on make-up sex."

Cameron unexpectedly arched his eyebrow and folded his arms, "Make-up sex, huh?"

I rolled my eyes, something I'd been doing a lot lately. "Don't get too excited. It's Nat, and in the hour total that I've known the woman, I've learned that anything sex-related is not off limits to that woman," I laughed.

"No, absolutely nothing sexual or otherwise can frighten or embarrass that woman."

"Oh?" I studied his flushed cheeks and laughed. It had to have been the look of exhaustion and annoyance in his eyes.

"No," he instantly shot back, "not like that. I've never been with Nat like that. It's just that—"

Now I was a bit concerned because Cameron was falling over his words too much, and Natalia was every woman's envy of a natural goddess. Her unshakable confidence was the icing on the cake. The woman was a unique personality, to be sure, but she was also sincerely a fun, likable woman.

"Cameron, we're broken up, and Nat is like every man's dream. It's okay if you—"

"I didn't, and no, it's not okay, and it would not be okay if I were with another woman. Aside from being focused on Jacks and his recovery, I gave my heart to you and only you. I don't just take that shit back."

Fuck, that escalated quickly.

"Cameron, I know it seems like that's what I did, but—"

"Isn't it, though, Jess? Isn't *that* what you did by shutting down on me, as if we had nothing, and jumping back into the arms of the man who made you feel safe?"

If I hadn't had these last thirty minutes or so with Elena for her to open my brain up and pull out some trauma issues I'd been dealing with in all my past relationships, then I wouldn't have known how to answer Cameron.

I crossed the room and took his hand, leading him to the sofa. Once we sat, I twisted and hugged him. I felt tears in my eyes as I inhaled Cameron's robust scent. I'd missed it terribly.

"I love you more than words, Jessa," he said, his lips gently pressing into my neck while his sturdy arms pulled me tightly into him. "I miss you. I'm sorry this happened to us, and I lost you to him."

I pulled back. "No," I shook my head and locked eyes with his sapphire blue ones, "you didn't lose me to *him*, Cameron." I ran my hand along the dark scruff on his face, "You lost me to my fears and the need to heal from the pain in my past."

He looked at me with a confused smile. "You sound like you've been talking to Elena," he said.

"How would you know?" I chuckled.

"The whole *lost to fears* and *healing from pain and past issues*. That has Dr. Elena Brooks written all over it."

I grinned, "It's the truth, though. Thank God I did talk to her because if I hadn't, I'd probably be wearing my engagement ring again, playing the victim and living comfortably miserable for the rest of my life."

"I could see any woman being miserable with that dick," he said, and I silenced him with a smile, placing a finger over his perfect lips.

"I know," I said. "However, that's all Warren has ever been to me, really. He's someone who took care of Jacks and me when I knew I couldn't have *you*. When you left me in college, it only messed me up so badly because I dealt with shit like that from my parents." I exhaled, still shocked that Elena had pulled this shit out of my head so quickly. No wonder St. John's hired her as their top neuropsychologist. The woman was practically a soul-reader or something.

"In the home where I grew up, I was made to understand that my feelings weren't valid. When my parents wanted me to do something, I had to do it no matter how it made me feel. There were times when I rebelled against that but going against their *rule* meant being cut off from them for years."

"You've never said a bad thing about your parents, Jessa. But then again, you never really talked about them at all."

"I know, it was best not to bring them up because if I did, I would get upset or anxious. The one time I stood up to them was when I got pregnant with Jacks. I thought I could go to them for advice, for help."

"And?"

"And they told me I needed to contact you, hold you accountable, and not let you off so easily by letting you dump me to pursue your dreams. They insisted that you and your parents had money, and long story short, they thought I should make *you* suffer for getting me pregnant, not them."

"Jesus," he said, reaching down to hold my fidgeting hands.

"This made much more sense when Elena pulled it out of my head, so bear with me."

"I'm just sorry I put you in a position to be told that by your parents. I feel like the biggest piece of shit alive over that."

"Speaking of apologies, that's probably why all I've done since you've seen me again is apologize for things. Not only did my parents make me feel ashamed about my actions, but Warren jumped in there and picked up where they took off. I've always felt responsible for everyone's feelings and comfort, but not my own. People-pleasing was all I knew. So, when you got me out and kept me out of that zone, taking me on trips and pampering me, that was foreign to me. It felt wrong," I felt my voice lower. It was so weird how things that had happened in my life affected me so profoundly, and I never saw that it was unhealthy. "I felt guilty for being with you because everything was about *me*."

"It'll always be about you, Jessa. You're my lady, and—"

"I'm going to lose my train of thought," I laughed and cut him off. "When you made life about what I wanted, it felt wrong. Don't get me wrong, I loved it, but deep down, there was guilt. And when Jacks got into trouble, and I wasn't there because I was doing something *for me*, all those buried guilty feelings exploded to the surface. I freaked, and in my mind, I believed Warren was the one who could make me feel right about dealing with Jacks and the medical issues. In my mind, Warren was responsible because he didn't put me first. He put himself and his accomplishments first, making me believe that was a healthy way to live.

In reality, Warren was putting work first for himself, and I was expected to respect that and appreciate that because work bankrolled a roof over my head, food in my mouth, and medical care for my son. There was no love. There was no happiness. It was a very lonely relationship, and strangely enough, I was comfortable being lonely like that."

"Shit, Jessa."

"All that said to say this," I turned my hands to hold his. "I was scared, Cameron. I wasn't raised in an environment where I had my voice heard or my feelings validated. All I've ever known to do was to make everyone else happy but me. I'm happy when they're happy if that makes sense."

"Makes perfect sense, beautiful," he said. "You were afraid of making me unhappy if you told me about the pregnancy because it would interfere with my career."

"I would've ruined your life, Cam. We both know you would not have been the surgeon you are today." I rubbed my forehead, "Can you imagine where all those children would be, especially our son if I would've told you that I was pregnant? And what if—"

"No more *what if's*, Jessa. People have worried themselves into early graves over the statement *what if*. I've missed too much of my son's life and nearly lost you again because of it too." He repositioned himself to face me better. "I know I placed you in a position to question everything, but you aren't responsible for my feelings or reactions. I hate that you felt responsible for all of that."

"Well, I did become estranged from my parents for about four years because of it," I laughed. "And it made me think I'd found love with Warren, but it's not just all that. It's my baggage, my damage, and I just need to start owning it now instead of casting blame or trying to please everyone but myself by doing what they want instead of what I want."

"Is that why you're still with Warren?"

"It's why I have to move on from Warren," I said. "I need to take this time to heal. To heal alone, and to heal with our son."

His once hopeful expression grew somber. "Somehow, I was hoping all these revelations would bring you back to me."

I felt tears in my eyes again. "Cam, you don't want me like this. Trust me. I'm damaged, seriously, and I'm not just saying that. I will hurt you, if not now, then later. Something else will come up, and I will blame myself for trusting you when you put me first and loved me the right way. I must face things and learn to be strong on my own. The very fact that I ran back to Warren when the storm hit me full blast is enough to tell me that I would do it again. And it's not because I don't love *you*; it's because I *don't* really love *me*."

"I don't agree with that," he said.

"I didn't want to either, but it makes too much sense not to be true. How can I honestly say I love myself when I allow other people's happiness to overrule my own? That's not self-love, and even now, when I see this look of sadness on your face, I feel responsible for it. And knowing that I'll hurt you until I'm healed makes me want to take back everything I just said so that I can end your suffering."

I didn't know if what I was saying made sense. It made sense when Elena pulled it all out of my head, though. She laid it all out like a puzzle, and I needed to put the pieces back together again. I had to stop living like this even though I knew no other way, especially because I knew no other way.

Even now, it was killing me that Cam wanted me back, and as much I wanted to be with him too, I knew I needed time to figure out how I would start putting myself first.

"Hurt people, hurt people," Cameron said. Then, as if a light had been flipped on, he looked at me with a smile. "I will support any decision you make, but know this, Jessica Stein: if you plan to stay single for the rest of your life, then I'm going to be the old bachelor living in the single-wide trailer across the street, hitting on you while you prune your rose bushes every day."

"I never said I wanted to be single for the rest of my life," I answered with a laugh. "And even if I am, I can't imagine my billionaire-ex living in a single-wide trailer across the street."

"Oh, you'd be shocked at how us crazy-rich people roll," he laughed. "We go incognito all the time. Besides, those trailers can be very nice."

I patted his hand and rose. "Thank you," I said, hugging him after he stood with me, "for understanding."

He kissed the top of my head. "I'm doing my best to understand, which means I'll be kicking Collin's ass for allowing his wife to pull my girl farther away from me," I felt him laugh as I pulled away.

"Cam, this isn't her fault."

"Jessa," he said as he smiled down at me, "I know it's not her fault, but that doesn't mean I'm not going to give her hell for it. However," he arched his eyebrow and smiled at me, "I'm here for you, and I'm not going anywhere. When you're ready, and I pray to God that it will be soon, I'm ready to show you the love I know you deserve. I just wish I could help you on this journey."

"You're helping me by being understanding. I need to see my potential, doing things for our son and me without leaning on anyone else. I just need to figure shit out on my own."

"And Jacks?"

"If you have days that you're not at the hospital and want him to be with you, then I know nothing would make him happier."

"And Warren?"

"He'll be more difficult than you're being, that's for sure. But I'm positive he'll move back to New York."

"Jessa, if you don't have a place to live—"

"I'll figure this out, Cam," I said. "This is all part of the healing journey so I can be the best version of myself and have a promising future for a solid, equal relationship."

"I understand. As I said, I'm here for anything you need. I love you for putting yourself first, even if it means kicking me in the balls."

I felt him laugh, but I hugged him tighter. I was scared shitless. I didn't want to lose Cam, but I knew now why I pushed him away and ran back to Warren as I had. Things in my childhood and previous relationships made me nearly marry a man I'd be miserable with just to say I had a hero.

Now, I was almost thirty-eight years old, and I had no direction. All I knew to do was to take care of Jacks, and up until recently, be a support system to Warren. How would I ever take these first steps? I didn't know where to start, but I hoped it would come to me.

Chapter Forty-Seven

Cam

I walked Jessa out to her car, feeling that all hope for us getting back together was slipping farther away with each step I took. I wasn't happy with the arrangement, but I had no say in it. I told her I would give her time to get things right for herself, and I truly meant that. Hell, I loved the woman; if I didn't know that before, I knew that now.

Before, I might've taken this rejection as a *fuck you* and walked out of her life forever. But something told me to give her the time and space and allow her to heal. I honestly had no idea what she needed to heal from, but it wasn't my place to question her feelings.

Jessa had always had a good head on her shoulders, so if something didn't seem right to her, I trusted her instincts.

It's not that I didn't have the fight in me to win her heart back; it was that I loved the woman so much that I was willing to honor her request and let her go.

I just had to hope that whatever journey she was on would lead her back to me.

"Where's Jessa?" Bree asked, taking a sip of her martini.

"A better question would be, why the fuck aren't you with Jessa right now?" Collin said, sitting casually on Jim's massive ass sofa that was situated in this room to do nothing more than offering a perfect seat to take in all the lights of Downtown LA.

"Ask your wife," I said, grabbing a beer out of the bar fridge in the corner, my pathetic voice halting all conversation in the room.

"What happened, Cam?" Elena asked while I twisted off the top of the beer and worked to down the whole thing in a few gulps.

I wiped the back of my lips, everyone staring at me where I stood by the mahogany bar. I leaned back against it, elbow on the bar and legs casually crossed. I stared into the dark bottle, searching for words to say because I wasn't really mad; I was just fucking confused.

"She doesn't want a relationship," I smiled at everyone in the room. "She needs to work on herself first."

"The upside of that," Jake started after a moment of silence, "is Warren is fucked, too, right?"

"I hope so," I said, taking another drink of my beer. "Who the fuck knows? I'm confused as hell." I pointed the top of my beer to where all my friends sat, staring at me, "I'm also sure that you all played some part in trying to get us back together. Sorry, that backfired on you."

"All right," Collin stood. "You're not even drunk, and you sound like a man who's been drowning his sorrows for a week. Fuck that. Yes, we were all trying to get you back together, and the best part is, she didn't fully reject you," he said, grabbing a drink from the bar. "She didn't. She's working on herself, and there's nothing fucking wrong with that."

"I know. I'm just confused. I have no idea—"

"Cam," Elena said, joining her husband, "you need to understand that so much had happened in her life to cause deep trauma, even before you left her in college. I applaud her for having the strength to choose herself first. I applaud you for giving her that opportunity."

"Well, thanks for the applause, Laney, but I don't feel like this is something to celebrate."

"It's because you're feeling sorry for yourself," she hit back. "Seriously, this is not about you, Cameron. It's about her. It's about her being able to resolve some behaviors and things she's afraid she will take into her next relationship. She will hurt that man, be it you or whomever else."

"I just feel like she's mine, you know?" I answered Laney as if it were just her and me sitting in her office in a therapy session. "It's hard to let her go again, especially after I just got her back. We barely had any time together before everything went sideways, and now?" I ran a hand through my hair, frustrated, "Now, here we fucking are."

"Remember what we talked about that day on that yacht," Jim spoke.

I eyed him and then looked away. "Right."

"Slow, go, and no," he said. "Cameron?"

I felt like my dad was speaking through one of my best friends.

"Yep," I said, hoping to end this.

The beer wasn't helping, and neither was talking about this. I needed to get out of here. I wanted to get on my motorcycle and drive dangerously to feel the adrenaline surge through my veins, taking away all these emotions.

"You're at a point where she's said *no*," Jim went on as if he had my full attention. "I'm guaranteeing that if you give her the space she needs, she'll bump you into the slow range," I turned to look at him, seeing that all of this may have a light at the end of the tunnel. "By that point, when she's ready to move slow with you, support her. Be there for her and build on a friendship."

"But tread lightly in Jim's *slow* category," Spence said with some humor, "because if she starts drawing the friend zone boundaries on your ass, you're fucked, and you never make it to the go category."

Jim rolled his eyes. "You would know, I'm sure," he said. We all knew how Spence was. He proudly *fucked 'em and left 'em*. I was sure the man broke the friendzone laws and fucked those women, too.

"I've been in all sorts of categories that Jim loves pulling out of his ass with his relationship bullshit," Spence said with a laugh.

"Yeah, no shit," Jake said, laughing with Spence and then looking at me. "Okay, enough of this therapeutic bullshit," he nodded at Collin. "Give her the space she needs. You're a hot piece of ass, and whether you two ever tell your boy the truth, you're an amazing father. I could go on and on about your sexy blue eyes," he said, acting animated with his arms, "your tight ass, and those biceps that make me want you to fuck me like Elena fucked Collin with some dildo in Jim's spare room earlier, but I have a much better idea—"

"The fuck are you talking about?" Collin asked, bringing to mind the lie I told Nat, who was conveniently in the kitchen with the rest of the ladies to avoid being around Spence. Lucky for Elena, she'd excused herself just before this started.

Jake held his hands up, "Not my thing, man. I'm not shaming you. If you like taking it up the ass so fucking bad that you'd do it at Jim's house because you can't even wait to get home? Hey, that's your kink."

"The *only* shit I've taken up my ass is *your* bullshit when I'm not in the mood for it. Other than that, I wouldn't last a minute in prison," Collin defended himself, and I couldn't help but smile at how this lame lie had taken off.

"You're letting Laney fuck you with a dildo in my house?" Jim said.

"Hell, it seems like marriage can be quite adventurous," Spence stood, "but not enough to tempt me." He walked over and patted me on my shoulder. "Hang in there. She'll come back. They always do," he chuckled. "I'm out, guys. My driver is here, and I have the Bartholomew project to tidy up first thing tomorrow."

"When do you fly out to London?" Jim asked. "Those bastards at Green Gate are trying to come in hard on that deal, and I want them leveled. You're the fucker who can get it done."

"I'm not drunk enough to listen to you boss my ass around while I'm not on the clock," Spence said, and then he looked over at me. "Seriously, let her go for now and focus on your boy. This will work out. It's refreshing to hear that someone wants to fix themselves for a change. Sex will probably be even better for it, too."

"Sex is always your end game and final thought," I said.

"Yep," Spence said, disappearing through the side door.

"And since your ass ain't getting any, up it or near it," Jake said with a mischievous grin, "we're going out tomorrow night after work, taking your plane or the bikes, or whatever."

"If I don't get held over," I said. "Work has been crazy."

"Find a way to get out of there." He looked at his brother, then me,

"We're not letting you bury yourself in your job like Jim did while he waited for Avery. We're going to live, and yes," he smiled wider, "the ladies already have a plan to help your lady live, too. It's all taken care of."

"What?"

Collin smiled, "This is going to be one long-ass bachelor party, and Jessa is going to have a long-ass bachelorette party, too." He raised his glass of gin to me. "So, you're welcome for Elena, knowing Jessa wouldn't take you back immediately. Laney had a backup plan to keep her close, taken care of, and all but gift wrapped for you when she's at Jim's *go* moment." He looked at Jim. "Where *do* you come up with that shit?"

"My wife owns a women's shelter that helps in these situations, and I run a global empire, dickhead. So, this shit just rolls off my tongue," Jim answered.

While the room settled a bit, I felt better about where all of this would go. Thank God Laney and the others would be there for Jessa as friends for whatever she needed.

After this pep talk, I felt solid. This would work, and like I told Jessa, I was here for her when she was ready for me. I just hoped it wouldn't take forever, but I could play the friend game so long as it meant I could see her. And, of course, Warren's ass could run back to New York City, where he belonged.

Chapter Forty-Eight

Jessa

Who would have ever thought that in all of this—letting Cam go, letting Warren go, and more importantly, putting myself first—I'd end up working with the children who came to Elena's equine rehabilitation center?

I decided to take Elena up on her job offer since I'd been there almost daily. Jacks had nearly fully recovered after six months of busting his ass at Laney's equine rehab center, and when she offered, there couldn't have been a better solution to my employment problem.

It was practically a fairytale, maybe not to everyone else, but it was to me. I didn't end up with Prince Charming, sweeping my son and me off our feet, though. That prince being Cameron, of course. Because in every perfect scenario in my head, Cam was the only man who could make me feel whole if I were to factor romance into my fairy tale.

But I was neither happy nor sad about losing Cameron. Jacks learned that Cameron was his father about a month after Warren was officially out of our lives. I can't say he seemed surprised by the revelation, so even though he didn't come out and say he already knew, it was obvious to me that he'd put two and two together long ago, which was no slight relief.

Dealing with Warren was a struggle, but I ripped that fucking Band-Aid off. He was angry and demanded to know why I'd do this to him after he'd given me a second chance. His tirade ended with the good, old-fashioned *you'll regret this* because he'd never grace me with a third chance. I let him say his piece, and he stopped fuming after he realized his words didn't have their usual manipulative effect. I think I tuned him out after he insinuated that he'd done me a favor by being with me again.

It was striking how a little insight could change my outlook entirely. How could I have thought he'd felt happy to be with me? In his mind, it was I who should be thanking him, and for too many years, I felt the same. But no longer. Never again would I allow myself to be treated as anything but an equal. I'd damn near broken my back from carrying a disproportionate emotional load in all my relationships.

Warren wanted me to believe I would be single, unfulfilled, and alone for the rest of my life because no one could love or take care of me as he could.

Well, if living single for the rest of my life resulted in me feeling excellent, strong, and accomplished like this, then I'd take it any day of the week.

"How's Millie?" Elena asked after I walked out of the office where I did reports and financials for the equine center.

I stretched, having stood for the first time in what felt like hours. "Jacks said she can now close her hands over both reins. She's riding the pony without him leading her around the coral," I said, walking through the lodge-like center.

This place was gorgeous in every way, but the story of what made Elena and Collin establish this as an equine rehab center was even more beautiful.

"That girl reminds me of him," Elena smiled, wearing riding boots that came up to her knees. "Do you want to take a ride with me? The ocean looks amazing from the top of those mountains," she said, pointing toward the back of her estate. "It's my favorite place to go after a long day."

"Nah," I said. "Jacks is putting that pony away, and we're going to head home. I'm starved and—"

"I'm getting you on one of these horses one day," she laughed in her contagious and youthful Elena way. "You can't only bury yourself in spreadsheets and all that boring office stuff while you work here."

"It pays great," I said with a laugh.

"Right," she answered as we walked outside. She pointed at the vomit green 1980s station wagon I'd bought with my first, well-earned paycheck. "That piece of junk would speak otherwise about how much I pay you. Collin has even questioned it."

I chuckled and stepped down the stone steps to the car. "I'm sure he has, and because of him and Jake, I hang onto the thing. It drives them insane."

Elena laughed, crossing her arms and looking down at me as I got in the car and pulled out my phone to text Jacks. "It's honestly the *only* reason I'm cool with that hunk of junk," she laughed. "Those dipshits need to be humbled in the car area of their lives if you ask me."

"Exactly."

I picked up my phone as soon as it rang. "Jacks, I'm taking off. And if you want to take your driver's license test tomorrow, I suggest you step it up so we don't miss dinner with your dad."

"Be out front in a second," he said.

Cameron said he'd loan Jackson his Maserati for the test. I swear, I didn't know if putting Jacks in the station wagon would be a bad idea compared to the damn sports car. Either way, I wasn't going to argue. Arguing with Cameron about doing things for his son these days was pointless.

I guess the sad part of this was that I felt Cameron and I had become amazing best friends and co-parents. It wasn't necessarily because I wasn't trying to take things further. Trust me, my hormones raged insanely when I was around him. Tonight, after we went to dinner, I'd be envisioning the way his eyes would get glossy as he came inside me or how much I craved his enormous cock. His moans, his growls, his teeth grazing over my nipples.

"Mom," Jacks said, making me jump and clear my throat, scaring the shit out of me for getting horny while thinking about Cam again.

Goddammit, why couldn't Cam just hit on me or something? Anything. I'd take sex without commitment at this point. But Cameron showed no interest, and I wasn't going to push him to do anything he didn't want.

"Let's go," Jacks said. "Or is this piece of junk even going to start?"

"Stop," I said. "It takes a few tries before the transmission turns over. You know how it goes."

"Thank God Cameron is letting me borrow his car," Jacks laughed, and his eyes brightened as I put the car into gear and drove down the driveway. "And I'm almost at my budget for buying my *own* car, too."

"I'm so proud of you, Jacks. I really am. I feel like you've turned into such an amazing, responsible young man. It's sorta mind-blowing," I said, leaving a trail of black smoke as we left the enormous Malibu estate.

"Well, maybe Cam's right," Jacks said. "Maybe disconnecting that crappy side of my brain allowed me to stop having seizures *and* think sharper, too."

"Don't get me started on that," I said, knowing that Cam and Jacks had a million and fifty jokes about how Jackson's right hemisphere was the only half of his brain that worked.

"Well, I'm thinking at least fifty percent better with half my brain by considering buying a Toyota pickup instead of this hunk of junk."

"You know what?" I said, eying him. "Leave the car alone."

"Ha," he reached over and rubbed my shoulder. "I love you no matter what, Mom."

* * *

Cameron

"All right, deuces. I'm out," I said to my secretary, grateful this long-ass day was over.

I was scheduled to be in the office all day, but after two emergency calls and determining whether my patients were candidates for emergency surgery or not, I'd been spinning in circles.

I was exhausted, but the thrill of seeing Jessa and staring into those crystal blue eyes tonight at dinner, on top of being with my son, was what drove me to nearly skip out of my office.

"Hey, Dr. Brandt," I heard a male voice call out, pretending to be a female fawning over me.

I turned back, knowing it was Collin since the neurological office center was one floor above me. "Hey, handsome," I teased. Luckily there were no patients around to catch me acting like some whacko.

"You and me tonight, right? I know you're lonely, and Elena is working late at the center," he teased.

"Perhaps you and Jake can play these dumb games until the end of time, but my ass can't."

"Speaking of your ass," Collin said, shifting his leather briefcase in his hand and loosening his tie, "any progress with Jessa?"

I sighed. "No," I answered truthfully. "None at all. Amazingly enough, I haven't been laid and have been single for an entire fucking year. I've got no idea how I'm doing this."

Collin smirked, "That's why your hands have been smooth as butter. It's all that lotion in the late hours of that night."

"Shut the hell up," I said, having become way too accustomed to helping myself out these days. "I feel stuck on this one. I don't want to pressure her, but I don't know where she is with wanting relationships anymore. She seems like she is so happy not being in one."

"Why don't you ask her?" Collin said. "I swear, you've gone soft."

"I'm not pressuring her. I'm just looking to see if there's any progress between us."

"Jacks mentioned something about you guys going to dinner tonight before his driver's test tomorrow," Collin said as we walked to the physicians' parking garage together. "That's progress, I think?"

I stopped before entering the structure and ran my hand through my hair in frustration, "I can't find an angle in. She's closed off, and I swear she friend-zoned my ass months ago after she bought that piece of shit car."

"Friend zone, my ass," Collin said. "And what is it with that damn station wagon and her anyway?"

"God knows," I said, having wanted that answer since the day she proudly pulled that thing up to my beach house to pick up Jacks in it.

"She reminds me of Bella, being all proud of that piece of fucking crap truck her dad bought her when she had to go live with him," Collin said.

"Who the fuck is Bella? An ex-girlfriend of yours?"

"That chick from Twilight," Collin said as if I knew what the hell he was talking about.

"Is that a bar?"

"Jesus, dude," Collin said as if I'd missed something in life that I should've known about. "Well, I can't fault you for not knowing. Unfortunately, you are quite dumb when it comes to making a woman want you."

"Again, completely lost," I said.

"You know, Twilight. It's that teenage vampire shit. Either way, Bella drove me fucking crazy with that goddamn truck. She insisted on driving that rust bucket when her boyfriend could've bought her a new car. It's stupid, right?"

"He had plenty of money, too. He was a fucking vampire!" Jake's voice resounded from behind me.

I looked at him with even more confusion. "You guys are fucking with me, right?" I said with a laugh. "Sorry, I missed the Twilight craze; however, I'm shocked you two did not."

Collin traded some knowingly amused expression with Jake, "Hey, the way to a lady's heart is through her mind, and if she's in love with, let's say vampire novels, and she wants to discuss that shit at the end of the day during pillow talk time, you fucking do it."

"Do you know how many times I got laid after agreeing with Ash that Edward was acting like a bitch in that book?" Jake said.

"Which one, first or second?" Collin answered.

"Or third or fourth? Eclipse was like *peak* bitch," Jake said as Collin nodded knowingly. "Don't get me wrong. I'm not saying I'm team Jacob or anything."

"It's cool, dude. The Quileute—" Collin started, these two obviously forgetting I was standing here.

"Can we honestly?" I said. "I mean, if you guys want to talk book clubs, please, go ahead. I'm trying to figure out how to get my girl back. It's been a goddamn year."

Jake gripped my shoulder. "Easily answered, man," he said, smiling at me. "Stop acting like a bitch and communicate."

"We do communicate," I answered. "Like fucking friends."

"Then it's time to put your balls on the table and communicate more. Make a better fucking effort, and tell her you want more," Collin said. "Seriously, be a man about it."

"*Not* a vampire, obviously," Jake added under his breath, amusing himself immensely.

I rolled my eyes and responded to Collin, "I am. I'm respecting her boundaries. Staying off that subject is doing that."

"Bullshit," Jake immediately said. "Has she asked you to stay off that subject when you approached it?"

"No, but she made it clear she wasn't going to be in a relationship a year ago," I answered.

"Unless she turned into a nun," Collin said, "I think she may have some wants and desires by now."

"You respect boundaries when she throws down that line, and then you stay on your side. So, unless she's told you she doesn't want anything to do with you aside from having a friendship, you need to step that shit up. Be a man and ask. If you don't, you could lose her to a werewolf," Jake said.

"Someone else could imprint on her, bro," Collin added immediately. "You don't want that to happen."

I couldn't help but laugh at how passionately they spoke about these characters that *"their wives made them talk about."* My friends were such idiots, but they were mine, nonetheless. "I'll never understand how you both make perfect sense with the stupidest analogies. It's like being at a circus with you two sometimes."

"Would you rather have Jim help your sorry ass out or us two clowns?" Collin answered.

"Debatable," I answered. "I'm going to get my girl back."

"There's the spirit that won Edward his girl, or did he?" Jake arched his eyebrow. "Maybe you and Jessa can read a few chapters tonight before you get laid for the first time in a fucking year."

"Oh," Collin said, walking toward his Bugatti, "by the way, Elena says that Jessa wants you, has now for a while, but she thought your dumb ass moved on."

"You're just now fucking telling me this?" I answered, knowing that Elena and Jessa were practically best friends now.

"You never brought it up, and I'm not one to play matchmaker," he shrugged. "Have fun getting laid tonight, Edward."

My heart, mind, and soul just became lighter, knowing that this long as fuck year was over, and things might work beyond friendship with Jessa.

* * *

I pulled up to the apartment Jessa had rented about a month after Warren left like the little bitch he was.

I was more than thankful Elena had insisted on giving Jessa an opportunity to work with her at the estate. I'd noticed that all my friends' wives were looking out for Jessa and Jacks, which relieved me so much. I loved that they all took to Jessa so quickly, and that was the thing with all these extraordinary ladies; they kept our spoiled asses grounded, and with their levelheaded way of seeing the world, they formed a wonderful bond of sisterhood.

"Be right there," Jessa said, whirling around and locking the apartment door after she exited.

I smiled, loving the view I had from the curb. I watched her dance down the steps happily, wearing a black, strapless dress and her golden blonde hair bouncing over her perfectly pronounced breasts.

"Where is Jacks?" I questioned with confusion.

She slid into the passenger seat, and my hungry eyes roamed over her toned and smooth legs. It took everything I had to keep my dick from jumping to attention, remembering kissing along the insides of those thighs and tasting the delicious flavor of her.

Fuck! Stop, you dumb-fucker! I halted all thoughts, and my eyes went straight to hers, resisting the urge to run my hands over the silky-smooth flesh of her legs.

Did she have to wear a short dress? Collin better be right because I won't make it another night without you, Jessa!

"Cameron," she laughed and rubbed my arm like a schoolgirl friend. "Did you hear me?"

I'm too busy wondering why the fuck you're treating me like we're besties and dressed like I'm taking you to your hot date with another man.

I'd *never* been this mother fucking insecure in all my damn life.

"I didn't, actually. I was distracted by how beautiful you look tonight," I answered honestly.

She looked away. My God, I couldn't do this shit. Every tiny little thing I did now made me so fucking worried I was doing the wrong thing. How many chances can a guy get before the woman realizes she just doesn't love him? And won't love him?

"Jacks is going with Collin and Jake," she laughed. "I'm shocked you were cool with them going over the driver's license stuff with him."

"Hold up," I said, snapping out of my pity party. "Those dipfucks are teaching my son the final driver's training shit?"

"Jacks wasn't mad about it," she shrugged.

"He'll be livid if he fails his written test at the DMV tomorrow," I said with a laugh, realizing my friends were at it again.

My phone buzzed, and I opened it.

The notification was from the group chat, and there was no way I would open that shit with Jessa sitting next to me. The guys took Jacks so she and I could have a night alone together, the first time in a year, and God only knew what they were going on about.

"Okay," I said, wishing I could mute the chat.

"Okay," she said, smacking her palms on her knees, "let's go grab a burger, then. I have to tell you about my day, though. It was so fucking funny..."

Jessa went into an adorable story, telling me all the details with her usual cute animation.

I had to gain confidence with this brilliant and very confident woman.

I had to make something of this. The pressure was on like fucking game day, and if there was one area I did well in, it was sports. I had to keep my focus and stay sharp.

No more of this bitchiness. I'd been wallowing in my pity for nearly a year, waiting for the day Jessa would take me back. Tonight, that all ended.

I just had to find a way to open up things. Drinks and dinner at Darcy's would loosen us up. I just had to get our asses out of La Habra and back to Downtown LA.

Chapter Forty-Nine

Cam

We walked into Darcy's, and I was quickly reminded why I'd never taken a woman I was serious about to this place—the ghosts of one-night stands and ex-girlfriends seemed to lurk in every shadow.

"Right this way, Dr. Brandt. It's good to see you again." The hostess smiled at me, her bronze eyes peering into my soul. She probably remembered me from the last time I was dumb enough to take a woman home from this place.

I snatched Jessa's hand protectively into mine and kept her close. I don't know why I was feeling nervous. Who gave a shit if an ex showed up? It would suck, but not enough to park that concern in my head when I had this beautiful woman walking by my side.

We were seated, and I ordered us a bottle of Screaming Eagle Cabernet, one of the finest wines from Napa Valley. Of course, I had to keep my game smooth, and my woman impressed, so what came out of my mouth after I ordered the wine I never expected.

"So, when will you stop acting like Bella from *Twilight* and get rid of that piece of shit car?"

"Bella from Twilight?" Jessa said, her head snapping up from where she'd been looking at the candle's flame dancing in the crystal in the middle of our table. She covered her mouth, rightfully stopping herself from laughing out loud. "Since when did you start reading ladies' vampire novels, Cam?"

The wine arrived, and I dismissed the waitress after she poured it. That woman had enough dirt on my ass and surely didn't need this shit, too.

"Since you and I became *friends only,* and I stopped dating women," I said, happy I could recover myself.

"You stopped dating women?" she asked, taking a sip, her smile knowing more than she was saying.

"Yep," I proclaimed proudly. I took a sip of my wine, happy that I could make it clear that I'd locked up *Hotel Brandt* for good because my heart belonged to this woman and this woman alone.

"So, if you stopped dating women, and you and I are friends *only,* then I guess you're into guys now?"

I choked on the wine as it tried to run smoothly down my throat.

"So, did your new boyfriend introduce you to the Twilight series?"

Oh, this was straight-up bullshit. Jessa wore the cute little expression, *knowing* I was nervous, and she was kicking my balls for trying to be cool. But, hell no, I wasn't going down this easily.

"First off," I held my hand up, pausing while the waitress placed hot bread and butter in front of us and then dismissed herself until we were ready to order. "I'm not gay, and one doesn't *have* to be gay to enjoy a good vampire book."

I defended myself against this cute little doe-eyed vixen sitting in front of me.

This book series had better be identical to Interview with a Vampire. It has to be. There's no fucking way Collin and Jake would know shit about a chick-flick book.

"Really?" she questioned. "So, you like the Twilight series, then?"

"You've heard of it, I'm sure."

"Don't know too many people who haven't," she said.

I wasn't backing down.

"So, then you'd understand why I compared your shitty car to Bella's," I recovered, taking another sip of wine.

She challenged me with an arch of her eyebrow, to which I laughed but kept my game pulled in tightly.

"My car is nothing like hers," she said.

I reached into the basket for the bread, buttered a piece, and handed it to Jessa, "It's everything like hers. It's like, she had that car just because Edward had money—"

Jessa's eyes squinted in humor, and she covered her mouth with her napkin after looking out the windows to the right of our secluded table.

Something wasn't right. What the fuck was so funny?

Her face dropped into her hands, and something told me I wasn't proudly defending a vampire novel near as hardcore as Interview with the Vampire.

"My God, Cameron, I love you. I really do," she said, tears in her eyes as she shook her head. "But please stop acting like you've read and loved Twilight, or I'll lose my shit and choke on this bread and die or something."

"At least I know that acting like a jackass is what brings the words *I love you* out of your mouth," I said, folding my arms and finding my adorable Jessa more beautiful with this laugh and humorous expression than anything in the world. "Now, please tell me what this book series is about."

"You honestly don't know?"

"I remember the craze or whatever, but I was buried more in medical terminology books than best-selling books at the time," I said. "Are the vampires gay or something?"

She lost it, and I wanted to read the fucking books to figure out what Collin and Jake read with their wives more than ever.

"Who compared my car to Bella's truck in that book? Which, by the way, it's a pretty damn good comparison. I didn't see that until now, but who told you that?"

"Collin and Jake. They've made it sound like all I had to do was read that with you, and voila! I'd have my beautiful woman back."

Her eyes grew serious, but she quickly recovered her expression.

"First of all, they're right." She smiled warmly at me and reached her hand across the table, and I quickly responded by placing my hand out to cover hers.

"Second?" I questioned, not knowing if this would get serious or funny again.

"Second, the vampire thing has a lot to do with Collin and Elena getting back together. Well, not Twilight, but The Vampire Diaries. Elena told me how Collin was just as clueless with that series as you are about Twilight. Anyway," she said, speeding through this explanation, "Collin got into it after Laney's accident, and then he and Jake admitted to everyone they were closeted teen vampire junkies. It got Collin through some pretty dark times, I guess. But," she squeezed my hand, "since that show was Collin's help while Elena was gone, I'm going to assume that Twilight was your comfort while I've been gone."

"I'm never living this shit down, am I?" I questioned. "I've never read it, Jessa. So, I don't even know who anyone is."

"Well, no better time than now to prove your love to me," she teased.

"And what will Jackson think about his mother and father reading Twilight alone in their room?" I said, feeling more confident, relieved, and happy than I had in over a year.

The look in Jessa's eyes, the smile on her face, and the slow way she rubbed her thumb over my hand let me know the love of my life was back.

"Our room, eh?"

"I love you, Jessa," I said, feeling it in my core. "I can't go another day, not knowing if I will ever *really* have you back. Not knowing if you truly love me or not?"

"It's been a very interesting year, you know? Learning what I wanted for myself. I made huge decisions on my own, purchased station wagons like Bella's, and did not know where my future would lead me. Would I be single or in another bad relationship that I trusted would be good? I didn't know. I learned that my heart has always been yours, Cameron," she said, and my own heart nearly stopped. "I just needed to learn to love and trust myself before I could trust you, or anyone else, with it again."

"So, you're giving me a third chance?" I said, standing up and walking over to her. "For the first time in my life, I honestly don't know what to do."

"Tell you what," she said, pulling the napkin from her lap and placing it on the table, "take me home, and we can figure it out from there."

I helped her from her chair and paid for what we'd hardly nibbled on and drank at this dinner. I couldn't get her out of here fast enough.

I had no intention of *ever* losing her again, and I planned to prove that the second we walked through the door once we got to my place in Malibu.

Chapter Fifty

Jessa

We couldn't get to Cam's place fast enough. After coming to the conclusion that he wanted me back through more vampire talk than I expected, I couldn't wait for us to get out of there. I didn't care about dinner at that point. I was damn hungry, but not for food.

"Jacks is spending the night with Collin and Elena tonight," I informed Cam as we walked up the steps to his beach house.

My breath was caught, and a shiver spiked up my spine when Cam looked back at me after unlocking the door. "Okay," was all he said.

Cam's eyes were darker than the night sky. I'd never seen him look so passionate. I was expecting to be scooped up in the man's arms, but instead, I was pressed against the front door after he closed it.

His hands immediately went to the zipper of my strapless dress. I exhaled, my eyes heavy with a rush of euphoric energy. His lips teased mine with a gentle kiss while his hands slid down to my hips, gently and effectively pulling the dress up and over my head.

"I love you," he said, his hands sliding over my ass and cupping it.

Our lips crashed into each other, hungry and desperate. Our kiss was wild and heated, and my senses were so blissfully assaulted by the sandalwood fragrance of his cologne that I hardly felt him pick me up.

My feet were placed gently on the floor of his bedroom—*I think that's where we were*—and Cameron turned me to face the enormous bright moon filling the skies over the ocean. Goosebumps covered every square inch of my body, recognizing that this would be different from any other time I'd been with Cameron.

His shirt was off, and his warm hard chest pressed against my back. Time stood still. And I was utterly at the mercy of this strong man standing behind me. I melted into him while he slid a hand around my belly, and his other came up over my forehead, gently bringing my head to rest against his sturdy chest.

The smell of Cameron's cologne intoxicated me as I fell deeper under this erotic spell. A warm sensation swirled in my belly as his lips gingerly pressed against my neck, his warm tongue tasting where his lips left a sizzling trail up my neck and to my earlobe.

"Fuck," I whispered in a breath I didn't realize I'd been holding.

Cameron said nothing. All I could feel was an energy of dominance and determination coming from him. We'd waited almost a year for this, and it felt more intense than when we were reunited for the first time since college.

Something was different. I was coming undone from the inside out as he held me, his lips steadily claiming my neck with a determination that drove me wild with desire.

He slid his hand from my belly, my naked body exposed to him for anything he wanted, and he was taking it the way he wanted it. And I loved this.

His large hand slid over my pussy, massaging my clit between his thumb and fingers.

Holy shit.

My knees buckled as he maneuvered my clit between his fingers like he created the body part himself. He caught me with his other hand, pressing my belly and plugging me into his chest.

"I'll never lose you again," he said in a low, husky voice. "Never."

The sound of his voice matched the way his hands held me, loving me. I wasn't going to be able to stand much longer with my entire body trembling under the hold of this man.

His warm breath covered the back of my neck before he pressed his lips against it. I exhaled and forced my eyes open. I was lightheaded, weak, and fully immersed in the pleasures and sensations only this man could ignite in my body.

His fingers dipped into my hot entrance while his thumb continued to work my clit in circles, and instead of being able to focus on the ocean sparkling under the light of the enormous moon outside Cam's bedroom windows, my eyes rolled back in my head.

"Jesus," I said, reaching my hands back and gripping his slacks.

A deep aching need for Cam to be inside me pulsed between my legs, and I pressed my ass firmly against his hard cock.

"Fuck yes," I said while Cameron moaned and moved his lips from my shoulder to the back of my neck.

His lips made a scorching trail as they gently kissed on top of my shoulders to the base of my neck. I couldn't speak as he continued to kiss over to the tip of my shoulder and his teeth gently stroked along my jaw.

I tilted my head to allow him more access, just to feel his lips while he continued to roll my clit between his thumb and fingers. His movements were firm but soft, and his rhythm forced the buildup of what I knew would be an explosive orgasm.

I moaned in half agony and half pleasure, unable to move or do anything for fear that the intense sensation building in me would go away.

"Harder," I groaned, moving my hips to compel his hand to follow my lead.

Cam's fingers were firm in their movements, and his other hand gripped the inside of my thigh as I moaned.

I needed more.

His fingers dipped inside of me and searched greedily for my G-spot. My eyes rolled back in my head while my breath was stolen by gripping and fiery pleasure. I would have fallen to the floor, writhing in desire while the spasm continued to swarm and erupt through my body, but Cam had a steady grip on me.

While my lips grew parched from panting through the intense orgasm, Cam turned me to face him. His moist lips captured mine, and his deep kiss swallowed me up effusively.

I couldn't gain my bearings. I couldn't do anything but relish the sweet flavor of the lips and kiss I'd missed desperately for all these long months.

"It's been too fucking long, baby," he said, cradling my naked body and returning his lips to mine.

My head was spinning from when we walked into this house to when Cam slipped my dress off me and began working me over in ways I'd needed since the last time we were together.

I couldn't even focus on what he was doing to my body because I was so enveloped with the sensations making me crumble.

I was back on his bed, his vibrant blue eyes searching mine. "I love you more than I can express, Jessa," he said, his voice low and raspy.

I reached my hands up and ran my fingers through his hair. This man was perfect in every way, and we were about to make up for a very long year without one another. There was no way thoughts of ecstasy would consume me as they'd done when we first walked into this room.

I maneuvered myself to roll Cam onto his back, and he did without a fight. His smile was lazy, matching his expression, seeming like he was lost in some trance. I straddled him and traced over the firm lines of his stomach and chest.

His body was perfect, and there were so many times when I saw him at the hospital in his dark scrubs that I wanted to take him just like this. There was nothing sexier than seeing this man in his work clothes or when he'd tease my eyes while playing football shirtless on the beach with his friends.

Now, he was mine. The separation and the healing from old wounds was over, and I could fully enjoy him without feelings of worry and guilt threatening to ruin everything constantly.

His hands ran up the sides of my legs. "Well, now you have me, gorgeous. I'm hoping you're not planning on being gentle?"

His eyebrow arched while he smiled.

"Does it look like I'm planning on being gentle with your sexy ass, Dr. Brandt?"

His face scrunched up in a humorous expression that made me laugh. "Dr. Brandt, eh? I suppose you worked up some fantasies, and now you're finally fucking the hot doctor?"

I shook my head and pressed my finger to his lips, and he kissed it gently, "And how would you know?"

"I saw how you checked out my tight ass at the hospital." He squeezed the outsides of my thighs. "And the way you drooled when I went through charts," he said in some silly, sexy voice.

"Oh, yeah?" I said, reaching behind me for his hard dick and using the precum to lubricate where my hand tightened around him, sliding up and down.

"Mm-hmm," he said, catching his bottom lips between his teeth and stroking my hand on his shaft. "And the way—" he paused when I pressed my fingers just under the head of his cock.

"The way?"

"Fuck, yeah, the way..." he said, eyes closed and breathless. "Fuck baby." He sounded so sexy that I felt myself getting wet and hungry for another orgasm.

I wished I could say that Cameron was just a hot doctor, but he was so much more than that to me. He was a good man—the best man. The best father and the most loving, compassionate, caring individual I'd ever known. I loved this man more than anything in my world, and I was so damn thankful we'd somehow managed to survive everything that we'd gone through from the moment he'd left me in college until we reunited to save Jackson—and everything that was madness in between.

I wish we could've worked a year ago, but I knew our journey wouldn't have lasted. I had too much baggage that would've fucked with my mind while I tried to build a perfect family with this man. Now, I felt stronger and happier than ever, and the best part was that it didn't take a relationship to find my happiness. The relationship that Cam and I were about to begin only *added* to my joy, making all this so beautiful and perfect.

Loving someone the right way was more rewarding than I imagined. But the most essential gift out of all this was that Cameron waited for me, proving that he was indeed the most amazing human being on the planet. Now, all I wanted to do was reward him for that.

* * *

Cam

I gripped Jessa's slender waist as she slid onto my throbbing cock. It was a damn surprise I hadn't come just by touching her for the first time in so long. I honestly didn't think I'd get a moment like this again, and part of me thought it might be a dream.

I licked my dry lips, watching her eyes roll back into her head while she rocked back and forth. Then, I pulled my legs up, positioning my dick to roll up and against her deep spot.

She leaned back against my legs while I pumped up into her, jolting with pleasure every time the tip of my dick reached her spot. Fuck, this was amazing.

Jessa's moans and tight pussy drove me crazy, and her perfect tits bouncing shamelessly in the air made me want to suck them.

I couldn't resist this perfect woman any longer, so I leaned up and captured her breast in my mouth. She moaned as my teeth nipped at her nipple, hardening it even more. I licked underneath her breast, closing my lips around it. I rolled my tongue in circles, pressing against her nipple as Jessa's hand came up into my hair, gripping and pulling it while her hips moved faster and faster, giving my cock precisely what it wanted.

I moaned loudly against her hot flesh, knowing that this woman's movements would make me come, and there was nothing I could do about that now. I wanted it. I wanted pleasure from my woman riding me hard and fast. Jessa gripped my shoulders, pushing me back so our eyes could meet.

"Come," she ordered, "I want your cum inside me." She smiled seductively.

My balls were tighter than fuck, ready to send my cum directly into her, but I didn't want this sensation to end. The rippling pleasure from her moving made me numb to everything but her tight pussy and the boiling of extreme pleasure ready to explode out of me.

"That's it. Are you coming with me?" I managed.

She practically left claw marks on my shoulders as she forced her hips backward, bringing my cock deeper into her.

Shit.

Fuck, I was done. I grabbed her perfect ass and jerked up into her, slamming in hard and deep, joining her pleasure with a growl and groaning of my own.

The orgasm was so fucking intense, and it wouldn't fucking stop. While her pussy clenched around my cock, sending my cum into her, I rolled her onto her back.

This was more than I expected, and the ecstasy streaming through my system was just a warm-up.

As I came down from the orgasm, Jessa massaged her fingers through my hair and offered me a lazy smile.

"You're so fucking perfect," I said.

I kissed her lips, and then I noticed we weren't in the room I thought we were. "The fuck?" I said with a small laugh. "Well, shit," I dropped my forehead between her breasts. "Looks like Jacks will be taking another room."

"Is this where he stays in when he comes over?"

I laughed and looked around at all the shit Jacks and I had bought together to help make this room his for when Jessa was cool with him staying with me.

I was never so fucking happy when we told Jacks I was his father, and Jacks responded as if he found out he was the son of some celebrity. I never questioned him for not being upset about why he'd learned so late in life. I was just thankful he responded the way he did.

"The only room in the house with Knicks paraphernalia on the walls and shelves," I said, knowing that I'd probably never convert my boy into a Lakers fan.

Jessa laughed then her eyes met mine. "You are the best man and father that Jacks and I could ever ask for. I'm sorry it took me so long to realize that."

I narrowed my eyes at her, my dick soft enough to slide out of her warm pussy. "The only thing I regret, aside from not being in his life for so long, is that you raised him to be a Knicks fan when he's got the genetics of a Lakers fan."

She rolled her eyes. "You're such a nerd sometimes," she said, running her finger down the length of my nose.

"I know this is wild and probably the worst thing to say after fucking on our son's bed—"

"Then don't say it," she smiled and laughed.

Perhaps it was best if I waited. *Fuck it.* We'd waited too long, and life was passing us by each day that we didn't seize a moment.

"Marry me, Jessa," I blurted out. I suddenly wished I'd been a little bit more romantic, but hell, maybe proposing to your love with a soft dick after just fucking on your kid's bed was romantic too?

Jessa laughed and squeezed my head between her arms. "You're on one of your after-sex highs, and I'm hungry," she said, kissing the top of my head.

"I will get on my knees here and now and beg for your hand, baby," I said, nuzzling her neck with my lips. "But if you would like, I will make all of this right by proposing to you on the beach."

"Naked?" she teased.

"Anything, I don't give a shit, just be my wife."

I sounded like a desperate idiot, but I was dead set on this.

"Honestly, Jessa, I need you in my life. You and Jacks are my family. You both belong here with me. Make my life complete and become my wife, baby."

"I should send you a thumbs-up emoji response just to bring our entire relationship full circle," she said. Then she grew serious. "Yes, Cameron. I would love nothing more than for you, me, and Jacks to become the family we've waited too long to be. I love you completely, now and forever."

She would never have any idea how much I loved her and our son, but I vowed in my heart to prove it with more than words. She was my treasure and something I'd never planned to lose or take for granted.

Chapter Fifty-One

Jessa

Cameron and I spent that weekend wrapped in each other's arms until we couldn't resist picking up Jacks and telling him that his parents would be getting married and we were going to become a family.

"How do you think Jacks will take the news? I'm thinking he'll at least dig settling down out here—you know, to finally pull off from this online schooling bullshit and start gaining friends at a new school," Cam said.

"Yes," I answered with a smile, "I know he'll be happy to learn he's no longer going to need to do school remotely, now that his mom has made a decision to live in Southern California."

I was thankful that the school issue could at least be resolved. Since Jackson's surgery, I wouldn't settle down and force Jacks into a new school—especially with him going through rehab, and with me not too certain where I truly wanted to live.

Even though the school system in New York worked well with us for him attending remotely like he'd been, I knew it was something that needed to be worked out and soon.

I knew that Jacks wouldn't have a problem making new friends, or possibly even challenging himself to pursue sports again, even if he wasn't playing like he used to. I also knew that he needed to be around kids his age to thrive. So, with this year that we had, both healing in our own ways, I knew I had to decide on a school for him to attend in person.

I never imagined this decision would be made because I said yes to marrying his father, and our home would officially be here in Southern California. I had to admit, this was more than I could ask for in moving forward with my life, yet something still had me contemplating how to reveal all of it to Jackson...school attendance was now the furthest thing from my mind. Instead I was more concerned about his reaction to me saying I would marry Cam.

"I don't know why I'm so nervous," I said, biting my nails, something I never did.

"Truth be told, I am, too," Cam said, bringing the back of my hand to his lips while he drove. "Think I should give him the Bronco in case things go sideways and I need to buy my love?"

I smiled at him, winking at his joke. "Because I *certainly* raised him to take bribes for love."

"I couldn't possibly be more grateful for how you raised that boy. Seriously," he said, changing lanes to get off the freeway, "I probably would've fucked him up just by how irresponsible I was at the age. I don't talk about him much anymore, but my father would've been damn proud of how his grandson turned out," he kissed my hand again, "and proud of you for raising him so well. No doubt about that at all."

"I'm sorry about your parents, Cameron. I know you don't bring it up much, but since you did, I want you to know you can talk about them whenever you like."

"I've grieved them well, I think," he smiled over at me. "I used to go to the cemetery all the time, trying to talk to them and work out my frustrations, but I realized it was stalling me in life. I know I take them with me wherever I go, and you know as well as I do my dad would've kicked my ass if he knew I stayed stagnant and in that dark place."

"He had a profound touch on everyone's lives. I remember walking into the room with all those stiff, powerful, rich men; somehow, your dad commanded every single one of them."

Cam smirked, "I see some of my dad in Jacks." He glanced over at me, his dark Ray Bans hiding his eyes, "It's so strange how genetics work, you know?"

I smiled, but then a certain sadness washed over me. "I want to say something because I need to put it to rest."

"Go ahead," Cam said, and I realized I sorta hated when we both got serious. Especially Cameron.

I shook my head, pushing the awkward nerves away. "I'm sorry I never told you about being pregnant," I said.

"Don't do that, baby," he said.

"No, I'm deadly serious, and this is something I need to say. I've watched you with Jackson this past year, and you are such an incredible father. I see how you are with the kids when we get together, and they are drawn to you like a moth to a flame. You have such a wonderful personality, and beyond feeling like I robbed Jacks of you during his important years growing up, I feel like I robbed you too. I did that because I put an idea in my head about how you would take it, not trusting myself or you, and I didn't allow you to decide for yourself whether you wanted to be in his life. It was wrong of me, and I can't take any of it back, but I can acknowledge it and apologize. And hope that the years ahead will make up for it."

That was more than I expected to say, but it had bothered me for years that I'd never given Cam a chance to make his own decision about our son. I never gave him a chance at anything, and over this last year, I'd seen him at work and with all the kids; it was so obvious why he'd chosen to work with children and why his patients adored him. He loved children, and I never gave him a chance with his own because of my insecurities.

"Jessica," Cameron said, stopping at the red light, "I want you to really understand that I know why you never told me. I get it and feel like an even bigger piece of shit, realizing it was due to how I left you. It was bullshit. I put you in a position to believe I would've lost my shit or something. Who knows? But I guess that thumbs-up emoji response fucked up more things than I would have ever imagined. It worked as a full stop, and I'd never thought that's how it came across."

"It's in the past for good, so let's keep it there from now on." I'd worked through this pain. We had no reason to revisit it again, and he agreed with a nod. "So long as we're on the topic of emoji thumbs-up responses," I said with a smirk, "let's talk about how it's going to be forbidden for us to use in our texting from this point forward."

He shook his head. "You finally had me serious in conversation, and now, we're going to make fake laws about a damn emoji," he said with a laugh, pulling up to Elena and Collin's estate in the Hollywood Hills.

"Okay," I chuckled and laughed, "let's let Collin, Elena, and Jacks decide whether we keep or ditch that emoji."

"What are you planning? God, do not tell Collin that that is how I ended things with you."

I smiled at him as we pulled up to the side of the house next to a bright orange Lamborghini. "Relax," I said, getting out of the Bronco.

"Relax," he huffed, opening his door and walking over to me.

"Damn," Collin said, walking out of the front door as soon as we approached. "I trust everything is kosher between you two? I'm presumably looking at two flames reunited in the fiery combustion of love?"

"Yeah, Dad," Cameron mocked. "All is fair in love and war."

"I see it is," he said.

"Where's Elena and Jacks?" Cam asked.

"In the kitchen making pizza," Collin said, turning to walk into their impressive home. "He's teaching A-man how to make pizza or something."

"How's that working for Alex?" I questioned with a laugh, knowing how Collin and Elena's two-year-old loved Jacks.

"Alex thinks he's the one teaching Jacks. It's an entire shit parade, but hell if I care. My son seems to have written the manual on the terrible twos, and whatever works to keep his destructive little butt under control, I'm down."

"It's half the reason you were eager to come up with some crazy lie to keep Jacks until this afternoon," Cam interjected while we walked through the large home.

"It's the entire reason, my brother," he said. "It's the *only* reason I'm thankful you two needed some *alone* time. Speaking of which, it's all good, and no more break-ups, right?" Collin asked with a mischievous smile.

"I think we're going to survive this one," I answered as we turned a final corner and walked into the enormous chef's kitchen.

"And thank the gods for that," Collin said.

"Who are you, Thor?" Elena laughed as she pulled a hot, fresh-baked pizza from the oven. "The gods!"

"Hey," Collin walked over to the fridge, pulled out two beers, and then looked at me, "beer or wine, hun? What's your flavor tonight?"

"I'll have a beer," I said, watching Cam meet Collin at the fridge, grabbing his own beer.

"That's my girl," Elena said as I walked over to her and hugged her. "How'd it go?"

"Well," I smiled, but then pulled it back, realizing Jacks wasn't even in here, "where's Jacks? We have news."

"Goddamn right, you do," Collin said, smacking Cam on the back while he took a sip of beer. "Choke it down because I want to hear all about it."

"We'd like Jacks to know about it before your ass finds out," he grinned.

"Oh, dammit," Elena giggled. "Okay, okay. I get it, but we sort of know." She squinted with a *please tell us* expression on her face.

"Okay," I said, unable to contain my excitement, knowing Jacks wouldn't be upset. "But where's Jacks?"

"They're out back, throwing the ball around," Collin said, then he looked at Cam. "Before we get into the juicy details, I have to say that Jacks has got a mean left-handed throw. Unlike your dumb ass, he hits his target when he fires one off."

Cam smiled with pride. Jacks could throw well with his right arm, but the boy didn't stop until he worked out the left-hand throwing. It's like he welcomed every challenge thrown his way, so that he could conquer them. It's just who Jacks was, and it was most certainly something he got from his father and, no doubt, from Henry Brandt.

"I'm beyond impressed with his skill. The kid seriously never ceases to amaze me."

"We'll go more into that later," Collin said. "Back to how this lovely lady never ceases to amaze you."

"How did it all go down?" Elena asked before looking at Cam. "Did you have rose petals all over the room, you know, all that cute romantic stuff?" she said, nudging him as she walked by and put another pizza into the oven.

"Something like that," Cameron looked at me nervously. I could only laugh because I didn't consider that we'd have to share our engagement story, and we hadn't discussed an alternative to the naked, sweaty reality.

"He was pretty cute about it," I said, my eyes locking with Cam, urging him to follow my lead.

"Bullshit," Collin said, looking like the cat who ate the canary. "Spill it, Cammy. Were you sappy, or was this a dud proposal?"

Cam and I locked eyes. There was no getting around this. These guys could sniff out a lie like a bloodhound on the hunt. And Collin was onto the game.

"It was a dud," I said, thinking I might save this. There was no way I would tell them about Cam proposing, *still naked*, directly after sex. It would never stop there. Ever.

"Total dud," Cameron said, drinking his beer while Collin and Elena stared at us as if we'd robbed a bank and lied about it.

"Just how dud-like are we talking here?" Elena chimed in. The beautiful woman would roast us if we veered the tiniest bit off track.

"Right," Collin pretended to act interested, "on a scale of dipfuck to dud, where'd your ass land? Dipfuck, of course, being at the bottom."

"Right around the dipfuck portion of the dumbass scale you just created," Cameron answered.

"Mm-hmm." Collin eyed me, trying to get me to crack. "Go on," he said dramatically, pulling Elena close to his side. "This shit is so hot and romantic, I'm—"

"Don't interrupt, Col," Elena said, both husband and wife trying to play Cam and me. "She's just getting started."

"So, I agree with Cam. It was very close to the dipfuck part on the scale," I said.

"One would argue that *I was the reason* it all fucking flopped," Cam played along, and now I had to hope I could hang with him.

"*You* fucked up the proposal?" Collin asked me.

I shrugged and took a sip of my beer.

"So, we're having this amazing sex. Amazing, off the fucking charts," Cam said, and I kept a straight face while Collin and Elena knew they were being bullshitted. In fact, I don't think they knew what to think. "Jessa practically needs a nap after I prove my worth to her—once again," Cam said seriously. "Then, my lady rolls over, and while I'm trying to spoon and shit—being romantic, you know? It's been a fucking year since I had her in my arms—and, to my surprise, she reaches for the phone."

"Fuck you," Collin responded to Cam. "How the hell did this shit go down, you two little bandits trying to keep shit a secret."

"I grabbed my phone to see if Jacks was okay," I said, playing into the lie. They seemed to start buying it now. "And, of course, I didn't have any missed calls or texts from him."

"So, I texted her," Cam said, shrugging at Collin and Elena. "I should've been pissed, I know." He shook his head, "But I wasn't. She was just so beautiful, laying there, naked polished body—"

"Skip the details that would make us sinners blush," Collin said. "You texted?"

"Anyway, with profound love, I texted her, *Marry me?*" Cam said, acting emotional.

All eyes were on me for my portion of the proposal lie.

"Well, I was about to locate Jacks on the GPS tracker, but I saw Cam's text come through, and I checked it first."

"Good damn thing because he might have smacked your bare ass while lying by you on the bed," Elena said.

"Right," I smiled, "I read the text and knew in my heart the answer was yes, but I wanted to verify Jacks was with you guys and didn't drive off looking for a party like teens do. So, I just hit the thumbs-up emoji, and that was it. We're engaged."

"Oh, for the love of all fucks, hot and sweet. That is the biggest load of shit I've ever allowed anyone to go on about in my presence. The thumbs-up emoji as a yes?" Collin interjected.

"Hey, that thumbs-up emoji stole my damn heart," Cam said, crossing his arms.

"That emoji is dismissive, and I hate it almost as much as I hate that lie," Elena said, walking over to pull the pizza out of the oven.

"Not the thumbs-up emoji again," Jacks said. I turned and crashed into my boy as soon as I saw him, hugging him tightly. "Did Cam do it again to you, Mom?"

"Do it *again*? What are we talking about here? Seriously?" Collin asked.

"Mom and—" Jacks paused, and he'd done this from time to time since learning Cam was his dad. It's like he wanted to officially call him dad but hesitated out of uncertainty.

"You better call me dad," Cameron teased.

I leaned into Jackson's side, shocked at how much he'd grown in the past year. Jacks had a proud smile on his face.

"Mom and *Dad*," he said. "It's how he dumped her in college or whatever. Mom hates that emoji more than anything in the world."

"Yet, you said *yes* to *him* with it?" Collin said, pointing his thumb toward Cameron.

"Yeah," I said. "I have no idea, but he got the point just like I got the point when he dumped me."

"It was an *emoticon* back then, okay?" Cam insisted.

"This had better be one massive and irritating lie, or I will insist you both hire me as your full-time therapist," Elena said.

"Lie about what?" Jackson said as Alex ran to Collin, only to be flipped in his arms and hoisted onto his dad's shoulders. "What's up with you two?" Jackson's eyes shifted from me to Cameron.

"I know it's been a long year," Cameron started, "and too long of a lifetime, not having me in your lives as I should have been. My selfish immaturity is why I didn't experience the best years of your life growing up, but I vow to you and your mom that I will never miss another day. I want, more than anything else, to have you both in my life forever and for us to be a family."

"I accepted your dad's marriage proposal," I said, overcome with emotion after seeing tears in Jackson's eyes.

He only nodded to Cameron and turned to me. My son's strong, muscular arms enveloped me, and his silent sobs rendered me an emotional mess. Jacks and I had held each other so many times like this, during good and bad times. Funny times and sad. And now, as we held each other again, I knew my son, who'd been through so much, had a full and happy heart.

We didn't need to exchange words. We just knew. We knew what we'd been through and how fortunate we were. Jackson was seizure free and healthy, and the man we both loved, who treasured us as much as we treasured him, was here to stay.

We were complete. We were a family now, and our lives would forever be blessed.

Cameron's arms came around us where Jacks and I stood, crying and holding each other. In some funny little way, it was like putting a big bow on this gift of *us*. I'd learned to appreciate every struggle in the journey that'd pulled us apart because, in the end, it brought us to now. Together.

This was our happily ever after.

The End...

Afterword

Thank you for reading Dr. Brandt! I hope you enjoyed Cam and Jessa's story.

And even though their story may have come to a close, Nat and Spencer's story is ready to ignite your kindles on fire! Once I get those two out of the bedroom, we'll get their story up and published for all of you who would like to read it, at least by December or January.

For those of you who have been following me writing the Billionaires' Club series, I want to thank you all from the bottom of my heart. You all have waited almost a year for this book, and were so patient while I was going through the hardest year of my life. And though it was a tough year, I absolutely wouldn't let it beat me, by giving up on telling my stories (these stories) and continuing in writing for you all.

I have so many ideas in furthering this series, or perhaps writing in a very similar series. I'm not too sure where I'll take my future stories, after I finish writing Mr. Monroe, but I am sure you will enjoy reading them as you may have enjoyed reading, Jake, Jim, Collin, Alex, Cam, and Spencer's stories.

So stick with me, and here's a link to my email sign-up exclusively for news and updates on my future books in this series and perhaps in another series.

AFTERWORD

So for all the updates, click the link below to sign up for emails on any news I have in my writing journey.

Thank you all again for your support and trust in my writing. You all mean more to me than you'll ever know.

All of my love,

Raylin

(Link to email sign up on next page)

Scan or click on the QR code to be take to the email sign-up form.

About the Author

Raylin Marks is the author of the Billionaires' Club Series. She enjoys writing, adventures, and good wholesome love...in all of that (well, some of that) she orchestrates timeless and exciting romance novels for anyone who dares to read them.

When Raylin Marks is not writing, she's usually found out in nature, either on the shores of California's West Coast, or up in the majestic mountains—somewhere or anywhere out in nature, gathering ideas for a new fun and exciting adventure to write for her readers.

Oh, and yeah, so she drinks too much coffee too.

Keep up with Raylin at any one of the sites below. Oh, P.S., she LOVES her fans, so don't be afraid to contact her personally if you want at: raylinmarks99@gmail.com.

Billionaires' Club Series Books

Each one of the books in the Billionaires' Club Series ends with an HEA and can be read in any order. Click on the links below to read any of the books in the series.

Dr. Mitchell: Book 1 (Jake and Ash's story)

Description:

Billionaires like him have a type. And it's *not* me...

I'm not the kind of girl who has one-night stands.

Except...I did.

What can I say? After a few drinks with a gorgeous man who made me feel *alive* for the first time since losing my mom, I was powerless to say no.

And I didn't regret it. Not one minute of our hot, mind-melting night together.

But he wasn't a *forever* kind of guy. So I walked away. I wasn't supposed to ever see him again.

Then I did.

Turns out my sexy one-night stand is Dr. Jacob Mitchell—and he's the cardiothoracic surgeon who just saved my dad's life.

The shocking part?

He never forgot about me or a single *minute* of our night together.

And he wants more.

Actually, he wants it *all*.

But I'm no fool. And just because he handles hearts every day doesn't mean I'm going to give him mine.

Not without a fight, anyway ...

Dr. Mitchell is a spicy contemporary romance featuring an alpha billionaire/reformed player, and the feisty free spirit who steals his heart. Sexy times are *definitely* included, and a happily ever after is guaranteed. Download today!

Mr. Mitchell: Book 2 (Jim and Avery's story)

The billionaire *always* gets what he wants. This time, he wants me...

My trip to London was the first lucky break I've had in years. It came at *just* the right time, allowing me to escape my sad reality for a bit. And the guy I met on the flight?

Perfection.

The short week we spent together was filled with raw, unbridled, and passionate nights. But it couldn't last. I'm a single mom with a troubled past and a shady ex. Romance just isn't in the cards for me.

Which is why I walked away from Jim and didn't look back.

That was before I landed my new job. Before I met the boss.

Before I discovered that Mr. James Mitchell, CEO, was *my* Jim—my unforgettable Jim from our week together in England.

Judging by the smile on his face when he sees me, he remembers *everything*.

And now he wants more.

He wants *me*.

The timing is terrible. My life's a mess, and I just *know* my ex will do *something* to ruin me. Again.

But none of that matters when I'm in Jim's arms.

So, what are the odds that I'm *finally* due for my very own happily ever after?

With my luck?

Not bloody likely.

Mr. Mitchell, a sexy contemporary romance, is book 2 in the Billionaires' Club series, but can be read as a standalone. It features an alpha male hero with a heart of gold, and the feisty, resilient heroine who easily runs away with his heart. Download today to start binge reading!

Dr. Brooks: Book 3 (Collin and Elena's Story)

We shared the love of a lifetime. Too bad I don't remember any of it.

Pieces of my life were ripped away without warning. My career, my control, my sense of self…it's gone.

So are my memories of *him*.

I now know him as the handsome doctor who was there for me when I first woke up after the accident. But before that, he was the love of my life. My everything.

Or so I'm told.

I'm not the woman he remembers. I'm just a ghost with her face. An unfortunate remnant of the happily ever after, fairy tale kind of romance we *apparently* had together.

He says he'll wait for me. That he won't stop fighting for us, even if he has to make me fall in love with him all over again.

I think he's right. I *will* fall for him.

But the real question is, can he truly ever love me for who I am *now*? Or will his heart always belong to the memory of who I *used* to be?

Dr. Brooks, an angsty, sexy, contemporary romance, is book 3 in the Billionaire's Club series, but it can be read as a standalone. It features a strong heroine struggling with amnesia, and the protective alpha male doctor who somehow manages to win her heart *twice*. Download today to meet your new favorite book boyfriend.

Mr. Grayson: Book 4 (Alex and Bree's Story)

I never should've let my guard down. Especially not with him.

I'm used to being strong. In control. I have to be to run my corporation. So, I should've been able to hold my own against him. Against his relentless charm and devastating good looks.

But I couldn't.

I didn't.

It doesn't matter that our companies are irrevocably tied together, or that being with him is beyond inappropriate. It doesn't matter that he's a known player and I don't tolerate games. It doesn't even matter that he makes me lose my prized control with every heated glance, stolen touch, and dirty whisper.

I crave him.

Being with him could cost me everything I've worked so hard to build. But as strong as I am, I can't seem to walk away.

Now, all I have to do is decide whether the cost of following my heart--which is pushing me straight into Alex Grayson's arms--is more than I'm willing to pay.

Mr. Grayson, book 4 in the Billionaire's Club series, is a spicy, office, contemporary romance designed to steam up your Kindle. This book features a sexy, alpha hero and the alpha CEO heroine of his dreams. It also includes plenty of witty banter and a guaranteed happily ever after. Download today, because you needMr. Grayson in your life.

Dr. Brandt: Book 5 (Cam and Jessa's story)

Letting her go was a mistake. I never repeat my mistakes...

It was just going to be a quick vacation. A break from the demands of my job as a pediatric surgeon.

I never thought she'd be there.

Jessica Stein. *My* Jessa. The woman I left behind all those years ago is every bit as sexy now as she was then. I want her more than ever.

Too bad she doesn't feel the same way.

To her, I'm the guy who broke her heart and let her down. She thinks I'm the same player I used to be.

She's wrong.

But the only thing she wants from me is my medical expertise. See, her son is sick.

I'll do everything I can for the boy, and eventually, I *will* convince her to trust me with the secrets I know she's keeping. I need her to give me a second chance, because I am the man she's been waiting for.

All I have to do now is convince her of that...

Mr. Monroe: Book 6 (Spencer and Nat's Story)

In what world does a failed one-night stand lead to a fake marriage? *This* one...

Our night together? It could've gone better. For example, he could've chosen to *not* take a phone call in the middle of the...final act.

But I'm willing to give him another chance. I'm a giver like that.

And Spencer Monroe is, after all, one of southern California's hottest, wealthiest, and most influential men. He's *exactly* the kind of player I like to bring to his knees—in the bedroom *and* out of it.

I never expected him to propose a fake marriage, though.

I *really* never thought I'd accept.

But here I am, at his brother's wedding, with a fake husband, clutching the stupid bridal bouquet I *should've* let hit the floor.

So, what the hell am I supposed to do *now*?

Well, I can tell you what I'm *not* going to do. I'm *not* going to fall in love with the ridiculously handsome, annoyingly charming billionaire.

That's what I keep telling myself, at least...

Mr. Monroe is the sixth book in the billionaires club series by Raylin Marks and can be read as a stand alone novel. A sensual and satisfying read about a CEO who is brought to his knees when his idea of a fake marriage is the one business deal that will change his bachelor ways and his life...forever. This alpha male has finally met his match, literally.

Printed in Great Britain
by Amazon